the HiDden liFe of HumAns

a nOvel

Erika Ritter

KEY PORTER BOOKS

Library and Archives Canada Cataloguing in Publication

Ritter, Erika, 1948–
     The hidden life of humans : a novel / Erika Ritter.

Originally published: 1997.
ISBN 978-1-55470-080-6

    I. Title.

PS8585.I81H53 2008   C813'.54   C2008-902274-2

ONTARIO ARTS COUNCIL
CONSEIL DES ARTS DE L'ONTARIO

The publisher gratefully acknowledges the support of the Canada Council for the Arts and
the Ontario Arts Council for its publishing program. We acknowledge the support of the
Government of Ontario through the Ontario Media Development Corporation's Ontario
Book Initiative.

We acknowledge the financial support of the Government of Canada through the Book
Publishing Industry Development Program (BPIDP) for our publishing activities.

Key Porter Books Limited
Six Adelaide Street East, Tenth Floor
Toronto, Ontario
Canada M5C 1H6

www.keyporter.com

Printed and bound in Canada
09 10 11 12 13   5 4 3 2 1

Printed on 30% recycled paper

2̶7̶
trees were saved
for our forests

Preserving our environment
Key Porter chose to use recycled paper
to print this book and saved these resources[1]:

energy	water	greenhouse gases	solid waste
124 million BTUs	231,154 L	8,517 kg	3,270 kg

Printed by **Webcom Inc.**
on Legacy TB White 30% post-consumer waste.

FSC

Mixed Sources
Product group from well-managed
forests, and recycled wood or fiber

Cert no. SW-COC-002358
www.fsc.org
© 1996 Forest Stewardship Council

[1]Estimates were made using the Environmental Defense Paper Calculator.

For Shannon, who's taught me what I know about dogs.
And for Butler, who's taught me what I don't.

the
HiDden
liFe of
HumAns

PART ONE

Saving Grace

Chapter One

From my living-room window I watch the man with whom I've spent the past two nights head down the front walk to his waiting taxi. Nothing too poignant about the parting, though. Leonard's just another one of the Marrieds—as I tend to refer to my revolving-door assemblage of other women's husbands. Men who come roaring into town at unscheduled intervals, like a fleet of aging buses pulling off the highway for a quick fill-up and a change of oil before carrying on to the end of the line. Men who make love to me with gratifying zest, as if this were their last chance to get gas before once more facing the endless desert of conjugal life stretching in every direction.

I'd be lying if I said I was love with Leonard, who is leaving me for the airport. No more than I'm in love with any of the Marrieds—whom I in fact *prefer* on a special-occasion basis, if only to be spared ever seeing any of them in the clothes they must surely wear to mow the lawn. Or perched on the edge of the tub, cutting their corns. Or caught in any of the other homely, unguarded poses that belong to the domain of ongoing involvement, as opposed to the realm of the sometimes fling. I don't know whether it's through good luck or good judgment, or what, that I've so far managed to skim over the surface of my illicit alliances with the impunity of a water-bug. What I *do* know is that, to date, there have been no tearful showdowns with wives, no insincere promises of imminent divorce, nor any tawdry recriminations on either side once it's time to call the whole thing off.

Meanwhile, from my post at the window, it's obvious that Leonard has already moved into another gear. Sitting in the back of the cab, fumbling for his Pocket Organizer—maybe to recheck the flight departure time, or to look up a phone number relevant to his next port of call, or to make a note to himself to call home from the airport. Though I'm not yet out of sight—or wouldn't be, if he'd glance in my direction—I am apparently already out of mind. Filed away for future reference, even as the cab continues to idle in front of my very door.

Of course, there's bound to be that one brief instant, that moment—just as the cab driver is stowing the luggage, or slamming the trunk with unnecessary force, or dusting his hands with that air of finality common to cab drivers—in which Leonard will pull himself back from the brink of forgetfulness. Just long enough to—Yes, yes, here it comes—Just long enough to look up at my window, to confirm that I'm still waiting there to see him well and truly off.

Okay, so now the driver has the cab in gear and is pulling away from the curb. Allowing Leonard only that one bare moment I predicted to flash a final smile at me—brief, self-conscious, somewhat automatic, as any smile flashed through the window of a departing taxi is probably doomed to be.

And in that same instant, just as the cab is speeding away, as I stand there with my hand arrested in mid-wave, I find myself experiencing a stab of...what? Loneliness? No, not quite. More like a feeling of blankness. As vacant as the space at the curbside where the cab used to be. Or the empty chairs in my dining room, where, a mere half-hour ago, Leonard and I sat sharing a farewell cup of coffee. Or the barrenness of my disheveled bed in which, earlier this very morning, I awoke to watch Leonard as he lay asleep, his broad freckled back turned to me, and the pillow crushed in his arms like a phantom lover.

Well, I know what to do next, of course. Once I've disengaged my hand from its waving mode, and turned away from my station at the living-room window, I will simply set about the task of obliterating all remaining evidence of male occupancy from the premises.

I rinse the cold coffee from the cups, smooth out the indentations left in the bed by our two slumbering bodies, toss Leonard's damp towels into the hamper, and wipe a blob of his shaving foam from the rim of my sink. After that, I go outside and unshackle my bicycle from the drainpipe beside the porch in order to take myself as far away as I can get from the conspicuous emptiness left in Leonard's wake. Striving with every rotation of the pedals, every singing revolution of the spokes, to convert that sensation of blankness into a sense of freedom, like straw spun magically into gold.

I live in one of those uptown neighborhoods lined with prosperous houses of brick and stone, each with a smooth lawn sloping up to the front door, like a napkin tucked under a well-fed chin. Single-family dwellings for the most part, grown-up homes inhabited by grown-up people. Many of them younger by far than me. Imagine! It's a realization that still has the power to shock me afresh, every time it occurs to me: the consciousness that I am no longer as young as I have been so long in the habit of assuming myself to be, over decades of arrested adolescence. Instead of simply facing myself for what I am: A single woman who continues to rent, when all around her have long since bought. A loose cannon rolling along a quiet residential street, past the homes of those whose goals and mortgages have become firmly fixed.

More and more, in fact, I've begun to think of myself as the feckless grasshopper in the fable, trapped in a neighborhood where—increasingly—the industrious ants hold sway. Armies of renovation ants, with a dumpster in the front yard and a carpenter in coveralls hammering up on the deck. French-immersion-camp-for-the-kiddies ants, unloading groceries from the tailgate of the Taurus, with an able assist from the undocumented Filipina nanny. Never-too-early-to-plan-for-retirement ants, returning from the video outlet with the latest Tom Hanks hit in hand, to be fed into the electronic fireplace.

Of course, in the fable the grasshopper freezes to death come wintertime, while the ants cluster oblivious around the radiant warmth of the VCR. It's not as though the profligate insect can change his improvident nature, any more than the ants could choose to be other than prudent planners.

Which means that, even if I should be settled by now—or should, at the very least, have the decency to repent the fact that I'm not—there's nothing I can do to change the scene. Nothing beyond what I'm doing right this minute: Pedaling away the after-effects of two lubricious days with Leonard, which would have cloyed if they'd gone on two days longer. Telling myself as I pedal, meanwhile, that playing in the traffic—at the busy intersection of Fuck and Forget—is still a game that's fun for all ages.

Chapter Two

O'Ryan's first name is Mick, although I've never heard anyone call him that. "O'Ryan" suits him right down to the ground—no mean distance, given the length of his lanky legs.

I ought to make it clear at the outset that it's been years since O'Ryan and I slept together. When we did, it was back in the days when a savvy Clint Eastwood squint still *meant* something, and there was still indisputable appeal in those ain't-nobody's-brand-on-this-here-cayoose types. No, seriously. There was.

Truth to tell, O'Ryan appeals to some part of me yet. The part fed up to here with nervous number-crunchers of the nineties, intent on balancing the budget on the backs of the urban poor. And unsuccessful graduates of the Institute of Advanced Hair Replacement. As well as *zaftig* Spielberg wannabes, whose voices are centered high in their adenoids while their hearts can be found down in the basement rec room, alongside their expensive electronic toys.

O'Ryan is nothing at all like those guys. Even so, he and I don't sleep together anymore. Despite the fact—or maybe because of the fact—that both of us are still more often available than not. Both still renters in the bargain, in the same increasingly gentrified neighborhood.

Although O'Ryan's work takes him out of town a lot more than mine does, he holds on to his bachelor apartment over on Bertrand—barely furnished, except for a stain-repellent tartan couch that looks about as cozy to loll on as a Scotch-tape dispenser, and a fish tank in which there's always one lone gourami swimming endlessly around and around, like something that didn't quite flush. O'Ryan also holds on to that car of his—a gas-guzzling relic from the bad old pre-unleaded days, its hood tied more or less shut with a length of toaster cord.

Most of which is really beside the point, since the point I started out to make is that O'Ryan and I are no longer lovers. Even in our heyday, "lovers" was far too flurried a term for what went on between us, and nowadays, all that goes on between us is that, whenever O'Ryan happens to be around, we sometimes hang out together. His term for it, not mine. To me, "hanging out together" has always suggested two shirts flapping listlessly on the same clothesline. Besides, in more up-to-the-minute parlance, it's been abbreviated to "hanging together."

Any point, I wonder, in pointing that out to O'Ryan? Who is sprawled on his back on my living-room rug, with his improbably huge Frye-booted feet propped up against one end of the old steamer trunk that I took with me to college, and which has since continued to serve, from eon to eon, as my coffee table. As if to add to the air of anachronism, O'Ryan is rolling himself a cigarette. An honest-to-God homemade rollie, fashioned from the contents of a dark-blue packet of Drum, and a paler blue packet of Zig-Zag papers. Not only has no one apparently bothered to inform him that the tobacco era is over, it appears he's equally unaware that hand-rolled cigarettes are even more atavistic. Way out there somewhere in approximately the same orbit of obscurity occupied by Beatle boots, the Patti-Stacker, and nickel bags of Acapulco Gold.

"'Hangin' together'?" O'Ryan repeats, once I decide to opt for pointlessness by bringing this neologism to his attention. "That's what people say these days? Well, fine. Let's hang here, Dana. Let's hang 'em high. Let's—" But then he breaks off, shaking his head. "Nope. Sorry, but I just can't leave that 'out' out. 'Sides, at our age, hangin' out is what we do—in all directions. And we're durned lucky we can still manage even that."

"Good God," I answer, a little more testily than I intended. "Speak for yourself as a pensioner. Myself, I never felt better. Nor *looked* better, thank you very much—at least, according to my die-hard fans. The few who haven't died and are still somewhat hard."

"Bullshit," O'Ryan says. "You and I were both a lot cuter twenty years back. No harm in admitting it—so long as we're prepared for whatever the future might bring."

"Jesus! The future? What kind of talk is that from *you*? It sounds as if you've taken up the sale of life insurance door to door. And here I thought it was going to be just like old times: you stopping by to put your feet on my furniture and drop your ash all over the floor."

"It *is* like old times. Only these days, it's my *ass* that mostly drops. Dana, all I'm sayin' is, I might have some good advice to shove your way. On a proposition that could help you stockpile for your old age, if 'n you run 'er right."

This may be as good a moment as any to make it clear that O'Ryan is not a cowboy. In fact, despite his heavy reliance on they-went-thataway locutions, he isn't even from the West. Of course, when you're long and lean and as weathered as a split-rail fence, with a drooping Wyatt Earp mustache and shrewd blue eyes as faded as your jeans...Well, shuckins. What choice have you got, except to present yourself as the all-walkin', all-talkin', all-chawin', all-spittin' reincarnation of Rowdy Yates?

I understand that I'm free to ask O'Ryan what proposition it is that he's referring to. Or I could simply wait for him to fill me in in his own good time, serene in the knowledge that, like most laconic types, O'Ryan is perfectly capable of debriefing himself, provided that you're in no particular hurry. Which, as it happens, I'm not.

"What I mean," he continues at length—as I knew he would—"is that you might get rich writin' scrips for this here show I'm workin' on now up to Winzigdorf. 'Less, of course, you're too high and mighty these days to do teevee."

Who, me? High and mighty? I doubt if anybody's ever devised a television program too bad for me to consider writing for. In fact, to most of the worst, I've already submitted so many "scrips"—as O'Ryan would have it—over the years that a number of them have even been deemed ghastly enough to be produced.

My only problem with what O'Ryan is saying is in figuring out exactly which execrable series he is currently working on, and why I haven't heard about it before now.

Something revolving around animals is a safe bet. Like a lot of lean and lanky range-rider types, O'Ryan commenced his own career on the cathode-ray tube working for those kinds of outdoorsy kiddie-hour shows that often require extras who look plausible in the company of horses. From there, he's gone on to work as a wrangler in a far more general sense—helping to handle the animals for that never-ending supply of family programs on weekend nights that feature a clairvoyant coatimundi or a precognitive porpoise, or a... oh, I don't know, an eland with ESP. The kinds of programs, in other words, alongside which *America's Funniest Home Videos* compares favorably to the early work of Marcel Ophuls.

"It's *Amazing Grace*," O'Ryan explains, once he gets tired of waiting for me to ask.

"Pardon?"

"Starts three Sundays from now, on the Family Fare Channel."

"Oh, you mean that's the name of the program. Well, I'll be sure to tune in."

"You don't mean that, Dana, but you oughta. It's bound to be a big hit. Amazing Grace is this dog. Actually, 'bout a half-dozen dogs. All named Major in real life, and most of 'em he. Well, you know how Brady works."

I do indeed. Brady Olsson is O'Ryan's boss, who heads up a company called Canis Major and is famous for training not only dogs, but all kinds of animals, in lookalike bunches. Each with a special set of tricks, so that the group adds up to one multi-talented TV mammal *extraordinaire*. In this case, the truly amazing *Überhund* Amazing Grace.

"I told you I'd watch, and I will. At least once, anyway."

"No, you don't wait for it to go to *air*, fer chrissake. What you do is get in touch with DogStar Productions. That's the outfit whose baby this is. Hell, I'll git ya some names and numbers to call, an' a copy of the bible, with all the characters and storylines an' shit."

"Thanks, O'Ryan. I appreciate the tip. At the moment, though, I've pretty well got as much on my plate as I can handle." A true statement, provided one doesn't mind handling platefuls of projects that run heavily to greetings-card verse, supplying captions for pictorial desk calendars with a Maritime theme, or editing the in-house newsletter of a small, environment-friendly cosmetics chain in exchange for a free monthly supply of their products.

"Yeah, I'm sure." O'Ryan nods, genuinely respectful of my talent, as few are—or should be. "You're always up to yer butt in work. So what is it this week? You ghost-ridin' another autobiography of some corporate kingfish?"

O'Ryan's drawling pronunciation supplies me with a captivatingly yipee-ty-yi-yo image of myself plunging on horseback across the bygone plains, in the midst of a spectral herd of stampeding metaphors and wildly snorting similes. By comparison, my real life as a sometimes ghost-writer, as well as calendar captionist and TV hack, seems tame indeed.

"Not exactly." Not exactly is right. Truth to tell, I would jump at just about anything. After everything I've done over the years, how much more demeaning could it be to write dialogue for a dog? Even so, something in me bridles at the idea, for reasons I can barely make clear to myself, much less to O'Ryan.

"Then what's yer problem? Tell you what, I'm gonna pass yer name on to some of the people up at DogStar who—"

"No! I mean, no thanks. It's just not me, okay? I don't do animals. The odd corporate kingfish notwithstanding."

O'Ryan is looking at me as if I'd just admitted to stifling puppies for fun. Animals, after all, are a lot of his livelihood. And it's not as if, up until this minute, I've ever seemed to aspire to standards. "You mean you don't like dogs? C'mon, Dana, fer chrissake. *Every-body likes dogs.*"

Do I not like dogs? No, that's not quite it. There's just something about the thought of working for them that makes me uncomfortable. Never more so than right this minute. "I told you, I appreciate the tip, and...well, who knows when I'll get hungry enough to change my mind."

Who knows? In the fullness of time and after a few more weeks of virtual nonemployment, I may think more kindly of DogStar Productions and less scrupulously about my own disdain for dog-oriented drama. In the meantime, I prefer not to clutter my head with any thought more complex than the appreciation of how pleasant it is to be lounging on the carpeted floor of my living room, with a nostalgic haze of tobacco smoke hanging in the air. And with the soothing continuity of O'Ryan's ageless, timeless, and wholly undemanding presence to reassure me—however deceptively—that some things *do* go on, year in and year out, perennially unchanged, and always what they seem.

Chapter Three

When Jerry started dating Marta, I overheard him telling his friend Mel that Marta might well be the answer for him. To which Mel replied that, as far as he was concerned, Marta was the answer only if the question happened to be: What's tall and Nordic, and about as cozy as midnight in a meat locker?

It may well be that I, like Mel, have been biased against Marta from the kickoff. If for no other reason than the fact that she hates me. Nothing personal, you understand. Marta just seems to disapprove of me on principle. The same way she frowns on jimmies on her frozen yogurt, the prospect of an impromptu game of Frisbee, and everything else in the world that serves no apparently useful purpose.

For example, right off the bat, Marta told Jerry that I'm badly trained. Which I regard as a slander, since I'm not trained at all.

"Oh, come on," Jerry cajoled her, the first time she came to his place and found me stretched out on the couch in my favorite position, with my chin resting on the arm, and my back nails hooked into the cushions in that way that makes me feel luxuriously safe. "Come on. Murphy doesn't like to sleep on a hard floor any better than you or I would."

"On the contrary," Marta said, rapping out the words like someone giving correct change. "I like very much to sleep on the floor for the sake of my spine. So should you, Jerry. Although not when the dog leaves so many hairs on the carpet."

The funny thing is, knowing the degree of disgust Marta feels for me, I find myself playing to that worst-case scenario. Actually confirming her harshest judgments, by acting like an out-and-out boor. You

19

know how you'll catch yourself doing that—not intentionally, but because you can't help it? Like the old jumping-up-with-muddy-paws bit, even though you know better. Or barking into someone's face, especially when your breath is at its doggiest.

Even if you *don't* know, I can give you a rough idea: Automatically, whenever Marta is around, I leap into whatever chair she is about to sit in. Or I set out to stick my nose in her hand, just to be friendly—and wind up burying it in her crotch by mistake. One day, I'm ashamed to say, I even grabbed her leg and tried to hump it. I'm ashamed to say it, because there is nothing about Marta that inspires that kind of response, even in someone as basically irrepressible as myself.

All of which causes me—and Mel—to wonder: What's Jerry doing with a woman like this?

"Marta is a real adult" is the way Jerry explains it to Mel, as we three tool along the Bronx River Parkway in Jerry's car. Jerry's at the wheel, of course, with Mel beside him, and I'm in the back—with my head out the window and my tongue blowing in the breeze.

"No argument there." Mel nods. "The Swedish Snowball's got to be forty, if she's a day."

"I mean," says Jerry painstakingly, "that after a lifetime of dating girls, I'm finally with a grown-up woman. Who *doesn't* feel the need to tape Aerosmith posters to my bedroom walls, or leave bobby-pins on the sink, or...well, let's see...forget to turn on the answering machine, or—"

"Enough," says Mel. "Before you herniate yourself trying to come up with any more of Marta's selling points. Look, it's your business, after all. If you want to wind up in the deadly embrace of some Scandinavian lady dentist who can freeze without Novocaine."

"Go ahead and snipe from the sidelines," Jerry tells him. "Anybody can do that."

Mel shakes his head. "I beg to differ, Glass. As an art form, sniping from the sidelines is vastly underrated."

"Yes? Well, okay, as long as we're both feeling free to snipe: It wouldn't kill *you*, either, Arlen, to try dating a woman old enough to vote. You know, just as a change of pace from the heartbreak of satyriasis?"

Apparently, Mel and Jerry are allowed to rib each other this way because they're old, old friends. Buddies from boyhood, now well into their forties. Bound by their common quest for a lasting relationship, and their common complaint that a good woman is hard to find. My hunch, personally, is that both of them like things just the way they are: doodling together down the parkway of life in Jerry's Honda, with no more serious goal in mind than finding someplace sunny to throw the Frisbee around while they commiserate about how lonely it is to be an aging bachelor looking for love—or for a decent frozen yogurt, whichever shows up first. Meanwhile serene in the knowledge that a good frozen yogurt is a lot easier to come by—and a lot easier to jettison if it disappoints.

Now, however, with the advent of Marta, something seems about to change in the long-standing alliance of Jerry and Mel. Mel must sense it too, because as the three of us sun ourselves against the wrought-iron fence in the park, licking our yogurt cones, he continues to needle Jerry about his new romance.

"I'm all for mature relationships, as I said," says Mel—who has, according to my recollection, never said any such thing. "But the downside is, women of a certain age tend to become desperate. It won't be as simple as you think, when the time comes to show Miss Norway the doorway."

"You talk as if it's a foregone conclusion," Jerry says. "Me dumping Marta. Who's to say she may not be the one to give *me* the gate?"

"Ha! Don't hold your breath on that one, Glass."

"No, seriously. Marta's got some real reservations about our relationship. Murphy, for one thing. Ugh, don't eat the cone, by the way. 'Wholewheat health cone' my ass. It's laced with sugar, and—according to Marta—we never really get beyond our cavity-prone years."

"Yeah?" Mel continues to nibble defiantly at the rim of his cone. "So Marta's got reservations about Murphy here? That's the first thing I've ever heard in his favor. Frankly, I never thought much of the mutt, as you know. But, hey, if he can save you from a permanent alliance with the Danish Prune, then I say, 'Murphy, you're a good, good dog.'"

"Sure, he's a good dog," Jerry says, but without much conviction. "You know I think the world of him."

"What I know," says Mel, "is that you've complained about the poor bastard from the day you got saddled. For which, as I say, I haven't blamed you. I mean, let's face it: Wonder Dog, Murphy ain't exactly. In fact, if you were lying unconscious on the back forty, pinned under the tractor or whatever, Murphy is *not* a dog who would run back to the farmhouse to summon Gramps. This is a dog who'd stop off someplace to call his lawyer—to assess his own liability in the whole situation."

"You don't know what you're talking about" is Jerry's response to that.

In fact, neither do I, entirely, although the gist of Mel's remarks about me seems to be negative. Which is confirmed when—almost by way of apology—Mel feeds me the remnants of his too-sugary cone, my cavity-prone years be damned.

"Look, Glass, I'm going to put this to you as clearly as I can." As if to absolve himself of responsibility for Jerry's fate, Mel wipes his fingers ostentatiously on a paper napkin. "The way I see it, you made your first big mistake the day you let this animal in your life. But he's in your life now, and heck, that's Burgerbits under the bridge. Just don't compound that initial error with *another* mistake. Such as working on some way for the pooch and the prune to co-exist."

"There you go again, Arlen." Jerry is shaking his head. "Jumping to foregone conclusions. Marta has never said one word about wanting to co-exist. Why should she? What would impel her to move all the way to Westchester when her practice and most of her private life are in the city?"

"Right!" Mel claps Jerry heartily on the shoulder as we saunter back to the car. "That's absolutely right. Keep those facts in mind. Write them down if you have to. Tattoo them on your arm. Because, trust me, you're gonna *need* to have 'em right on tap. Once the Ice Queen starts mentally measuring the windows of your apartment for some heavy velvet drapes."

Jerry still looks mystified, although Mel is now speaking in words that even I can readily understand. In fact, I almost wish he'd go back to al-

lusions way above my head, since I don't like to hear these prognostica-
tions. When it comes to forecasts about Marta, it's Mel's judgment I
trust, much more than Jerry's. Not only because Mel, like me, can't
stand the woman. But also because I feel a certain regret in the face of
the possibility that—as far as Jerry and I are concerned—the days of
girlfriends who come and go are now mostly gone, thanks to Marta.
Irrespective of whether Jerry is willing to admit it or not.

Chapter Four

As Karen bounds up onto the stage at the Canada Goose, brandishing a cordless microphone, her "I Raped Mike Tyson" T-shirt elicits barely a snort of recognition from the audience. Not too surprising, given the predominantly teenage demographic of this house—many of whom are barely old enough to recall the criminal conviction that temporarily derailed Tyson's career. Much less sympathize with the sentiments behind the slogan.

Typical Karen, of course, misjudging the mood of a crowd. Even so, I can't help acknowledging with admiration her stubborn refusal to admit that what matters so intensely to her doesn't mean a fireman's fart to anyone else. Except, possibly, to me—her old, if still somewhat equivocal, friend.

"Hi, my name is Connie Casserole, and I suffer from goiter." What Karen has done, I observe, is to poke holes in the rind of half an orange, in order to attach it by a length of string to her throat. Not funny. Not to this group, certainly, who likely have even less familiarity with the old-fashioned phenomenon of goiter than with the now-yellowing rap sheet on Mike Tyson.

Nevertheless, in the face of puzzled silence, Karen carries gamely on. Perhaps pitching her routine at some idealized audience in her head, rather than at this throng of over-privileged teenyboppers more intent on impressing each other by ordering alcohol with illicit ID than on trying to fathom the comedy of this skinny blond adult from another planet.

"Please, pay no attention to my crippling DEFORMITY, folks.

Just go on having a good TIME on your evening out. You DESERVE it. I only want to call your attention to my affliction so that you'll feel perfectly COMFORTABLE with it for the rest of my act. No need, either, to laugh at any of my jokes just out of PITY. We goiter sufferers are too PROUD for that."

Well, you had to be there. And the problem with this crowd is that they're mostly not. Puzzled silence is rapidly turning to noisy indifference, and I have the sinking feeling that before Karen's act is even half over, it'll *be* over, in every way except nominally. How does she do it? How has she gone *on* doing it, all these seasons, night after night? Presenting herself, year in and year out, under that ridiculous stage-name Connie Casserole, to endless successions of audiences whose tastes, interests, and ages only become more and more divergent from her own with the passage of time?

Of course, if Karen's comedy were in the zanily ingratiating mode of Robin Williams, or cheerfully low-brow like Roseanne's, the age difference between her and the crowd might not matter so much. But the problem is that Karen is often stiff-necked, angry, confrontational. Comedy on the edge, hostility on the half-shell, humor with a hot-foot—that's our retrograde Karen. Eternally intent on getting something off her bony chest, motivated more by the gasp of outrage than by the friendly laugh of recognition. You can't even assume that she derives pleasure from the work, or wants to have fun. Not when she consistently refers to it as "the work," and continually comes offstage feigning satisfaction at having inspired more walkouts than rounds of applause.

"No, seriously," she is continuing now, though the bit is dying. "You should absolutely NOT feel sorry for me. Nor should you assume, for one single SECOND, that this unsightly lump on my neck is something YOU could catch. Not as long as you play it safe, and never, EVER under any circumstances lie about the length of your DICK, you guys out there. And as for you ladies, no fair faking OR-GASMS now, or else goiter's gonna get you for SURE, all right?"

By the time Karen bows and flounces off with her microphone, several more eternities have passed. And if I'm not the *only* person in the house who's clapping, then I'm certainly a member of a select minority. Karen, by her own admission, is the oldest living regular at the Canada Goose who has never been accorded the honor of headlining. In fact, on a given night, she is likely to be the oldest person in the *room*. With the exception of Granpa Billy, who mops the floors after the last set, or the occasional van-load of Rotarians who sometimes arrive at the club under the mistaken impression that this is where a dinner-theater production of *Man of La Mancha* is in its fourteenth smash month. And as well, the occasional exception of an old, old friend like me, who—at Karen's request—can be counted on to turn up to give her feedback on material that she has no intention of changing.

When Karen emerges from the stage door into the alley, she looks a whole lot better to me than in her onstage guise, under the glare of the spotlight. Karen's really a very attractive woman; I have forgotten how attractive she can look, in her black leather jacket, with her white-blond hair brushed out around her shoulders instead of pulled back in that dowdy half-mast ponytail. And with her long swan's neck no longer accessorized by an orange rind.

Inarguably, the Karen who steps out into the alley to walk with me to a nearby deli is an infinitely more appealing apparition than scratchy, strident Connie Casserole, with her Olive Oyl elbows and fluorescent ankle socks. However, when I venture to voice that opinion over cappuccino, in a tone of halting deference—as befits a mere TV hack daring to address a true creative artist—Karen dismisses it out of hand.

"You are SO wrong," she declares, without a flicker of hesitation. "Alienation is part of *mein Effekt*—in the purely Brechtian sense. I mean, we're talking performance ART here, Katie. Not prime-time TV standup-turned-sitdown in the whiny, banal Ellen DeGeneres mode."

"Katie" is a nickname that still has the power to grate my nerves, even after the passage of...Christ, a quarter-century. "Okay," I agree peevishly, "so you know what you're doing up there with that—what is it, quinsy?—routine. All's right with your comedic approach—or, excuse me, your Brechtian *Entfremdungseffekt.* In which case, why invite me down to the Canada Goose to look at your stuff in the first place?"

"Because," Karen says, directing upon me the full force of her unblinking eyes, as unnaturally blue as the Technicolor gaze of a character in a comic book, "I TRUST you, Katie. Somewhere down deep, there's a writer in you dying to get out, who could also help ME out. Provided you were willing to put what's left of your mind to it. Instead of tapping out 'Arf, arf, woof, woof' on the computer screen and regarding THAT as a good day's work."

Ouch. To say that I regret ever having admitted to Karen that I'm now writing scripts for *Amazing Grace* doesn't even begin to plumb the depths of my remorse. What I regret, *au fond*, is having admitted to her, way back when, that I ever had ambitions to become a writer of any greater consequence. "I don't regard it as a good day's work. It's a good day's *pay*. There's a big difference."

"Come on," Karen insists. "You've GOT to dream of a life beyond dog TV and aspirations calculated in multiples of thirteen WEEKS."

"Come on yourself. You're the one with the creative mission, not me." Still, she's right about one thing, though I'd die rather than fess up: I had absolutely intended to draw the line before descending to "dog TV," instead of somehow slipping across it when my back was turned.

"Katie," she says, "I know you better. Underneath, you're a born hellraiser, an *agente provocateuse*, one of the last of the red-hot ballbusting mamas, just like me."

"Bullshit." And it is. I can't remember when I ever raised hell, provoked any agency, or even came remotely close to so much as bruising a ball. "I told you, no missionary impulses here. In fact, I'm with Samuel Johnson, who said, 'A woman preaching is like a dog walking on its hinder legs. It is not that it is done well; you are surprised to find it done at all.'"

At that, Karen grins—the white-toothed gleaming grin of the Crest Perfect Checkup Child she undoubtedly once was. "Now, don't tell ME that walking on its hind legs isn't the LEAST of the stunts you're forced to script for that Wonder Dog."

"Karen, let's not go there. I mean it. Me writing material for you isn't going to happen, not in this universe."

In fact, Karen's act—as she clearly knows—could benefit from some outsider's input. Not mine, though. What's required is some writer younger than either of us to bring her up to speed. Some savvy slacker, reeking of attitude, a Generation Xer with X-ray eyes, capable of convincing Karen to lose the goiter routine and jump off altogether from the bandwagon of bargain-basement Antonin Artaudism on which, at her age, she no longer belongs.

"Katie, Katie..." Karen is no longer grinning as she shakes her head. "It's not my ACT I'm concerned about. It's YOU."

"The hell you are."

"I'm serious. You're way too SMART for Woofie the Wonder Dog, and at the rate you're going, that big fat brain of yours is liable to RUST out before it WEARS out. Like everything ELSE in this god-awful climate."

Ouch again. Come to think of it, maybe what I really regret, more than anything before or since, is having made the mistake of meeting up with Karen in the first place. Thereby allowing her to attach herself to my conscience—seemingly for all eternity—like a fishhook embedded in my tender flesh.

Not that I can envision, even with the benefit of hindsight, how it might have been possible to bypass encountering her at McGill all those years ago, quite by accident. It was early in our first term, as we both lounged with pretended nonchalance on the front steps of the women's residence, under the scrutiny of the statue of Queen Victoria. Both of us waiting for our dates to descend the hill from the men's residence and spirit us away for the evening.

A late September evening, as I recall it. Moist, misty, as oppressive as summer, with the cars honking and screeching along Sherbrooke Street in celebration of Saturday night. In fact, there were three of us on the steps that night—me, Karen, and some other fledgling freshwoman whose name and place of origin I forget.

Even as I recall how painfully chubby she was, and how nervously she—like us—had elected to wager her one twelve-o'clock leave of the week on Mr. Maybe-Right, in hopes that he'd prove worthy of the gamble.

Not that Karen, nor I, nor that third girl knew much about the boys we'd all separately agreed to see on that same Saturday. As I remember, each of us had only briefly met her beau *du jour* at some "mixer" held earlier in the week. Now, here we were, on a sultry September night, each pretending for the others' benefit that the evening's outcome mattered not one whit, one way or the other.

"I'm from Skokie, Illinois," Karen announced to pass the time. "Which may well BE the armpit of the universe, but which, so far—I have to say—leaves Canada here right in the DUST on the sophistication scale. Of course, nobody in my family wanted me to come up here for college, and I can't say my dad didn't WARN me. Pa Larkin is sixty-three years young, and he volunteered for the war, way before Pearl Harbor. Which explains how he happened to do some hard time up in Canuckland, on his way overseas to join up with the RAF. It's Pa Larkin who told me that Canadians subsist almost EXCLUSIVELY on a diet of turnips and cabbage. A chesterfield, he says, is what they sit on, not smoke. Otherwise, according to my pa, there's not a hell of a lot to KNOW about Canucks.

"And so far, I'd say he's right. Which is NO surprise, since Pa Larkin is just about the smartest old guy in the WORLD—even if all he does for a living is run a liquor store in the armpit of Skokie, which, in turn, is the armpit of the universe. Present country excepted, of COURSE."

I think I was too distracted about my upcoming date to be offended. Chances are, I would not even have remembered that initial encounter with Karen had not she and I and the other girl whose name I forget all found ourselves once more—as if by prior arrangement—back on those self-same steps no more than two hours later. Still far in advance of the midnight curfew for which we'd all three signed out in our youthful optimism. The chubby girl whose name I don't remember confided in tears that she'd cut short her evening out after her date remarked, unchivalrously, on the way his motor-scooter sagged under her weight. While *my* knight in shining armor had metamorphosed into a churl in a too-shiny suit when he pointed to the hair on my forearms as a "genetic throwback."

"Too fat? Too hairy?" Karen mocked us. "Ha! That's NOTHING! The geek I wasted MY twelve-o'clock on wants to know if the reason I'm so 'scrawny' has to do with some DISORDER his father-the-shrink warned him is the coming thing among college girls. The dink even wrote the name DOWN for me, in case I wanted to seek out treatment. It's called... if I can read this... *anorexia nervosa*. Either of you ever hear about it?"

"Sure," I shot back. "If you water it twice weekly and keep it out of the sun, it'll bloom for you all year round."

At that feeble sally, Karen grinned the white-toothed grin I've come to know so well. What became of that forlorn chubby girl, I can't recall. What I do remember is how Karen and I celebrated our newfound friendship and our newly lost dates by sitting up together way past midnight, drinking a bottle of syrupy wine she'd swiped from the bottom of her absent roommate's garment bag. Eventually, we got around to introducing ourselves.

"Your name is DANA? Come on!" Karen started right in. "Don't tell me you're SERIOUSLY interested in spending the rest of your life answering to some frozen-faced, turnip-eating, candy-assed CANADIAN kind of name like Dana. Tell you what, as a personal favor to you, and from the very depths of this Dixie cup of Mogen David wine, I dub thee Katie. A REAL name, a name that suits thee, forsooth. An AMERICAN name."

Typical of her, she didn't bother asking me what I thought of "Katie." Typical of me, I didn't object. I was, in fact, somehow flattered that my first friend at McGill would think well enough of me to make me over. In her own image, as it turned out—with a name that sounded closer to "Karen," and a new nationality to match her own.

"Katie Jaeger?" I giggled. "From Omaha?" That was still in our first term, after Karen had taken to introducing me under the identity she'd chosen for me. "You've just decided who I am and where I'm from?"

"Sure, honey." Karen shrugged. "I'm sure Omaha is MUCH nicer than Gopher Prairie, or wherever you're REALLY from."

No doubt. But as time went on, I began to make feeble complaints. "You know, you really shouldn't assume that making me an honorary American is such a compliment. Not with what's going on over in Southeast Asia."

Only in our final year as undergraduates did I become adamant. "Karen, please stop introducing me as Katie, Princess of the Platte, all right?"

But it wasn't all right. Somehow, in that final year, things were no longer the same between us. I now had a boyfriend that Karen hadn't met who knew me as Dana. And when Karen made her campus debut as a standup—relying on material cribbed from the late Lenny Bruce—she made a point of receiving my backstage congratulations with chilly reserve.

After graduation, we drifted completely apart. And it wasn't until years later that we ran into each other—not in Montreal, but here. In the lobby of a small experimental theater where Karen was now performing material more like Sandra Bernhard's than Lenny Bruce's.

"You became a WRITER!" she squealed, after I murmured something about a script I was working on. "Which only goes to show what a PERFECT pair we still are, Katie, honey. You can write some stuff for ME—all about the assholes we were dating the night we met. If that's not a prime example of dogma chasing karma, what is?"

Whatever it was, I found myself so glad to see her that I neglected to object to being Katie again. And also neglected to speak too specifically about what I was writing, as a hack-for-hire whose true karma was to embrace no dogma at all. As a result, I let Karen—always stronger on paper than in performance—start lobbying me, right there in the lobby, to help her with her act. And she continues to lobby me to this very day.

"You know," I say to her now, quietly, "I'm not what you think. I never was."

She regards me with wide-open cornflower-blue eyes. "You're EXACTLY what I think, and I'm NEVER wrong."

Is it affection or mere obstinacy that fuels her feelings for me? To this day, I can't say for sure. There's something about the combined effect of the pale hair and black biker jacket that enhances the sense of paradox that she perpetually presents.

While I'm still mulling it over, a white-shirted waiter appears and hovers helpfully.

"Where it says 'free-range' chicken?" I direct his attention to the menu. "What exactly do they mean by that?"

He shrugs. "Maybe they cook it...on top of the range, or whatever."

"No, no, it's *free* range. As in ranging free. Oh, hell, skip it. Give me egg-salad, okay? And I promise not to ask where those eggs spent their formative weeks."

"Katie! Honestly, honey. What do you CARE? I mean, since when are you some lapsed VEGETARIAN who cheats with chicken?"

"No, you're the one who cheats with chicken. All those little boys you lure away from their paper routes?"

That's not quite true, but not quite not. From what I've seen of her dating life, Karen seldom picks on men over thirty. And, despite her own age, still gets away with robbing the nest. Not that many of her romances appear to lead anywhere lasting. For all I know, she simply devours her dates at the end of the evening, like some insect removing her mate-of-the-moment from wider circulation as soon as he's serviced her.

Karen smiles a smile of private predation. "Never mind ME. It's your feathered friends we're talking about."

"Oh, I don't know. If I'm going to eat them, I at least like to think the lives they've lost were somewhat worth living."

"Honey, you're too much." She is shaking her head again, in what now appears to be genuine despair of me. "You think that's the POINT of free-range chickens—for THEM to have a good time?

The idea is that they TASTE better. Not whether it's NICER for some bird not to be nailed to the perch in its battery box before they lop off its HEAD."

Funny, but I could swear she's actually angry with me. God knows, her own idiosyncrasies are every bit as bizarre as mine. More so. That house of hers, for instance—as scrupulously scrubbed as the waiting room of a top-of-the-line oral surgeon. Dishes and cutlery whisked into the dishwasher immediately after use, and sometimes during.

To my certain knowledge, Karen does a wash every single day, loading up her washer-dryer with any article of attire—as well as towels and bedsheets—that may have come in contact with her body during the course of the previous twenty-four hours. In fact, the minute she parts company with me, I know precisely what she'll do: hurry home in her assiduously vacuumed Volkswagen Bug to throw the clothes she's wearing into the washer. Along with the dishtowel she may have used to buff a drinking glass at some earlier point in the day, and the already laundered nightgown that she wishes to put through the cycle once more for good measure before bedding down in it.

"Can we not discuss chickens nailed to their perches?" I admonish her. "At least, not in front of my egg-salad sandwich."

"I mean," Karen continues as if I hadn't spoken, "I just wonder if it's some weird byproduct of writing lines for that dumb dog. Like, starting to relate to them all as if they were HUMAN?"

"All *who*, for God's sake? Anyway, I don't give the dog lines! If you ever watched the show you'd know Amazing Grace is too busy saving the day to stop and palaver."

Although it is funny, now that I think about it, how the inner lives of chickens have lately begun to matter to me. Maybe Karen's right, and it all stems from putting directions in my scripts like "Grace feels that Tommy is in danger," "Grace's first thought is for the safety of the kids on the schoolbus."

By the time we part, Karen has apparently forgotten all about my overweening concern for chickens, and my continued underachievement as a creative artist. She's firmly back in her chirpy mode as she pecks me on the cheek, bids me "Safe home, honey!" and gives me a final flash of her white white smile. All vestiges of annoyance evaporated, leaving no telltale trace behind. I am, once more, exactly who Karen thinks I am, and once again, she's never wrong.

What is it about me, I wonder, that invites those kinds of assumptions? When I was a kid, my brother, Paul, would turn off and on like Karen, inexplicably enraged at me one moment, and eagerly protective the next. The kind of brother who might tear the heads off your dolls, but who could also be counted on to wheel you home in your wagon in a thunderstorm, when all the other kids were deriding you for being afraid. And with Paul—just as with Karen—I found it impossible to work out precisely what it was about me that inspired these shifts.

We are twins, but somehow Paul's always seemed older. In fact, by the time we were eleven and I was still firmly locked into let's-pretend, Paul had graduated to hanging around on the corner with his friends, posing as a tough. Which meant that every day on the way home from school, I had no other choice but to ride right past him, mounted on the back of my imaginary horse.

At first, Paul made a feeble effort to defend me from the scornful hoots of his friends. But when I showed no sign of giving up the horse, he became utterly furious, and appealed to my mother. Who was no help at all, and in fact could always be counted on, in the crunch, to come down foursquare on the side of Imagination and Creativity, and in staunch opposition to Dull-Witted Conformity.

Eventually, when Paul had had enough of his friends' derision of his nutty twin sister, he took the law into his own hands. One day, instead of simply standing there on the corner humiliated as my horse Hightail and I cantered past, he followed us home. And confronted me in the garage, which served as a makeshift stable for my invisible horse. "Where is he?" he demanded. "Where's the god-damn horse?"

I was too terrified by the "goddamn" not to tell him. "There." I indicated the general area where Hightail stood, contentedly munching his invisible oats.

From behind his back, my brother produced the Daisy air rifle he'd been given for Christmas on the clear understanding that he was never, ever to point it at any living thing. Now, however, he was not only pointing it at my horse, he was squeezing the trigger. There was a sharp report, and the next thing I knew, my imaginary horse lay on the concrete floor of the family garage, as dead as any flesh-and-blood steed.

Even Paul seemed momentarily mesmerized, and stood gaping at the spot where he'd fired, for all the world as though he, too, could see the havoc he'd wrought. It was, quite possibly, fantasy's darkest yet most impressive hour.

My brother flung aside his rifle, ran out of the garage and, to his credit, seemed truly repentant. Until the next day—when I came careering past him and his friends once more, this time on the back of a brand-new steed I called Black Magic. Poor Paul. From the look on his face, it was clear that he now understood what I must have known all along: as a weapon, even a Daisy air rifle is no match for imagination unbridled.

My twinship with Paul was mere biological fact. We were not—and are not to this day—remotely alike. We don't want the same things; we probably never did. Killing my horse was only a way for Paul to prove it.

Twinship with Karen, on the other hand, is a concept she keeps thrusting on me. But we are not, at base, the same. No more alike than I and my brother. Karen probably knows it too. Yet, unlike Paul, stubbornly refuses to prove it outright.

Hightail is dead; long live Black Magic. That's apparently all on Earth I know, and all I need to know. Despite the expectations I occasionally arouse in others that there ought to be more to me than that.

Chapter Five

I have no clear recollection of which of Jerry's girls it was who sprang me from the Shelter, and then moved herself and me in with Jerry. If I seem like an ingrate for forgetting her name, you have to understand that she didn't last all that long. Jerry is the sort of guy to whom relationships simply happen. And then—just as quickly—*un*happen. I guess it's an irony of his life that, among all those incidental entanglements, *I'm* the only one that so far seems to be a keeper. In spite of the fact that our involvement is the only one that Jerry didn't choose.

Boy, did he not choose me. My clearest recollection of the day I arrived is his horrified expression as he opened the door of his apartment to find me standing on the mat, at the end of a frayed rope, fresh from stir. Not that I stayed standing on the mat for long. Before the girl on the other end of the rope could even get it off my neck, I pulled it right out of her hand, skittered across the bare parquet, and—without even thinking—lifted my leg against the nearest vertical object.

Which happened to be one of Jerry's prized Bang and Olufsen speakers. At first, there was a muffled fizz. Then a bang—or was it an olufsen?—followed by a yelp of pain from Jerry, and an instantaneous apology from the girl, who'd apparently hoped to present me as a surprise.

Some surprise. It was very soon after that the girl departed. "Temporarily." The deal being, as she promised through her tears, that as soon as she got settled at her sister's, she'd be back for her stuff, and me. Needless to say, she never came back. And when Jerry phoned the number she'd left him, it turned out to be disconnected. "Temporarily."

All that was some time back. The girl's stuff is still in the apartment, and so am I. Looks as if Jerry's been left holding the stoop-and-scoop bag. Not so temporarily.

Since then, as I say, many other girls have come and gone—mostly gone. Apparently getting stuck with me was a freak example of Jerry zigging when he should have zagged, because when it comes to his other relationships, he appears to possess an uncanny talent for taking on the sort of women who can just as easily be taken off again.

Or "girls," I should say. With the recent exception of Marta, the females in Jerry's life tend to be: (1) young enough to be required to show ID; (2) anxious about their future careers in modern dance, art history, or French translation; and (3) exceedingly temporary.

One minute, there's the girl in the kitchen, popping another herbal teabag into Jerry's cup and spreading Fleischmann's Lite on his toast. Then—boom. The next minute, he's taking her aside for a murmured conference, after which, all of a sudden, she's crying quietly as she throws her dance leotards, her big art books, or her language-learning tapes into her American Tourister suitcases. While Jerry—always inclined to allergy attacks when under stress—reaches for his Ventolin with one hand and dials a cab with the other.

"I'll call you tonight," he always promises the girl, as he helps her pilot her American Touristers out of the apartment and into the elevator. True to his word, he always does call that night. Stretched out on his bed, cradling the receiver with one hand, while operating the TV remote with the other.

All the time he's talking soothingly into the telephone, he keeps changing channels, summoning a succession of images to life on the screen. A brand-new car revolving on a spotlit platform; two wrestlers, circling each other warily. Then, with a flick of the button, Jerry can transform them into two tiny men adrift in a tiny boat, on the lapping tide of a very large toilet bowl.

Out of deference to the girl on the other end of the phone, Jerry keeps the volume on the set right down. But just watching the pictures that merge into each other on the screen apparently inspires him to know what to say to ease the girl's pain, as he speaks in a comforting low-key murmur. I can never quite catch the words, but whatever Jerry murmurs seems to do the trick. Because the next day, or the day after that, when the girl shows up at the apartment for the stuff that didn't fit into her American Touristers, she's always smiling bravely. And if there are any hard feelings toward Jerry, she manages to keep them under wraps—at least until she swoops down on me to give me a showy farewell kiss.

"Murphy, you big goof," the girl is more likely than not to whisper into my ear, a bit too loudly for comfort. "You know, it's *you* I'm going to miss the most."

If Jerry overhears this, he gives no sign. He merely stands there massaging his temples to relieve the sinus pressure as he waits politely for the girl to go.

This time, once she's on her way, it's forever. Leaving the decks clear for whoever shows up next, with hope in her heart, an L.L. Bean bag full of hot-rollers under her arm, and a diaphragm tucked in her purse. In advance of the American Touristers that will surely follow a day or two later. And then—just as surely—follow her out again.

Through it all there's been me, the only constant. Although I suspect that if I had a suitcase to pack and someplace for the cab to drop me, Jerry would have long since seen me on my way, too. In a heartbeat. Believe me, whatever illusions I might have had about the sanctity of my bond with mankind, I left back there at the Shelter. Which is not to put the knock on Jerry, you understand—who's hardly the type who'd ever beat me, or starve me to death. But the fact is, if he ever *did* decide to dispose of me in some permanent way, he'd never be held accountable. And when you live the way I do—on the continued goodwill of someone who never actually *wanted* to live with you in the first place—you tend to keep such facts in mind.

So far, though, so good. Jerry does his best by me, most of the time. And in return, I try to do my best by him whenever I'm able. Which may not make it sound like a partnership exactly made in heaven. Still, we carry on with it, one day at a time.

In the evening, for instance, when Jerry comes home, and we take our walk together in the park. During which I always attempt to liven things up by seeing if I can jerk his arm from its socket before he manages to rein me in.

"Murphy, please!" he always complains, just as if he had something better to do. "You've got five minutes before Jim Lehrer to get down to business."

The business I'm supposed to get down to is finding a spot to shit, but Jerry can't bring himself to refer to that activity by name. Instead, he calls it "getting down to business"—which makes it sound more like a career choice than a bodily function.

Then, when I finally do my business, he always stares down at it critically for a moment, before dropping a Baggie over it and easing it into the nearest trashcan. Whatever I've produced, I get the impression, is never quite what he had in mind. But then, as I told you, life with me altogether has never been quite what Jerry had in mind. 🐾

Chapter Six

Ring!

It's the phone, but that's okay. Let the machine pick up. That's the whole point of having a machine when you work at home. To keep the outside world at bay, where it belongs.

Ring!

At least, that's been my story to the folks at the income tax department, when claiming my answering machine as a business expense. My time being money, and all that shit. For my home is my office, and I detest interruptions.

Ring!

Well, "detest" may be too strong a word. The truth is, I love interruptions, *especially* when working. And I suspect that the nice folks at the income tax department feel exactly the same as I do about taking a little break every now and then.

Ri—

Oh, the hell with it. Who am I kidding? Girls just want to have tax-deductible fun. "Hello?"

"Hello yourself," comes a familiar rumble at the other end.

It's Derek Matthews, who constitutes precisely the sort of interruption to my work that I got the answering machine in order to prevent. "Derek! How lovely to hear from you." Well, it is, goddamn it. To the extent that I can't help smiling, and letting the smile show in my voice.

"I just got into town. So when the hell are you going to drop over?"

"Drop over? Usually when you call, it's from the next corner to ask if it's okay to stay *here*."

"Don't be a nitwit, Jaegerschnitzel. I'm at the Arlington."

"Don't call me Jaegerschnitzel."

"What about nitwit?"

"That I'm okay with. It's the corny little endearments I take exception to."

"Look, the point is, I have a corner suite. Paid for by my publisher."

"Oh, right. And I'm supposed to drop everything, and rush right over?"

"No, you're supposed to rush right over, *then* drop everything."

"Har-dee-har. When would you like me to come? And if you say 'About ten minutes after you get here,' I'm slamming this phone."

Sadly, this is what passes for repartee between Derek and me. A little Tracy, a little Hepburn, a lot of mutually self-indulgent re-bop. Still, if I had to pick a favorite from among the Marrieds, it would be Derek. Especially today, with a hotel suite to offer me—instead of the prospect of yet another male houseguest to clean up after, and feel the absence of, once he's hit the road.

"Look," Derek's voice is growling in my ear, "I'm phoning you from the hotel bar. Why don't you join me here, and we'll have a drink or two and take it from there?"

I know precisely where Derek will want to take it from there. On the other hand, should I happen to decide to make it clear to him that a drink is all I have in mind, he's not the type to get obnoxious about it. Of all the married philanderers I've ever met, Derek comes closest to qualifying as one who genuinely enjoys the company of women for its own sake, irrespective of whether or not he scores. Just so long as it's understood at the outset that his preferred option is always to score.

"Okay, let's say I meet you there at six. You can pencil in some back-up babes for later in the evening, in case I decide to kack out on you early."

"Jaegerschnitzel! You really ought to give me more credit."

"You're right. It wouldn't occur to you, for one single second, that there's any possibility of my kacking out. By the way, have I told you lately how much I hate it when you call me cute names?"

Okay, so now I've hung up the phone and still have until six o'clock to figure out whether I'll stay over at the Arlington or not. Although, why am I kidding myself that it's really in question? Being in bed with Derek has always been fun, in any locality. From harmless horseplay, to languorous kisses, right through to more explicit contraventions of the indecency statutes, Derek knows, as they say, the right moves. As well as the moves that keep the moves from *seeming* like moves. Plus, he's unstintingly appreciative. "Those legs," he'll murmur, as he watches me dress for dinner once we've made love. "That ass. The way those legs meet that ass."

"Bullshit," I'll scoff. But even so, I'll try to treat him to a sexy little wriggle as I struggle into my pantihose—at the same time regretting that I once more forgot to wear stockings and garters instead.

Those legs. That ass. That's right. So how come I feel so goddamn... equivocal this time out, as I go through the familiar ritual of surveying my attributes in my full-length mirror while getting dressed? After all, the legs still meet the ass, more or less. And even though the effect undoubtedly isn't what it once was, it's not as if Derek's getting any younger, either.

Oh, come on, now. Fully dressed and wearing lipstick, isn't the total package presentable enough to at least prompt a rush of affection for the woman smiling back at me from the mirror? We've been through a lot together, me and my smiling reflection. Certainly enough to have earned us the right to congratulate each other for the way we've both managed to keep from looking as if we've been through very much of anything. I mean, maybe I *am* getting older, and God knows I can't claim to be getting any better. But at this point, isn't it something of a minor triumph that I don't yet seem to be actually getting any *worse?*

Besides, tonight, no matter how I play it, I'm bound to come out ahead on the deal with Derek. Simply by virtue of the fact that, for once, it's me who gets to decide whether to stay or go—and someone else who gets left, whenever I eventually leave.

Chapter Seven

In the pink-and-buff interior of Suite 1911 at the Arlington Hotel, I am resting my head on the furry mat of Derek's chest as he reclines on a bank of pillows, puffing a cigar and sipping Scotch. "Now isn't this nice?" he remarks, his voice an agreeable rumble against my ear.

"Very nice," I agree. Which it is. Whenever Derek stirs himself to tap his cigar in the ashtray, I feel the starchy, worldly kiss of hotel bedsheets. On the flesh-colored nightstand on my side of the bed sits my own ration of Scotch in a hotel glass, with the "Sanitized For Your Protection" wrapper crumpled alongside. Through the sealed hotel window, I can hear the late-night sounds of the city below— close enough to make me feel at the sophisticated heart of things, yet sufficiently remote to keep me far above the level of the madding crowd.

I am glad that I elected—after a none-too-suspenseful struggle— to stay the night. There is nothing like the smooth impersonality of a decent hotel to restore my sense of myself as the kind of worldly-wise woman who still gets called up for such agreeable overnight assignments. I raise my glass, clink it against Derek's, sip my whiskey—then make a decidedly unworldly-wise face. "God, I hate the taste of Scotch."

"Everybody does," Derek informs me. "How the distilling industry prospers regardless is one of life's enduring mysteries. In fact, I'm thinking of doing my next book on that subject. Christ knows, I've got the research."

"What about the book you're doing now? How's that going?"

"The book," says Derek, "is killing me."

By which I understand—as I am meant to—that the book is going very well indeed. Which is more than can be said for its author, who looks terrible this trip, even in the flattering pinkish glow of the bedside lamp. Unless he's genuinely tired from months of writing. To say nothing of his long flight today from the Coast, "researching" God knows how many Scotches while on board.

"Derek," I say gently, "it's awfully late. Don't you think you need to turn out the light and get some sleep?"

Defiantly, he reaches to pour himself another drink. "What I need is to cut back on these christly cigars." The mattress heaves a little as he props himself more firmly against his bulwark of pillows to sip from the glass.

"Or," I venture, "cut back on the Scotch?"

"No, no, it's the cigars. Give me a kind of... clutch in the chest." He rubs the affected area, his fingers half submerging in a carpet of gray-blond hairs.

I sit up too, feeling faintly alarmed. "What do you mean?" Derek is not a tall man, but he has always seemed big to me, and indestructible. Larger than life, with his full-bodied laugh, broad beefy chest, and seemingly limitless capacity for all forms of excess. A vulnerable Derek, on the other hand, strikes me as no Derek at all. It's a thought I'm not particularly proud of, as it forms in my head. Quickly as I can, I try to mask it with a look of maternal concern. "Gee, it's probably heartburn, don't you think? You were—"

"Don't strain yourself, Jaegerschnitzel," he growls, "with the I-give-a-crap act." Whereupon, he rolls toward me, to plant a Scotchy kiss on my mouth. "We all know what you're in this for, and on *that* score, you don't have a thing to worry about. Old Matthews is hardly dead meat yet." To prove the point, he reaches under the covers to fondle my naked hip.

"Seriously." I pick up his hand and replace it firmly on his side of the bed. "You've worn me out already, and I, for one, have got to sleep. There's always tomorrow morning, once we get our second wind."

Although Derek continues to make a show of reluctance to close down the party, I can tell he's secretly grateful to lay his head down on the pillows, switch off the lamp, close his eyes, and drift into oblivion. As I've reassured him, he's already made love to me quite respectably, and I find myself happy to fall asleep, too.

The next thing I know, I'm in the midst of a familiar dream. In this dream, I'm waving goodbye to Derek from my own front window as he settles into the backseat of the taxicab at the curb. Wait a minute, I think, sound asleep. Wasn't this trip going to be different? This time, wasn't *he* going to be the one left behind, in his prepaid suite at the Arlington?

But in my dream, there's really nothing I can do, except what I always do in waking life, after being left: get out on my bicycle, push away from the curb, and speed off to escape the onslaught of emptiness. *Try to catch me*, rasp the gears, as I pump the pedals in a customary attempt to dissipate the customary sense of loss, with each forward turn of the front wheel. Feeling, in one moment, like a rider clinging to the saddle over uneven ground. And in the next, like the horse—sturdy legs churning resolutely up the slope. A cycling centaur, I marvel fuzzily. A member in good standing of some species that interlocks man and beast. Aligned to both, yet possessed of a freedom unknown to either, as I—

I awaken, rudely, in the darkness, with a jerk. Which reminds me of a joke of sorts that my friend Karen likes to make: "I awoke with a jerk, and it was no one I knew." Well, I guess you had to be there...

Meanwhile, I'm *here*, and still no more than half-awake, I am gradually becoming aware of something pinching my arm, as though my flesh were caught in a vise. As if someone had suddenly grabbed hold of me, in an effort to drag me down off my bike. Then, with a sharp intake of breath, I sit up in bed, breaking once and for all through the surface of my dream—which falls away around me, like shards of ice splintering on a frozen pond.

Now I'm fully awake—in bed in Derek's suite at the Arlington. Beside me in the dark is Derek, breathing harshly as he squeezes his fingers convulsively around my arm. He is, I try to assure myself, only having some kind of dream himself. Though, of course, I know better than that. Derek, rasping beside me in the darkness, is caught up in something far more menacing than any nightmare. Derek may, in fact, be dying. And there is nobody here but me to help.

I wrench free of his grip and propel myself out of the bed. Only to waste precious seconds groping vainly in the dark for the lightswitch. Instead, what my fumbling fingers find is Derek's shirt—still damp with his sweat—on the back of a chair. I pull it on and blunder toward the door, locate the knob, turn it—then wince, as the light from the corridor comes stabbing in.

Even as I stumble into the brightness of the hallway, it occurs to me that I have no idea what I'm doing. Derek, if not actually dying, is certainly ill. So why am I standing out *here*, when I should be in *there*, phoning for an ambulance?

I stand gazing stupidly along the carpeted corridor, with its endless succession of doors, each closed indifferently to my distress. Then I glance back at Derek's door—suddenly terrified that I've locked myself out, wearing nothing but his shirt.

But no. The door, thank God, is ajar, the Do Not Disturb sign still swinging festively from the knob, as testimony to the force with which I flung open the door and launched myself into the corridor. I have to go back in there and call somebody. Call somebody, and tell them....

What? That I just happened to be passing Suite 1911 in the middle of the night, clad only in a man's shirt, when I overheard panicked breathing behind the door? Derek, after all, is not only very married, he is also something of a celebrity. While I—although strikingly single and not at all celebrated—also have some kind of stake in this, since it's *my* clothes all over the floor of Derek's room, and the stain of *my* lipstick on one of the Scotch glasses beside his bed. Okay, so we weren't actually making love when Derek was stricken. So what? Since nobody—and now it's Derek's wife that I have specifically in mind—is likely to believe for one solitary second that my role in this moth-eaten mini-drama is as anything other than the bimbo sent over by Central Casting. Upon whom—in the worst tradition of comic cliché—Derek literally collapsed in mid-screw.

In the few nanoseconds that it's taken me to formulate these thoughts, the door directly across the hall has opened wide. A man dressed in a casual jacket and slacks steps out, looking, despite the hour, as fresh as the proverbial daisy. And so eagerly expectant, you might almost think he'd been *waiting* behind his door for hours in hopes of just such a nocturnal emergency erupting across the hall.

"Something the matter?" he asks me politely. Just as if he's prepared equally to entertain the possibility that there could be any number of quietly quotidian reasons for a barely clad female to be standing in a hotel corridor in the wee morning hours looking somewhat electrocuted.

"I...yes!" I manage to blurt. "It's—it's my, uh, friend." I gesture over my shoulder. "He's suddenly very sick."

Without waiting to hear more, the stranger pushes past me and into Derek's room, where he finds the switch to the bedside lamp with embarrassing ease. Derek is still gasping, but less hoarsely, and as the glare of the lamp strikes his face, he squeezes his closed eyelids tighter like a child and moans a faint, reflexive protest.

"Is he conscious?" I ask the stranger, for some reason trusting him to know.

He shrugs, and reaches for Derek's wrist to feel the pulse. In the process, pulling back the bedclothes, and exposing Derek's vulnerable nakedness—for which I blush complicitously.

"What's his name?" the man demands of me.

"It's Derek Math—" But then, remembering Derek's celebrity status, I quickly amend my response. "His name is Derek. Derek's his, uh, name."

"Derek? Can you hear me?" The man addresses Derek loudly and distinctly, as if they were both under water. There's a slight accent, I note irrelevantly. Something residually British, perhaps. But faded, as if with the passage of years. "Derek, you're going to be all right."

Is he? "Can you tell what's wrong?" I whisper to the helpful stranger.

Who shrugs once more, modestly. "Heart, at a guess. But you'll want a more expert opinion. I don't suppose you've thought to ring down to the desk?" Meanwhile, anticipating the answer, he's already reaching for the phone.

"No, wait!" The desperation in my voice arrests the man's hand on the receiver. "I...Look, I'm not his wife, okay? He has one, but I'm not it."

"I see." The man nods, clearly not surprised. "Well, I doubt that either of you ladies is likely to wind up a widow. But he needs help. Then we'll get *you* sorted out, all right?"

All right? I'm not at all certain that I want to be sorted out. On the other hand, what choice have I got? As the stranger phones the front desk, I stand by stupidly. Longing to take Derek's hand, to whisper something comforting, whether he can hear me or not. But my illicitness in the situation makes me self-conscious. To the point where I feel inhibited from taking any initiative, even to the extent of picking up my clothes and retiring to the bathroom to put them on.

"Good. Thanks." The man concludes his conversation, then cradles the receiver and turns back to me. "Right, then, sweetheart. You've got, I should estimate, all of ninety-seven seconds to make your getaway." With impressive economy of motion, he casts about the room, correctly pinpointing each and every object in it that pertains to me. Which he gathers up and crams into my arms. "Coat, skirt, blouse, underthings, purse. Now, you take all this, as well as this, this, and this"—to the burgeoning pile he adds my shoes, my watch, and lipsticked drinking-glass—"and you scarper across to my room. Shut the door, get dressed, and then off you go once the coast is clear. Without so much as a backward glance. Got it? Well? Don't stand here gaping. He's not your husband, remember?"

Even so, I continue to stand here gaping, unable to articulate my reluctance to leave Derek like this—unconscious, and in the dubious care of a complete stranger. "But if I just take off, how will I find out if he's okay?"

"Ah!" This time, in the man's nod, there is a faint suggestion of approval—presumably for this unexpected display of devotion. "Well, then, I'll tell you what: just stay in my room. Don't so much as peek out the door—not even when the paramedics come thundering up here with all their emergency gear. I'll go with your friend—Derek, is it?—to the hospital. Then, as soon as there's news, I'll ring you in my room. Now, I can't do fairer than that, can I? Look lively, sweetheart, and skedaddle. If you truly want to stay out of this."

I long to take a moment to explain to this man that it's not what he thinks. That it's not my own skin I'm trying to save, but Derek's. There is, however, no time to explain. On top of that, what difference could it make to this smugly smiling man who calls me "sweetheart" and winks collusively at me as he hands me my underclothes?

Without another word, I juggle my possessions into a manageable bundle and hurry across the hall into Suite 1912. Slamming the door behind me only seconds—or so it seems to me—in advance of a cheerful *ding!* that announces the arrival of an elevator car.

In accordance with instructions, I resist any temptation to look out the door, even when I hear the ambulance crew arrive. Or when, soon afterward, I hear them depart—with gratifying speed—bearing what I hope is a still-salvageable Derek. Only once the elevator has begun its descent do I dare open the door and glance along the corridor.

Every door is closed; everyone is abed; all is silence on the nineteenth floor of the Arlington Hotel. It's as if the paramedics, the anonymous Good Samaritan who summoned them, and even Derek himself have all dissolved in air, like the insubstantial elements of one of my dreams. Only my delayed sense of nervous shock betrays the fact that something untoward has occurred this night.

>-+-+›--O--‹›-+-‹

With a concentration intended to steady my trembling hands, I begin to put on my clothes. My upper arm is still sore and pink where Derek's fingers grasped me so desperately. Poor Derek. Will all of this seem like some hectic nightmare to him too, once he re-emerges into consciousness? Assuming, of course, that he *does* re-emerge...

By now, the trembling has spread to my knees, as I make my way over to the window and gaze out at a cityscape almost beatified by the pre-dawn light. The sky, suggestive of neither night nor morning, spreads like a vast purplish bruise. The windows of uninhabited office towers blaze with empty self-importance. Far below, the On Duty lights of taxis twinkle along the pavement. And somewhere out there—in the midst of it all—is Derek.

I try to will away an image of his blanketed body—either dying or dead—slung on a gurney in some forgotten hospital corridor. Perhaps I should have gone with him in the ambulance, if only to plead his case. "Don't you know who this is?" I might have demanded of an indifferent nurse at the Admitting desk. "It's Derek Matthews, the well-known investigative journalist. Author of numerous best-selling exposés—including his recent blockbuster on hospital mismanagement. Not that I know him *personally*, of course..."

But no. I did do the right thing in electing to remain uninvolved. And even if Derek is dead right this minute, I feel certain he would agree with me. As he looks down—like a hairy-chested, cigar-smoking Blessed Damozel—from whatever realm of heaven is reserved for husbands who cheat but endeavor to keep their wives from finding out. *Way to go*, the Blessed Derek might commend me, with a seraphic smile—his gray-blondish head adorned with a crown of stars, a stalk of lilies in his hand in place of the customary tumbler of Scotch. *Way to keep cool, Jaegerschnitzel, under fire. After all, just because a guy deals with his mid-wife crisis by screwing his leggy mistress(es) whenever his publisher sends him on the road, it doesn't mean that...*

Not that I believe for a second that Derek is dead. On the other hand, I have no way of knowing how long it might be before the helpful, fresh-as-a-daisy stranger phones from the hospital. Nor what exactly I am going to do if the guy never does phone and leaves me dangling here for hours—in a hotel room that isn't mine, awaiting a call from an anonymous man whose general reliability I have no way to assess.

Nervously, I glance around the room, in search of some visible testimony to the earthly existence of its erstwhile occupant. There is nothing in evidence. Nothing in the closet, apart from a few clanging hangers. No suitcase yawning on the canvas luggage-stand. Nothing in the drawers, either, not so much as a pair of socks. On the flesh-colored nightstand—identical to the one in Derek's room, I note somewhat sadly—there is a half-empty can of Diet Coke, the sole evidence of recent habitation.

When I check out the bathroom, I turn up nothing resembling a toothbrush, shaving kit, or unwrapped bar of soap. Not even the towels on the rack are askew to offer proof of this guy's corporality.

So who is he? I begin to wonder in earnest, once I've completed my fruitless inventory. What's he doing, living like a squatter in a corner suite at the Arlington? Conveniently right across the hall from Derek, and perfectly positioned to pounce from behind the door, fully dressed, in the middle of the night, in response to some cue of mine that I have no awareness of having transmitted.

When I put it to myself like this, it all starts to sound increasingly sinister. Like the intricate underpinnings of one of Derek's true-life espionage plots—which invariably lose me somewhere around page fifteen in a thicket of informants, and spies, and counterspies, and suspicious moles even more numerous than those you'd find among the clientele of a prospering dermatologist. If this were one of Derek's books, a man checking in without luggage right across the hall would turn out to be a paid assassin for some drug cartel, or the Mafia, or worse.

Truly jittery now, I move abruptly away from the window, to avoid being caught in the cross-hairs by some sharpshooter in an adjacent building. After all, suppose Derek's sudden "illness" was induced by something slipped into his Scotch? Well, okay, not in his Scotch—considering that I drank some myself. Let's suppose instead that something got slipped to him on the plane. Then, when he collapsed in the hotel—bingo! Suddenly, this helpful stranger shows up, calls down to the desk, and before you know it, a squad of Colombian hit men posing as ambulance attendants turns up at the door of the suite to spirit Derek away. But not to any hospital. Oh, no. To some secret location, high up in the Andes, where he—

Jesus! At the sound of a key turning in the lock, I gasp and wheel to face the door, half-expecting to catch a round of semi-automatic gunfire in the chest. Instead, in the open doorway stands the helpful stranger—smiling, ruddy-cheeked from the early-morning chill, and brandishing in his hand nothing more lethal than a steaming Styrofoam beverage cup.

"Coffee?" He proffers the cup. "You look on edge. A spot of caffeine should settle your nerves."

"No, thanks." Meanwhile, I attempt to recover the rhythms of normal respiration. "My nerves are fine. Only, you said you'd call me from the hospital."

"I would have done. Except I thought you might be pleased if I reported in person. As well, it occurred to me that there's a small detail I should take care of."

"And what detail is that?" If I sound short-tempered, I feel that it's forgivable, in the circumstances.

"Just this." The man picks up Derek's crumpled shirt from the bed and waves it at me, like an exhibit for the prosecution. "It might be an idea for me to slip this back into his room, mightn't it? Before his wife turns up to collect his things."

"His wife?" I feel certain that I'm being jerked around here, quite deliberately being fed bits of information one tantalizing bite at a time. "Is Beth on her way? Why? Isn't he okay? You haven't said."

"Derek's 'resting comfortably,' as they say. Lucky bastard." The man sinks into the armchair beside the bed and closes his eyes. It occurs to me for the first time how tired he must be. And how attractive he is. I'm ashamed of myself for noticing that at this moment, but I do. He's rather short, but very good looking, despite the blue hollows of fatigue under his eyes, and the dark stubble that advertises him as overdue for a shave. Under the circumstances, this is *not* someone that I wish to find appealing. But I do. And in deference to his evident exhaustion, I permit myself to soften a little.

"Here." I push the Styrofoam cup of coffee across the nightstand toward him. "I'm sure you need this more than I do. It's been an awfully busy night."

He opens his eyes, apparently surprised by my sudden sympathy. "That it has. He's going to come through it, though, your burly cigar-smoking friend. Mr. Derek Matthews, the noted spinner of taut and truthful yarns. D'you know, he looked familiar when I first rushed into his room? But it wasn't until the paramedics fished his ID from his trousers that the penny dropped. Christ! I even bought one of his books one time—in hardcover, no less. Just between us, it tailed off a bit. Reckon it was round about page fifteen that I bogged down. At any rate, once I worked out who he was, I understood why you might have been disinclined to turn in the alarm yourself."

There's something in the way he puts this—in the sidelong look he gives me at the same time—that causes my nervous antennae to stand at attention once more. Could this possibly be an approach to…what do they call it in the old movies? A "shakedown"? After all, given the fact that Derek is well known, and given the further fact that this smiling stranger is letting me know that *he* knows that, too…

"Yes," I say, "Derek is pretty prominent in his field. And, of course, there's the fact that he's married." Fuck it. Let's put *all* the cards right out here on the table and see who picks them up. "So, you were telling me that his wife is on her way East?"

"Yes, but you needn't worry. According to what anyone knows, I was the solo Samaritan who happened to hear his groans from across the corridor, and miraculously found his door unlocked. Not a word in my plausible narrative about a sylph-like creature wandering the hallways of the Arlington clad only in Mr. Matthews's shirt, which, as I say, I plan to replace in his room before its absence is noted."

"Thanks." My teeth are gritted, and my temper has shorted out again.

"Don't mention it. All in a night's work, sort of style."

All in a...Uh-oh. "And what sort of work might that be?"

"Well, let me put it like this: I'm a bit miffed with myself for failing to recognize your friend straightaway from his book-jacket photo. Never forget a face, and all that Magnum, P.I. malarkey."

"P.I.? You mean you're a..." I grope for a word, not at all certain what word it is I'm groping for.

"Yes, so it would seem." From the inside pocket of his jacket, he comes up with a business card, which he hands to me.

"'Carl Hart and Associates,'" I read aloud. "'Efficient. Experienced. Confidential.'" Then I sit down on the bed, with the card between my fingers. "You mean you're a...private detective of some sort?" The words come out sounding accusatory. As though I've been tricked somehow—which, come to think of it, I may have been. "And you've been...shadowing Derek for some reason or other?"

"I beg your pardon?" The man's dark eyebrows shoot up. "You got all that from reading my card?" He plucks it from my hand and stares at it for a moment before pocketing it.

"Look, Mr. Hart—assuming that's who you are, and not just one of the 'associates'—all of a sudden, I feel kind of vulnerable here. I mean, this kindly stranger, who just *happened* to appear in the hallway in the middle of the night, sort of camping out across from Derek's suite, it turns out, keeping track of who went in and who went out. Well, you know what, Mr. Hart? I liked you better when I thought you were a Colombian hit man." And, somewhat disgusted, I get up and move away from him.

"I...beg your pardon?"

"Will you stop saying that? It should have been obvious to me right off the bat. Here you are, so conveniently located in Suite 1912, without any luggage, in a room where the bed hasn't even been sat on by anyone but me. So who hired you to spy? Derek's wife? Not that I blame her. It's about time Beth cottoned on."

"My." The man's eyebrows have climbed even higher. "So you cased my room pretty thoroughly. Still, I expect there's a bit of detective in all of us. Even those of us who draw the wrong conclusions."

"Well, you must be here for *some* reason."

"True enough. But nothing that has any connection to Mr. Matthews."

"No? Then why did you volunteer to go with him to the hospital? And why come back, when you could just as easily have phoned? You really might as well come right out and tell me what it is that you want."

"What do I *want?*" He gets up from the armchair, to sprawl wearily on the bed. "What I want is to lie down and sleep. On this bloody bed, which—as you so astutely point out—hasn't been so much as sat on, except by yourself. What I want is to close my eyes. Assuming that there is no further thankless task I can perform, that is—either for you or for the estimable Mr. Matthews. After having already chased round half the night on the ungrateful behalf of you and your philandering friend. Whose wife, incidentally, is not my employer. Since keyhole work is something I leave to those much newer and much more desperate in this line of work than myself."

Oh, dear. I can feel my face growing hot with embarrassment. "I'm sorry. I guess what you were doing in this suite in the first place is none of my business. It's just...I've had a pretty rough night myself, one way and another."

Carl Hart looks at me—for the first time in our brief acquaintanceship—with an expression that is neither droll nor mocking, but merely evaluative. "Yes, I expect you have, at that. But you needn't worry, same as I said. Derek's going to pull through. And if he's half as clever in person as he is in print, he's already worked out that your name need not come up at all. So you can relax. For all intents and purposes, you don't exist."

I don't exist. It's the Other Woman's epitaph. No more than I deserve, of course. "And you got word on his condition from an actual doctor?"

"Yes. He'll be fine, if he minds his manners. I gather it's what they call angina pectoris. A warning of what's to come for real if he doesn't cut back on the hard drink and the cigars, along with all the other indulgences that—" Carl Hart cuts himself off abruptly, suddenly sensitive to the fact that he is speaking to one of Derek's more unhealthy vices.

"Look," I say, "not that it matters one way or another, but Derek and I weren't... that is, I was asleep when he had his attack."

"Ah!" The detective nods. "Well, that's fine. Not, as you say, that it matters, one way or another."

There's a sudden awkwardness between us. We are now both standing beside the bed, facing each other, and seem mutually reluctant to call it a night—or morning.

"Anyway," I temporize, "I wonder when precisely Beth is arriving? Because I'd like to drop in on Derek at the hospital. But not if..." I shrug eloquently.

"No, of course not if. I understand. Well, my impression is that she's planning to take the first available flight. So I doubt you should risk just dropping in on him. Even if you ring his room, make sure you do it before she arrives. Since, theoretically, you ought not to have any way of knowing he's ill."

"Yes, of course." Once more, the illegitimacy of my situation hits me like a humbling slap in the face. So much for airily preferring to keep things casual with the Marrieds. The fact is, once a wife is summoned to the scene, not even the most superficial sort of sentiment is permissible for me. I am *persona non grata*, and that's all there is to it.

Carl Hart coughs delicately. "Look, I'll tell you what. If you like, I'll ring the hospital later on, to check on Derek's condition, in my Samaritan way. Then, I could ring *you*, to let you know how he's doing."

The expression on his face is all innocence as he takes a pen from his jacket pocket in order to jot down my phone number. It would be easy to give it to him. So much easier than just walking out. Even so, the fact that the guy is a private investigator still makes me somewhat qualmy. He's also extremely attractive—which for some reason makes me qualmier still.

"No, that's okay. I'll take a chance on calling Derek's room before his wife arrives."

Carl Hart nods. "Suit yourself." Although he does not put his pen away. "Still, if you're at all inclined to give me your number, perhaps I could ring you, anyway."

It infuriates me that I find this offer so tempting. "Now, now," I josh him. "I thought we agreed I don't exist."

"Well, that might be remedied..." He continues to stand here, pen in hand, with an expression as open and ingenuous as the new day dawning outside the hotel window. For the first time, it occurs to me that *this* may be why he elected to come back to the suite, instead of merely phoning: to explore the possibility of seeing me under less absurd circumstances. "In any case, I'll give you back my card. In case you feel like ringing me sometime."

God, but I find him likable now, genuinely likable. As well as attractive. For a moment, I feel my resolve beginning to waver. "Well, maybe I..."

But as he fumbles in his pocket for the card, he brings out with it a small rectangular object, no bigger than a calculator, and sets it on the table.

I point to it uneasily. "What's that for?"

"That? Oh, it's just a tape recorder."

"I see what it is. But what's it for?"

Carl Hart shrugs with indifference. "Nothing much. I tape things sometimes. Does that seem so peculiar?"

I hardly know what it seems. All of a sudden, though, I'm qualmy again. "On second thought, keep your card."

"Why? What's the matter?"

Not a thing, most likely. I can't blame him for looking at me as if I've lost my mind. All the same, that tape recorder—whatever its purpose—has put my nerves back on a state of alert. "I'll just be on my way, all right? Thank you, though, for saving my bacon."

"I'm sure it's bacon worth saving. Look..." He takes a step toward me. "Even if you don't exist, you must have a name. Where's the harm in telling me what it is? No tape running, I promise."

Where's the harm? Clearly, this guy hasn't been monitoring my reactions as astutely as he should. "No harm. But where's the point?"

"I don't know. Let's find out. What's your name?"

"It's...Grace."

"Grace?" Carl Hart notes my hesitation—then notes me noting him note it, and smiles. "Now, you're certain about that?"

"Of course."

"Grace what?"

"Oh, just Grace. You know us good-time girls. One name is generally all we need."

"Come on. You know I think better of you than that. No more cracks at your expense, I promise."

"Jesus, Carl—if that's *your* name. You're really persistent, you know that?"

"And you're really interested, Grace. Do you know *that?*"

For a moment, I face head-on the brashness of his too-perfect smile. Then I extend my hand with what I hope is becoming hauteur. "Goodbye. Thanks again."

"You're entirely welcome. Goodbye, Grace."

As I walk to the door, I notice that he makes no move to follow. I shut the door behind me and manage to walk all the way to the elevators without so much as a glance back. Only once I've pushed the button to summon a car do I risk a quick backward look. Nope. The door of Suite 1912 appears to be—like all the other doors on the nineteenth floor at this early hour—closed as tightly as a drum. Carl Hart, P.I., seems to be back on whatever case he's been hired to crack. And off mine, once and for all.

On the whole, I feel less pleased about that than I ought to, and catch myself wishing I'd given him my name. Before coming to my senses, and sternly recalling poor Derek. Lying white-faced and helpless in his lonely hospital bed, his out-of-town adventure cut cruelly short, and only the arrival of his wife to look forward to.

Not that there's much I owe Derek, mind you—apart from my continued discretion. But one thing, at least, I feel I ought to do is to think about him—and only him. Instead of asking myself whether I made a mistake in passing up a second adventure at the Arlington, in the suite right across the hall from the one in which Derek was stricken.

The elevator deposits me in the lobby, and I walk past the bar where Derek and I met for drinks a hundred years ago. Then I step out into the daylight blossoming on the other side of the Arlington's tinted revolving doors. Into a realm where I'm free to think about whatever I want—and nurture whatever regrets I choose. Now that the danger is well and truly past.

Chapter Eight

When Marta announced her intention of bringing a few things over to Jerry's apartment, I somehow knew enough to expect something more than the arrival of a new set of hot-rollers. Or a second toothbrush snuggling cozily in the bathroom next to Jerry's. Or a fresh rock-group poster Krazy-Glued to the bedroom wall like the flag of yet another temporary army of occupation. After all, since Marta is nothing like any of Jerry's previous girls, it stands to reason that her notion of what constitutes "a few things" would, likewise, in no way resemble anyone else's.

Sure enough. Since her announcement, whenever she arrives to spend the night, Marta is never without a cardboard carton under her arm—to add to the growing collection that already stretches all along the back hall like a string of freight cars ripe for unloading.

Unload them she does, on the nights that she stays over. And the contents are, so far, frankly staggering. One by one is how these boxes got in the door, but if you total up what's now warehoused in Jerry's apartment, you've got an inventory equivalent to the spoils of several sacked civilizations. Chinaware, silverware, glassware, and cooking ware have all been offloaded into the cupboards. Along with an omelet pan, a vegetable steamer, some chafing dishes—and an espresso machine, which had Jerry reaching for his Ventolin spray the moment he saw it, because, of course, among his many allergies, coffee is king.

In what used to be the spare room, Marta's installed a halogen lamp, her posturepedic office chair, her personal computer, and trays of files. In what was once the living room, she's appreciably lowered the quality of life by moving the couch (*my* couch!) in order to make room for a case of books and a large Oriental vase full of dried flowers—that started Jerry sneezing afresh, before he'd even begun to recover from his encounter with the espresso-maker.

In the bedroom—where Mel once direly predicted the advent of heavy velvet drapes—Marta has proved him wrong with the installation of blinds and lace curtains. Even in the bathroom, she's staked her claim, by hanging something called a "loofah" from the showerhead and parking something called a "rubber plant" on the windowsill. In fact, it's hard to feature what can be left in *her* apartment, apart from the major appliances—which are probably also bound to show up here sooner or later.

Why Jerry isn't more alarmed than he is, I cannot figure out. Unless he's simply in shock, as he lies on the bed in his usual posture—half-watching a half-dozen or so TV channels while talking on the phone. Marta is right down the hall, meanwhile—more or less within earshot—flattening newly emptied boxes. As if she never expects to need them again, now that they've served to truck her entire life over here and impose it on myself and Jerry.

Still, to hear Jerry tell it—or mutter it—on the phone to Mel, the situation is well in hand. "Seriously, Arlen, this in no way resembles moving in *qua* moving in. So Marta's bringing over a few personal items. So what? She's here a couple nights a week, and she needs some stuff. Besides, that apartment of hers is practically a broom closet. Anyway, it's kind of nice having her things around. As . . . a way of gradually getting to know her better."

Uh-huh. Or, as a way for Jerry to gradually become better acquainted with an increasingly bewildering array of items to which, it turns out, he's violently allergic.

Mel, meanwhile, seems no more inclined than I am to buy Jerry's line—at least judging from the strenuousness with which Jerry is forced to stem what are obviously objections issuing from the other end of the phone. "No, no, Arlen, of *course* not. Marta's no keener to co-habitate with Murphy than she ever was, nor any crazier than she's ever been for the idea of living way out in the burbs. There's no incursion under way here, I'm telling you."

Yeah, right, I can imagine Mel rejoining. And old Murphy there is Prince Norodom Sihanouk in a cunning disguise.

Meanwhile, as Jerry continues to assure Mel that everything's under control, his ever-restless channel-changer pauses briefly on a nature program, where an examination of courtship rituals of various animals is in progress. As far as I can tell, there doesn't appear to be a single species that stakes out its new territory by hanging up a loofah, or seeks to lure a mate by flashing a bright, shiny object, such as an omelet pan. However, there *is* this one busy-looking bird that reminds me of Marta as it weaves its nest. Same determined glint in the eye, same briskly purposeful movements... The next thing I know, that bird'll be crushing cartons under the heel of its sensible Scandinavian shoe.

Jerry's paying no attention to this program. Which is too bad. There's a lot to be learned from TV, which has made an enormous difference in my own development. Especially since I don't get out much, and have no access to books. Of course, even with television, there are limits, since I'm pretty much doomed to watch what Jerry's watching, and only when he watches it. But even operating within those constraints, it's obvious to me that, at the current moment, I'm picking up a lot more from the TV than Jerry is—information that, in this case, could safeguard his independence.

But no. The next thing I know, he's flicked the remote to another channel. And at the same time, continues to insist to Mel that there is absolutely no cause for alarm. "Jesus, Arlen! How clear can I make this? There is no call to catastrophize. If there's any development at all in the status of the relationship, it's only that Marta and I might—and I emphasize *might*—make a trip to Norway sometime to meet her family. But that's— Look, will you kindly back off? 'Might meet the family.' That's all I said. Hardly the opening bars of 'Here Comes the Bride.' Besides, until I can get Murphy off my hands, how am I going any place? I can hardly take him to Europe. I can hardly take him around the *block*. And who in their right mind would babysit him for me?"

My God. It only gets better. From down the hallway, I can still hear Marta stomping cartons flat. Bang! Bang! Each report of leather heel in decisive contact with cardboard is like a gunshot fired into my own heart. One way or another, Marta will wedge herself in here, even as she forces me out. A trip home to the folks with her new beau, or a gradual insinuation of herself into Jerry's home...The tactic Marta chooses to accomplish her goal will, in the end, be incidental. What matters is that she's on the march—as inexorable as Fate, as sure as shooting.

While Jerry, still unwitting, continues to reassure Mel—and maybe himself—there's nothing afoot he can't handle. Continuing to flick inattentively from channel to channel, learning nothing he can use as he continues to explain into the receiver, with soothing monotony, the advantages of an involvement with a mature woman. Who can bring to a relationship so much in the way of durable goods, and so little in the way of clinging dependency. 🐾

Chapter Nine

Of course, there's a reason why—when pressed for my name by Carl Hart—I came up with Grace as...what would I call it...my *nom-de-nuit*? The Grace I had in mind, I'm sure, was Grace Goldberg. A friend of mine, one long-ago summer in London. I wonder what ever happened to her? For some reason, I've always felt that if I knew the answer to that, I'd know a lot.

Grace and I shared a bedroom in one of those over-crowded Earls Court flats crammed with colonials back in the days when the "British invasion" of pop stars to our shores was being answered by a corresponding influx of North American youth to the swinging streets of London. Right off the bat, Grace and I noticed that we looked alike. Even more than that, according to Grace, she and I were "psychic soulmates, transcendental twins, the last surviving members of the Doppel Gang."

Well, perhaps not quite. But it's interesting to me to remember how readily I bought that line. Despite the fact that, for me, mere twinship was no novelty. Besides, I had also only recently resisted the efforts of another friend—Karen, back at McGill—to make me over according to her specifications.

With Grace Goldberg, however, it was a whole different proposition. And it was true that, when we wore similar clothes, matching earrings, and copycat hairstyles, we were able to produce what Grace liked to call a "Hayley Mills moment." Meaning that we could actually pass for each other—at least, in the dusk with the light behind us.

To Grace, it was all a terrific lark: arranging a date with some guy she'd bewitched at the local pub, then sending *me* to answer the door when the guy came calling for her at our flat. Amazingly, the substitution seemed to work. So long as the man in question never actually saw Grace and me side by side, it didn't appear to cross his mind that he'd fallen victim to the old bait-and-switch.

For me, the romantic benefits that accrued from looking like Grace were only part of the payoff. It was the unbearable rightness of *being* Grace, even temporarily, that constituted my real reward. Not only did I have more dates that summer—albeit secondhand dates—than I could shake a stick at, I had a brand-new personality that I could, at will, don like a jazzy new jacket.

Grace's Long Island accent—full of vowels that throbbed and clanging consonants—was fun to imitate. More than that, she had a zestiness, a spirit of bravado, a sort of dazzle, that I could truly capture—but only in those moments when I was actively involved in taking her place. As if, once I entered the State of Grace, I found myself on a well-deserved holiday from my sober self.

The sober self I'd left at home with my boyfriend, Mark. Whom I was seriously slated to marry the minute I came back from my sojourn in Jolly Old. It wasn't that I'd gone to England with prenuptial plans to sow wild oats. How could I possibly have planned to meet someone like Grace, and embark with her on an idyll of multiple, meaningless whirlwind romances?

An idyll that came abruptly to an end, late that summer, when Grace unexpectedly fell in love with one of our favorite timeshares—a pretty French boy named Jules. Suddenly, she and I were no longer members of equal standing in the Doppel Gang.

I knew my vacation in Graceland was officially over the night she announced that she and Jules were on their way to the Continent, with vague plans to hike in the Pyrenees. Being Grace, she assumed no consultation with me was required. Being me, I also assumed Jules was hers by right. Despite the fact that my claim on him was as good as hers.

For some masochistic reason, I went to the railway station to see the lovebirds off on their train to Dover. Now that the jig was up, and Jules was permitted to see Grace and me together, the notion of any resemblance between us seemed preposterous. Clearly, Jules was mad for her, and viewed me as—if anything at all—merely some species of Not-Grace, vastly inferior, like every other girl on the platform that night who was not his beloved.

Grace, on the other hand, surprised me by clinging to me piteously, crying like a kitten. Much more extravagant in her grief than I, even though she was the one moving onward and upward, and I was the one left behind. "It's been a gas," she managed to quaver through her tears, "being your better half."

Better half was right. After Grace left, I couldn't seem to hold on to any of the men she'd trawled for me, and I lacked the enterprise to restock the pond from scratch. Oh sure, when I applied myself to it in front of the mirror, I could still make myself look like her. But somehow—lacking Grace as a point of reference—I'd lost the knack of simulating that particular combination of breeziness and breathlessness that had made her (had made *me*) such a winner.

Meanwhile, Grace's place in the flat had been taken by the elder sister of one of our flatmates, apparently in shock from a sudden divorce. Poor woman. She must have been all of twenty-six—which, at the time, seemed to me tragically past it. We were sharing the same bedroom as Grace and I had, and at night I would awaken to muffled sobs emanating from the bed I still thought of as Grace's.

I'd lie awake in the darkness, feeling helpless to offer any comfort to this lonely, stoical English woman whose life appeared over. At the same time, I'd worry all through the night that my new roommate's misery would prove contagious—just as Grace's *joie de vivre* had been. Suppose I were to stop looking even remotely like Grace, and start to look like this desprised divorcee?

Meantime, I'd heard not a word from Grace. My inclination was to go back home, to my boyfriend, Mark. And yet, without Grace to release me from my thralldom, I continued to linger in London, like an indecisive ghost.

Except now, instead of flirting away my evenings at the local, I was staying home. To gape at television with the divorcee's younger sister—who never dated, sucked her thumb although she was in her twenties, and always kept fresh flowers in her room, next to a framed photo of Gregory Peck.

As summer withered into fall, and I began to consider a photograph of Gregory Peck for my own bureau top, I realized I'd let things go too far. Mark was ringing me almost nightly now, demanding to know if I'd booked my flight back. And yet I remained, trapped in apathy.

"Grace, where *are* you?" I scrawled on a card, and mailed it to the poste restante address in France she had left me. "I thought you were going to write me, posthaste (ha ha). Am thinking of heading back home—unless you let me know by return mail that you and Jules can't live without me. (Ha ha again.)"

I never heard anything back. Somehow, falling out of touch with her felt like losing contact with a part of myself. My better half, as Grace had quipped before disappearing from my life forever, in the company of a cute blond boy with a cuter accent and a canvas backpack.

What if *I'd* been the one to go off with Jules, instead of Grace? I wonder about that sometimes—how my life might have been different had I not returned to Canada to marry Mark. At the same time, I wonder what ever happened to Grace and Jules after they left me behind, waving despondently on the platform.

Out in some parallel galaxy, is Grace Goldberg living my life? Undergoing the same embarrassments, identical triumphs, and reasonable facsimiles of my trials and tribulations? Presuming that we are, at base, "transcendental twins," just as she once pronounced us.

Or—as seems more likely—what if Grace is living an *alternative* life? The existence that I forfeited, in my craven inability to fight for possession of Jules? Suppose Grace is out there somewhere, reaping the rewards of my aspirations. And doing a far better job of playing Dana Jaeger than I ever did pretending to be Grace Goldberg.

If that seems preposterous, there is this to consider: how more or less preposterous is it that two college-age women from two different countries would meet up in a third country—to discover that they looked alike? Alike enough to fool an entire summer's quota of men, both in and out of bed.

In subsequent years, I made sporadic efforts to track Grace down. Even to the extent—once, when I found myself on Long Island—of calling all the Goldbergs listed in various local directories, in hopes of happening on one who was a relative. No luck.

Clearly, however, I have not yet given up. Why else, so many years later, would I find myself making an instinctive decision to pass myself off as Grace, one more time, to a man I found attractive? Yes, I still wonder whatever happened to Grace Goldberg. Believe me, if I knew the answer to that, I'd know an awful lot.

Chapter Ten

Ring!

"Hello?"

"Dana? Hi, it's Mel Arlen."

"Mel! What a surprise!" Which it is. Mel is Jerry Glass's best friend. But how long has it been since I saw Jerry, or even thought about him long and hard? "Are you in town?"

"No, I'm in the city." By which Mel means Manhattan—with the geocentricity of a true New Yorker, for whom all other urban centers are merely so many inconsequential collections of huts. "Glass doesn't even know I'm cwalling you."

"Oh? Is...is there something wrong with Jerry?" A bolt of panic shoots into my stomach, ricochets off my heart, then exits, via my arm. Oh please, don't let anything bad happen to Jerry. Not now, not ever, amen. Even though he and I are only a casual out-of-town item these days.

"No, nothing wrong with Glass, no more than usual. By rights, he should be cwalling you himself, but you know how he is: cannot, positively cannot, bring himself to ask for a favor. Hates being indebted, even more than he hates shorts that bind. Am I right here, Dana? Is this the Jerry Glass we both know and love?"

My surge of panic now under control, I am beginning to feel faintly suspicious of the too-chummy tone of Mel's call. "Favor?" I echo, knowing I shouldn't. "What favor exactly are you referring to?"

"Nothing so major. In fact, when Glass admitted to me he hadn't brought himself to ask you himself...well, I was thunderstruck. Considering what great rapport you have with the dwog."

For a moment I don't know what Mel means by "dwog." Then, all of a sudden I do, and my faint suspicion begins to crystallize into something cold and hard. "You mean, what's-his-name...Murphy? This is the dwog—dog—with whom I supposedly have such rapport? Mel, I only met the creature once, the last time I was down there, and as I recall it, he ate my brand-new Amalfi espadrilles, with my Vuarnet sunglasses for a chaser. Is this your notion of rapport, the spectacle of some big old mongrel bonding with the few designer items in the meager wardrobe of an impoverished freelancer?"

"Come on, not so freelance anymore, and I bet not so impoverished. Didn't Glass tell me you now write regularly for some TV dwog show up there?"

For the life of me, I can't imagine why Jerry's friend Mel is phoning me long-distance at daytime rates to commend me for my contributions to *Amazing Grace*. "Oh, well, what can I tell you, Mel? It's a living of sorts."

"Hey, more important than *that*, writing for dwogs only goes to show you must have special insight into...canine psychology. Besides, Murphy isn't so bad once you get to know him, and it'd only be for a couple weeks."

"A couple...?" Uh-oh. Here it came, the payoff pitch, and I was caught looking. "Slow down here, Mel, and let me get this straight." Although, for the life of me, I can't imagine why I'd want to. "Are you, by some chance, asking me to take care of Jerry's dog?"

"Bingo! You took the words right out of my mouth."

"Well, you can put the words right back *in* your mouth, because—my special literary insight into canine psychology notwithstanding—there is no place in my life for a dog. If Jerry needs a sitter, why not board Murphy at a kennel? Where he can eat his weight in Frost fencing and cedar chips?"

"Board him? Never. You know how Glass is."

Yes, I know how Jerry is. Aversive to commitment to a point that is almost allergic. And at the same time, paradoxically, indentured to the point of imprisonment to the few responsibilities he does take on. "But, Mel, if it's only for a couple of weeks, why don't you take Murphy yourself?"

"Don't I wish I could?" Mel sighs heavily into the receiver, for all the world as if he really did wish he could. "I'm Glass's best friend for thirty years. Why wouldn't I take on the hairy bastard, to help Glass out? Except there's this no-pets clause in my lease."

"Oh? Lucky you. You're off the hook."

"That's not the way I look at it, Dana." Oh, no, not much. "Besides, before *you* weigh in with a definite no, there's maybe one question you should ask yourself: If the shoe were on the other foot, would Glass be prepared to undertake a hassle of similar magnitude on *your* behalf?"

Ouch. With rhetorical skills like these, Mel is wasted as a tax attorney. The criminal court is where he belongs. I can imagine him arguing persuasively in front of a jury that several hours of community service would be sufficient punishment for his client, a remorseless serial killer. The fact is, Jerry's still in love with me, despite all the time that's elapsed since I felt that way about him. He *would* help me out, no questions asked, if I ever needed him, and Mel apparently knows that as well as I do.

"If the shoe were on the other foot," I feebly stall, "Murphy would have chewed it by now, clear up to the shank." But the battle, I sense, is already lost.

"Ah! Is that a conditional yes I'm hearing?" Sure enough, Mel is shameless, now that he has me on the ropes.

"Not so fast. I have to think this over. I mean, it's hardly like taking on a Boston fern."

"Come on, what's the big deal, once a day you pour some kibble in a dish?"

"There's more to it than that, Mel. Walks, for instance."

"Okay, fine. At the rate of two walks a day, over three–four weeks, how many walks are we talking? No more than—"

"Whoa! Three or *four* weeks, did you just say? I could swear, when we started out, it was only two."

"Two, three, four, five...what's the difference? Before you know it—boom. Glass is back."

"Back already? My, my. You haven't even told me where he's going."

A pause, for the first time, on Mel's end of the line. As he evidently tries to work out how much to divulge about Jerry's upcoming absence. And precisely because Mel isn't saying anything, I find myself swallowing hard. As I contemplate the possibility of being faced with the existence of a rival for Jerry's affections even more formidable than my own ambivalence. "Mel, where is Jerry going? And with whom?"

"No place. With no one. To Europe, on some radio producer's conference in...Barcelona, I think he said. What do I know? Anyway, the point is Glass needs a dogsitter *mucho pronto*, as the Barcaloungers say. And if I remember right, Glass tells me you got this nice big backyard up there in Kyanada?"

"Oh, right. Up here in Canada, it's nothing but one big backyard."

"Come on, Dana. All I'm saying is that a dwog might be terrific company. I mean, you still live alone, right?"

Double ouch. Presumably, someone who lives alone is desperate for company in whatever form she can find it. Any minute, he's going to add that, since I also work alone at home, I've got nothing better to do all day than open up dogfood and vacuum pet hair from the furniture. "Mel, I don't even *like* dogs." Even to my own ears, it sounds categorical. But possibly true. At least, for the purposes of this conversation.

"Jesus, Dana. For a couple of weeks? What's not to like? For Glass's sake?"

Uh-oh, here we go again. "Since you mention Jerry...Why didn't he phone me for this favor himself?"

"I told you why not. Christ, he doesn't even know I'm cwalling you."

"Yes, you told me that too." But even my suspiciousness is proving no defense—argues, in fact, the degree to which Jerry still matters to me. "Look, at least give me some time to think this over, okay?"

"What's to think? I told you, Dana, it's a piece of cake. Couple times a day, you throw some chow in a dish, maybe let 'im out for a..."

But as Mel rattles on, I can tell he's no longer listening to himself. Why should he, when he senses that he's got me boxed in a corner of my own construction? From which—he and I can both tell—I will approach my dumb decision one cautious step at a time. Pretending to think it over very carefully—before placing my foot down squarely on the land mine.

Chapter Eleven

Actually, the way I first met Jerry was kind of cute. He picked me up at some media writers' colloquium in New York City—but not with anything X-rated in mind, at least not initially. What Jerry wanted, he said, was to interview me on the radio program he hosts at American Public Broadcasting. Not because I was famous, he made a point—perhaps too *much* of a point—of explaining. In fact, he wanted to talk to me precisely because I wasn't. "A typical working wordsmith" was how he described me to myself. "A faceless foot-soldier slogging it out in the trenches of write-and-rewrite-and-I'll-get-back-to-you. Totally unsung, and occasionally unemployed."

When I broke the news to him that I was a faceless *Canadian* foot-soldier, he thought that was even better. "Since conditions, as I understand it, are even worse up there. What with all the U.S. pro-ductions bringing in imported talent. I mean, your people are lucky to work as gofers, aren't you?"

"Don't make it sound *quite* that glamorous," I told him. "My ego's over-inflated enough as it is."

Of course, that was long before my gig on *Amazing Grace*. Even so, there seemed plenty to talk about on air, and being interviewed by Jerry in the studio turned out to be more fun than he'd made it sound up front.

Some place, I still have a tape of that conversation. Jerry sent it to me very soon after. But not, as it turned out, quite soon enough. Be-cause, by the time the audio record of our initial encounter arrived in my mailbox, the most intensive phase of the relationship was already effectively over. "You should have overnighted it," I remember joking to Jerry via long-distance the day the tape showed up in the mail. "If you expected to get it here while you and I were still hot."

It's not that our entire relationship came and went during that very first weekend in New York. It's just that our peak point was where we started from, and after that it all began to slide downhill.

But, God, when I listen to the two of us on that tape...How on top of my game I sounded that day, full of confidence that I was coming across cute enough—but not *too* cute—to charm the auditory pants off Jerry's listeners. At the same time, charming Jerry even more—judging from how an approach to a date was written all over his voice, right from his first taped "Hello."

The tape ends, predictably, with an exchange of thank-yous. Like a polite interaction at a Red Cross clinic between the donor of a pint of blood and the technician who's managed to extract it with a minimum of pain.

"You're very good at your job," I recall telling Jerry as I got up from the interviewee's chair, feeling a little light-headed—as if I *had* given blood, and was now feeling the effect of the procedure on my equilibrium.

"Would you care for some tea or something?" Jerry asked, still in the spirit of a conscientious health care professional.

As it turned out, the suggestion was an invitation to linger. Lingering in the cafeteria progressed to my staying on in New York— no longer at the hotel where the media colloquium was still in session, but at Jerry's apartment, out in Westchester.

In spite of the whirlwind nature of the courtship, I could not fail to notice, right off the bat, that Jerry and I were, in certain essential ways, nothing alike. Jerry misted the plants on his windowsill religiously once a day. He took pride in telling me that he rotated the tires on his Honda every five thousand miles. He had mastered the arcane art of folding a fitted bedsheet into a perfect rectangle, could gauge the ripeness of a cantaloupe solely by smell, and knew how to repair a Rolex watch using no other tool than the miniature nail file on his Swiss Army knife. On top of that, his racks of compact discs were all cataloged, the old movies he'd taped from television were tidily tabulated, and tapes of every interview he'd ever conducted in a career of twenty-odd years were systematically filed.

By way of gruesome contrast, how could I help thinking about my own disordered life? The poinsettia left over from Christmas, grown leggy and yellow under a tent of cobwebs. The refrigerator, empty of anything except the lightbulb and a half-consumed jar of Baco-Bits. My poor bicycle, left out in all weathers to rust beside the porch, and the five-speed blender that my parents had mailed me four birthdays ago, still sealed up in its box.

Not that I was worrying, specifically, about Jerry venturing north of the border to discover he'd aligned himself with a pig. It wasn't that I really cared what he might think of the few scraggling perennials on my windowledge that I always contrive, through arrant neglect, to turn into annuals in no time flat. Nor was I all that apprehensive about revealing myself as a woman whose entire audio system consists of eight old Mothers of Invention LPs, hopelessly warped from years of leaning against the speakers that I purchased from that electronics store that went out of business in the early eighties—shortly after promising to explain to me how to hook the damn things up.

No, what *really* bothered me, right at the outset, about the Felix-and-Oscar aspect to the differences between Jerry and me was the greater gulf that they symbolized. We were, I felt sure, proceeding down the road of life in two totally different gears. Jerry, slowly but surely, with a Dustbuster at the ready, and his Rolodex file on the seat beside him. And me, jerking and jolting at all the wrong speeds, while attempting to squint through the streaks on my windshield.

Precisely how it was that Jerry and I backed off each other, I can't say for certain. It was as if our budding relationship died of some mysterious syndrome, along the lines of sudden infant crib death. Puzzling, somewhat. But perhaps what's more puzzling—especially when studied in hindsight's rearview mirror—is how on we both were before we backed off. Virtually prepared, I swear, on that very first weekend, to get married or take whatever other extreme measure was required to cement the bonds of our quirkily improbable union.

No, seriously. Hard to feature now, but so true then: me, on the cusp of renouncing my Marrieds in favor of becoming a Married myself; Jerry, the busy bachelor, willing to at least entertain the prospect of abandoning his endless succession of doe-eyed girls whose glossy headshots seemed to spill out of every available drawer or gaze down on me guilelessly from the top of each bookcase.

And then . . . we both recovered our senses. Or, more accurately, I recovered mine, and Jerry pretended to follow suit. Not to flatter myself unduly, but that was the way of it, I think. Which is what accounts for that particular mixture of affection and guilt I feel whenever—

God, why am I still talking about this as if it mattered? Because it did, and it does. It's as if Jerry and I tacitly continue to hold each other in reserve. Just as though either of us could, at any moment, regain that first, fine, careless rapture and recall the other to active romantic duty.

I doubt if it makes any sense. I mean, Jerry and I rarely see each other upwards of once a year, and we talk on the phone twice a month, max. I know he continues to date on his standard revolving-door basis. (After all, that awful dog he's acquired, that Murphy, has got to be the four-legged love child of some misbegotten union or other.) For Jerry's part, what he likely suspects about the disreputable nature of my love life is probably close enough to the truth.

Even so, even so, our absurd kinship appears to endure. To the point where Jerry's friend Mel takes it for granted that he can phone me up out of the blue and lobby for favors on Jerry's behalf.

It's not that I've committed myself, yet, to taking on Murphy. It's just that . . . well, of course, if I do, Jerry will likely bring him. And somehow, the idea of seeing Jerry here—right here on my own unkempt turf—suddenly has a certain appeal. Particularly when I envision it by tilting my head at a particular angle and squinting through my lashes just so—in a way that conveniently edits the dog right out of the picture.

Chapter Twelve

Apparently, there's some essential difference between telling an outright lie and merely putting a creative spin on the truth. At least, that's how Mel seems bent on explaining it to Jerry, on one of our customary excursions along the parkway. From the backseat, it's difficult for me to evaluate the merit of Mel's intricately worded argument—what with the traffic noise and all the distracting aromas wafting in through my window. However, I'll at least make an effort to relay what I manage to pick up.

"Besides," Mel is currently propounding with conviction, "it's not like you're *not* going on a trip. So, the spirit, if not the letter, of the truth is intact, so to speak."

"So to speak? So to *new*speak. Jesus, Arlen!" This, of course, is Jerry, shaking his head in what might be disgust—although, without being able to see his face, it's hard for me to know for sure. "The spirit, the letter...the mile-high pile of bullshit. The fact is, you *lied* to Dana on the phone. There is no radio producers' conference in Barcelona. What there is, in fact, is a gang of Marta's near-relations waiting on the outskirts of Oslo to give me the old once-over."

Mel snorts. "And that's what I should have told your dear friend Dana? Good plan, Glass. Makes me wonder why you didn't place the call yourself and just ask her flat-out to facilitate your *amour* with the Finnish Frigidaire by stepping in as your babysitter."

"Look, don't get me wrong." Jerry takes a sudden soothing tack. "It's not that I don't appreciate what you did. Personally, I wouldn't have had the faintest idea how to broach it."

"That's right." Even while agreeing, Mel still manages to sound aggrieved. "You wouldn't have the faintest idea. I suppose, in your book, old Dana there is gonna be overjoyed by the news that you're happy in the arms of someone new. Well, in the vise-like grip, more like it, and happy only in the sense that a rodent may well be happy in the belly of the boa constrictor. And as for new, Marta's hardly the *latest* model to come down the ramp of—"

"Come on, let up a little, will you? Of course it's not like Dana would be overjoyed to hear about Marta. What woman ever is, regardless of the status of her own involvement with the man in question? And as far as Dana and I are concerned...Well, there's still some kind of status there. Damned if I know what, but *some*thing."

"Well, sure. You still have a kind of thing for that one. Not so hard to figure out: The girl that got away and so on and so forth."

Jerry shifts uncomfortably in the driver's seat. "Ugh, Arlen, will you *please*? You have this way of rendering legitimate feeling in the cheesiest possible terms. Dana's not a 'girl,' she didn't 'get away,' and I have no kind of 'thing,' believe me."

"Okay, fine. But don't try to tell me Dana's got no kind of thing for *you*."

"I know she does," says Jerry miserably. "Which is why lying to her feels all wrong. Meanwhile, telling her the truth—in this instance—feels even wronger."

"Precisely," says Mel. "Which is why *I'm* the poor schlub who undertook to make the call. And, in the process, decided on my own initiative to edit out any references to the Icelandic Iceberg as the moving inspiration behind your sudden urge to take a trip abroad. However, if you're so goddamn conscience-stricken, you can always call Ms. Canada yourself and come clean—at the peril of losing out on one very big favor."

"Some favor." Jerry seems more miserable by the minute. "Autumn in Oslo, on some frozen fjord, surrounded by a pack of marriage-minded Norwegians."

"Sorry, pal. *That* grave you dug yourself. I did my best to lock up the shovels. Besides, it's never too late to back out."

"It is when the tickets are nonrefundable. Anyway, I'm going. Marta would kill me otherwise."

"I'd kill you myself," grumbles Mel. "After the trouble I took to sweet-talk the sitter."

Jerry merely concentrates his attention on weaving from lane to lane through the late-afternoon traffic.

What is going on here? What exactly has been decided, and what impact, if any, will that decision have on me? I wish I knew. And at this point, neither Jerry nor Mel—each staring silently out of his own separate window—shows the slightest inclination to pursue the topic any further.

Leaving me—as sometimes happens on these afternoon excursions from here to there and back again—knowing less by the time we head back home than I did when the three of us initially hit the road.

Chapter Thirteen

Every once in a while, I am invited to dinner over at Mark and Ted's, and tonight is one of those occasions. Which explains how I happen to be seated on a sumptuous floral sectional sofa in a corner of the living room of their penthouse apartment, which is furnished with a general lavishness that would do credit to a pair of Spanish grandees.

There are expensive, intricately patterned Oriental rugs on the floors and heavily valanced drapes across the big picture windows. Along one entire wall of the living room runs a gigantic aquarium, in which (I would guess) several thousand dollars' worth of glittering species of fish shimmer and dive in elusive flashes of Technicolor. In a wrought-iron cage resides a screaming, squawking family of equally brilliant birds, who clutch chunks of papaya between their scaly toes and spit pomegranate seeds onto the newspaper liner below, with the disdainful hauteur of dowager duchesses.

The walls of the apartment are covered with expensive works of art, some on lease from the provincial gallery, but others purchased outright by Mark and Ted for what seem to me incalculable sums of money. I have no idea, frankly, how the two of them manage to live so grandly. Mark grew up well-to-do, but since the death of his parents, most of his share of the fortune has been tied up in a nasty intra-familial litigation straight out of *The Little Foxes*. While Ted, a latecomer to medical school, is still in his residency at the hospital. Oh sure, one day he'll be raking it in, but meanwhile, how do they do it? Especially now, with Mark able only to work part-time.

When I first knew him, Mark seemed at home with the un-framed posters, lengths of ugly carpet scored for a song at the Sally Ann, and the strange rickety furniture that still graces my own apartment, even as he moved on to loftier labels. But that is Mark, of course. Always able to curl himself as comfortably as a cat in the lap of whatever lifestyle presents itself. What gets left behind he does not often seem to lament. Although, of course, he does—for reasons of his own—continue to invite me over, every couple of months or so, for one of Ted's highly produced dinners. And for reasons of my own I continue to accept. And so, *voici*. Here I am again.

Opposite me, on another aggressively flowered couch, sits Ted's mother, Gertie, afflicted in old age by a tremor that causes her head to wobble waggishly. I like Gertie. Still evident are vestiges of the blushing English rose who came to this country as a war bride more than half a century ago. Perhaps even then aware—or perhaps not—that her entire quota of positive karma would be consumed by the extraordinary good luck of meeting Ted's soldier father, sail-ing to the New World after the Armistice, and then—after numer-ous miscarriages—finally giving birth to a happy, healthy son.

At the point when Ted's father died, it may have occurred to Gertie that the lease on her good fortune was about to expire. Or, perhaps not. I'm inclined to doubt Gertie's capacity to absorb the knowledge of her only child's homosexuality. I believe that she honestly believes in Mark as Ted's longtime roommate, and in me as some equally longtime girlfriend of Mark's patiently waiting in the wings, like Miss Brooks lingering after class in hopes Mr. Boynton will twig to her charms at last.

How else to explain the placidity with which Gertie reigns as the empress of the dinner table, listening to her son and Mark quarrel amiably about whether it's Key West or Fire Island next summer, and who did or did not remember to decant the wine properly tonight? I wonder if she even notices how sick Mark is looking now—particularly tonight. His Italianate complexion, with its per-manent tan, has faded to a waxy yellow; his hair—which he wears in one of those Bergen-Belsen razor-cuts still in favor among some gays—is more flecked with gray than it was last time I was here; his close-cropped beard, now similarly grizzled, gives him an attenuated El Grecoish look, like some aspiring saint not long for this world.

>─┤◄▶─O─◄▶┤─◄

"Does Gertie know?" I demand of Mark.

Dinner is over; Ted and his mother have insisted on clearing up, and Mark—who barely ate a bite—has ushered me out onto one of the penthouse's four spectacular balconies. It's a warm evening for the season—so absurdly warm that the lights of the city spread out beyond us seem not so much to twinkle as to throb through the mist.

"Know what?" Mark, sipping a cognac, feigns ignorance.

"Well, anything. Let's start with tonight. The four of us all having one of our ritual Sunday dinners, like the most oddly constituted nuclear family of all time. Does she *seriously* never wonder about it?"

Mark shrugs. "If she does, she keeps it to herself. Anyway, at this point, Whippet, who cares?" "Whippet" is a nickname Mark coined for me when we first met—and I was a lot quicker, and a lot sleeker, than I am now.

"I care. Particularly now, in view of...Well, how *are* you doing these days?"

"Ah, so this is why you begged me, with eloquent eyes, to conduct you out here. To ask me how I'm holding up?"

"Would you prefer I do it in front of Gertie?"

"No." He glances away from me, and down at the gauzy-looking streets. "Since you ask, I have no idea how I'm doing. I could go on for years. I could be dead in months. This—as Ted explains it to me so illuminatingly—is how these things go."

These things. In the half-light of the balcony, where Mark's face is shadowy like the face of a stranger, I can only dimly connect him to the robust boy I used to know. It isn't Ted's fault that Mark contracted HIV. It was through an ill-advised dalliance with someone Mark picked up. Ted had gone out of town, against Mark's wishes, to attend some medically oriented event—an AIDS awareness conference, for all I know. For revenge, Mark slept with some stranger named Miles. "As in Miles to go before I sleep" is the way Mark put it when he told me about it much later. "And now Miles is sleeping the big sleep, and I tested positive eight months ago."

It was some time after that, that the virus manifested itself as an opportunistic infection, which, in turn, heralded Mark's arrival into the wonderful world of full-blown AIDS. What a healthy ring "full-blown" has. In no way suggestive of the gaunt ascetic sitting beside me on his balcony, gazing down at nothing in particular, with no discernible expression on his once-handsome face.

"And how long do you and Ted plan to pass this off to his mother as . . . what, a persistent cold?"

"Whippet, I told you: Gertie knows what she wants to know, and what difference does it make, anyway?"

None, perhaps, except to me. After all, what Ted and Mark are to each other is their own business, if they want to keep it from his mother. It's who *I* am to Mark—or who I used to be—that I seem to want acknowledged, particularly as his life visibly ebbs.

I'd like to say so, but I don't. Confrontation has never been Mark and me. Perhaps part of what has kept us close, in spite of it all, is our joint reluctance to play any other role together, apart from that of college sweethearts. Politely nostalgic for those bygone days— untouched either by the scourge of AIDS or by any memories except those of the good times.

Not all of which were, by the way, so good. In my first year living off-campus, for instance, with several other girls, in one of those long railway apartments so plentiful in the McGill ghetto. I liked the other girls, and I liked the apartment; the only problem was, I was in love—bootlessly—with a broad-shouldered boy named Mark Bannerman, who was engaged, it was said, to a beautiful sophomore down at Mount Holyoke. And at the same time, trifling openly at McGill with another girl, named Gloria Geller.

The fact that Mark was more than taken did nothing to dampen my enthusiasm for him. One day, in a fit of girlish masochism, I invited him and Gloria to the apartment for dinner. I wanted my roommates to observe up close the miracle that was Mark Bannerman. I wanted them to assure me—however falsely—that I had some right to hope. I wanted, I suppose, to erect some sort of public altar on which to consecrate myself to eternally unrequited love. And to that sad and desperate end, I spent the better part of the late afternoon in the kitchen, whipping up the best goddamn pot of chili Mark—or Gloria—would ever taste.

It was one of those autumn evenings in the ghetto that I remember as utterly elegiac. The thick twilight was beginning to drift over the trees, and from some other suffering soul's open window down the street wafted Donovan's castrated wail: "Oh-h-h no-o-o...Must be the see-sun of the witch, ye-ah..." Outside the Campus Market, a block away, I could hear the bell on the delivery boy's bicycle as he headed off from the store, with his basket full of cigarettes, quarts of beer, cans of cockroach killer, and all the other staples of life vital to residents of the McGill ghetto—a rag-tag assembly of students, anglophone pensioners, and newly arrived immigrants from Greece and Asia.

It seemed a blessed neighborhood in those days. A congenial mosaic, a small and fabulous kingdom. Those of us who lived there, in that high-flying post–Expo 67 era, knew how lucky we were to be in such a neighborhood, in such a city. Even if, for some of us, it meant doing penance from time to time, by standing in the kitchen over a pan of hot oil and onions, embroiled in preparation of a meal to be consumed by both the object of our fierce obsession and the girl he was screwing instead of us.

It was at that moment, as I was listening to Donovan, to the bell on the delivery boy's bike, and to the snap of onions frying in the pan, that Mark came quietly in the door and up behind me. Before I was actually aware of his presence, he grasped my shoulders and turned me around to face him. Startled, I clapped my hands to my mouth, and smelled the reek of raw onion. To this day, the odor of onions takes me back to that moment. There was a star shining outside the window, caught on the edge of a cloud, like a brooch tangled in the hem of a shawl. There was the moan of Donovan's lonely lament, drifting across the alley like a lost-sounding cat. And there was Mark Bannerman, the gray-eyed embodiment of college romance, gazing at me and smiling—for all the world like a man who cared.

"Gloria can't make it for dinner," he reported. "I hope you don't mind if I come stag?"

Stag? No problem.

Later that evening—much later—I lounged with my roommates and their boyfriends and Mark on the floor of the living room, with its perennial pile of beer bottles shoveled like landfill into a corner beside the couch. I recall a Glad sandwich bag full of twiggy-looking marijuana making the rounds, and an atmosphere of yearning hanging heavily in the room—at least, over that part of the room occupied by myself. I didn't dare glance at any of my roommates—all of whom were waiting to see what move I'd make on Mark, and when. Suddenly, the telephone rang. We all jumped, but in that delayed way you react in the wake of dope. Finally, one of the roommates reached, in slow-motion, to answer it.

Then the roommate avoided my eyes as she handed the receiver to Mark. "It's Gloria."

Mark did not glance my way, either, as he spoke tersely into the phone. "What's up, Glo? Oh, yeah, great dinner. We're all just kind of…sitting around and—What? Oh, come on. Of course. You know I do."

Okay, so you heard him, I told myself silently. He says he loves Gloria, and even if he doesn't sound as if he does, let's not forget his *real* girlfriend, down in Massachusetts, whom he's slated to marry when he graduates. So, if you're in love with Mark Bannerman too, you'd better take a number.

"Oh, Christ." Meanwhile, on the phone, things seemed not to be going too well. "Look, Gloria," Mark was muttering, "can we not get into that right now, while—Hello?" He took the receiver away from his ear and stared at it for a moment, in a puzzled, stoned way, before hanging up. "Shit," he said to the room at large. "I believe this calls for a cigarette. Uh, Whippet, would you mind? My pack's in my coat in the dining room."

It took me a moment to register the fact that I was being dispatched on an errand, like his valet. Without looking at any of my roommates, I scrambled to my feet and hurried to where Mark's expensive leather jacket hung from the back of a chair. Along with a pack of du Mauriers, I found a heavy silver lighter engraved "To M.B. from S.S. with love." I knew that S.S. was Sally Styles, Mark's fiancée down at Mount Holyoke. Rage quite suddenly overcame me. I felt my cheeks flaming as I read and reread the inscription, and I was choked with emotions I knew I had no right to feel.

I tucked the lighter inside the cigarette box, then marched back down the long corridor to the living room, where Mark still sprawled on the threadbare rug like a basking cat. He looked up at me, and smiled an elegant feline smile. "You find my smokes?"

"Yes," I said in a muffled voice. "And your lighter."

"Good stuff. Toss 'em over, will you, Whippet?"

"You bet I will." As I side-armed the weighted deck of cigarettes through the air at him, I had a momentary image of his face, smiling and expectant, in that split second before the cigarette pack and lighter came whizzing together through the air, end over end, and a corner of the box caught him right between the eyes. In the next second, there was a stream of blood gushing from between his brows.

My roommates and their boyfriends, meanwhile, were staring goggle-eyed, first at me, then at Mark, then at me again. Mark, in a daze, clasped his forehead as blood seeped out between his fingers.

"Dana! Jesus! Why did you do that?"

My mouth seemed to open and shut again and again, forming and reforming silent syllables, as if I were a foreigner unable to speak in any known language. At last, I found my tongue, and my words came out in a blurt of anguish: "What's so goddamn good about Gloria?"

That, of course, cleared the room. As my roommates and their boyfriends beat a speedy retreat down the hall, Mark struggled to his feet, like a boxer uncertain of his ability to answer the bell for the upcoming round.

"Oh, Mark, I'm so sorry..." I sprang over to him and pressed my hand to his brow. The sharp corner of the pack had nicked him decisively, and bright drops of his blood spattered the floor like poker chips. He was still swaying a little, and I couldn't tell which had stunned him more deeply—the force of my assault, or the angry outburst that had followed it.

From a great way off, I could hear the front door of the apartment open and shut as the roommates and their boyfriends exited severally into the night. God love them, I thought. I owe them all one.

"Sorry?" Mark took hold of my wrist, and looked into my eyes, seeming oblivious to the blood still trickling down his face. "For what? For being in love with me? You are, aren't you?"

"Oh, Mark, your poor head..."

"Shush." He leaned toward me, and gave me a kiss that tasted tangily of blood. "Each man kills the thing he loves, hadn't you heard? With a sword, or a kiss, or—in the case of some women—with a loaded deck of du Mauriers."

With surprising handiness, Mark freed himself from his involvement with Gloria Geller. And then, more painfully, from his engagement to Sally Styles. Sally I never did meet, but Gloria, amazingly, wound up as a friend. In fact, the next year, when Mark and I got married, she sent us a fondue set—one of only seven that we received. Six months after that, when I got word from Gloria that she was about to be wed, I rewrapped one of the fondue sets and mailed it to her with a note: "May you and Stuart be as happy in your marriage as Mark and I are in ours."

In spite of everything that happened later, I would still say that Mark and I *were* happy in our marriage—just perhaps not quite quick enough in extricating ourselves when we stopped being happy. But even now, sitting out on the balcony of the apartment that he shares with Ted, my overriding feeling is one of affection for him, and all we briefly were together.

In the dim light, his face—although hollow-cheeked—is still quite beautiful. There is no evidence, in the smooth space between his perfectly arched brows, of the sharp corner of a weighted cigarette pack that caught him unawares. But then, Mark is not the sort who scars easily.

"Mark..." Out of the blue, I put my hand on his arm, and ask, "Do you still have that silver lighter? The one with Sally's initials, that I threw in your face?"

He smiles. "My God! That lighter! Who knows where it is? Of course, I quit smoking years ago—when Ted told me that cigarettes would kill me." Abruptly, he stops smiling, and fixes his gaze on the orange glow of a sodium streetlamp down below. "Maybe I should dig out that old lighter and start again. If cigarettes were going to do me in, that pack you shied at me would have done the trick."

"Don't talk like that. You may well outlive us all." It's a funny thing. Having urged Mark to talk to me frankly about his illness, I find myself—in the face of frankness—fobbing him off with cheerful platitudes.

"Bullshit I will." But he is good-humored about it, as if comfortable dealing with my denial. "I'm on my way out. But—believe this or not—I really don't mind that much. I've had a good life. I just wish I could see you happy, Whippet. Happiness would look good on you."

Ugh. There's nothing like the feeling that your fucked-up life somehow constitutes a piece of unfinished business for someone else—who apparently won't rest in the grave until he gets *you* settled. "Don't worry about me, Mark. I'm happy enough."

"The hell you are. What is it, you still wasting your time with married men?"

"Only you, sweetie-pie." After all these years, Mark and I still have never got it together to come formally apart by getting divorced.

Mark grins, for a moment looking quite like his old self. "Lucky for me. If I were single, you wouldn't give me a second look."

We both laugh—but not so loudly as to attract Ted and his mother out onto the balcony. Tacitly, Mark and I have elected never to abuse the privileges Ted has granted us. A heterosexual partner, of course, would never allow me such license to share Mark's life, even to the extent that I still do.

"Seriously." Suddenly, Mark is no longer laughing. "I wonder if we should get divorced. Late in the day or not."

"What on earth are you talking about?" I feel my face growing hot, as if I were being accused of something.

"You know what, Whippet. You need to move on."

"Move on?" Now I'm angry, barely able to keep my voice pitched at a discreet level. "It's hardly as if you're keeping me back."

"I hope not," he says simply. "It's just...Dana, after all these years, when are you going to get real with someone else?"

Real? I tamp down a sudden, unbidden image of that detective, Carl Hart, stretched out in the armchair in his suite at the Arlington, his eyes closed, his face attractive and vulnerable. "As a matter of fact, I do have some single guys on file."

"Really?" Mark looks interested, almost hopeful. "Such as?"

"Well, there's my friend Jerry, down in New York. He and I may be heating up again."

"How so?"

"Well...he might be coming up to see me. With his...dog."

"With his...?"

Oh, shut up, Dana, I think. "Jerry's going on a business trip," I explain, feeling more and more uncomfortable. "I'm thinking it might be fun to look after the dog while he's away."

"Fun?" Mark is clearly disgusted. "Sounds to me like the guy is just ripping you off."

In spite of myself, I snap back. "You're a fine one to talk about ripping me off!"

The expression on Mark's face is surprised, pained, bewildered—as if I'd suddenly clipped him between the eyes with a cigarette pack. "You think I asked for the hand I've been dealt?"

"No, you didn't ask. But neither did I. And I'm doing the best I can, goddamn it. For all you know, Jerry could be the one." This is nothing I intended to say. Nor even something that I think I think. But there is a quality in the waxy translucence of Mark's skin that reminds me, suddenly, of Derek Matthews, ashen even in the pink glow of the lamp at the Arlington. Derek, of course, has emerged more or less unscathed from his ordeal, even phoned me from the hospital to tell me so. Nevertheless, I feel myself somehow clutching at life in the midst of death. Trying to grasp at something to hold on to, come what will—and there is Jerry, more vital to me than I generally like to admit. And a less dangerous direction to go than any other.

"Now, don't just say that," says Mark, "to appease me."

"Appease you?" I'm grinning at him, good-natured again. "Hell, I'm saying it to make you jealous."

"And of course I am." Mark leans over to kiss my cheek. "I hope that's always understood."

Ted appears at the balcony door, just in time to catch the tag end of the kiss. But there's nothing in his expression to suggest that he minds. "Well, washing up's all done. Now, Mum's for Parcheesi, unless you'd prefer *La Traviata* on laser disc?"

Coughing along with *La Traviata*. How apt. "Actually, Parcheesi might be a treat. I'd like Mark here to see that there are some games I can actually win." And I continue to smile at Mark wickedly, but the smile he returns to me is abstracted, automatic, as if he no longer remembers what we've been talking about. The moment that we shared has passed, and that's all right with him. He can let it go, like everything else, not because he's uncaring but because he, for one, has moved on.

Chapter Fourteen

It's at times like these that I really begin to fear that "mankind" may be a contradiction in terms. There's something even more businesslike than usual about Jerry on our walks, and every once in a while I catch him looking at me in a way that suggests there's bad news afoot.

It may be that—despite my best efforts—I'm finally pushing him to the end of his rope. Lately, even little things appear to make him ultra-irritable, as if he's looking for reasons to find fault and need not look far.

"You want to get sick?" he screamed at me—actually screamed—just the other day, after I swallowed some rubber bands I found on the sidewalk. "You want to end up at the vet? Is that the idea?"

Oh, sure, that's absolutely the idea. I love the vet; who does not? I especially look forward to having my nails cut to the quick and beyond, and my ears gouged out *for no apparent reason* by some State-sanctioned sociopath who apparently doesn't even need to know me personally in order to want to hurt me. You see what I mean about how unbalanced Jerry has become. And there's more.

"Supposing," he continued raving at me right out there in public, "I filled your dish with rubber bands, rodent parts, Popsicle wrappers, broken crayons, and all that other schmutz you scarf up from the street. Would you eat it, just because it's *there*?"

No, of course I wouldn't eat that stuff if I found it in my dish. That's not the point. The point—which Jerry clearly doesn't get—is that with refuse, as with real estate, it all comes down to three basic things: location, location, location. Food eaten outdoors just tastes better. Don't ask me why. Whereas, in an indoor setting, even its claim to *be* food might be open to question.

No use explaining that to Jerry, who is becoming less and less interested in grasping the point, and more and more interested in picking fights with me about inconsequentials. Possibly in order to sop his conscience, once the time comes to give me the old heave-ho. "See how hard I tried?" will be his plaintive defense. "Unfortunately, the animal became impossible..."

No, seriously. Something that major is on tap, I can tell. And if this were television instead of real life, I might mount some sort of protest against the inequities of my situation. Organize a Dozen Dog March on Washington, or proclaim Puppy Pride Day from the edge of the Reflecting Pool. Unfortunately, what looks easy on TV does not fall so readily into place in the here-and-now. How the hell am I supposed to organize, when I've yet to figure out how to work the deadbolt on the apartment door?

In real life, it's Jerry who works the locks, and in the end—with an assist from Marta—he's liable to slide that bolt firmly into place. Leaving me on the other side of the door. For good. After all, from the Animal Shelter I came, and to the Animal Shelter, yea verily, I can return. Ashes to ashes, and all that circle-of-life schmaltz.

I'm sure I'm on to something, because nowadays even Marta's acting differently toward me—almost nice. As though she suspects it's an effort she won't be required to keep up for long. So, any way you look at it, that's how it adds up: a one-way ticket back into stir.

Not that the Shelter is entirely awful, from what I recall. Fresh newspapers delivered daily, regular meals, and, of course, the perennial hope of moving on to better things. Precisely *what* things don't matter in a place like that—so long as "moving on" does not entail a long, long walk down that dark passageway that ends at a door restricted to Authorized Personnel.

What lurks behind that door, I learned, my first time around, from this cat in the cage across the aisle from me. Who was apparently taking bets all over the Adoption Area that my luck would run out before I got sprung. In fact, I soon saw why the cat liked the odds so much: I was bigger than most, I shed profusely, and my manners—then as now—left a lot to be desired.

In the highly competitive adoption market, I knew the best I could hope for was a junkyard gig, spending the rest of my life cultivating an attitude at the end of a length of tire-chain. Not much of a prospect— although it beat hell out of the alternative. In fact, as he continually re-iterated that alternative, there was always a big smirk on the cat's face. His idea of a real kick was to make hissing noises at me in the middle of the night, like the sound of escaping fumes. "Pss, psss...Hear that, boy? Ask not for whom the gas flows; it flows for *thee.*"

God, how I wanted a way out. I remember those afternoons, during adoption hours, when the public came in to look for pets. That was my cue to go into action: rolling on my back in my cage, waving my feet in the air, lolling my tongue like an idiot. Heck, I would have stood on my head humming the theme from *Old Yeller*, if that's what it took to make a good impression.

When that failed to click, I started trying to work on some routine more refined than an impersonation of a slobbering moron, bicycling on his back. Something...well, along the lines of: "Hi, there, my name is Murphy, and I'm the type who'd rather listen than talk. My hobbies include rescuing small children from raging rivers; the last book I de-voured—binding and all—was *War and Peace*, and my Scotch is..."

No, seriously. I was almost that desperate. Trying to figure out how to make a good-enough first impression to get sprung by someone gen-uinely looking for what I pretended to offer. Forget congenial personali-ties. Forget compatible dreams. What was at stake for me was matching needs. If I could have taken out an ad, I would have: "You're looking for someone to come home to. I'm the someone who'd like to be at home when you get there. You like early-morning walks in the rain. You don't mind tossing a slimy tennis ball forty times in succession. You know how to operate a can opener, and you've got twenty-five bucks in your wallet to buy my way out of this gulag. Me: Tall, good-natured, outgoing. Plus I have all my own teeth. There you go. It's Kismet."

Or something. In the end, I have no idea what winning combination of qualities I did manage to muster in order to convince that long-gone girlfriend of Jerry's whose name I forget to take me. But whatever the magic formula was, I doubt that I'd be able to duplicate it a second time around.

Of course, it may be that Jerry's desire to dump me will just blow over. Maybe he'll decide to stop looking at me as if he were mentally measuring me for a concrete crate. Maybe he'll decide to scrap his plans to sell me down the river at Marta's request. And if he does decide to do all that...Well, what can I tell you? That would be Kismet too. But I wouldn't bet on it. No, not even if some cat were to offer me odds of fifteen-to-one. 🐾

PART TWO

....

Sleeping Dogs
Don't Lie

Chapter One

Even before I can make out the New York plates, I am able to iden-
tify the Honda as Jerry's, merely by the circumspect way it moves
along my street in quest of a place to park. Good old Jerry. I feel a
rush of affection for his Big Apple suspiciousness—evident even
from my living-room window—in his obvious reluctance to trust
the apparent tranquility of a residential Canadian street. The
minute he turns his back, he is no doubt expecting an army of
hubcap thieves, tire-slashers, radio-boosters, or worse to leap from
behind the nearest Watch for Children sign.

At last, however, he's selected a berth. Then, it's with a heavy
heart, I must confess, that I continue to watch from my window as
he fights Murphy out of the car. Or, more accurately, they fight
each other, in order to determine whether the dog will exit via the
hatchback—Jerry's choice—or through the front windshield,
which appears to be Murphy's preference.

Oh, my God, what have I gotten myself into by agreeing to keep
this animal, who would obviously best be kept in the freezer? Rue-
fully, I think about that well-behaved battery of lookalike dogs
named Major, whom I've glimpsed on those occasions when I've
been summoned to the studio where *Amazing Grace* is shot. Of
course, the Majors are creatures of showbiz. No more akin to every-
day dogs than television resembles real life. Even so, I do *not* like the
way Murphy's straining bug-eyed at the end of his leash as he drags
Jerry, like an afterthought, up my front walk. Is it too late, I wonder,
simply to lock the door and pretend that I've moved away?

But, of course, I can't do that. I agreed to this servitude, after all. Agreed for all kinds of reasons I can't recollect right now, except they must have had something to do with my residual feelings for Jerry. Who is presently being towed with panting determination up the steps of my porch by a creature whose eye-bulging, tongue-lolling aspect puts me in mind of some primitive dog totem.

With my welcoming smile firmly affixed, I fling open the door. "Hi! How was your—?"

Seeming to recognize me as a long-lost friend, Murphy lunges against me with a happy chortle. In spite of myself I'm somewhat charmed. Maybe Mel was right. Maybe there is some sort of special rapport between me and—But as Murphy stiff-arms me with his front paws he simultaneously sends out a jet of pee to wet the front of my jeans. And suddenly, I'm no longer charmed.

"I'll pay for the cleaning," Jerry offers, with the speedy reflex of one obviously accustomed to having to make such instantaneous promises of reparation.

"It's okay." Still smiling, I offer him my cheek to kiss. "I'll just throw them in the wash. Come in and make yourselves at home."

Murphy, for one, needs no further invitation. He barrels through the open door like a sailor joyously returned from years at sea. In some ways, his buffoonish presence is a blessing. A momentary deflection of the awkwardness of seeing Jerry after so many months, and having to usher him, at long last, into my chaotic domain.

"Nice place," Jerry says, trying to sound as if he really means it.

"Thanks. I'll go change my jeans. It's great to see you, Jerry."

And it is. Even exhausted from his long drive, Jerry looks good to me, with his crisply curling hair and earnest hornrims. A good-looking man, and a nice one. Too nice to let get away again, so casually...

The rush of feeling is almost disorienting, and I'm glad of the excuse to retire to the bedroom, close the door, and regain my composure as I hunt up other jeans.

I can hear Murphy's toenails clattering up and down the bare hardwood as he checks out his new accommodations. Quite probably, Jerry's doing some checking of his own, examining my apartment room by room, as though expecting to unearth some evidence to explain the puzzling turn our relationship took so long ago. I wonder how I look to him, viewed in my scruffy natural habitat. "Up in Kyanada," as Mel would say—as though referring to some bleak, unalleviated tract of Royal Doulton outlets bordering an endless expanse of tundra.

I know, of course, that this is only an overnight bivouac before Jerry hits the highway again—this time unencumbered by Murphy—as a prelude to his even lengthier journey to Spain. Who he and I are to each other at this point hasn't been discussed, and I've got a camp cot set up in my office, just in case our inclination is to play it platonic. On this occasion I'm strictly the dogsitter, and it may be that when he gazes at me, all Jerry sees is the face of a willing patsy. On the other hand...Well, as I hinted to Mark, who knows what can happen on the other hand?

Pinched by my fresh pair of jeans, I emerge from the bedroom to discover Jerry in the kitchen, attempting to keep Murphy from swiping the countertops with his tongue. Ugh. Not that there aren't crumbs aplenty on those counters ripe for swiping, but...Suddenly, the prospect of co-habitation with someone whose standards of hygiene are even more casual than my own overwhelms me with a shock of reality. How was it again that I ever agreed to this?

"Uh, look, Jerry, let's just send Murphy out into the backyard, okay? I put some toys out there to amuse him."

"Is the yard such a good idea?" Jerry trails me anxiously to the kitchen door. "I mean, you don't think somebody's liable to come by and steal him, do you?"

"No, I don't, but we can always hope." I open the door and gently nudge the dog outside. "Relax, he'll be perfectly safe. This is Canada, remember? Now, how about some coffee?"

"Coffee?" Jerry's expression is now one of wide-eyed horror. "Coffee is complete poison to me. You know that."

Yes, of course, I do know that. But for some reason, it slipped my mind. Or perhaps I've merely assumed, illogically, that Jerry's allergies might not apply on this side of the border. "Right. Sorry. How about herbal tea instead?"

>─┤◆>─O─<◆├─<

All right, all right. So obviously I was mistaken about the Animal Shelter. Five minutes into the car trip, it came clear to me that Jerry and I were headed someplace uncharted. But as the journey went on and on, mile after mile and hour after hour, I began to grow even more apprehensive, wondering where in hell I *would* wind up. Then, when we finally arrived, and I got out and saw this woman I faintly recognize... Well, what can I tell you? The relief just came flooding—until, the next thing I knew, it was the Bang and Olufsen incident all over again. All over *her*, to be more precise.

Okay, she was a little annoyed with that, and now I'm stuck out in the yard. But hey, it's a yard. All to myself, no less. With grass and trees and the whole ball of wax. So, whatever I'm doing here—or, for that matter, whatever "here" is—it certainly beats a three-by-five-foot cell down at the Shelter carpeted in yesterday's Classifieds. I may not be home, exactly, but I am—at least for the moment—definitely dry.

>─┤◆>─O─<◆├─<

As the kettle is heating up, I sit down at the dining-room table opposite Jerry, willing myself not to think about what Murphy might be doing to my backyard. Out of the corner of my eye, I have caught a glimpse through the window of a tree limb shaking mysteriously. I stifle my impulse to investigate. No point making Jerry even more nervous about the hazards of the great outdoors.

"So," I say, cheerfully conversational. "Here you are, on my turf at last. Does it seem weird?"

"Not too weird. Dana, I really appreciate what you're doing."

"Doing? What am I doing? Nothing so major. Whoops!" In response to the whistle of the kettle, I jump up too abruptly, like something being jerked on a rusted pulley. "I'll go make tea."

The last thing I need to hear right this minute is how huge a favor I'm doing Jerry. He seem so nervous—guilty, almost—and I don't want that. What I want is to get off the topic of the dog altogether and open up the discussion to the subject of him and me.

Alone in the kitchen, pouring boiling water into the teapot, I permit myself a good look out into the yard. Where I am greeted by the sight of Murphy, his eyes closed in what looks like a transport of bliss, as he chews on an important branch of the lilac tree. I'm fond of that tree. Still, I force myself *not* to run out and drag the dog into the house, where he might do worse. Sternly, I harden my heart against the gentle sensibilities of trees everywhere, and resolve to let the harsh laws of a dog-eat-tree world prevail, at least for now. Better some lilac bush than me.

"How's Murphy doing out there?" Jerry wants to know as soon as I return with the pot and a couple of mugs.

"Just fine," I assure him, in the on-top-of-it tone I've been affecting since his arrival.

"Good." With a grateful sigh, Jerry accepts a freshly poured mug of Tension Tamer. "I can't tell you what a favor you're doing for me."

"Jerry! Will you stop making such a big deal of it? I write scripts for that dog series now, after all. Murphy practically counts as research."

"That's good." Still, he doesn't sound very convinced.

"Besides..." Why do I seem so bound and determined to make Jerry feel *good* about exploiting me? "You can hardly help the fact that you're being sent on this course or whatever in...where did Mel say? Barcelona?"

Jerry's only response to that is a pained wince, as though some nerve has been struck. Which makes me nervous too, but somehow I can't resist venturing where I know I should not, at least not until after a few more cups of Tension Tamer. "Unless...there's something you're not telling me. In which case, you should. What are casual, out-of-town women friends for, except to stand *in loco sororis*, as it were, and listen nonjudgmentally to your confidences?"

"*In loco sororis?* Is that actual Latin?"

"Jerry, the point is, you ought not keep secrets from me."

Although maybe he ought. Because I don't like that edgy expression that's playing around his mouth as he sips his tea.

"I'm not," he says, still without much conviction. "This is hard, though. Seeing each other face-to-face for the first time in months. And meanwhile, I'm dumping my dog, then leaving tomorrow morning."

Murphy, I can sense without even glancing out the window, has broken off the lilac branch and left it lying on the ground like a cruelly fractured arm. Now he is at work on some of the smaller branches—the fingers, so to speak. Hard? No kidding. My backyard is being pulped at the same time as Jerry is playing up his enormous gratitude to me, while downplaying any more flattering responses. "Jerry...are you seeing somebody?"

Another wince. "Well, you know I see...people. So do you, right?"

"Never mind me. Are you seeing somebody in particular?"

"Well, I...Mostly, lately, there's this woman named Marta. She's a dentist. From Norway."

"Ah!" In this dispassionate-sounding monosyllable, I hope I've revealed none of what I feel on hearing this news. Meanwhile, even though the dining-room windows are closed, I am vaguely aware of a grinding sawmill sound that can only be Murphy's jaws hard at work. "And is it serious? With Marta?" Somehow, with a Scandinavian lady dentist, I can't see how it could be anything but.

"I'm not sure. Yet. Dana, can't we just—"

"No. Please. Tell me about Marta. What's she like?"

Jerry considers this, his head to one side, apparently intrigued by the extraordinary originality of the question. "What's she like? Well, you know, blond. Willowy. Sort of crisp and cool. Very tidy, of course."

Of course. I steal a glance around my dining room, which, despite the efforts I've made in advance of Jerry's arrival, still gives a general impression of dingy wallpaper and lurking dust-mice. "And how," I continue in a clinical tone, "does Marta feel about you coming up here to visit me?"

Jerry looks at me, perhaps trying to evaluate the correct course to steer. "Uh, well, she knows you're taking care of Murphy for me. While I'm, uh, away."

"I see." And don't I just? I get up and move over to the window, to take a franker look at what Murphy is up to. The sight that now greets me is a truly sobering one: Murphy, sprawled on the grass with the painted metal handle of the Toro power mower between his paws as he chews with furious concentration through the rubber handgrip.

My landlord, who drops over every Sunday to mow the grass whatever the season, adores that Toro mower the way another man might dote on a child. Horrified, I continue to stand at the window, trying and failing to imagine how I will break to him the news of what has befallen his favorite. How is it that a dog with brand-new rawhide bones and old tennis balls left strewn for him appetizingly around the yard would deliberately choose a gas-powered lawnmower to gnaw upon? Briefly, as I press my forehead against the coolness of the windowpane, I try to recollect when I might ever have felt more wretched than I do right this minute.

Marta, the Norwegian lady dentist—cool and willowy and blond and tidy—is aware of me only as some nonthreatening back-number who's undertaken to babysit Jerry's dog. While Jerry gets set to fandango his way across the Iberian peninsula—planning, no doubt, to cheat on us both along the way. Why Marta hasn't herself volunteered for dog detail I can only attribute to the fact that she's obviously smarter than I am, as well as blonder.

"Dana...?" Jerry approaches me from behind, tentatively. "Is Murphy still okay out there?"

"Perfectly okay. Why not?" I turn from the window to face him. "I'll make more tea, shall I?"

Without waiting for his response, I snatch up the pot and stalk back into the kitchen.

"Dana..." Jerry has followed me, and reaches out to touch my arm with concern. "Look, if I've said something to upset you, I'm sorry. This really is hard for me."

"Whereas for me, it's a picnic—getting to hear all about the woman I've lost you to."

Jerry steps back from me in surprise, as well he might. "*You're* the one who asked." Still, mixed with the surprise on his face is another expression, closer to pained puzzlement. "As for who lost who, well, as ridiculous as this may sound under the circumstances, I miss you, Dana. I still wonder why things never worked out the way we first thought."

I set the kettle down sharply on the stove, like a judge ruling on the inadmissibility of this testimony. "Oh, come on. For you, I'd say things have worked out swimmingly. Why the hell should you want to start all over with *me?*"

A new expression—more guarded—has now taken charge of his face. "I didn't say anything about starting over."

"No, you didn't." Yet, somewhere, I sense the stirring of some-thing faintly hopeful, and the possible abatement of my current woe. "I guess what you said that bothers me is that nothing could ever work out between us."

"Come on, I didn't say that, either. Anyway, what's so terrible about the way we *have* ended up? I mean, here I am, right? And I'm still allowed to miss you, aren't I?"

"I don't know. How do you think Marta would feel about you missing me?" I have no idea where I'm going with this. But right at the moment, I seem to require confirmation from Jerry's own lips that something unassailable still exists between us, Marta be damned.

"I don't know," Jerry replies carefully, "how things between me and Marta are going to go in the long run. I can't even explain our relationship. It's just…well, it's not even so much that I want to be in it as I feel that it's where I ought to be. Did you ever get that feel-ing about anyone?"

Unexpectedly and for no good reason, there's that recollection once more of that night at the Arlington Hotel, and Carl Hart, cramming my clothes into my arms. *Right, then, sweetheart. You've got, I should estimate, all of ninety-seven seconds...*

"No!" I declare with unnecessary vehemence. "I've never had a feeling like that."

"Ah." His point scored, Jerry nods.

"Except," I amend quickly, "that time in New York, when I first met you."

"Me? Come on, you were backpedaling from the word go."

"So what? As a cyclist, let me tell you, that doesn't mean necessarily there's no way forward."

"Jesus!" Jerry is rubbing the bridge of his nose where his glasses pinch, in a gesture so characteristically his that I want to wrap him in my arms and press him to my heart.

"Jerry, about Marta...Is it such a good thing—being in a relationship you 'ought' to be in?"

The fact that I'm the one who's scored this time is evident in the way Jerry continues to massage the bridge of his nose as he studiously avoids my gaze. When he speaks at last, his voice is muffled with emotion. "Dana, please. Let's not bullshit each other here in the name of nostalgia. You know you were never in love with me."

Do I know that? Tears have begun to smart at the corners of my eyes, and as I unfurl a length of paper towel to dab my face inelegantly, it feels very much to me as if I am in love with Jerry, and always have been. Not merely because loving him and being loved in return would simplify my life so enormously. But also because it might help explain what we're both doing here in my kitchen— while on the other side of the wall, in my backyard, Jerry's dog is gradually consuming everything in his path, as he makes his inexorable way toward the house.

"But I do love you, Jerry." The words sound good aloud. So good that I dare to try out a variation, just to see how that might resonate. "I've always loved you." And I'm vastly relieved to discover that these words sound good too, as well as near enough to truth as makes no difference.

"Yes?" Jerry still sounds doubtful, but at least willing to walk this concept around the block. He fixes me with an expression that I recognize from our first encounter: his unflinching interviewer look. "And what precisely is it about me that you love? I'd be interested to hear."

Oh, God. A little off-guard, I take a deep breath and prepare to make my response. What do I love about Jerry? The question buzzes in my brain, around and around, like a fly trapped in an empty jar. I am quite suddenly a student again, caught short by a pop quiz for which I should have known enough to study. *List all the reasons for which you love Jerry Glass, giving examples where relevant. Be sure to compare and contrast your feelings for Jerry Glass with passions aroused in you by any other men, before or since...*

Dear God, I lament silently, why oh why didn't I study for this? Borrow the notes from someone else in the class, look stuff up at the library...

"Well?" Jerry prompts, after an interlude of silence. "Is it so tough to come up with an answer?" Meanwhile, I notice that he suddenly appears relaxed—on top of things, almost light-hearted. As if some danger has, at the last minute, been averted.

"Of course it's tough. Nobody can answer a question like that. I wouldn't dream of asking you why you love *me*."

"I could tell you," he answers, firmly. "If you were to ask, I could absolutely tell you what I love about you, without allowing one single second of dead air to elapse."

"Ah!" I nod. "And it's not as if you 'ought' to feel this way about me?"

No longer light-hearted, Jerry looks straight at me—straight into the heart of danger. "No," he says. "It's not how I ought to feel, but I do."

The only reasonable response to that is to give him a long long kiss. I reach my hand around the back of his neck—the slender stalk of his neck, the crop of curling brown hair, boyish and vulnerable. "Let's not ask each other a goddamn thing," I breathe. "Let's just keep feeling the way we do." And I kiss him.

In spite of the tenderness of the moment, I can't help stealing another glance out the window. Having finished off the lawn-mower and most of the trees, Murphy is now nibbling at the footings of the fire escape, tentatively, to see what nourishment they might afford. After they're dispatched, what next? The cindercrete foundation of the toolshed?

"Jerry…" I shift a little in his embrace.

"What's the matter?"

"About Marta…"

"I thought we agreed." Jerry takes a firm but tender grip on my shoulder. "No more questions. For now. We're going to work this out, I promise."

Does he mean it? From the dazed look in his eyes, it's hard to tell. Even harder for me to evaluate my own preferences and priorities in a situation that has so rapidly escalated from a standing start straight into high gear. What is it about me and Jerry, that every time we choose to fall for each other, it has to be at the speed of light?

"Tell you what," I say, smiling gamely. "This is all a bit confusing. I could use a walk to clear my head, and—something tells me—so could Murphy."

>─┤◆>─O─<◆├─<

I have to say we make a cute couple, Jerry and I, out for a promenade in the park with our big floppy dog. The picture of perfect domestic harmony—marred only by this alarming tendency of Murphy's to strain and slaver at the end of his leash in his eagerness to be out and doing. For which I can't wholly blame him, since the park is thronging with both dogs and kids, all running free in a cheerful welter. As the new custodian of the leash, I feel authorized to make a suggestion.

"Jerry, why don't I let him off for a minute? Look how he's dying to make new friends."

Jerry stops and stares at me as though I've just proposed that we drop Murphy from a helicopter to determine whether he can fly.

"That's rule number one, Dana. You must never, ever, under any circumstances, let him loose outdoors. I can't emphasize that enough."

Okay, so that's rule number one. And yet, in the dappled dusk settling over the park, all the other dogs are gamboling gaily, like rambunctious kids cramming in as much playtime as possible before supper.

"I'm serious," Jerry appends ominously. "You have no idea what a mistake it would be to let Murphy off that leash."

"I understand," I assure him. Although I don't. The tender, vulnerable face that Jerry showed me mere minutes ago in the kitchen has turned hard and cold outdoors. And as I struggle to keep Murphy reined in, I can't help thinking: What's the point? What's the point of being a dog if you never, ever get the chance to run?

It's a mutinous thought, completely at odds with my indifference to the dog. And suddenly, it's as if Murphy's intercepted it. Or has simply chosen to take advantage of my momentary inattention to tug the loop end of the leash out of my hand. However it's happened, in a trice he is spinning crazily off across the park with his leash flying out behind him like Isadora Duncan's trademark scarf.

"Murphy!" Jerry pauses just long enough to fix me with a reproachful glare—"I *told* you not to let him loose!"—before sprinting away in none-too-close pursuit of his fleeting dog.

I join the chase, but with a curiously detached sensation. Joggers, nannies, groundskeepers, children, even squirrels all seem to be watching me from a great way off, like frozen spectators lining the length of the racecourse at Ascot, their expressionless faces turned with equal uninterest on the winners and losers thundering past. As I come panting around the clubhouse turn, they all recede from my field of vision, shrinking to indistinguishable dots in a pointillist landscape.

Murphy, meanwhile, is also a dot, but more distinct—a tiny black-and-white ball bouncing in a random trajectory across the grass. From afar, I am forced to watch in helpless horror as that distant dot leaps—playfully, I presume—on a child, and tears the hat neatly from his or her head. Then, with the hat in his mouth, he capers clownishly for the crowd thickening at his end of the park.

Jerry is nowhere to be seen—not, at least, by me. Meanwhile, I am panting in earnest as I attempt to gain ground on Murphy's antic black-and-white shape. Which, no matter how I hurry toward it, appears always to remain the same tantalizing distance away. Now he's dropped the hat and is making a run at the kiddies' play area. Where he somehow manages to tangle his leash around a toddler and take him—in a bellyflop—down the slide.

Hunched over now, gasping for breath, I can hardly bear to continue to look at the swath of mayhem being cut up ahead. When I next dare to raise my head, it is to discover that Murphy has freed the child, mercifully unhurt, and is off again, with Jerry now in visible pursuit. Standing winded at the sidelines, it seems to me as if several hours have elapsed since Murphy began his zigzagging tour of the park.

Next thing I see, he's buzzing a group of other dogs. Who stare at him for a moment, then elect, *en masse*, to join in his madcap sport. As though they've been waiting in bondage for countless centuries for just such a messiah to arise in their midst and take personal charge of their emancipation.

Jerry meanwhile has been steadily gaining ground, and now he tackles Murphy by the tennis court. Then manages to reel him in on his leash, like a marlin—to the apparent edification of the ever-enlarging crowd of onlookers.

Still hovering on the periphery like the coward I am, I do my best to ignore the comments—both amused and annoyed—of the assembled throng. And when Jerry—too breathless or too angry to speak to me—exits the park with Murphy more or less in tow, I simply fall in behind, at a meek and respectful distance.

Several minutes of silence elapse before Jerry, still toiling purposefully across the grass, can bring himself to fling a few words at me over his shoulder. "I don't want to fight about this," he gasps hoarsely. "Fighting fucks my respiration up."

Ah, yes. Jerry's bronchial byword always—at least, for as long as I've known him. Were it not for his legion of allergies, I wonder, would he be more of a confrontationist? More than once in the course of our strange and spasmodic relationship, I've caught myself wishing that Jerry, when provoked, would holler back—instead of merely misting his plants very rapidly, with a fatalistic sneeze. Maybe if he'd fought with me, right at the outset—respiration be damned—he and I might not have downshifted as rapidly as we did into anemic nothingness. Maybe we would not be engaged, right this minute, in attempting to kick-start the old *amour* once more—especially while encumbered with the canine byproduct of one of the many other involvements that ensued in the wake of our original romantic dissolution.

"We don't have to fight," I concur wimpishly. "I'm sorry Murphy got away on me. It won't happen again."

"Good."

But it's not until we're back at my front door that Jerry can bring himself to look me in the eye. "You know..." He pauses on the porch, the better to intensify his searching let's-cut-the-bullshit interviewer expression. "You took me totally by surprise before. Announcing out of the blue that you still miss me."

"No, you're the one who misses *me*. You said it first, remember?" Having gained the advantage of that long kiss and his fervent assurance that we'll work things out, I now find myself...not backpedaling, precisely. Just hesitating to rush headlong through the door I've opened. At the same time, I avoid his gaze as I grope in my pocket for the key to unlock the actual, nonfigurative, door that leads into my apartment.

"Yes, all right, so I said it first. But you're the one who upped it to 'love.'"

"Jerry, are you backpedaling? You can admit it." And I almost wish he would. If only to crank up the level of my own ardor once more.

"No, no, I just...Look, I think I still have to go ahead with my trip."

"Well, of course!" I can't help staring at him, amazed. "I mean, it's a business thing. I understand. You can't just back out."

"That's right," he agrees, but with a surprising lack of assertiveness. "So. We'll just put everything on ice till I get back from Madrid."

"I thought it was Barcelona."

"Oh, well, I…change planes at Madrid or someplace. Anyway, what's the difference?" He takes my hand tenderly. "The point is, I still have to go. I'm sorry."

If he's sorry about sticking me with Murphy, he can't be any sorrier than me. Otherwise, I have to acknowledge that I'm somewhat relieved at the prospect of putting things on ice. If only to slow down this rapid play of events. And it's not as if Marta is going to pose any threat while Jerry's in Spain, safely away from both of us.

"It's okay," I tell him. Out here on the porch in the deepening twilight—even with Murphy's bony head bumping between our two sets of knees—it's remarkably nice to be kissing Jerry some more, really kissing him. As a prelude to an exchange of intimacies even more assuring, once we go into the house and get into—

"So, good." Abruptly, Jerry has pulled away, and is now regarding me somewhat awkwardly from a distance. "We won't talk about this anymore till I'm back. Or *do* anything about it, either. If you catch my drift."

I catch his drift, all right. Just another kiss or two out here on the porch is what he means. And after that…by no manner of means does Jerry plan to bed down for the night any place except on the camp cot in my office. Which is, I gather, some chivalrous concession of his to the ambiguousness of our present circumstances. The sort of chivalry, in my opinion, that can't die out quickly enough.

⊳━◄◊⊱━○━⊰◊►━◄

 I'd like to describe the feeling, but I can't. What it was like to go giddy with the realization that, for the first time ever, I was free to run. Sure, I realize my liberation was inadvertent. A question of me pulling free, as opposed to being set loose. I mean, it's far too early in the game to count this woman as any kind of ally. Whereas it was nice of her to give me those trees and that power mower to chew on out in the yard, I can tell she's actually far more interested in Jerry than she is in me.

Which is fair enough, if it means I can take advantage of her inattention to bust loose again. There was something so addictive about it. Awe-inspiring almost, thundering through the park on my own recognizance. A dog among dogs, so to speak. No, more than that: a kind of *god* among dogs. I mean, I had the rest of the pack following me—straight into the jaws of hell, I suspect, if I'd been headed that way.

Now that I've tasted liberty on that level, the question is: Can I ever feel satisfied again with those sedate little strolls under close confinement, that used to seem like the be-and-end-all? You could, of course, argue that I was better off before, in my indentured ignorance. You *could* argue that, but I won't be listening.

Instead, I'll just be lying here, rerunning again and again my late, great adventure in independent living. With a sappy little smile on my face—and seditious dreams in my heart. Dreams in which I watch and wait for the next chance to rise up and run, a god among dogs. 🐾

⋟⋯⊙⋯⋞

In the morning light, I awaken groggily to the sight of a dark, tousled head on the pillow next to mine. And I smile. Sweet sentimental Jerry of the chivalrous resolves, unable, evidently, in the deep of night to hold firm to his vows, when he could—instead—be holding me.

"Jerry?" Gently, I tap the shoulder of the blanketed body beside me. "Jerry, I'm so glad you—"

A black-gummed, grinning gargoyle face lolls back to greet me, one eye rolling hideously in its head. "Murphy!" Sheesh!

But as the dog scrambles to his feet, I have to laugh. "Well, Murphy. Was it good for you? Can't say it was good for me. In fact, I must have nodded off in the middle. Let's keep this from Jerry, though, okay? I mean, he thinks I'm back with him."

When Jerry emerges from my office, he seems quite delighted to discover that Murphy took the initiative to bunk in with me. "Wow, he's really *bonded* with you! That's terrific."

Uh-huh. I set a mug of tea before him, and some hypoallergenic muffins I bought, which to me taste as if they've been made from old overcoats.

"What this means," Jerry continues to bubble, as he scarfs his tweedy muffins with real enthusiasm, "is that I can leave him here with a clear conscience."

It seems to me that Jerry is making ready to leave with a light step along with his clear conscience. This morning, there are no searching looks, no allusions to what may ensue between us upon his return.

It's not until he's actually at my front door, shifting his overnight bag from one hand to the other, that he betrays any hint of hesitation. "You know, I really do appreciate what you're—"

"Jerry! Will you can the gratitude, once and for all? I agreed to take Murphy, and I'm doing it. It's nothing for you to act guilty about."

He is acting guilty again, goddamn it—as if he were about to perpetrate some enormous scam. For a panicked moment, it occurs to me: What if he's intending to stick me with the dog forever? "I mean, heh heh, you are planning to come back, right? It's not as if you're headed to Barcelona under the Witness Protection Program or something?"

"Of course I'm coming back," he assures me. "Dana, I...Oh, hell." He wavers for a moment, seemingly on the brink of some utterance, then pulls back from the precipice. "It'll keep till I get back."

"Jerry, is there something you're still not telling me?"

"No. Let's stick to the original plan here, okay? Shelve this conversation for a couple weeks."

I consider putting up an argument. Then, just as quickly, think better of it. After all, it's not as though I'm entirely prepared myself to look him in the eye and reiterate the things I said last night.

Ambivalence, thy name is Jaeger. "All right," I agree. "The sooner you leave, the sooner you'll be back." Not that I believe for a single second his "couple weeks" guesstimate. A month, at least, is bound to elapse before Jerry will be able to bring himself to come back to claim his dog like a piece of left luggage.

There are bright tears standing in his eyes as he leans down to kiss me—rather chastely—goodbye. Then, as he takes Murphy aside, I discreetly avert my gaze. However Jerry feels about his dog down deep, on the surface he is a sentimentalist. "So long, old buddy," he mumbles into Murphy's furry neck, like a boy in some children's classic, forced to abandon his pet on the road to manhood. "Behave yourself. For a change."

"He'll be fine," I tell him, with a heartiness I'm far from feeling.

Nodding wordless acknowledgment, Jerry gathers up his bag and hurries out the door.

I move to the living-room window—my customary post from which to watch men depart. Murphy trails after me. He rears up on his hind legs, puts his paws on the sill, and gazes out, his nose further smudging the already clouded windowpane.

By now, it must be clear to him that Jerry is leaving. Unless, of course, Murphy's the sort for whom delayed response tells the tale. I picture him hurling himself through the window long after Jerry has driven away. Or moping for days beside his untouched food, nose resting tragically on the rim of the dish.

For now, though, there's absolute equanimity in his manner as he observes Jerry stowing his valise in the rear of the Honda. Even as the car pulls away, Murphy continues to stare unperturbed out the window, his strangely pale eyes as inscrutable as a wolf's.

"You okay with this, Murphy? You handling this?"

At the sound of his name, he turns his harlequin face toward me, and his yellow-eyed gaze seems to say: *Handling this? Of course. Don't kid yourself for a minute that you're the one handling things around here.*

"Well, good. Because here we are, Murphy. Stuck with each other for…well, who knows how long?"

Even as I utter the words aloud, the sickening reality begins to settle in my stomach, like a sinking anvil.

>−!−◆>−O−◆−!−◂

Stuck with each other? I can live with that. I can live with anything, except possibly Marta, and I doubt she's likely to come calling. Meanwhile, this place is good enough for me—certainly a damn sight better than a stretch at the Shelter.

As for Jerry, he'll be back, I'm sure, to squelch any fun that occurs in his absence. If I want to work in another run in the park before he shows up, I better start lobbying this lady right away.

>−!−◆>−O−◆−!−◂

I continue to stare at the dog, who continues to stare back at me. I swallow hard, and as I do, I can envision—in a word-balloon over my head—a single desperate syllable: "Ulp!" Which more or less sums up the situation.

Chapter Two

🐾 Jerry, it now appears, is not coming back. How I feel about that, I'm not quite certain. On the one hand, the palpable proof of Marta's victory over me leaves a galling aftertaste. On the other hand, I have to face the fact that at least some of the impetus to cut and run came from Jerry himself. In which case, so be it. After all, Jerry's and mine has never been a match made in heaven.

Not that my extended sleepover here is, so far, exactly the honeymoon suite. Clearly, Dana's in this strictly to curry favor with Jerry, and seems to have no idea that she's wasting her time. After all, wherever Jerry is right this minute, you can rest assured that Marta can't be far behind. Or, more accurately, on top—her favorite position from which to assume command. Sitting on Jerry, so to speak, as if he were a suitcase she wants to cram shut. Which leaves Dana-the-dog-minder...where? Out in left field, with a leash in one hand and a poop-scoop bag in the other.

Sadly, there's been no further indication of the free-Willy spirit that characterized our first outing in the park. Ever since, she's kept me on a short lead and a tight schedule that would do credit to Jerry himself, that rajah of repression, that high pooh-bah of party-pooperism. Unlike Jerry, however, Dana appears to have some faint glimmering of sensitivity to my situation. The other day, for example, when she was running late and bundled me out into the backyard to do my business in five seconds or less...At least she was decent enough to appreciate how indecent it was. All of a sudden, out of the blue, she started talking right out loud about some prisoner, taken out of his cell by his captors every morning and ordered to crap on cue. 🐾

>⊷•⊙•⊶◁

It's not that the dog is someone I feel I can talk to. But there's something about him that makes me talk to myself. For instance, the other day when I put him out with stern injunctions to perform the sole trick in his repertoire—which is defecation more or less on demand—I had a sudden flash of this story I'd heard years ago, in my prairie childhood, about Louis Riel—or was it Chief Poundmaker?—being held by the Mounties in some squalid prison hut, from which he was frog-marched every morning by his guards into the yard. To endure the humiliation of pants pulled down, and an angry voice screaming at too-close range: "On your mark, set, squat!" As if shit not only happens but should happen right on the spot.

So this is what dog ownership—even on an interim basis—evidently means to my psyche: being condemned to play the part of a Mountie—after a lifetime of fancying myself more the Riel or Poundmaker type. In this relationship, I am the overbearing adult. The hidebound, humorless representative of law and order, in only nominal command of this furry, four-legged child.

Now, the canine characters on *Amazing Grace* don't consume a lot of onscreen time shitting in the yard, or biting their fleas, or licking their balls. No, dogs on *Amazing Grace* are up and doing, with a bushy-tailed sense of purpose that would do credit to a Mary Kay Cosmetics rep. And any scriptwriter in search of ideas for future episodes would be better advised to spend her time speed-reading *Bob, Son of Battle* rather than squandering valuable time hanging out with old Murphy here.

Although, there are times when he looks at me with a solemn, aggrieved air that puts me in mind of some noble primitive. Like Black Elk, sizing up the white man's potential as a recording secretary—now that there's nothing left of his own culture, apart from the stories that were never written down. Or like a time-traveler who might have passed this particular checkpoint before, in some previous life.

><del>·◆·─O─◆·</del>·<

A lot of what I know, I've learned from television. But since I'm never the one in charge of the controls, much of what I piece together tends to be hit-and-miss. I do know there was a period B.C. (Before Conquest) in which my ancestors pretty much ran things for ourselves. Then came A.D. (After Domestication), which brought with it not only captivity, but a sort of dog diaspora, when human beings broke up our packs, in accordance with their basic operating principle of divide and conquer.

I'd like to think that this woman I've wound up living with could feel some sympathy for my situation, but apart from her occasional flashes of insight, I get no indication that she does. So far, the only TV time we've spent together was with *Greyfriars Bobby*. She brought it home on video and forced me to watch it with her. Meanwhile, she talked through the whole thing, wondering how they got the dog to do the kirkyard scenes, and figuring out how she might plagiarize the plot unobtrusively.

I, meanwhile, am imbibing this heartwarming crap, and asking myself what's the big deal about Wonder Dogs? When she could be cribbing material from someone like me—a dog who wonders. I mean, my life is full of marvels that put Greyfriars Bobby right in the shade. The paradox of my leash, for instance: Why it is, when she reaches my leash down from the shelf, I surge with such excitement. Even though the leash represents what reins me in as much as what sets me free. That's the mystery inherent in my leash, both my liberation and my oppression, my boonest companion and my strictest chaperone.

How is it that I am able to celebrate both of these things together, on one long keening note? Without my leash, let it be clearly understood, there is no such thing as a walk. Yet with my leash, there is no such thing as a walk on the wild side, ever. And for me, the wonder of that contradiction will never cease.

><del>·◆·─O─◆·</del>·<

Wasn't it F. Scott Fitzgerald who observed that the mark of a true intellectual is his ability to hold two opposing ideas in his mind at the same time? Being no intellectual, I have no idea what that means. Still, I'm beginning to suspect that Murphy does.

When he reacts to his leash, for instance, I note that the response is distinctly twofold. First, his impression of a Publishers Clearing House grand-prize winner—when he leaps and yodels and slavers and sobs. Followed almost immediately by the suddenly drooped ears, the submissive crouch as I clip the leash to his collar—as he recalls that this five-foot length of leather is actually a two-edged sword.

Of course, it may be that Fitzgerald was as wrong in his definition of the intellectual as he was about the comedic possibilities inherent in cutting off people's neckties at dinner parties and eating soup with a fork. It may be that the ability to hold two opposing ideas in the mind at the same time means squat. A parlor trick that can be performed by the veriest imbecile—as witness, Murphy. Who may simply be too stupid to understand that the leash that signals "walk" is the same leash that keeps him from running. Or else is too much of a cockeyed optimist to surrender the notion that every walk, however tightly reined, is one step closer to breaking free to run, forever and ever.

Chapter Three

"The way I see it," Karen is confiding to her audience, "middle age has one real advantage. No, make that TWO. 'Cause, whoo-ee, looka here at THESE twin beauties. Breasts, right? For the first time in my life, I'm starting to develop boobs worthy of the name. Honkers. Knockers. Jugs. Bazoombas. Only problem with these hooters you sprout in later life is, they're hanging down around my MIDRIFF. See? Like, could this be why they call it MIDDLE age?"

Christ, how does Karen do this? Stand up on stage jutting her chest at a bunch of youthful strangers. Could there be catharsis of some kind in it, a paradoxical denial of the facts by proclaiming them? No, I don't believe that. Even under the harsh spotlight, Karen still looks far younger than she is. Her bosom, while modest, still rides as high as a girl's. And I've never met anyone less hung up on aging than she is.

"No, seriously, now that I finally HAVE a bust—it's a BUST. My body is sagging so SERIOUSLY I should start wearing a product-warning label: 'Some Settling of Contents May Have Occurred Due to Handling.'

"Jesus! Wouldn't you think I'm ENTITLED to a brief interlude—an HOUR, say—during which my new breasts would have the decency to poke out PERKILY? You know, before beginning that long trek SOUTH? Like this old retired couple, right, weighed down with luggage, trudging slowly, SLOWLY toward the Miami departure gate?"

Do I wish I could do what Karen does—pick up a microphone and compulsively confess my fears, real or imagined, in hopes of receiving absolution in a tidal wave of laughter? No, I don't wish that, not really. Especially when the tsunami of hilarity—in Karen's case—is generally little more than a spattering of embarrassed titters.

What I do envy is the apparent candor she brings to "the work." Unlike myself, dutifully forging words in my far-from-redhot smithy, Karen really says what she means, and (presumably) means what she says.

"Okay, okay, suppose I WAS granted that one brief hour of poking perkily? Like, can you DIG it? Me, driving all my old boyfriends CRAZY with my new, improved pair of pointies! I mean, I am talking about every guy I EVER dated, right? In my younger, less-ENDOWED days. Those guys who always wound up rejecting me with the five CRUELEST words in English: 'Sorry, babe, I'm a tit-man.' Okay, that's SIX words if you count 'tit' and 'man' as separate. Which, unfortunately, I've OFTEN had to do...

"But, hey, never MIND. 'Cause now I'm STACKED, right? And now I'm calling UP those bozos, one by one, in order to TAUNT them over the phone about what they're missing. 'Oh, hi, Dave. It's Connie. Connie Casserole? That's right—the Human Hatrack. That's what you used to call me, didn't you, honey? Only, guess WHAT, Davey? Now I've got these, like, HONEYDEW MELONS, okay? And they are jutting SO jauntily that I could hardly see OVER them to dial your number. Oh, yes, Dave, these boobs of mine are the real thing. No synthetics here. Suck on THAT—you should live so long, you SCHMUCK.'"

No, I take it back. Her candor—if I can call it that—is not to be envied at all. As Karen, in the guise of Connie Casserole, bows and tries to make if offstage before the pallid applause has completely expired, I sit numbly in my chair, wondering what I'll say to her.

Does she have any idea in the world, I wonder, how naked is this fantasy of revenge? Which may *be* a fantasy—although the vengefulness that fuels it seems real enough.

Could Karen really make such a phone call? I'm embarrassed even to think that she could. And so, as her old friend Katie, what am I supposed to do: commend her for her creativity, or snicker along with her at the expense of all the tit-men named Dave?

⪦━◦━◦━◦━⪧

Karen, as it turns out, is too caught up in anger at her audience to bother asking me what I thought of the act. "Fuck 'em," she declares as she pilots her Volkswagen Bug, pedal to the metal, up Varsity Avenue. "Fuck the Canucks if they can't take a joke, eh? Like, if I'm gonna be forever doomed to cast my pearls before underaged SWINE, they might as well be swine with a SUNtan. California, Katie. California is calling."

Of course, I've heard the "California Here I Come" song before. Some years back, Karen even made good on the threat by heading out to Los Angeles in her vintage Volkswagen, with big plans to break into the comedy scene. Apparently unaware that the scene was no longer what it once was.

However, Southern California did at least provide her with unparalleled opportunities to spend her copious free time logging long restorative miles behind the wheel of the Bug. No wonder she still talks about going back. Since driving, to Karen, represents the same sort of spiritual rejuvenation Abe Lincoln is reputed to have derived from splitting rails.

"Uh-huh" is my understated response to Karen's threat to blow town. Meanwhile, I worry about blowing dinner as I shrink down in the passenger seat while she muscles her way from lane to lane. Karen drives *well*, I remind myself, as naturally as most other people breathe. Just so goddamn *fast*—with "Don't Cry for Me, Argentina" cranked up on the car stereo, and an expression of kamikaze fervor on her face—that the naturalness of my own breathing is in jeopardy, on those rare occasions when, as now, I make the mistake of taking up her offer of a lift home.

"What's the matter?" She takes her eyes off the road to give me a long look—far too long for safety, in my opinion. "Don't you think L.A.'s the right career move for me?"

"Will you please concentrate on your moves up this street? Karen, you and I have had the California conversation a million times."

"Honey, at this point, there isn't any conversation we HAVEN'T had a million times. Which is what makes us so US. Which is also why you should come WITH me this time."

"To Los Angeles? Oh, sure, I can feature it. I bet I can step into the head writer's job on *Friends*. And, of course, Hollywood's always looking for forty-plus nobodies to knock out multimillion-dollar epics. Provided the writer has no scruples about sleeping with Harrison Ford, to get a feel for his character."

"Katie, I'm not kidding. We would be the BEST together in California. And the BRIGHTEST. The climate out there PRESERVES things, you know. Especially cars. This one time on Santa Monica Boulevard? I spotted a '52 bullet-nose Studebaker sedan. A dead RINGER for my daddy's old car back in Skokie."

Yes, I know all about the Studebaker back in Skokie. As well as its identical twin on Santa Monica Boulevard. Karen apparently does not remember, but I was with her one night when she'd just returned from L.A. and decided to call up her dad.

Of course, by that time, Pa Larkin was a very old man. So perhaps it's understandable that he had some difficulty grasping the point of Karen's call. All the same, as a silent bystander, I found it painful to listen to normally chirpy Karen as she struggled to bridge a gap evidently wider than all the miles between here and Illinois.

"Daddy? Hi, it's me. It's Karen. How're you doing, hon? I—No, Karen. KAREN. Up in Canada? But, guess what, I just got BACK from California, and I—CALIFORNIA. Los Angeles? Where the comedy clubs are? I had some terrific bookings, Daddy, and I—No, not BOOKS, *bookings*. I don't write books, I write comedy, so I—Daddy, let's never MIND about that right now. Guess what I saw in L.A.? This is what I phoned to tell you. I saw the old Studie! No, STUDIE. Stu-duh-bay-ker. Your old BULLET-nose, Daddy. Remember?

It was the only time I've ever seen Karen like that: forlorn, desperate, with the veins working in her skinny neck as she strove with all her might to be recognized—and loved—by that befuddled old man on the other end of the phone. Eventually, the old man must have turned the phone over to Karen's mother, because the next thing I knew, Karen had banged down the receiver and turned to me angrily. "I HATE that woman. I can SMELL her, right through the receiver. That musty, mildewy, CHURCHY smell. Fuck, I need a BATH."

I couldn't think of a thing to say that wasn't inane. However, for the first time, Karen's compulsive need to scrub and rub suddenly made a sort of sense.

Tonight it's clear that Karen has forgotten that sad phone conversation ever took place, or that I was on hand to witness it. Her father died last spring, and in the intervening months, he has been completely wrapped by his daughter in a golden mantle of memory that becomes him better than the truth ever did. "A dead RINGER," she repeats now, reveling. "You know, I even phoned Pa Larkin UP one night, to tell him I'd seen a '52 Studie in L.A.? He got SUCH a kick, Katie. His little Karen, calling him up just to tell her dear old dad she'd spotted his CAR."

I glance out the window to note the provincial legislative buildings whipping by at enormous speed.

"Honey—seriously. Come with me to the Coast. We'd have SUCH a blast in a rented bungalow on the beach, and you could borrow the Bug whenever you wanted."

Karen forgets that I don't drive, and also forgets that beach bungalows never figured too prominently in her L.A. life when she found herself much more a should-have-been than a wannabe. Hanging around the fringes of a comedy scene that was—like her— no longer as fresh or as flourishing as it used to be.

"Tell you what. If you really do go back down there, I'll come visit you in the beach house. How about that?"

"Mint. If you MEAN it, Katie. Which you don't."

No, but then neither does she. "Karen, you've driven past my street three times now. At this point, I'll promise you anything."

When she lets me off at my corner, I scramble out of the Bug, believing I am home free. But no such luck.

"Katie, not so fast. You haven't told me how you liked the bit."

"Bit?"

"Don't be LAME. The breast bit."

"Oh. Well, I...I think there's real courage there."

"Excuse me? COURAGE?"

As I hover uncomfortably at the curbside, holding the car door open, Karen peers out at me like a cabbie scrutinizing a cheapskate fare. "What's COURAGE got to do with anything, for fuck's sake? Does it work or not? God knows, I can't depend on the AUDIENCE to let me know."

"Well, as I say, I think it's sort of brave. To...go along with your anger like that."

"Anger?" Karen's eyes are as wide open, and as blue, as the portals of heaven. "Honey, who would I be ANGRY at?"

Oh, God. "Well... men?"

"Men! Katie, men are the BEST. Who else could be so stupid, and so SWEET?"

"Oh." I nod, trying to convince myself to leave well enough alone.

"I mean, it's all a JOKE, honey. You, of ALL people, should get it."

Even now, she doesn't sound particularly jokey. Maybe that's the problem with the act. "Karen, it's late. Let's talk about it more tomorrow, okay? Now, don't look at me that way."

But as I close the car door and turn away, she's still looking at me that way. As if I were out in the audience—staring back at her without comprehension, like a pig contemplating a pearl.

>━◆>━O━<◆━<

Turning up my front walk, I can make out Murphy, a prick-eared presence at the window of my dimly lit living room. So absolutely expected that I am struck by how much for granted I now take him.

"Hi there, Murphy. Miss me?"

He never acts as if he did. Merely surveys me with that level yellow-eyed gaze. I never ask him if he misses Jerry. Nor, I notice, is it a question I ask myself. It's not that I was lying when I told Jerry I loved him. It's more that the person who claims to love him is in abeyance. Frozen in time, like some candidate for cryonics. On ice, as Jerry said. Or under it.

Surely down there somewhere, Murphy has feelings. Resentment at Jerry for leaving him? Annoyance with me for failing to fill the breach? Murphy doesn't seem to get mad; he doesn't get even. He doesn't even get off—except at the sight of his leash, or the sound of a fresh avalanche of kibble into his dish. Or, occasionally, *in flagrante delicto* with my laundry bag. But what's he thinking?

Murphy, meanwhile, continues to regard me—not cutely, with his head cocked to one side, like His Master's Voice. But levelly, coolly, almost judgmentally. And I feel exposed by that stare of his, as if I were onstage myself. Being silently heckled from the back of the room by a sadistic clairvoyant in a fur suit.

Chapter Four

Of course, even those lucky sons of bitches who get to run in the park on a regular basis are seldom permitted what I would term genuine freedom of assembly. And it doesn't take a genius to figure out the strategy behind it. Divide and conquer, just like I told you. Keep 'em in line by keeping 'em apart. Above all, keep them loyal by keeping their eyes firmly on the prize: human approval, the ultimate accolade.

No, it doesn't take a genius to figure it out. Unfortunately, every day I see underachievers in that park who could benefit from an IQ transplant to bring them up to speed. Real mouth-breather types— Labradors, mostly, or spaniels. You know the type I'm talking about: "Jump, you say, boss? Yassuh—how high?" "Fetch that dead feathered thing? No problem!" I mean, some of these good-old-boy boys are so simple, they should wear signs: "Will salivate for food."

Even so, it's my firm belief that there's no dumb animal so dumb as to be beyond reach of *some* improvement. Trouble is, reaching out is a tough nut to crack when, like me, you're kept on a short, short leash.

Offhand, I would have thought a woman would be a lot easier to get over on than a man. Well, she should be, but believe me, this one's not. Tense, dutiful, mirthless, uptight . . . measuring out meals by the cupful, measuring out walks step by step.

Who knows? She may have her reasons. The other day, I overheard her complaining on the phone that the only man who shows up in her life on a reliable basis has "Culligan" stitched on his pocket. In which case, I say: Let's find this woman a date. Anything to keep her from taking out her disappointments on me.

Frankly, the problem could be in her presentation. She seems to spend a lot of her time in T-shirts and jeans and sneakers, with this dumb little backpack she sports instead of a purse. And then there's the bike. The first time I got a load of her heading out the door in her little-girl getup, my immediate thought was that she must have offspring somewhere, and was trying to decoy danger away from them. I saw something about that on the Nature Channel one time: this species of lizard that protects its young by taking on their adolescent coloring in order to draw off potential predators.

However, in Dana's case, it turns out, there are no young. Unless you count her—as she so evidently wishes you would. To be fair, everyone else in her age group in the park seems similarly immature. The only way I can separate the football-playing men from the football-playing boys is by figuring out which bald heads are merely a fashion state-ment. Meanwhile, the middle-aged women are jogging in outfits that look like kiddy pajamas—while the teenage girls sit hunched up on the edge of the fountain, dressed in black and bitterly smoking cigarettes. No wonder Dana's unsure about which generation to join.

As for me, I have no access to any peer group whatsoever. Nights, I lie awake—well, for at least a minute—turning the problem over in my mind. Only to fall asleep, problem unsolved. Except in my dreams, where I always manage to find a way to gather my fellows around me—mouth-breathers and Wonder Dogs alike—in order to exhort them to rise up and break free of their choke chains. 🐾

Chapter Five

Not to make too big a deal of it, but I loathe and despise making the long trek to the offices of DogStar Productions. Which are located at a studio complex up in Winzigdorf, a kitschy Aryan-looking hamlet about twenty inconvenient miles north of downtown. Inconvenient to me, certainly, since it's too far to bicycle, I don't drive, and I am ill-disposed to evince enthusiasm for any job-site accessible only by commuter train.

To be fair, Winzigdorf is a job-site I am not often required to commute to. In fact, DogStar Productions actively discourages authors of episodes of *Amazing Grace* from dropping up to the set, on the grounds that our presence might prove "disruptive" to the shooting schedule. Meaning that DogStar fears if any of us writer types ever got an up-close gander at the liberties taken with our work, we might disrupt the shooting schedule but good—by shooting into the assembled cast and crew.

Personally, I don't much care what is done to my scripts. Nor do I have any particular desire to see it done. Which is why, on those rare occasions when I am requested to front up, I resent wasting a perfectly good afternoon choo-chooing all the way to Winzigdorf Station, then walking a quarter mile to the studio, in order to applaud the evisceration of whatever turkey I submitted in the first place.

On previous, similarly compulsory, visits, I've had the tour of the soundstages, the back lot, and the several permanent outdoor locations that are scattered around the village. I've shaken paws, solemnly, with all the Majors who play various aspects of Amazing Grace. I've exchanged pleasantries with those far less pivotal personnel who play the human characters on the show. Clearly, no such social niceties are on tap for today. Today, nothing much will be expected of me, except complete acquiescence to the proposed changes to the script—and a complete rewrite before I'm allowed to get on the train and head back downtown, a sadder but wiser woman.

⤐⬩⬩⭘⬩⬩⬩⤏

By the time the script meeting breaks up, I've pretty much performed as requested: I've rolled on my back and exposed my underside, the way as-cast dogs in *Amazing Grace* do when required to demonstrate their submissiveness to the hairy heroine.

After that, the head writer, the script supervisors, the script coordinators, the script consultants, the script editors, and assorted assistant producers were all encouraged to take turns telling me how woefully unworkable my script was, as submitted. With which I eagerly agreed. But, just to make sure that I'm clear on the imperative of mending my ways, the script I submitted has been projected on the overhead, so that the many blue pencilings in various hands might be magnified hugely, for my further instruction.

At this point, I expect someone to bring out a rifle, order me to lay my writing hand on the table, and smash my fingers with the butt of the gun. However, I am spared this treatment—presumably reserved for writers who must be whittled down to size. Evidently, I'm now deemed to be the right size already: small enough to fit in anyone's pocket.

It's a tribute to my spirit of cheerful cooperation that I am personally escorted back to reception by the script supervisor—or is she the script consultant? Whoever she is, her name is Glenda and she offers me an invitation to drop by the set before I go home, to see a script (not mine) in production. "Terrific story," Glenda assures me. "Terrific suspense. Grace befriends a little boy who's been abducted by his own estranged father."

Wow. Terrific story, all right. As for suspense—well how, I wonder, does it all turn out? Happily, something tells me. "Uh, no, thanks. I have this, uh, appointment back downtown—"

But I am spared the necessity of further fleshing out this fib by the sudden arrival of two men in the reception area.

"Glenda!" one of the men—whom I recognize as a producer named Wesley—hails my companion. "Have you met our special consultant on this episode? He's an expert on abducted children. Meet Carl Hart."

It *is* Carl Hart. He looks much the same, although more freshly shaven. His smile, already wide and white, grows wider still as he meets my gaze. "Grace!" he says. "Nice to see you again."

"Grace?" Glenda looks at me, momentarily befuddled, then at Carl. "Terrific to meet you, Mr. Hart. Actually, this is Dana Jaeger, one of our terrific series writers. Wesley, we just had this terrific meeting on Dana's terrific script."

"Dana?" Carl Hart's eyebrows elevate. But no higher than mine, on hearing my much-abused script now described as terrific.

"Yes," I admit tersely.

"It's Dana, is it?" he persists. "Not Grace?" Of course, he knows damn well it's not Grace and never was, but can't seem to resist dragging the joke around the ring one more time.

"Grace is the name of the dog on the show. Maybe you're confusing me with her. I'm sure you've had a tiring day on the set, in your capacity as…what is it, child-abduction expert? Funny, I don't remember you in that line of work the first time we met."

"No more than I recall *you* as a scriptwriter. Of course, the circumstances were somewhat…fraught."

Meanwhile, here are Glenda and Wesley listening to Carl's and my conversation with a naked avidity that suggests this could be the most terrific story idea of all time in mid-pitch.

"Look," I tell Carl, "I've got a train to catch. Glenda, I'll fax you the rest of the changes. Nice to see you, Wesley. So long, Mr. Hart." With a wave of farewell for the group at large, I hurry out of the reception area, through the front doors and onto the long walkway that will lead me, eventually, out of the studio complex and in the direction of the Winzigdorf train station. Which—in keeping with the gingerbread-gothic architecture of this entire burg—looks like something Hansel and Gretel might have stopped to snack on.

But I'm not even halfway to the station when a nondescript car comes crawling up beside me, honking its horn politely. "Dana! Would you like a lift downtown?"

It's Carl Hart, of course, smiling at me with the cordiality of an old dear friend. This time of day, it's at least an hour and a half between trains, and for all I know, I just missed one. Oh, well, where's the harm?

><>•O•<>•<

"I'm surprised," he is saying, "that a big-time television writer such as yourself doesn't have her own car."

"Yeah. Maybe I should have stuck with being a good-time girl."

He laughs. "Actually, I never took you for a good-time girl— whatever that is, outside the confines of a forties film. Any more than I ever believed your name was Grace."

"Well, that's okay, because I never believed you were a private eye."

"Please. Private *investigator*. Private eyes went out with good-time girls."

"You don't say. And when they went out, did they have fun?"

"More fun than you and I are having right at the moment."

But the fact is, Carl and I *are* having fun, zooming together down the miles of twisting gray expressway that snake southward into the city. Now that he's elected to drop the nudge-nudge-wink-wink drollery that seems to be a favorite facade, he is turning once more into an appealing guy. Pretty much as he did back at the Arlington, when I declined his invitation to call him sometime. But since he's reappeared anyway, I might as well relax and enjoy the ride. "Seriously, though, private investigator or child-abduction expert. Which one's the scam? Or is it both?"

"Neither. I *am* an investigator, as it happens, and these days, more cases than you'd believe involve tracking down parents denied custody who snatch their own kids. The night I met you, for instance, I'd been tipped off by a 'reliable source,' as they say, that a bloke I was after had checked in to the Arlington with his pair of twins."

"Just twins," I tell him, still not sure whether I believe him, but determined to remain in command of the little I do know for certain.

"I beg your pardon?"

"'Pair of twins' is redundant. I happen to be a twin myself, so I should know."

"You've a twin? Truly?" Carl glances from the road to me, as though expecting to see me replicate myself right before his eyes. "So, it was your twin sister Grace at the hotel that night?"

"You got it. Grace, the sweet, self-effacing good twin. Whereas I'm the one who commits all the ax murders and tries to pin them on her."

He nods. "And what have you done with Grace, then? Killed her too, and stashed her someplace in your flat?"

"If you pull over here, you can find out. The house on the right. The ground floor's mine. You can come in if you like, and see for yourself where the bodies are buried."

"Well, that might be interesting."

"Oh, I should also warn you: I have a big dog. One false move—and he'll hump your leg."

>━◆>━O━◆━�<━<

It seems like the most natural thing in the world, sitting here in my living room with Carl Hart. For once, Murphy has risen to an occasion, and is behaving toward Carl with the grave dignity of Sunnybank Lad.

"Nice animal, this," says Carl. "Not all over the guest like a great bloody tent, the way some of these big bruisers are."

"He can be awful. God knows what's into him tonight. He isn't my dog, and I'm still trying to work out his full spectrum of moods."

"Not yours? Don't tell me he's a special consultant the DogStar people hired to help you with your scripts?"

"Helping isn't one of Murphy's strong suits. I'm just looking after him for a...friend." I'm annoyed with myself for that slight hesitation. And even more annoyed with myself for following up the hesitation with a coy locution like "friend." The same term I used, so lamely, to describe Derek the first time Carl and I met.

"Ah!"

As I force myself to meet his gaze, I am interested to note that his eyes—which I'd taken to be brown—turn out, on closer inspection, to be more of a hazel. "Now, don't say 'ah!' in that knowing way of yours. If there's something you want to know, why don't you come right out and ask?"

"All right, I'll ask. This friend—is it a man?"

"I fail to see how that is, in any way, relevant to anything."

Carl throws up his hands. "Christ! What am I supposed to do with you?"

We are sipping away on red wine; it's an index of my nervousness that I offered him alcohol at a time of day when coffee would be the more appropriate beverage. At first, he said he didn't drink, and launched into some story about being an army cadet in England years ago and getting drunk with a buddy. Who dared him to climb up onto a tank, from which Carl said he fell, breaking his nose and putting paid to his military career at one and the same moment. That was when he swore off liquor. Except, he amended, on special occasions—like this one.

"What do you mean?" I ask him. "What are you supposed to 'do' with me?" Meanwhile, it's taken me a moment to realize that he is no longer sitting opposite me, in the armchair. Now he's beside me on the couch, and so startled am I that he's made that move, I have no clear recollection of when he might have made it. "You're not required to do anything."

"Well, can I ask you whether you're involved with any of these 'friends'? Apart from that married writer chap with the wonky heart. Good old Derek."

"I'm not 'involved' with good old Derek. I haven't seen good old Derek since that night. I have talked to him on the phone, though. And he asked me to reiterate his gratitude to you, should I ever see you again. Well, here you are again, so consider it reiterated."

"He is entirely welcome. In fact, the next time you see good old Derek, you can iterate that."

"If I see him. I told you I'm not involved with him. Besides, I'm not sure I know how to iterate."

"And your other 'friends'? Are you involved with any of them?"

"I'm not involved with anybody." And, as I nullify Jerry's existence in a sentence, I deliberately avoid meeting the eyes of his dog.

"Good."

"Oh, yes? And what about you? While we're on the subject. Are you involved with anyone?"

"I could be. How do you like my chances?"

The brief silence that falls is full of significance, as if we've reached one of those watershed moments on which you look back and say: There. That was the point where the relationship began to happen. Or didn't. That was the moment when it could have gone either way.

"What do you mean?" I say at last. "I really have no idea what you mean."

"No? Then what chance has this involvement at all, if you keep on pretending not to know what I mean?"

"Oh, why don't you just fuck off?" I ask. But in a tone of voice that seems to succeed in suggesting exactly the opposite.

><+>-O-<+>-<

Making love. How many times have I made love over the years? Certainly often enough that this should merely be tabulated as one time more. I've made love to Donovan, to Donna Summer, to every species of background music from Bachman-Turner Overdrive to Bach cantatas. There was even a brief period back in the eighties during which my entire neighborhood seemed to be under complete reconstruction. Which meant that, all one spring and summer, I was forced to make love to the sound of pile drivers.

Yet, no matter who, what, when, where, why, how, and how often, "making love" was the term of choice. Even if, most of the time, it was only sex. And this time, of course, is just one time more.

Except...what if this time I find myself plunging deep, deep, deep, to the bottom of the sea? To glimpse the coral-encrusted remains of the wreck of some vessel rumored to have sunk centuries back, full of incalculable treasure? I've heard tell of the booty aboard all my life. Furred over with small oceangoing creatures, so exotically foreign, and yet, at the same time, so oddly familiar.

Is this what love looks like? These vaguely shimmering images, looming up at me from the bottom of the sea? Altered utterly by lying so many fathoms deep during all the years it's taken me to summon my courage, hold my breath, and submerge myself once more to these black, black depths of panicked surmise. In hopes, at long last, of a lingering look.

Now that we are alone in the bedroom, with Murphy safely on the other side of the door, Carl and I take all the time in the world to unbutton each other's clothes. Which seems only right to me, since his is a body, I discover, that would require all the centuries Andrew Marvell prescribed to do it justice. His beautifully molded shoulders, the delicate crosshatch of dark hairs along his belly that I follow in an unerring line with my lips, down to where his penis rises tenderly to greet my mouth...

I am lying on my very own bed, making love to a man I know nothing about, but about whom there seems to be nothing to learn that isn't printed on his fragrant skin, in the warm crook of his neck, behind the bend of his perfect knee, or in the gorgeous curve where muscled thigh meets velvety groin.

"You're beautiful," I hear myself murmur.

And he reaches down to raise my face gently to his, so that his lips are almost touching mine. "No, you are," he whispers. "Do you have any idea how lovely you are?"

No. But for the moment, I let myself have some idea, and even succeed, briefly, in seeing myself the way I'd like him to imagine me: flat of belly, pert of breast, long and lean and limber.

Carl has kissed me, over every inch of me, or so it seems to me, and run his tongue meditatively over all the parts his lips liked best. He's spread me open with his tongue, and taken me so gently between his teeth that by the time I come—either for the first time, or the fifty-first—my voice seems to cry from a great way off, as if it belongs to some distant spectator at an event too affecting to observe close up.

When he finally thrusts himself inside me, it's with such decisive pleasure that I have no choice but to hold him tight—already fearing what might become of me once he begins to slip away. But before he slips away, he comes at last. With an eloquent shudder that passes all along his body and into mine. And it's then that I can feel the flutter of his heart inside my own chest.

It's only sex, I marvel, stroking the damp hair at the back of his neck. That's all we can say so far for sure. Yet, it feels so much more like making love that I feel compelled to issue a silent apology to all the other men I ever took to bed under the mistaken impression that making love was what we were doing.

>-+-+>-+-O-+-+<-+-+<

Carl and I are sipping coffee across from each other at my dining-room table, just as though we've been doing this together all our lives. By which I mean there is nothing between us that seems self-conscious, or rushed, or tinged with regret. To the contrary, it's all just perfectly natural—as natural, that is, as things can be between two strangers whose bodies have become familiar terrain but whose hearts, thus far, remain uncharted.

"Of course," Carl explains to me, "these parental-abduction cases are not my only area of, ahem, expertise. It's just that these days, split-up or adoptive parents rowing over custody is a much steadier line than adultery wars, or insurance scams—and a lot less grubby, too. At least some of the time in an abduction case, I can end up feeling I've done worthwhile work.

"Mind you, I grew up an orphan myself. Which is a different sort of hell—but, arguably, less of a hell than bickering parents. I was shunted from one foster home to another till I ran off for good and all. But sad as it was, it doesn't compare to the misery of these supposedly 'lucky' kids that everyone wants.

"So, you see, I don't mind this work, since there seems to be some point to it. Nor do I mind—for a fee—sharing a little of my... well, expertise with producers of TV programs or whatever. All in a good cause sort of style."

It seems like a long speech for Carl, and has some of the quality *of* a speech. Yet, he delivers it so matter-of-factly that I can't help being impressed. An orphan... Well, certainly I can see that as a genesis for his involvement in what he regards as this meaningful work. Although there may be other explanations, too. "Have you got children of your own?" I ask, through rubbery lips.

"I do indeed. My daughter's school play is tonight, as a matter of fact."

I pause in the midst of clearing the table, a cup teetering perilously in my hand. "Oh, you have a daughter."

"Two, actually. Aged twelve and nine." And then, smiling at me quizzically: "Why? Do you mind?"

Do I mind? Of all the potential land mines, trapdoors, and hidden springs I feared any involvement with Carl Hart might lead to, I somehow failed to anticipate the most obvious: he's married. Well, of *course* he is. Given my history—and even my expressed preference—how could he be anything but? Brand-new leopard, same old spots. But for once, yes, I do mind, goddamn it. "Well, the thing is, you didn't let on you're married."

"What? Oh! No. The kids live with their mother. Vivien and I have been split up quite a while. So you see, when it comes to this familial breakdown business, I truly do know whereof I speak.

Though there's been no custody rows between us, thank God."

The sick sensation in my stomach has died down somewhat, and it occurs to me I may have over-reacted. Which, no doubt, is the real legacy of all these years of the Marrieds—to say nothing of the more recent saga of Jerry and Marta and me. Now, whenever I envision a relationship, it's automatically in the shape of a triangle. "So you and your ex-wife are still friends?"

After the briefest of hesitations, he nods. "Yes, I expect we are."

He "expects"? "Don't you ever talk about it?"

"Well, we talk about the kids, mostly. As for the rest of it, Viv's come to terms, I suppose you could say. Look, sweetheart..." He gets up from the table and comes over to me, arms extended appeasingly. "I'm not running away, truly I'm not, but I've got to run. There's work waiting for me that won't wait."

"I see." I am standing here holding a coffee cup in each hand, feeling more like someone left holding the bag.

"No, you *don't* see, but you will. Because the way I look at it is this: We've got all the time in the world, you and I, to find out all about each other. Whose father did what in the war sort of thing. Don't you agree?"

In spite of myself, I permit him to enfold me in his arms, and allow myself to experience the rough, not unpleasant, caress of his woolen lapel against my cheek. After a moment, he gently releases me and whispers in my ear: "I'm off. I'll ring you, shall I?"

Will he? Without waiting for my prediction—or my permission—he hurries down the hallway, to the front door. A moment later, I hear the door open and close. Then the hasty thump of footsteps as Carl—in his apparent eagerness to be off—takes the porch steps two at a time. For once, I do not go to the living-room window to watch a man drive away.

When I let Murphy in from the backyard, he seems surprised to find Carl gone; he even goes so far as to cast about looking for him.

"Forget it," I advise the dog. "He's not going to ring me. I've been through these things a lot more often than you, and believe me, I know. This one's not coming back, no matter what he said."

Chapter Six

The years roll swiftly by in dogdom, but perhaps that fact is offset by moments like this, which seem frozen in eternity. We are outdoors in the dark, Murphy and I—where, tonight, it feels we've been since the last glaciers retreated. Companionable together, in the darkness. With only the reddish glow of the burn-in-bag coals on my Perfekto Portable Backyard Bar-Bee-Kew to provide us with some source of commonality, around which to build this brief detente.

It's way off season for backyard barbecuing, but tonight is another weirdly warm one, and the whim just took me. A moon of sorts is disentangling itself from the treetops and telephone wires, and beginning to rise high enough to appear pristine against a more rarefied backdrop of sky and stars.

What's sizzling on the grill in my backyard is a soybean burger. But as I squat on my haunches to flip it over, I am the archetype of early human predation, cooking up the kill. While Murphy by moonlight awaits his portion of preformed protein as eagerly as if it were the very first chunk of charbroiled bison flung at the very first dog who ever helped in the hunt.

My upstairs neighbors are away this week; there is no one to stare down from on high and wonder what on earth. I am attempting, as best I can, to put out of mind any thoughts of why Carl Hart doesn't call—along with any thoughts of whether Jerry will. Tonight I am determined to make Murphy's and mine alone. An observance overdue, a date postponed from prehistory, a kind of truce between predomesticated woman and as-yet-untamed beast.

Of course, it's hard to say how long this idyll will last, given the essential contradictions in Murphy's position. He wants more freedom—that's clear to me whenever we head to the park. Or, more accurately, whenever I am dragged like a water-skier behind a speeding, erratic motorboat. At the same time, he depends on me for food. The canine equivalent, I suppose one could say, of those women who insist on equality but still expect men to pay for their meals and help them on with their coats.

One thing I will give Murphy, though: he is frank and forthright in his demands. He doesn't grovel; he doesn't ingratiate; he doesn't—not even during a companionable interlude like this—pretend to regard me as the centerpiece of his universe. In fact, I'm not even sure I'm *in* his universe, except as the disembodied hand that wields the can opener and the unattached legs that walk him out the front door. If he had his own credit card, I'm convinced, along with his own key, he wouldn't choose to see me at all, except for a duty lunch every so often. And even then, only if nothing better came up.

Which, of course, contradicts everything I've heard or read about dogs—including the gospel according to *Amazing Grace*. Dogs are supposed to be affectionate, loyal, obliging, and kind. While Murphy—at least in my experience of him—is gross, self-centered, gluttonous, judgmental, and sly. Unless all those other dogs (including that platoon of pooches named Major who pose as Grace) are only faking it. Every dog jack of them—except for Murphy here, honest in his awfulness and awesome in his honesty.

And if Murphy does indeed not lie—except like a rug, abjectly flat and furry on the hardwood floor—then whether he actually likes me or not doesn't much matter. Just so long as he doesn't pretend to. And as for lying outright to me...Well, when my husband, Mark, did that, it was by far the worst of the crimes he committed. Worse than the infidelities themselves—even worse than the truth about the gender of the persons with whom he was being unfaithful.

Lying is the deal-breaker, the sin *qua non*, the biggest of all the big-ticket items in the lottery of love. Murphy may not ever love me; I may not love him, or even aspire to. But this much, at least, he and I have got going: we do not lie to each other about the limitations of what we have got going. Nor about the limitless scope of what we do not.

➤—◆—○—◆—❰

Not only does everything taste better eaten outdoors, it tastes better cooked outdoors, too. Sadly, it tastes better *cooked*. Period. "Sadly," I say, because in that simple fact lies the downfall of a once-proud culture. For a haunch of seared flesh, we sold ourselves cheap. For a mouthful of burnt brisket, we cheerfully renounced all future claim to our autonomy, independence, and self-respect.

It was a bad bargain. But we made it, because we are gluttons. Which means that, for everything that has happened to us since the dawning of the Pot-Roast Period, we may have no one to blame but ourselves.

But deep in my sleep, down where I dream, it is a whole other story. The trick—which I have more or less perfected in sleeping up to twenty hours a day out of the twenty-four—is to be lying here, and at the same time to be somewhere else entirely. To be another Murphy altogether, if you want to put it like that. Or the real Murphy, as I like to put it to myself.

In this place called the Dreaming, where I truly live when I am living in it, there are no leash laws. No anxious owners, no garden walls too high to scale, no back fences that can't be dug under. In the Dreaming, there is only what I follow with my twitching nose, my trembling whiskers, my stiffly jerking legs.

➤—◆—○—◆—❰

Despite what is lacking in our waking life, I have to confess we like to sleep together. At least, I like it. Even when in the grip of some dream, Murphy shivers and moans against me like an unquiet spirit.

So deep down does he seem to go in his sleep that I find myself feeling the magnetic tug. As if I were in danger of plunging helplessly after, at the end of his leash, down whatever rabbit hole he chooses to drag me.

Until we wind up...where? In a kind of nameless nether world nothing like waking, that the dog has dreamed. While I only follow.

Sometimes, in the places I go in my sleep, I find myself already there waiting to greet me. Sometimes not. Sometimes, I am dreaming a landscape where I've never been, populated by creatures I haven't yet met who are living lives that have nothing to do with mine. Creatures to whom I may either catch up in time—or else have already left far behind, dreams and dreams ago.

A certain aroma, a brief encounter, a chance memory...it takes no more than that to lead me down the garden path, then over the garden wall, or the rainbow, or the crescent moon. To where I am part of all that I have dreamt.

Picking up Murphy's saliva-covered toys a dozen times a day; righting the plants that he up-ends; mourning the shoes, scarves, and socks that he routinely destroys...Friends of mine who waited too long to reproduce, and now feel too old for their unruly infants, complain to me about the endless custodial rounds, the constant crisis intervention, the mindlessness of the repetition, the scarcity of thanks they get. But at least with children, there's some larger goal in view. Some kind of reward—however illusory—up ahead. With Murphy, on the other hand, here and now is all there is. There is no forward motion, no hope of progress, as he bumbles obliviously on and on, always the same, eternally unimproved.

Whenever he thinks I'm not watching, he scuttles off to my bedroom, to feverishly hump the laundry bag hanging from the closet door. The first time I saw him pumping away like that, my response was purest disgust. My instinct was to speak to him sharply and drag him away, revoltingly erect. Gradually, however, I have acquired a kind of abashed sympathy for this lonely expense of spirit in a waste of shame.

God knows who it is he has to picture in order to spark the engines of his lust and bang away on the bag like that. But one thing I must concede: if Murphy can't be with the one he loves, he at least deserves credit for doing his best to do what the rest of us do—by simply loving the one he's with.

Not to speak of the stuff he appears willing to eat. In fact, I would prefer to say nothing about that stuff—not so much because I don't know for certain what it is, as because I rather suspect that I do: clumps of grayish grimy Kleenex in the gutter; bird-do daubing the pavement like oilpaint on a palette; the almost indistinguishable remains of a Tootsie Roll gruesomely squished; the almost too-distinguishable remains of a mouse that's met a similar mishap.

To Murphy, it's all the same, and all of it uniformly delicious. A bewildering, undifferentiated array of revolting *residua* that I choose to designate as "Splat." Somehow hoping that such cheerful unspecificity will help me shift my focus away from too-precise identification.

And yet, this same Murphy who grovels in garbage, pees on the peonies, and snacks on Splat is also the animal who has consented, tonight, to join me in quiet camaraderie, as we watch the moon shining down on Murphy and me with equal indifference while it struggles to transcend the trees.

Soon enough, this moment will pass. I'll extinguish the coals, and after that, it will be back to business as usual: Murphy chewing his way through a closetful of shoes, and gnawing out the crotches of my underpants. Murphy straining at the end of his leash, while I haul on his collar, crying, "Heel! Heel!" like some over-reaching evangelist calling down a cure on the sick. Murphy, ravener of refuse, lecher of laundry bags, despotic disrupter of domestic routines.

Yet, just one time, for this occasion only, on this one blessed and singular night, he is another Murphy altogether. Who is—and I blush to disclose it—as closely my companion as some dog in a dream.

Chapter Seven

"The Change, the Change, the Change..." As she turns the words over and over like loose coins, Karen prowls around my living room, brandishing a wrapped tampon as her improvised microphone. "I mean, change into WHAT? Hot flashes, dowager's hump, hormones from horses...let's see now...Like, try trading in those maxipads on Depends adult undergarments and presto! Oh, yeah, it's a whole DIFFERENT deal after the Change, all right!"

My eyes are following her pacing progress back and forth, back and forth. Murphy, too, is riveted, his head moving left to right, then right to left and back again in time to Karen's restless roaming. Though I can't imagine what he might make of the material. To be truthful, I'm somewhat nonplussed myself. Up close, creativity in progress—like childbirth—is not a pretty sight.

"Karen, I'm sorry. I just don't see where you want to go with this." Nor, I could add, why she wants to go wherever it is with me in tow. "I mean, you could lose that prop mike for starters. Not only is a Tampax not all that funny, surely it's all wrong for menopause?"

Karen pauses mid-prowl to regard me with edgy impatience. "Come on, Katie. Do you have to be so LITERAL?"

"Apparently. Which is why I am always absolutely the wrongest person for you to try out new riffs on. I mean, the middle-aged routine was one thing, but change of life? Isn't it a bit early for you to cover that base? Christ, all that is years away still, and no wonder you can't seem to generate jokes that either one of us gets."

"Years away." She shakes her head, and her ponytail along with it. "Honey, it's all HAPPENING. Sooner than you think. And if I can face that fact, why can't YOU? Personally, I can't WAIT to be rid of all this...sanitary shit. SANitary! THERE'S a misnomer, if there ever was one." She glares briefly at the tampon before launching it through the air like a miniature javelin.

"Don't be ridiculous." I don't quite know why this subject riles me, but it does. "You said it yourself. Once you're rid of all the 'shit,' as you call it, what's the alternative? Hot flashes, hormone replacement, incontinence, and osteoporosis. Change of life! I'll say. Lycanthropy for ladies. In the privacy of your own home, no full moon required."

The expression on Karen's face is now one of interest. "Lyc... what? Go on, Katie. Where are you heading here?"

"No place." All of a sudden, I'm annoyed with myself for revealing this level of vehemence about something I couldn't care less about. "It's just that expression, change of life. Like turning into a werewolf or something. And 'menopause'!" I shiver. "All I can see is this pair of furry paws—menopaws!—sprouting from the sleeves of my blouse. To go with the hair sprouting all over the rest of me, and the big Quasimodo hump!"

Karen shrieks with laughter. It really is a shriek—staccato and whinnying. "Menopaws! That is SO cool!" She bunches her hands into clumsy paws and inspects them in mock horror. "Like, morphing by moonlight. Can't you dig it? All these menopausal werewolf WOMEN out there, with the urge to stalk by night...Katie, what did I say? Down deep someplace, you've got the STUFF."

If so, down deep is where I prefer to keep it. But there's no deplaning Karen once she's on board with a concept she hopes might fly. "Well," I say modestly, "I guess there are a few places you could take it. Like, if menopause were a kind of syndrome. Middle-age... let's see... middle-age affective disorder. MAD, for short. Get it? It could have its own awareness day, like AIDS."

But I can see she is no longer listening to me, as she resumes pacing the room like something out of a bad horror film. "Out there, prowling in packs to—no, check that. NOT packs. Make it prowling all ALONE. The lone wolf. Yeah, like that. The NIGHT stalker. Very scary, on all fours, this humped back and one big bushy eyebrow STRAIGHT across...Tapping on the window of some two-timing GUY. Then ducking down in the shrubs, coiled to POUNCE the minute he comes out to see what..."

It's the same uncomfortable sensation I had that night at the Canada Goose when Karen was launched into her tit-man routine. Where is she going with this—in a very literal sense? And why on earth is it someplace that any sane person would want to go?

The peal of the doorbell saves me from the necessity of deciding whether even to pose the question. However, my gratitude is short-lived, once I open the front door to discover my dear friend O'Ryan standing on the other side.

Of all the people I know—with the possible exception of Carl Hart—Mick O'Ryan is the one I would least-willingly place alongside Karen in my living room. Since O'Ryan can generally be counted upon to turn all tongue-tied and aw-shucks in the presence of any woman who isn't prepared to smile a lot, say very little that is threatening to him—and, in general, show him the kind of quiet courtesy that one might employ in order to entice a very shy and very skittish horse to approach and eat oats from the crown of one's hat.

As for Karen's chances of creating a soothing impression...well, it occurs to me to begin to worry about whatever became of that tampon that she fired in the general direction of my sofa.

><+>-O-<+-<

Having declared at the outset that he couldn't stay but a minute, O'Ryan has been lingering for what now seems like hours. Surprising me by the ease with which he converses with Karen about his work on *Amazing Grace* and the essential role he played in getting me hired on, too.

"Oh, so YOU'RE the evil genius," Karen exclaims—to the evident bewilderment of O'Ryan, who has surely never before been accused of being either. "You know, Katie had a promising career as a REAL writer before TV destroyed her talent."

"Katie?" Even more bewildered, O'Ryan glances from Karen to me, as if he's somehow missed a change in casting.

"It's an old nickname," I explain to him. "Which I hate. Which my old friend Karen knows I hate. Which more or less sums up the basis of our long-standing friendship."

"I know what you mean." He nods sympathetically. "All the Majors hafta answer to 'Grace' while on set. They're trained to do it; they know how to do it. But, shoot, it does not mean they *like* to do it."

"You see," I translate for Karen's benefit, "all the dogs in the show are actually named Major. And most of them aren't even females."

"That's right," says O'Ryan. "Like the original Lassie? Now, he was a he. Some egg-suckin' disaster-area name of Pal. Till Rudd Weatherwax—the famous dog trainer?—got holt of him. And whipped him in shape in no time flat!"

O'Ryan is beaming as he recounts this marvel, and I wonder: What is the appeal of the old familiar story of the rough diamond? Is it identification with the trainer of legend, able to polish that diamond bright where all others have failed? Or the notion of being Pal himself, full of untapped potential, brimming with secret smarts—and only waiting for the right master to come along and issue the right commands?

Karen must surely be as bored as all get-out with the turn this conversation has taken. Nevertheless, she, as much as O'Ryan, confounds my predictions by reaching out with the toe of her sneaker to prod Murphy to some kind of attention. "Hey, hear that, poochie? Maybe there's even hope for YOU." Then she surprises me even more by smiling at O'Ryan, quite collegially. "No 'whipping' Murphy into shape, though. Katie here don't cotton to cruelty to dumb animals. Not even CHICKENS. ESPECIALLY not chickens."

O'Ryan grins back at her, to make it clear he knows she's funning. "Hey, I bet nobody in this room is in favor of whippin' old Murphy here. Not you, neither."

"Oh, well..." As Karen shrugs girlishly, I try—and fail—to rec-
oncile this purring kitten with the panther who was on the prowl
in this room mere minutes ago. "I guess he's not SO bad, for a
DOG."

O'Ryan surveys Murphy appraisingly. "He looks like one pretty
smart *hombre* to me. Reckon I could do a little somethin' with him.
I mean, heck. It took me half a hour—less, maybe—to teach one o'
the new Majors to 'speak.'"

I make a conscientious effort not to look at Karen. Since the concept of O'Ryan teaching anyone—animal, vegetable, or mineral—
how to speak must surely strike her as it does me: roughly as
creditable as the notion of Yasser Arafat holding a seminar on the
merits of maintaining a clean, close shave. "No, thanks," I tell
O'Ryan. "Murphy's got quite enough to say as it is. Besides, he's not
my dog."

"Maybe not, but I'll tell you somethin' fer free: he's sure the hell
itchin' to be told who's boss."

"He *knows* who's boss. That's just the trouble." And yet, as I look
down at Murphy, it's tempting all the same to fantasize: me in
charge, Murphy toeing the mark. Why does that seem so attractive?
When I don't even wish he was mine?

"...bunny back up to the studio," O'Ryan is informing Karen
when I force myself to focus once more on the conversation. "Big
scene to shoot this aft, with all the Majors. Y'know, you really
oughta come up to the set sometime as my guest, when—"

"Oh, Karen wouldn't be interested," I interject. "She doesn't
even watch TV."

"So WHAT?" Karen wants to know. "It would be SUCH a gas.
Really."

"Sure," O'Ryan agrees confidently. "Why, Dana was up there herself to Winzigdorf not so long back. Am I right, Dana? Seems to me I
saw you there, the same day that detective was on the set, to—"

"I don't remember." Abruptly, I get to my feet. "Why don't I
walk you to the door?"

"What detective?" Karen asks.

"I have no idea." The last thing on earth I want, of course, is to have this discussion with Karen. "O'Ryan? Don't you have to go?"

"What's wrong?" O'Ryan demands on the way to the door. "What'd I say?"

"Nothing. I just don't want you to be late to work."

"Too bad I hafta run." He tries and fails to lower his voice discreetly. "That friend of yours, that Karen? Wow. She strikes me as real neat."

Neat? Well, yes, in a literal sense. Nobody neater. But in the sense that O'Ryan is employing the term? "Well, I'm, uh, glad you think so," I tell him, praying meanwhile that Karen can't overhear.

But when I return to the living room, the first thing she says to me is: "What DID he say wrong?"

"Jesus Christ. You've got hearing like a fruitbat, don't you?"

"Seriously, Katie. Who's this DETECTIVE?"

Sheesh. "You are. And as of now, you're off the case." What is it about her that instinctively makes me feel I'd rather swallow cyanide than divulge a single detail about any man I've ever dated, including those who, like Carl, never called back? "In fact, I have no clue what O'Ryan was on about. I just figured he'd bored you long enough about his work up at wonderful Winzigdorf."

"Bored? Katie, are you CRAZY? The question is, Where have you been HIDING him?"

"I beg your pardon?" I stare at her in shock, trying to work out which one of us is, indeed, nuts. "I don't *hide* him. O'Ryan is just an old buddy of mine who—"

"An old buddy in the BIBLICAL sense?"

"Oh, for God's sake. Look, I've known him since the seventies—"

"The seventies! Aha. That means you DID screw him. Everybody did, back then."

"Karen! O'Ryan is hardly your type, and I—"

"Who SAYS he's not? Yum." And she actually licks her lips, with such vulpine relish that I feel my own protective hackles rising.

"Look, leave him alone, all right? He's no match for you."

"Are you KIDDING? This is made in HEAVEN."

"I mean intellectually."

She snorts. "I DON'T. And when it comes to sex, I never met a guy who couldn't look out for himself. It doesn't mean a THING to them, Katie. They'd fuck MUD if women went extinct."

"O'Ryan's not like that." I now feel genuinely alarmed on his behalf.

"Honey, I don't UNDERSTAND." Karen is regarding me suspiciously. "If YOU wanted him, it'd be strictly hands off. But since you don't..."

Since I don't, let's just heave the poor guy into the piranha tank. And yet, what real reason do I have to think that's what I'm doing? "Anyway, he's way too old for you. I mean, O'Ryan's as ancient as you and I are, practically. I thought you only dated the ones who still order from the children's menu."

She grins at me, with exaggerated carnality. "Nah, I only date them when they're ON the children's menu. Oh, relax, honey. I wouldn't hurt a fly, much less a GUY. Much less that long, lanky, yummy buddy of yours."

But when she lopes down the steps of my porch, her blond ponytail bouncing like Corliss Archer's, and her skinny ass swaying impudently, I stand gazing after her for a long minute, before closing the door.

In the living room, Murphy is sound asleep, stretched on his side, legs extended, looking like a toppled rocking horse. His lips are drawn back in a hideous rictus, and as I continue to look down at him, I detect a slight tremor beginning in his front paws. Prologue to a dream, no doubt. What can it be this time? Where does Murphy go in his sleep, and would he care if I followed? Yet another of those questions, I feel, that if I could only answer, I'd know a lot.

Chapter Eight

This must be a dream, because I seem to be in the backseat of Karen's Volkswagen—as if I were the family pet, rather than her dear friend Katie. But dream or no, Karen is driving with the customary belligerence of her waking life. I'm not sure where.

All I know is that it's late at night, the traffic is light, and every time the car jounces over another set of streetcar tracks, the top of my head whacks against the roof light. Not that Karen appears to even know I'm here. The volume of the radio is already too high, but as she drives, she continues to dial it higher and higher. So that even if I were to cry out in protest against the bumps, she'd be unlikely to hear me, much less care.

Then, when she turns abruptly down a sidestreet, I am flung painfully against the door. Which, at this point, I almost wish would open, to throw me clear of the car and out onto the pavement.

No such luck, however. Now Karen is cruising up and down the same block, over and over, as if she were pacing and repacing the stage at the Canada Goose. "There it is!" she exclaims. "Stupid muscle-headed Brad's stupid muscle car, parked on its stupid PAD, in front of stupid Brad's stupid HOUSE."

Brad? Who's Brad? I could try asking, though I see no point. Since Karen clearly isn't talking to me, but to herself, in a sullen singsong voice, its emphases petulant, almost childish. Besides, although I may not know who Brad is, I'm having no problem figuring out what he's done: he's kissed Karen off, the fool. And while his stupid car may be out on its stupid concrete pad in front of his stupid house, the stupid house itself is darkness. Suggesting that stupid Brad is inside, asleep.

"He's in there," Karen breathes, as if to confirm my supposition. Now she's parked in front of Brad's house, with her headlights doused and the radio off. "But he's not alone. Guys like Brad—guys NAMED Brad—are NEVER alone. Except in some sort of EXISTEN-TIAL way. Regardless of how many boozed-up buddies are crashed in a pool of their own VOMIT in the living room, and how many underage CHICKS are flagrantly DELICTO in Brad's way-cool WATERbed."

In the backseat, I shift nervously. Thinking that I really should do something to calm Karen down—even if her upset is only occur-ring in a dream. Which, being a dream, renders me incapable of doing much to help, apart from shifting nervously in the backseat and wishing I could be dreaming my friend Karen in some less-fraught situation, and myself entirely absent from the proceedings.

"Of course..." As she continues to muse, Karen gazes intently at Brad's house, as if expecting it to get up and walk off the lot. "I DO have my trusty Slim Jims. It would be, like, ZERO sweat to jimmy open the Trans Am and stuff a few DOG turds in Brad's glove com-partment. Or did I ALREADY dog-turd Brad's Trans Am? Or was that the Trans Am of some OTHER asshole also named Brad, who ALSO stood me up for absolutely no good reason?"

On her fingers, she starts tallying various forms of vengeance she either could visit, or has already visited, on this particular Brad. It's quite a list, and it includes: spattering raw eggs on his windshield; packaging roadkill and sending it to him Federal Express; plastering his name and phone number all over the neighborhood on Post-its advertising everything from piano lessons to cut firewood to kit-tens for free and used stereo speakers; sending the usual number of unrequested pizzas to his address; calling his mother long-distance and posing as his counselor at a drug-treatment center; and mailing literature from the local gay rights action league addressed to him at his place of work.

For my part, I'm horrified. Not in my wildest dream—which this surely must be—can I conceive of revenge on such a petty but oddly impressive scale. Although the fact that I am even dreaming these things lends them a certain ghastly creditability.

"What else?" Karen mutters, once she's run out of fingers on which to count her crimes. "What ELSE can I do? There's ALWAYS something...Aha!"

From the glove compartment she produces a spray can and shakes it vigorously. "Great CAR, Brad. Like, SO cool. Only, if you're gonna tint your WINDOWS, honey, you ought to REALLY tint 'em. Like, Rust-Oleum BLACK, okay? That way, you can just screw all your little girlfriends right there in the CAR, and nobody can see IN! Of course, once I'm finished, you might have a little trouble seeing OUT, too!"

Continuing to shake the can, Karen climbs out of her car, hurries over to Brad's, and starts in spraying. Suddenly, a light goes on upstairs in the house, and a male voice shouts: "Who's out there? Karen? Fuck, if that's you again, you bitch, so help me God, I'll—"

What Brad plans to do so help him God is drowned out by Karen's derisive screech in response: "Yeah? You and what ARMY, honey? That pack of BROWNIES you're banging up there in your ROOM?"

I am frightened for her, and I want to cry out to her to get the hell out of there. Yet my tongue seems numb, and the words refuse to leave my mouth. As dumb as the dumbest of animals, I hunch in the backseat, mutely staring out the window with large panicked eyes.

Quickly, Karen crosses the lawn, her long legs flying, and leaps back in behind the wheel. Then, in a rasp of gears and a squeal of hot-smelling rubber, we're out of there. Bouncing and jouncing along the street, jerking around corners, swerving on the curves...

Any minute now, I swear, I will awaken, tossing and thrashing in my own bed. With Murphy pressed up against me, like as not, trembling in response to his own private visions. Any minute now, but not quite yet. For now, I am still sound asleep, with nothing available to give reassurance that what might be is not the same as what is.

Chapter Nine

I doubt if Karen saw me staring. I doubt she'd have cared if she did. My opinion on any subject you'd care to name is, believe me, no very big deal to Karen. Still, I have to say I was impressed. Not so much with her material, which wasn't that funny. But with the idea that she can just...stand up there and do that.

God, what I'd give for the chance. Fifteen fleeting minutes of fame in front of a microphone, just like the pros I've seen on TV. Just like Karen, right up there in our very own living room. Giving the gears to whatever and whoever I please.

"Hi," I'd begin, peering out into the darkness beyond the stage lights. "Anybody here from another species? Come on, stick 'em up there, all you members of the master-race. Whoa! What's that, way at the back—a *hand*? You bet it is. That opposable thumb, folks. It gives you away every time. Riley, shine the follow-spot back there on Table Six, will you? Oh, yes, they're humans, all right. Who else would order a drink with a plastic palm tree?

"That's Riley the retriever on the follow-spot, by the way. And while we're at it, let's have a cheap laugh at the expense of whoever gave him that dorky name. I mean...*Riley*? What is up with this new trend in names? Forget the old days. Forget Rags; out, damn Spot; Rover's all over. Now it's...well, Riley. Plus, on the door tonight, we got Foster the fox terrier. Take a bow-wow, Foster. Who else? Oh, yeah, Tyler the Doberman is your bartender tonight—and of course, he doubles as the bouncer.

"My God! Riley, Foster, Tyler, and Murphy. With names like these, why are we wasting our lives chewing up slippers? Hey, you could buy *shares* in Riley, Foster, Tyler, and Murphy. I mean, with names like these, we could get *audited*!"

See, this is how I'd suck them in, with a light-hearted tack. First, get them laughing—then bring out the big guns and train 'em squarely on the humans in the house. "Whoops! What's going on back there at Table Six? You people there—I'm talking to you. Are you trying to sneak out? No need to stumble around in the shadows. Riley, why don't you hit Table Six with a little more light?

"Ah, that's better. Hey, whatsa matter, Table Six? I see you standing at the door; I hear you whimpering; I notice you begging with your eyes. But I'll be damned if I can figure out what you want! Lemme see, what could it be? Aw, now don't tell me! You folks want to go...*out*?

"My God, Table Six, if you want to go out, how come you don't do what the *rest* of us poor slobs have to do: give a polite little woof and hope for the best? Say, by the way, don't you just love that, everybody? You're standing at the back door with your bladder bursting, woofing away for all you're worth—and some two-legged turnip-head has to ask: 'What *is* it, fella? You wanna go *out*?' 'No, schmuck, of course not! What would give you *that* idea? I'm standing here barking to warn the doorknob not to try any funny business! Of course I goddamn well want to go *out*!'" 🐾

⊱──⊱◈⊰──⊰

The first thing I perceive, as I begin to awaken, is that I'm alone in bed. Even Murphy—my only regular bedfellow of late—has obviously gotten up and lumbered out to the living room. Yet, for some nagging reason, I feel that there ought to be someone here beside me this morning. Some guy, maybe, who...? Oh, shit. Wait a minute. That guy from Montreal...friend of my friend Deirdre...called me up out of the blue to tell me...what? Ah, right. That Deirdre had suggested he give me a buzz when he came into town...

One drink. Right. It's coming back to me now. One drink was what I countered with when he phoned to offer dinner. Nothing as risky as dinner, not sight unseen. Just one drink in a neutral location, over and out. But then...(I'm piecing this together, still slowly, but more surely as I go) we *did* have dinner. And much, much more than one drink.

Oh, God, I didn't get *drunk*? I haven't done that in years. Still, something must account for the fact that all I can remember about last night is about a bazillion drinks. Then ending up here, somehow, for a nightcap.

Right. One little nightcap. That must have been the way it went. Well, no harm done. Since here I am, in the gritty gray light of dawn, all alone, as we see. And yet...why is it that I can't exactly remember kissing the guy goodnight and sending him on his way?

And why is it that from somewhere off-camera, so to speak, I am gradually becoming aware of a sound very like my shower running? And while we're on that subject, what is *that* on the chair by the bed? Christ, I'm still bleary, out of focus, can't quite make out... Oh, shit. Or do I mean oh, shirt? For is that not a man's striped shirt, forsooth, and a pair of crumpled slacks?

Meanwhile, what have we here on the nightstand? Two brandy glasses, if I'm not mistaken. Empty now, but each with a residue of stale brown liquid ringing the bottom of the...Ugh.

But, soft. Now, what's *that*—that whistling sound coming from my bathroom? Like the sound of...well, whistling. That's exactly what it's like. Someone whistling above the cascade of water rushing from my shower. "A pretty girl...is like a melody..."

Oh, God, no. He stayed the night...We had sex...He's still here...

Why? What would possess me to do a thing like that with some friend of Deirdre's, for Christ's sake, some textbook salesman, or whatever the fuck he is, whose name I don't remember, and whose sexual technique can't be all that indelibly etched on my brain either...Oh, God, am I desperate? Is that what it comes down to? Have I become so desperate not to think about Carl Hart who has never called back that I'm willing to try to jam the circuitry of my memory bank by any means?

Okay, now, look. Let's get a grip. Maybe if I just burrow down under the covers, this whole unfortunate episode will blow over. Once this stranger in my shower has run through his entire repertoire of postcoital pop ditties, old and new. Once he finally towels off, dresses, and departs my life for good—having failed to rouse me from my slumbers, and eventually concluding that I've fallen into some kind of coma from which it might be dangerous to awaken me too abruptly. Yeah, that sounds like a viable plan, all right.

Of course, there's still Murphy to face. Although why I should have to explain myself to someone who gets it on regularly with a bag of my dirty wash is... I mean, it's not as if Murphy is likely to make the case that I owe some allegiance to Jerry, or to Carl, of all people, who not only promised he'd call but acted as if he planned to call within the next—

Oh, no. No, you don't. Stop right there. Block that thought. Focus your mind on the man who's currently occupying your showerstall, and is now whistling up a medley of Kenny Rogers's greatest hits. Think about something else—anything at all.

Think: men are assholes, every last one of them. And, God knows, after getting it on with the Whistling Gypsy Rover, I *must* be down to the very last one. But who cares? Men are so bad that, compared to men, dogs are starting to look good to me. Even Murphy.

Okay, so Murphy has been known to relieve an itch by rubbing his rectum inelegantly across the carpet. And maybe he does sleep with his tongue protruding unattractively between his teeth, and his eyeballs rolled back to the whites, like Fuseli's *Nightmare*. But let's look at the positives: he eats what I serve up, no questions asked; he never complains when I hog the remote, and he likes me even *more* when I have my period.

Ah, I'm getting drowsy now, thank God, inside the sheltering warmth of my duvet. Beginning to drift into that shadowed nether world where half-wakefulness and semi-slumber freely intertwine.

Who knows? Maybe this is the place where Murphy goes, when he goes to sleep.

I can picture him, lurching home at last, after one of his unexplained absences. Feet all muddy, a knowing glint in his eye, the odor of cheap cigars and cheaper cologne clinging to his collar. "Where have you been?" I demand. "No place." "Who were you with?" "Nobody." "What did you do?" "Nothing."

Or suppose he didn't come home at all? What would I do then— head out blindly to track him down? Where would a dog even go, in an upscale neighborhood like mine, where admission into virtually any decent establishment presupposes a jacket and tie?

Well, I'm asleep now, obviously. Not only am I not making any sense, I find myself traipsing fruitlessly down sidestreets and narrow back lanes, looking for some sign of my dog. With no idea where he might choose to go when the choice is his.

Eventually, I find myself in a part of town where I've never ventured before. Wandering along an ill-lit alley—until a jittery neon sign in a basement window catches my eye. "The Dog House" it reads, in palsied, buzzing letters.

The Dog House? I wonder if this is one of those havens of humiliation I've heard about. To which otherwise respectable folk repair in order to submit themselves to unspeakable indignities while down on all fours in a collar and leash? Even so, I ought to check it out—if for no other reason than it appears to be the only place available *to* check out.

I follow some steps descending from the street and push open the door. Inside, it's dimly lit and stuffy, and smells much like a...kennel. In the half-light, I can barely make out what seems to be a welter of furry bodies, clustered in small groups around some pint-sized restaurant tables.

But before I can accustom my eyes to the dark, a shaft of light cuts through the room like a laser. A spotlight, illuminating a small stage, bare except for a microphone stand. "Ladies and littermates!" From somewhere, a voice comes booming. "Welcome to the Dog House, distinguished home of canine comedy at human expense. Now, won't you put your two front paws together to welcome our featured performer, fresh from a successful tour of the neighborhood garbage cans... It's the one, the only... He-e-ere's Murphy!"

I stand stunned at the back of the room as a dog I instantly recognize—except for his jaunty little bowtie (or is that a fake goiter attached to his throat?)—comes bounding onstage to snatch up a microphone and greet a wildly yapping throng. So this is it. *This* is where Murphy goes when he sleeps. This is what he aspires to in his dreams, and perhaps wide awake: the opportunity to get up there and poke fun at me and my kind in a—

Ick! With a gasp, I come to, touched by a nose so wetly cold that the shock is almost electric. Whose nose is it, anyway? It can't belong to the shower-stud, can it, wet from his ablutions and hoping for seconds? But no. The water in the bathroom is still running, and I can hear the strains of yet another whistled ditty echoing off the tiled walls.

"Murphy?" I pry open my eyes—to confront at very close range a grinning, black-lipped countenance, with a pink tongue protruding like a length of lox. "Oh, shit," I croak, in a voice rusty from too many brandies. "So I'm awake."

>-+-<>-+-O-<>-+-<

Her smeared-looking face peers from beneath the bedclothes, an inch or less from mine. Her sleep-swollen eyes regard me with dismay—as if this entire awful escapade were somehow my fault. "Oh, shit," she says. "So I'm awake."

The fact that she's embarrassed melts me a little at first. But, just as I'm on the verge of commiseration, she pulls a sour face and rolls away from me. "Ugh, get out of here, will you, Murphy—with your awful breath?"

My breath? Excuse me, and what was she gargling last night—battery acid?

"I mean it, Murphy. Just get out. You know my bedroom is off-limits."

Oh, yes? Since when—and to whom? As if to prove my point, who should appear from the bathroom, right on cue, but the sap *du jour* himself, swaddled in a damp bathtowel.

"Hi there." He pads barefoot over to the bed, to claim its inhabitant as his rightful reward. "Hope you didn't mind me helping myself to the shower."

Mind? Heck. Why should we mind? Our *casa, su casa,* and all like that.

Shut up, she warns me telepathically. Or at least tries to, by fixing me with a bloodshot glare that she hopes makes clear how little she craves my input. Okay, fine. If that's how she wants it, I'll butt right out. Only...next time she's attempting to show me off to company with the old "Speak!" routine? She can forget it. Nothing. *Nada. Silenzio.* She'll hear a pin drop.

Meanwhile, here's this guy, attempting to advertise himself as an ambassador of goodwill by parking his damp butt on the bed, and at the same time holding his hand out to me to sniff. "And how is old Murphy this morning?"

Oh, right. We were introduced last night, at that. Frankly, I'd assumed the guy was too plastered—and too firmly wedded to his mission of getting laid—to remember making my acquaintance.

When I fail to respond to his extended hand, he withdraws it, and wraps it around Dana's bare shoulder in a proprietary way. "Now, you can just relax, big fella. Our mistress is in good hands."

Our *what*? Kind of getting ahead of ourselves here, aren't we—big fella?

"You know," the guy addresses himself to Dana in an authoritative tone. "It's natural your dog would be jealous of me."

Jealous. Right. That's what I am. I think it's those polyester-blend slacks of his on the chair there that I most envy.

"Maybe I'll just put Murphy out in the yard," she says, shooting me another dirty look as she starts to get out of bed—then remembering that she's completely naked, slides abruptly back under the covers.

"The yard? Naw. Why? Let 'im stay. He'll warm up to me. Everybody always does." But as the guy attempts to illustrate his point with a kiss, Dana shifts away from him adroitly. "Hey, what's wrong?" he demands. Then smiles. "Oh, I get it..." And winks at her confidentially, jerking his head in my direction. "*Pas devant le chien*, eh?"

Oh, brother. He's a linguist, too. So how did she come up with this winner—trolling the corridors of Berlitz?

Eventually, of course, I do get shunted out into the yard. Where I do my best not to imagine what might be going on in the bedroom in my absence. Then—surprisingly quickly—Dana reappears at the back door to assure me that the coast is clear. "Just a...wrong number," she informs me, with the air of someone who believes she has nothing to explain—but feels compelled to explain, anyway. "Look, it was a mistake, that's all. The good news with this one is that he's on his way back to Montreal. Not that I'm apologizing or anything. Certainly not to *you*."

No, no, of course not. Certainly not to me. I mean, I suppose *I'm* the one who lures in every Tom, Dick, and Harry—then fixes him a drink that would stun a mastodon?

"And you can wipe that look right off your face, mister. That other business, with that guy Carl, was completely different. Besides, that's not going to happen again, either. The point is, none of this has anything to do with you—or with Jerry, in case you're in the mood to play the part of the reproachful watchdog here. Anyway, that's my last word on this. I have no intention of getting into a protracted discussion with someone who doesn't even talk."

Maybe not. But at least I can think—which is kind of a novel reverse on how *she* does things.

"Anyway," she continues, as if someone had asked, "what's the point in attempting to explain the complexities of single female life in the waning moments of the twentieth century to someone for whom figuring out how to unwrap a leash from around a lamp-post evidently poses an overwhelming intellectual challenge?"

And with that, she turns on her heel and walks off. As if that's the only way she can assure herself of actually having absolutely the last word on this, or any other, subject. 🐾

Chapter Ten

One night, that's all it was. One night and one morning out of my life—and now he's out of my life, for good. For *good*, okay? Suicidal to assume anything else. Fatal to tell myself that it hasn't all worked out for the best. No different, really, than that brief one-off with that friend of Deirdre's.

Ridiculous, isn't it, to go back over it again and again, as if searching a patch of ground for clues that have long since disappeared? Why didn't he call? Why didn't he call? Going over it the way old Murphy here works over the park with his nose. Look at him go at it: immersing himself in...what? The scent of some female, no doubt, who passed by some time ago, but left a droplet of her pee trembling meaningfully on a blade of grass.

God, he's really perusing it, like a particularly provocative editorial in the morning paper. And he'll keep on reading, oblivious. Even when the *femme fatale* whose pee it is comes back into frame, as it were, and sashays past, right under Murphy's nose.

Neither Murphy nor his nose will notice her. Like Adele H., obsessively on the trail of her elusive lover, Murphy prefers to pursue his private truth in a droplet on a blade of grass. Even as the very object of his obsession passes right by him, and out of his life.

Out of my life...That's right. There's no evidence strewn about. No reasons to keep going back and back over the ground. Every reason to stop. For good. For your own good.

><+>-O-<+><

🐾 She could do worse than do what I do—which is to read the park with my nose. She could do worse, and she is. Mooning miserably over what barely was and is no more. While I, much more sensibly, lose myself in that companionable realm where past and present linger side by side, layer on layer. With no real distinction between what was Then and that which is Now.

There's the scent of that squirrel who raced by this morning—and was squashed flat by a truck this afternoon. Alongside the fetching aroma of that Pekingese who hesitated mere moments ago to deposit her essence delicately on the grass. Then toddled up the slope and out of sight. And the odor of old bones moldering many layers deep, under the mulched-over flowerbeds...

Last week's headlines, yesterday's news, today's hot topic. All equally alive to me as I breathe them in, and sort them out, utterly impartial. 🐾

>─┼─◆─•─○─•─◆─┼─<

Simply keep reminding myself that it's different for men. It comes, it goes, and all that lingers in mind's eye or memory's ear is some vague recollection of look, or sound, or taste, or touch. Or an unfulfilled promise to call.

Just the opposite of Murphy here, breathing in those ancient aromas as if they were here and now. It's more than a memory of an essence, that female odor on the grass. What he inhales is, for him, the very essence of essence itself. An olfactory record, a layered landscape of smell upon smell. Where what can no longer be seen, tasted, touched, or heard live on, in the afterlife of aroma. As vividly present as the here and now.

>─┼─◆─•─○─•─◆─┼─<

🐾 In the realm I call the Scenting, there's no such thing as Time. Only vast, variegated eternity, stretching like an endless veldt in every direction. I can track myself across it, scent my own spoor, follow my own aroma deep into a dreamscape, where nothing is lost and nothing is gone.

She could do worse than to follow me there. To find me already at home when she arrives—my eyes glittering in the depths of the cave I claimed as mine, long before she even dreamed her kind was on the scene.

No losses to mourn in that domain, where the Dreaming and the Scenting are one and the same. As I set out to follow my nose across all the acres of Earth that I have already covered in ten thousand lifetimes. As I search out the clues she and I missed the first nine thousand nine hundred and ninety-nine times around.

Chapter Eleven

One thing I'll say in Murphy's favor—and it *is* the one thing—is that, as someone to watch old movies with, he's generally unbeatable. He really does seem to watch—ears up, yellow eyes unblinking and attentive, as he scans the TV screen. Best of all, he doesn't drown out the best bits in some inane running patter about camera angles, who should or should not have had a facelift, and what's been lost or gained by reformatting the film for the small screen.

Actually, the inane patter is my department. Especially when—as today—the old movie that we're watching is on assignment: the original *Lassie Come Home*. Which just happened to catch my eye in the TV listing, on a drab, weepy weekday afternoon, when any excuse in the world will do to have a good cry and still call it work.

Work it is, believe me. Since there's evidently nothing Murphy has to teach me about love, loyalty, and all the other virtues ascribed to his species, I'm still forced to pick up my script ideas from secondhand sources. And thereby ruin the cinematic experience for both of us, as I make my notes aloud through all the sad parts.

Because it is raining today, because I already feel useless, woebegone, unlovely and unloved, I have elected to bring myself even lower by also doing my wash. I don't know exactly what it is about laundry that I so loathe—but I do know I am not alone in my deep detestation. My fellows in the local laundromat and I are a motley throng—reduced to shrunken-up sweats, paint-stained jeans, and what bears a suspicious resemblance to pajama cuffs peering from beneath the hems of misbuttoned macintoshes, as we fling every other article of clothing we own into the gaping maw of the washing machine or the dryer's wide-open hatch.

What is the true extent of the horror that lurks at the heart of this darkness, perhaps nobody at the laundromat is equipped to say. All we can say for sure is that we don't want to do this, we don't want to be here, and the quicker we can get out of here the better. Which means that—on this particular wet and woebegone afternoon—I have left the laundromat even sadder, but effectively no wiser, having repacked my newly washed and more-or-less dried laundry back in the bag in which I schlepped it all here.

Once back home, I let my laundry tumble from the bag into a moist welter onto my bed. As a prelude to indulging myself even deeper in my wallow. Snuffling self-pityingly with what feels like an incipient cold, dressed in the shabbiest clothes I possess, with my hair not only unwashed but frizzy from rain and the heat of the laundromat, I switch on the TV set and prepare—with a kind of loathsome relish—to tackle the tedium of matching unmated socks and pulling apart the sleeves of sweaters amorously entangled in transports of static cling.

As I stand staring at the TV screen, sorting and folding, all I can manage to do is marvel that, in the fifth decade of my existence, I'm still hauling my clothes to a coin laundry and bringing them back to an apartment I only rent, and temporarily share with someone else's dog. On a good day, I'd feel footloose. Today, I'm just depressed. Though not, as yet, teary-eyed.

Outside my window, the dusk is deepening. Rain is beating on the windowsills, gushing from the drainpipes, spattering loudly on the fire escape. Within the confines of the smaller window of my TV, meanwhile, Lassie—acting according to off-camera cues from the legendary beast-*meister* himself, Rudd Weatherwax—is hurrying ever homeward, across a make-believe Scotland of MGM's devising.

Now surely by the time that dog hits the schoolyard, limping, bedraggled, but triumphantly on time for the four-o'clock bell, I will have reached the point where I need to be—sniveling, and awash with tears.

When I glance over at Murphy, he appears to be equally unmoved. But then, what do I expect? Murphy is, after all, hardly the come-home type himself. And probably suspects that Lassie keeps on bolting back to Yorkshire purely to piss off Nigel Bruce.

As for me...well, am I any better? Dry-eyed, even as the closing credits crawl. Now, wasn't there a time, back in the mists of childhood, when I might have counted on a salutary sobfest over a movie like this? When I would have wailed like a banshee over *Lassie Come Home* on a rainy afternoon?

Then, perhaps, but clearly not now. I might just as well wash my face, apply some makeup, take a precautionary cold pill, and prepare to face the rest of my life with tearless resolution.

But no sooner have I turned off the TV and resolved to put this new plan into action than there is the unexpected sound of the doorbell. Which, on a day like today, I lack sufficient self-determination not to answer.

With a ball of rolled-up socks in my hand, I pad on despondent feet down the hallway to the front door. I wrench it open with effort, since the dampness has, of course, swollen the wood, and—there is Carl Hart. Standing under the leaky overhang on my front porch, with a curl of black hair plastered wetly against his forehead, and dark drops of rain spattering the lapel of his gabardine coat.

He allows me to observe a moment of stunned silence, and then says: "Well, I promised I'd ring. Or...did you think I meant the phone?"

More silence elapses, as I continue to stand in the doorway, staring at him, and hunting for responses that will not come.

"Aren't you going to ask me in? Your veranda leaks, in case you hadn't realized."

Of course, the total effect of my appearance must be horrendous. My Medusa-like hair, running nose, lack of makeup, and baggy sweatpants that are generally never on exhibit except at the laundromat. It's unbelievable to me that Carl has chosen this moment to re-enter my life. And equally unbelievable that—having seen what he must be seeing now—he won't choose the next moment for a speedy re-exit.

But he doesn't. "It's wonderful to see you," he says, smiling as if he's telling the truth. "I've missed you, sweetheart."

At that, the tears that have eluded me all day long overwhelm me, and I begin sobbing inelegantly into the wad of socks in my hand.

"Dana! Christ!" Carl sounds genuinely alarmed. "What's all this?" Then, as unlovely as I am at this moment, he steps toward me, and wraps me in his arms. "Tell me. What on earth is the matter?"

"I . . . was w-watching this movie," I bring out at last, burying my face against his coat, and further wetting it with my tears. "I always c-cry at the end, when they reunite."

Carl pats my back soothingly. I can feel the warmth of his body beneath his clothes, as I breathe in the mixture of soap, soft skin, and rough wool that conspire to make up his distinctive aroma. "But if they're reunited," he reasons, as if with a child, "why should you cry?"

Good question. Yet, standing here on my porch, with Carl's arms around me at long last, I find that I'm crying, all the same.

PART THREE

Running Dogs

Chapter One

"Sorry!" Carl seems out of breath when he finally arrives—an hour later than advertised. As if he's jogged, not driven, all the way uptown. "I should have let you know I was running late."

"No problem," I assure him. Which I suppose it isn't. Since what he's billed as a "leisurely drive in the country" surely does not require split-second timing. "Something go wrong at work?"

"It's all sorted out now. Where's Murphy? You'll want to bring the old flea-motel, won't you? Let him kick up his heels out in the wild, sort of style—assuming he's got heels to kick, and we find something wilder than the usual expressway snarl."

I snap on Murphy's leash and let him and Carl lead me out the door. Then, at the curb, I stop short—surprised by the sight of a large, rather dowdy-looking stationwagon hunkering there. "Where's your car?"

"Packed it in. That's why I'm late." Carl opens the passenger door, gestures me in, and then unlocks the tailgate for Murphy.

"So where'd *this* behemoth come from?" I ask, glancing dubiously around the well-worn interior.

"It's borrowed."

"Yeah, I'll just bet. What'd you do, hot-wire it at some suburban mall?"

"Not a bit of it." He jingles the keys in my face as a reproach to my suspiciousness. "It's mine, in actual fact. Or used to be. Viv's kept it on, mostly to chauffeur the kids."

"Oh." I shift in the seat, feeling uncomfortably closer to Carl's wife than I ever expected—or hoped—to get. This, then, is the car that belongs to the world of ballet classes, and soccer practice, and buying-in-bulk expeditions to the mega-mart. A world that Carl has avowedly left behind, and one which is utterly foreign to me. Yet here we are, Carl and I, bound for an afternoon of abandonment—in the most domesticated conveyance imaginable. Whether with or without his ex-wife's permission, I dare not even ask.

"The understanding being, I'm free to borrow this one when mine's on the blink."

An image leaps into my mind of Carl Hart, private eye, tailing sinister suspects down some alley—in this big bumbling car that screams "family" and lacks only a grimacing Garfield suction-cupped to one of the windows. "Wow," I comment. "Yours really is a civilized split-up."

Carl shrugs as he starts the engine and pulls away from the curb. "We've an understanding, Viv and I—about the car, at any rate. Now, look, I have no idea where we're headed here. So, if it's all the same to you, I propose that we get off the main highways at the first opportunity, and just see where the backroads lead us. What d'you think?"

I take one more look around the interior of Carl's ex-wife's suburban stationwagon—then make a quick decision to ignore its provenance for the rest of the afternoon. "What I think is that seeing where the backroads lead us is an admirable basis upon which to construct a philosophy of life."

He nods at me approvingly. "That's my girl."

And this is my guy. Of all the men I've met, only Carl drives a car exactly as I like to imagine I would myself—assuming that I had a car, and knew how to drive it. He seems content to give the stationwagon its head, allowing it to turn on impulse down whichever road it pleases. As though he and the car are operating on some agreement they've worked out that whatever path they choose will eventually take them home—or some better place.

Somewhat guiltily, I think of Jerry. A devotee of four-lane highways and the most efficient distance between two points. Then there's O'Ryan, who always seems to be wrangling whatever vehicle he's driving into submission. And of course Derek, and even Mark—careening along while squinting at the roadmaps spread out in their laps. As if pinpointing their current location meant more than arriving someplace else in one piece.

I reach out my hand, to nestle it between Carl's headrest and the warm hollow at the back of his neck. Without glancing away from the road, he slides his hand between my knees and tenderly squeezes my thigh.

"Happy, then?" he asks, his eyes fixed on a point just beyond the windshield.

"Happy," I say, studying his neatly sculpted profile, and believing that, at this moment, I am.

Today is one of those opaque, weakly sunlit days that late autumn sometimes affords. As the intertwining Plasticine strips of expressway give way to long, undeviating concession roads, I watch fields of frost-bitten pastureland streak past the car, and give myself over to the simplicity of this adventure. There is, as Carl has declared, no itinerary here. No agenda, no final destination. And only as much road ahead as what can be seen out the front window at any given moment.

He negotiates a jouncing rutted track that runs like a furrow between two fields of stubble. Then it abruptly peters out. Leaving him no choice but to bring the car to a stop. "Right," he says, undismayed. "So now we know. This is not the passage to the Orient after all."

"You're hopelessly lost, Carl. Why don't you just admit it?"

He turns to look me straight in the eye. "Too right I am. Hopelessly, utterly, completely lost. How about you?"

We make love as best we can—right there in the front seat of the stationwagon, with Murphy panting audibly in the seat behind. There's something tacky about it—ridiculous, even. But something exhilarating, too. To be doing what we're doing in the middle of some farmer's field, where we have no right to be. In a car begged for the occasion from Carl's wife, with my borrowed dog looking on.

"I love you."

The words, almost inaudible, come in a rich exhalation of breath against my ear. And when they come, have the effect on me of a live grenade—blowing to smithereens every illusion I've cherished about my capacity for detachment. Leaving me, in the aftermath, conscious of nothing except the fact of my arms around his neck, the sensation of his voice catching roughly at my ear like a burr on a blanket, and a scent of freshly scorched earth I must merely be imagining. So Carl Hart says he loves me. Now what? What can possibly happen next? This was not in the plan. At least, would not have been in the plan if there happened to be one. As it is—without any itinerary or any destination in view, I am tempted to tell him I love him, too. Yet can't somehow bring myself to say it, not right out loud. And find myself hoping like hell he won't ask me. Don't ask, don't tell, don't pursue. Surely that's the policy to follow.

Eventually, there's a whimpering from the back seat: Murphy's discreet reminder that any appetite for voyeurism—even his—has limits. Carl reaches to open the back door. "Off you go, then, mate."

"No!" I sit up, put an arresting hand on Carl's arm before he can release the door handle. "Don't do that."

"Why ever not? We're having our fun; why shouldn't the poor bugger have his?"

"Because I promised not to let him loose."

"Promised?" For the first time in our brief acquaintanceship, Carl seems slightly impatient with me. "Promised who?"

"My friend. Murphy's owner."

"Oh. Well, of course, your friend isn't here, is she? Or he."

"No." And I thank God for that. As I imagine Jerry crammed in the backseat of the stationwagon alongside his dog—watching me and Carl make love. "Carl, I can't just let him run."

"Christ, we're out in the middle of nowhere. There isn't another car for miles, and I doubt whether a bear's been spotted in these parts in the last hundred years. What on earth are you afraid of?"

I can feel myself blushing to the tips of my ears in the face of a situation even more absurd than Carl can appreciate. Here am I, clinging to my promise not to let Murphy loose—as if to a flimsy fragment of honor floating in the sea of my vast perfidy. Not so very long ago, after all, it was Jerry I claimed to love. No binding contract, of course. And certainly no pledge of troth that Jerry would have any right to hold me to. Even so, out here in what Carl calls the middle of nowhere—deep in the countryside and deeper in love—I feel required to assert what's left of my integrity, in some small way. Even if, on the larger level, my word so patently means nothing.

I begin pulling on my disarrayed clothing. "Look, I'll take Murphy for a quick walk. Since, as you say, he's entitled to his outing, too." Avoiding Carl's gaze, I lean into the back to clip on Murphy's leash. "Just wait in the car, okay? I won't be long."

A few minutes later, when Murphy and I return, I find Carl collapsed with laughter against the steering wheel.

"What's so funny?"

"Nothing. You. Your clothes half-unbuttoned, stumbling about in the stubble—with the dog decorously on his lead."

Now I'm laughing too as I slide in next to Carl. The first small bump on the rocky road to love, it seems, has been surmounted. There's a lingering aroma of sex in the car, musky and salty at the same moment—and I wonder whether Carl will attempt somehow to obliterate it before returning the stationwagon to his wife.

Then, as I reach back to unclip the dog's leash, I become aware of something else, which has escaped my notice till now: a child's stroller, folded in a corner of the cargo hold like some spiny, deceased insect. The sight is unnerving. As if I'd turned around to find one of Carl's offspring staring at me accusingly from the backseat.

"Carl...there's a baby stroller in the back."

With no indication of surprise, he turns to look. "Christ. I've told Viv to hide the bloody thing in the cellar, or give it away. Toby's far too big for it now."

"Toby?"

Carl is shaking his head, mock-impatient—although not with me. "He still craves a push, when he wants attention. And Vivien caves in to him. Well, the baby, after all."

Baby? I have no idea if I've repeated the word aloud or am merely asking a question of myself. The answer seems to be simple enough: the baby is another child of Carl's. Of whose existence I have been happily oblivious until this moment. "And how old is, uh, Toby now?"

"Let me see... getting on for four? Is that possible? Yes, four next birthday. Crikey."

Crikey is right. Somewhat in passing, I remark to myself how Carl's Britishness seems to escalate whenever we encounter a subject he suspects might be difficult. Steady on, not to worry, wait for it, it'll come right on the day, sort of style—and other poems. "Carl, are you telling me you have a child who's only three years old?"

"Well, four next birthday, same as I said." Carl appears not at all embarrassed to be caught attempting to smuggle extra offspring aboard our brand-new relationship.

"No, what you said, when you first mentioned your kids, was that they were twelve and nine."

"So they are. The girls, that is. Toby... well, he was a bit of an afterthought."

Just a bit. "Carl, the thing is... you never told me."

He is flatly disbelieving. "Certainly I told you about Toby. Why wouldn't I?" He reaches out to take my hand. "That morning, after we'd spent our first night together, remember?"

"Of course I remember." God, how could I not? The love we made that night, the very first time that we... "You told me you had two children. One had a school play that night." I allow my hand to remain in his, but lifelessly, like someone's discarded glove.

"Two *daughters*, I said. Sweetheart, if you forgot young Toby, or I did, it's natural enough. Since we were only getting to know each other, you and I. In any event, there's nothing to be upset about, is there?"

It's true, with Carl's fingers caressing my palm, I can no longer recall with precision what it was that he told me about his children, countless centuries ago, on our first morning together, when he sat at my dining-room table sipping coffee with the air of a man who belonged there and no place else. It's equally true that talking about his other life is not a habit in which Carl often indulges. Any more than I encourage such indulgence. As a veteran of lo these many Marrieds, if I have learned nothing else, I have learned this much: advise them to check the family photo album at the door.

On the other hand, Carl has striven to represent himself as anything *but* a Married. And how could recollection of a three-year-old child have slipped his mind, or mine? "Carl, tell me: How long have you and Vivien been split up?"

The briefest of pauses, or am I only imagining it? "I told you that, too. Quite a while."

"But if Toby is only three..."

"Viv and I were finished, in point of fact, even before he came along. Poor little chap. It's not his fault that he...happened when he did. But he happened nonetheless. And now I do what I can in the aftermath. Except remake what fell to pieces years ago. I can't do that."

No, of course not. Still, this is a far cry from the two cheerfully civilized adults I so infinitely prefer Carl and his ex-wife to be, strolling away from their marriage without even a momentary misstep.

Silence falls, and it's as if the leadenness of every unhappily married couple has descended on Carl and me like a curse. Because here he is, withdrawing his hand from mine. And here am I, gazing stonily out the passenger window of the stationwagon. Murphy, meanwhile—long since forgotten as the occasion of an earlier, pettier dispute—is now sound asleep in the back, his chin resting on one inert wheel of the stroller that was the genesis of this new contention.

I feel hollowed out, heartsick—unable to imagine that no more than half an hour ago, I was lying on the car seat in Carl's arms, with his lips against my ear, as he whispered that he was in love. Nothing, from that moment forward, seems to have gone right between us. The worst of it is that, even now, I am unable to explain to myself exactly what it is that has gone so irretrievably wrong. I mean, what am I accusing him of—deliberately courting me in a car littered with evidence of some concealed life? Surely, if Carl was lying to me, he'd go about it more adroitly than this.

"Dana…" This time, when he reaches across the seat to take my hand, I permit myself to press his fingers in response. "Whatever you want to ask me, just go ahead and ask, will you? Because the way I see it, we've managed, somehow or other, to blunder upon something quite splendid, you and I. I don't want to lose it. At least, not without knowing why."

Just outside the window, on my side of the car, a startled group of birds flies up—without warning and without apparent motivation—from the stubble. Like particles shot from the barrel of a gun. "Did you see those birds? Didn't they look like particles, shot—"

"Dana, answer me."

When I finally turn to answer him, I'm amazed that there are tears—bona fide tears—in his eyes, making them glint more green than hazel. "I love you, too," I say, and lean over to kiss him.

Which is not, of course, what I intended to do, right this minute. Nor what I intended to tell him, any time soon. And yet…why should I continue keeping secret the fact that I love him? If it ever has been—from the very first moment—a secret to either one of us.

"Oh, you do, do you? Well, you've been long enough owning up to it, I must say."

Dusk will soon be falling; it's suddenly turned chilly inside the car, and I shiver, chafing my hands together. "What were you planning to do? Keep me out here freezing to death in the middle of nowhere until I finally broke down and admitted I love you, too? Is that the point of this whole excursion?"

"Only a collateral benefit," he says. "Actually, the real point of this excursion, as I initially conceived it, was to teach you how to drive."

"Come again?" It's an expression I doubt I've used in thirty years. But it's an indication of how startled I am by this proposition that the only response I can muster is a kid's response.

"Teach. You. To drive. Didn't you tell me you've never learned how?"

"Maybe so, but I don't recall telling you that I wanted to learn. I have a bicycle, which is all I need in the city. Surely I told you all about that, too."

"I just took for granted that push-bike of yours was no more than some...environmentally correct affectation. Anyway, here we are today, out in the open, under optimal conditions—at least, until it starts to get dark. Which is why it occurs to me—"

"Occurs to you, my ass. You just finished telling me that a driving lesson was the real purpose of this entire trip, and you were only pretending to be in this for front-seat sex."

Carl grins. "Too right. I hated every minute of it. Still and all, I did a good job gritting my teeth and waiting for it to be over, didn't I? Now, can we get to the good part?" For all his jocularity, I can see that he is, in fact, serious.

"Carl, what is the big deal about everybody having to have a car? Have you got stock in General Motors or something?"

"No, sweetheart, I've got stock in you. You'd be a lot safer behind the wheel of a car than on that bike."

On the one hand, I'm touched by his concern for my well-being. On the other hand, there's an air of responsibility that I find annoying. As if I were one more dependent of his he'd forgotten to mention. "Look, if I'd ever actually wanted to drive a car...Well, heck, I grew up on the prairies, after all. Out there, everybody got their license at sixteen, as a matter of course."

Everybody but me, that is. In fact, this stubbled farmer's field, stretching in every direction, reminds me almost too acutely of the flat patch of pasture—parched and cracked like an old dinner plate—where my father took his children in succession to teach them how to drive. First, my older sister. Then my twin brother Paul and me. Well, not me. Since I broke the family mold by refusing to learn. Something about it—that prairie rite-of-passage thing, or something else—put me off. Perhaps it was my suspiciousness, in that closed-off culture, of the phony sort of freedom promised by possession of a car in wide open spaces that were merely empty. Or perhaps I was simply looking for some new way to piss my family off.

"Tell you what," Carl is still insisting. "All I want you to do is slide over behind the wheel, and just let me give you some idea of what's involved. It's dead easy; believe me, it is."

It's strange how he can't let go of this. Any more than I can let go of my resistance to being treated as if I were somehow dependent on him to teach me independence. "Look, I'll tell *you* what: next time we come out here, make love to me, just the way you did today, and I promise, I *will* slide over into the driver's seat. How's that?"

Carl looks both amused and despairing. "You drive a pretty hard bargain."

"Well, so long as I can drive something."

"All right." He sighs. "Next time. And I'm holding you to that."

"No, I'm holding *you*. Right now. Right here. Haven't you noticed?"

"It…hasn't entirely escaped my attention." He moves closer to me, presses his lips against my neck. "You'll do anything, won't you, to change the subject?"

"As far as I'm concerned, this is the subject."

When we finally relinquish each other, it is to gaze into the darkness beginning to fall across the landscape, as gently as a sigh. "Christ," murmurs Carl, "it would be something, wouldn't it, just to step on the gas pedal and head off over the horizon, forever and ever?"

It's uncharacteristic of him to sound so wistful, so yearning. And for that reason, I don't want him to let go of the thought. "Well, what are we waiting for? Let's step on the gas, by all means, and wipe that tear away."

But he shakes his head, smiling, and it's clear that the urgency of the moment has passed. "Tell you what: we'll put that plan on hold, too. Until it's your foot on the pedal."

"And then...? We will take off together? You'd do that—honestly?"

"Honestly." He raises his right hand. "There's no one I'd rather drive off into the sunset with."

Would he do it, though? As the stationwagon retraces our path through the field, out onto the gravel road that turns into a paved highway, which in turn melts into the expressways that will wind us back into the city, I rest my hand on Carl's knee and peer into the headlights of the passing cars. Trying to imagine what it might mean to run away with him. Right now. Just like this. Because, if we're actually going to go, my hunch is that it's now or never. In his wife's stationwagon, with his son's stroller in the back, along with my part-time dog. With no particular destination in mind, and nothing more in the way of baggage than the scant information about each other we already possess.

Chapter Two

I can only describe the sensation by comparing it to a faint alarm bell sounding in my head. Beware, the bell seems to say. Beware the man who appears to have walked away from his marriage with the casualness of someone leaving a barbershop: briskly, without a backward glance—pausing in the doorway only long enough to brush those lingering little hairs from the edge of his collar before hurrying on about the business of his day.

There ought to be someone with whom I can discuss my qualms about Carl. There ought to be, but... well, let's look at the available cast: O'Ryan? Great guy, but. Or Karen? Oh, please. Even if my bad dreams about her are only dreams... Well, let's just say what Karen doesn't know about Carl isn't going to hurt her. Or him.

Now, Mark used to make a top-notch confidant. In days of yore, when the man of the moment failed to pan out for me, I still have vivid recollections of weeping into the lapels of my ex-husband's favorite *disegnatore* jacket, and letting him soothe me with somewhat abstracted words of comfort. But that, as I say, was the Mark of old. Today, he's made of less substantial stuff, and I am less inclined to burden him with any adverse information about my life. Even if I am truly in love with Carl and scared to death... What's that to Mark, in his daily struggle not to be scared to death by death itself?

I find myself wishing, absurdly, that I could reach back through the layers of time to my old friend Grace Goldberg. Of all the people I've ever known, Grace still stands out, somehow, as someone uniquely qualified to see into the heart of me—the doppelgänger she left behind her.

I can picture her, I absolutely can—twenty-two years old for all eternity, with dangling earrings, a thigh-high miniskirt, and white Courrèges boots—sprawled in the Boston rocker across from me, with her long mesh-stockinged legs thrown up over one arm of the chair, and her skinny mini riding up unabashedly.

"The problem with *you* is..." That's how she'd start. Sailing right in, picking up her end of the conversation with magnificent disdain for the fact that fully a quarter-century has passed since she and I last spoke. "The problem with you is that you operate all the time like you're gonna get caught. Christ, like you *wanna* get caught."

Yes, that sounds like Grace, all right—those orotund vowels, richly rolled *r*s, and tortured Long Island diphthongs that I could, once upon a time, mimic to perfection.

"Not true," I retort, flatly Canadian, but more ready than I used to be to challenge her. Not only has she not changed a jot in twenty-plus years, she seems oblivious to the fact that some of us might have moved on. "This is not kids' stuff anymore, Grace—swapping outfits and identities to see how long we could fool the boys. I don't know how clear I have to make this, but it's gone past the point, with Carl, of treating him like some casual boff."

Grace snickers lavishly. "Oh, yeah? Well, far be it from me to remind you, but you weren't ever exactly casual with even the casual boffs. Not way back when."

"Come on!" I feel stung—just as if Grace Goldberg actually were here with me in my office, making such a crack to my face. "I wasn't the one who fell in love with that French boy Jules. And then disappeared with him into some damn mountain range or other."

"Come on yourself!" I can picture her grinning at me, and jangling her long earrings as she shakes her head. "You were more in love with Joowels than *I* was, truth be told. No, you were *not* casual. Not you, not then, not ever. Just scared shitless of getting hurt."

Jesus, and to think I've been waiting for more than twenty years for this infuriating little know-it-all to come back into my life. "You never even wrote to me, Grace," I point out, *apropos* of who-knows-what. "After promising me faithfully that you would."

"I meant to write, and besides, I thought today's topic was this Carl character. Pretty *hot* topic, too, if you ask me."

"Who's asking you? You've never even met him."

"I don't have to." As Grace licks her lips lasciviously, she reminds me, uncomfortably, of Karen. "I've *seen* the guy. God, but is he delicious. Especially in the morning, sound asleep."

I'm astonished, outraged almost. "Where have you seen him asleep?"

"Where else? In your bed, kiddo. When you're out in the park with the dwog at the crack of dawn, like a schmuck. Meantime, there's cute little Carl—nestled snug in your bed, with his hair all tousled, and his eyelashes...well, shit, those eyelashes, what can I say? They're so *long*, they're almost tousled, too, and—"

"All right, Grace. I've seen his eyelashes. I've seen Carl sleeping."

"Yeah, and you've *left* him there. That's the part I can't figure."

God, are none of my men ever safe, from anyone? "Is there some point here, Grace, that you're making?"

"My point?" Grace leans forward earnestly in the rocker, and suddenly lowers her voice, almost tenderly. "My point is that you're missing out on some of the primest times with Carl, while you sweat the small stuff. But, see, that's always been your stock-in-trade: missing out, because you're too busy covering your tush. Christ, even the night you met this guy, as I recall, you couldn't bring yourself to just be yourself and go for the gusto. Not you. 'My name is Grace,' you told him." Abandoning tenderness as a tactic, she permits herself a small snort of contempt. "'Grace'! Gimme a break. You should be so lucky to be me!"

"Well, I'm being myself now with Carl. Too much so, maybe. At the risk of blowing the whole thing sky-high."

"Oh, now..." Grace is back in her Ms. Nice-Guy mode once more. "Don't make it sound so much like *work*. Can't you have some fun with the guy?"

"I do have fun with the guy."

"Oh, yeah? When?"

"In bed. When I come *back* from the park."

"Oh, yeah?" Grace giggles smuttily, as I knew she would.

"Oh, yeah." My tongue is becoming thick with recollected lust. "In bed...I'm managing to just play it as it, uh, lays."

"Good for you. That's the way to play it—in bed, and every place." Then abruptly—as though her work here is done—Grace swings her long stockinged legs off the arm of the rocker and gets up, stretching elaborately. "There's no reason it shouldn't all turn out fine. Carl's too damn delectable for it to turn out any way else. Unless, of course, you fuck things up."

"Well, I'll do my best. Not to, I mean. And while we're on the subject of fucking things up..." There's a question, it occurs to me, that has been waiting in the wings to be answered, for a quarter of a century. "Whatever happened to Jules?"

But the rocking chair beside the desk in my office is, quite suddenly, empty—as indeed it has been all this time. Only rocking a little back and forth—or, at least, so it seems to me—to suggest that it might have been recently occupied. No sign of Grace, of course. Not even the sound of her purring *r*s fading away in my mind like the smile of the Cheshire cat evaporating in thin air.

I sit at my desk staring down at a wide white expanse of storyboard stretching before me as limitlessly as an Arctic landscape viewed from on high. What would it mean, to free-fall from some great height onto that vast, virginal expanse spread out below me so invitingly? Would I feel the brittleness of my middle-aged bones making violent contact with solid ground? With nothing, nothing on the way to break my fall. And no sound in my head, except the endless reverberation of the impact.

There's always the bottom at last—that eventual encounter with cold hard ground. But what would Grace Goldberg know about that? Imaginary Grace, wafting as weightless as any twenty-five-year-old memory ought to. Who—even if she could fall—would surely bounce on impact, with the carefree resiliency of a character in a cartoon.

I, on the other hand, will not bounce. Certainly not this time—if, in fact, I ever could. Casual? Not then, not ever. Not according to Grace Goldberg, who need not have come so far to tell me what I already know.

Chapter Three

🐾 No doubt you're agog to learn what *I* think of Carl. The fact is, I like him. He has on him the smell of truths unconfessed. Say what you will about that aroma, it's tantalizing.

Also on the plus side: Carl's no one-nighter who's going to suddenly start whistling in the shower, or sounding off in fractured French. On the other hand, he's not Jerry. I suppose that if I were any kind of loyal retainer, I'd express some indignation about the way Dana's allowed Carl to just step into her heart and make himself at home.

For instance, the other morning—when she decided to give him his very own doorkey. The way she trailed him nonchalantly to the front door to see him off to work. And then pretended to catch sight of a spare key lying—where it's always been—on the table in the hall.

"Oh!" It was cute, actually, watching her try to play it offhand. So casual that she's practically yawning. "Oh! Look what turned up. It's a spare. I guess you might as well have it, if you want."

"What's this?" Mind you, Carl's quite a sketch himself—the way he stares down at the object she places in his hand, as if he genuinely can't imagine what to call it.

"Don't make me say 'the key to my heart,'" she says. "Look, Carl, you don't have to take it, if it seems...well, premature."

"I will take it—as one of the few compliments I'm ever likely to get from you."

"It is. I don't make a habit of this. Believe me. I don't."

"No? I'm glad." Carl reaches out to touch her cheek. "Glad, in fact, doesn't begin to cover it."

Now, that was a genuinely meaningful moment between them. But also comical, in the way they both tried to pretend it was no big deal.

"Anyway," Dana says, still ultra-casual, "with your own key, you'll be able to drop in on me unannounced—and catch me in the act."

"I'll catch you in the act any time you like." Whereupon, Carl flips the key up in the air like a lucky coin, then slips it into his pocket. Before heading out the door, to take the porch steps, as usual, two at a time.

Now, the not-so-casual part: For a long moment after he left, Dana just stood there, smiling gamely and staring at the closed door. Then, her smile faded, and she sank down in the nearest chair, and covered her face with her hands. "Oh, God," she murmured between her fingers. "Oh, God, what on earth am I doing?"

What's she doing? Utterly losing her sense of humor, along with her heart. It seems to be a package deal. Since I'm the only one here who's apparently having a good time.

Sense of humor, after all, is such a fragile flower, so totally in the eye of whoever gets squirted by that bogus boutonniere. I mean, I have actually met people who think there's something funny about giving me a rubber mailman to chew. When, in fact, the real-life mailmen of my acquaintance have always been good-hearted types, like Dana's mailman, Doug. Who wears a toupee that looks like a muskrat, and brings biscuits for all the dogs on his walk.

Now, no dog would ever find it amusing to chew up Doug, even in effigy. Although, there was this one day when his toupee fell off, right on the porch. And I pretended to worry it, just for a joke. But I stopped as soon as I could see Doug was upset—and besides, that kind of thing only proves my point.

My point being that humor may be another one of those species-specific things. Which means that the gap between what makes *you* laugh and that which causes *me* to suppress a smile is as wide as the gulf that separates our divergent opinions about the pleasures afforded by rolling in fresh manure.

In fact, in the time that it took Dana to finish asking herself, with her face in her hands, what she's doing—when she knows damn well what—I managed to make a start on a list of some of the essential differences between your idea of a good wheeze and mine. See if you agree:

YOUR HUMOR	OUR HUMOR
Fake dog vomit on the stairs	Real dog vomit on the stairs
A dog smoking a brier pipe	A dog chewing up a brier pipe
A well-dressed person stepping in dog shit	A well-dressed person picking up dog shit
A dog catching a frisbee	An old hippie missing a frisbee
A dog growling at a dog on TV	A man swearing at an umpire on TV
A pet maternity boutique called Pregnant Paws	A pet maternity boutique
A T-shirt that says "Life Is a Bitch"	A T-shirt that says anything
A recording of dogs barking a popular song	A recording of Ethel Merman singing a popular song
A dog wearing antlers at Christmastime	A man wearing a Shriner's fez at any time
A comic strip in which dogs say funny things	Peeing on a comic strip in which dogs say funny things

Chapter Four

I do not, as a rule, cook. Which, if anything, understates the case. Generally, my larder is bare, and there's nothing in the freezer, apart from what looks suspiciously like the Ziplocked remains of Jimmy Hoffa.

Today, however, I have been seized without warning by the atavistic urge to cook dinner for Carl. Atavistic indeed, since as an urge it seems to belong back there with my long-lost student ghetto self, intent on finding the way to Mark Bannerman's heart through a vat of chili.

Not that I expect making a meal for Carl to achieve the same conclusive results. It's just... Well, my question is this: Can I pull it off? In view of the fact that it's been years and years since I involved myself in anything more elaborate in the way of culinary preparation than sprinkling a handful of Baco-Bits over cottage cheese, and can no longer even recollect what it was I used to try to cook, back when I could also remember offhand whether my stove is gas or electric.

No point in phoning up my mother for one of her recipes. Since my mother's only recipe has always been for those killer date squares of hers that effectively scared both my sister and myself away from the kitchen before we reached our teens, and prompted my brother to become the first kid in the history of our town to hire himself a food taster.

Ah yes, my mother's date squares... If not exactly a reliable shortcut from any man's stomach to his heart, then certainly a

190
•

fertile byway on the royal road to my own unconscious. Which I tend to picture as paved with Irene Jaeger's trademark date squares, like so many interlocking pieces of patio brick.

How fragrant they were, when piping hot from the oven. Then—once cooled—how tough and unscuffable, like some polymer byproduct of rocket research. Even my father—who, I'm convinced, would have readily snacked on plutonium if he'd come upon it in Tupperware in the fridge—was forced to make a separate peace with my mother's date squares.

One of my most vivid childhood memories—and I can almost swear to its accuracy—is of my father slipping a handful of adobe-like date squares into his pocket, for surreptitious transport out to the garage. Where he kept, as I remember, a wooden peach basket under a pile of paint rags, expressly as a receptacle into which to toss all the date squares he'd only pretended to eat over the years.

I have a further memory, of coming upon him in the act of taking date squares from the peach basket and wedging them under the wheels of his car, which was stuck in the lane. "Traction," I recall him explaining to me with a confidential wink. "Not a word to your mother, though, eh?"

Mind you, it's possible that I have made that story up. Although my mother's date squares were real enough. In fact, so corporeal is the weight of the evidence they constitute of a possible inherited domestic deficiency in me, that I feel I must either simply succumb for good and all—or else make one last valiant stand against my genetic makeup. It is precisely in that do-or-die frame of mind that I march to the telephone, to punch up Carl's number at work.

"Hart."

"Hi, Hart. So are you coming over tonight or what? I'm making dinner."

"You're...? Good God, whatever for?"

"Never mind what for. That's between me, my mother, and the support group for the culinarily challenged that I'm planning to start in her honor. Just tell me what time you can make it."

"Oh. Well, that's just it. I can't say for certain. In fact, one of the

192 • Erika Ritter

things I've most loved about you, to date, is that you never expect me to say for certain when I might turn up."

"*That's* one of the things you most love about me? Meaning what? If I were to die this afternoon, and you were asked to come up with a few words at the funeral, all you could be counted upon to share with the grieving multitude is your memories of me as this amiable pushover whose chief virtue resided in her singularly low level of expectation?"

"Something like that. Unless you'd prefer—on that doleful occasion—to be eulogized as a woman who always made the sweetest little noise in her throat when she was about to come? Although, on second thought, that may well be a fact about you already familiar to too many of the grieving multitude as it is."

"I'm making dinner, goddamn it, whether you're here or not. So *be* here, at seven sharp."

"Seven sharp it is. I shall look forward to it for the rest of the day."

>-+-<>-O-<>-+-<

I've barely embarked upon the hoary ritual of setting my dining-room table with candles, real cloth napkins, and cutlery that actually matches, when the phone rings.

"Hello?"

"Hullo, sweetheart."

"Uh-oh. You're running late."

"A bit. I'm just now leaving my office, and—"

"Which means you'll be here in what? Twenty minutes or so?"

"Not quite. I'll be stopping at my—at Vivien's on my way. Seems she's having some sort of…something with one of the girls. I'm not clear what; she sounds a bit hysterical. Viv does, I mean. Still, I should be at your place no later than half-past. How's that?"

How's that? Somewhat at odds with my preferred picture of Carl's ex-wife as a hearty I-say-who's-for-Horlicks type, utterly incapable of hysterics. Especially today, of all days—with the warm crusty smell of perfectly browning biscuits wafting from my oven.

"Well, I'll try to push everything back by an hour. But after that, dinner's on the table, whether you're here or not."

>-+-<>-O-<>-+-<

It's eighteen minutes past eight, the dinner rolls—long since out of the oven—are now cooled to the consistency of paving stones, and I am trying not to give in to a growing conviction that the curse of my mother lives on in me. Instead, I am making a positive effort to channel my energies toward the creation of the perfect soufflé—a dish which I've actually had numerous chances to rehearse this week. Since this is the third night that I've attempted to schedule Carl for dinner, the third night he's failed to show up at the appointed time, and the third night that I am being forced to face the eventuality of simply sliding my creation into the garbage can, untouched and decidedly deflated.

>-+-<>-O-<>-+-<

It's twelve minutes to ten. Just as my fifth soufflé in almost as many days finishes collapsing in a tragic heap, the telephone rings. Don't let it be Carl.

"Hello?"

"Oh, Christ, sweetheart, I'm so sorry. Small problem's come up with Andrea, who's had a serious setback at Brownies." Carl's voice is low and furtive, as if he were speaking to me on a telephone line that he has reason to suspect may not be secure. "But I'll do my utmost to be there within the hour."

"What? Carl, I can hardly hear you. Where are you—inside a laundry hamper or something?"

"Look, the sooner I ring off, the sooner I'll be on my way. I only hope you haven't gone to any trouble."

>-+-<>-O-<>-+-<

At eleven-oh-six p.m., give or take a minute, the phone starts to ring. Just as I am wrapping what I can salvage of the chicken shashlik in foil, and attempting to wedge a four-quart container of bouillabaisse into a freezer compartment too long overdue for defrosting—and already filled to the brim with dinners I have previously prepared, only to shelve, untouched. The salad, thank God, never *has* gotten dressed for its several false debuts this week, and may still be crisp enough to fight another day. However, yet another of my soufflés (I'm getting really good at them) has been consigned to the garbage—where it clings scummily to the sides of the pail, like some mad-science mutation that refuses to give up without a struggle its dream of becoming a viable life form capable of eating Toledo.

"Hello?"

"Dana, if you decide to slam the phone and never speak to me again, I shan't blame you."

"I won't do that—provided you're calling to say you're on your way."

"In a tick, sweetheart, in a tick. I know this sounds so... but this time it's Gemma. Some difficult homework that apparently only Daddy can be—"

"Homework? At this hour? Shouldn't she be in bed? Shouldn't *we?*"

"I'll be along as soon as I can. Unless... Look, at this point, truthfully: Would you prefer I not come at all?"

Wearily, I survey the countertops laden with unconsumed food, and the sink heaped with the unwashed vessels I cooked it all in. "No, I'd prefer that you come, whenever you can."

>─◆─○─◆─◁

It must be well after midnight by the time I once more (I'm getting good at this, too) remove the unlit candles, still-folded napkins, and the pristinely gleaming cutlery from the dining-room table. Then turn out the porch light, lock the front door, and head off to bed.

The next thing I know, there is the metallic scratch of a key in the front-door lock, a gruff welcoming "woof" from Murphy, and then Carl comes crawling into bed beside me, to wrap me penitently in his arms. "I'm so sorry," he whispers into the back of my neck. "God, it's nice to be here at last."

"Carl...I can't make love now. I'm too tired, just too tired..."

"Yes, I know. So'm I."

Yet, three-quarters asleep, I realize that we are making love anyway—or some somnambulistic facsimile thereof. When I come awake at last, it is to find that I've just come, with Carl's head drooped sleepily against my shoulder. I don't have the heart to ask him what time it is.

"You did go to an enormous amount of bother, didn't you?" he murmurs in the dark.

"No, not really. I think I just...opened my legs, and you did the rest."

"I mean with the cooking and whatnot. I took a look in the kitchen when I came in. Another soufflé sacrificed. Christ, you really shouldn't, you know."

Suddenly, I'm wider awake in the dark than I want to be. "Why? Why shouldn't I? It might make a nice change some night—provided I can actually get you over here—to sit down to dinner, at home, like normal people."

Carl stirs, and although I can't see his face, I know instinctively what's wrong with what I've just said. "Normal" is what he's sought to escape, and somehow can't seem to, quite. "Normal" is the last thing he desires of me, and the last thing he ever expected to encounter in the good-time girl who introduced herself as "just Grace."

"Don't worry." I'm striving for lightness. "I know when I'm licked. From now on, it's back to living on love. I can't imagine what got into me, coming over all Betty Crocker all of a sudden."

Although, I can imagine what got into me, and frankly it scares me to death—the extent to which I've allowed myself to slip into some wistful fantasy of playing house. The extent to which I—of all people, and at this late date—have allowed myself to *want* to slip into such a fantasy, with Carl or with anyone else.

"No, it's my fault." Carl rolls away from me, sits up in bed, and runs his hands through his hair. Even without turning on the light, I can tell that he's completely exhausted, and closer to defeat than I ever could have imagined he might get.

"Carl...do you want to talk about it?" I hope against hope that he doesn't—not right this minute.

"No, not actually," he says. "No more than you want to hear about it."

———○———

This time, when Carl comes tiptoeing into my bedroom in the dark—as usual far later arriving than he promised he'd be—I sit up and switch on the light. Freezing him midway to the bed, with his shoes in his hand, like some freshman caught by the floor don hours past his curfew.

"Christ." Embarrassed, he drops his shoes with a thud. "You've got more than you bargained for, haven't you, old darling?"

In apprehension of a showdown, my heart is pounding. But I force myself to shrug—like the casual, noncensorious, nothing-on-earth-like-a-hysterical-ex-wife type that I still style myself. "Somewhat less than I bargained for just lately. By the way, you might want to give the 'old darling' routine a miss. Since I believe I am still two years, eight months, and sixteen days your junior. Old darling."

I am bantering bravely, as if facing grave medical news. But Carl doesn't seem to be fooled. He sits down on the bed, and reaches across the blanket to squeeze my hand. "So you want to hear about it, do you?"

"I...suppose it's your—it's Vivien, isn't it? Who's obviously *not* as okay with the situation as you first let on." I am careful to sound matter-of-fact, nonjudgmental. Or perhaps I am merely being careful to speak in a manner calm enough to slow the beating of my own heart. Carl is right, and he isn't. I want to hear; at the same time, I most decidedly don't. Most of all, I want not to care.

"She *was* okay with it, at first. Even now, in her more honest moments, she knows the split-up was for the best. Christ, how could she not? Chaos, uproar, endless bickering. No stone left unturned—or untossed."

He is not looking at me, but seems to be addressing himself to a dark corner by the bookcase, well beyond the pool of light cast by the bedside lamp. As if hoping to locate there in the shadows some solution to the commonplace and debilitating dreariness of the life he can't manage to get past. "'Look,' I said to her—when it came clear to me that I had to move out. 'I need a place to live in that's *mine*. Some place where I can think my own thoughts, read a book, or *not* read it as the spirit moves me. Some place where I can hunt up a clean *shirt*, for God's sake, without it triggering another row.'

"At first, she seemed to agree with all that. But as time passed, and the separation became more and more permanent... Well, she's become frightened now, you see, that she's lost me for good. And it's that fear that's making her so impossible just at present."

I do not have any idea how to respond. Although it does occur to me, somewhat dully, that if a measure of peace and privacy is all that Carl has been seeking, what sense did it make to go to all the trouble of ridding himself of one set of entanglements, only to declare himself "involved" with me?

"Of course, I wasn't expecting *this*." Apparently reading my silence and the thoughts that underlie it, he turns to me, unsmiling, but emphatically tender. "You must understand: nothing I've said is meant to suggest that I'm sorry about anything that's happened. At least, insofar as you and I are concerned."

Be that as it may, nothing he's said suggests, either, that he wishes to re-encounter in me another version of his wife: Reproachful and stormy by turns, in her constant struggle against her perfectly reasonable expectation of a normal life with a man she undoubtedly still loves.

Which leaves me...where, precisely? In my oh-so-familiar role as the Other Woman. Back by popular demand—irrespective of whether I feel inclined to bring the act out of retirement. Aligned once more with a man who seeks nothing from me except uncomplication, and cheerful countervail to the weight of long-term domesticity. The only difference between Carl Hart and the Marrieds being: I happen to be in love with Carl. Which, on the one hand, creates demands. And which, on the other hand, makes it impossible for me to shrug and simply walk away when my demands cannot be met.

"Carl, you can't go on like this—running back and forth between her house and mine. You're worn out. Something's got to give."

"I know that. But not this." He is almost angry, although not at me. "I have no intention of giving you up. I don't see why I should."

"Neither do I," I tell him. And then—because I don't know what else to say—I allow him to put his arms around me. Just as if we've come to some resolution of this problem, and have earned the right to seal it with a kiss.

Chapter Five

So You Want to Teach Your Dog Who's Boss! is the name of the book that's recently made a sudden and unwelcome entry into my life. I know that's what it's called, because Dana makes a point of reading the title out to me every time she hauls me out into the yard for a crash course in basic obedience.

"So You Want to Teach Your Dog Who's Boss!" And again. You know, just in case I missed it the first four hundred times? Meanwhile, utterly sidestepping the question of how I got to be "her" dog all of a sudden, and what exactly there is in her demeanor that cries out for nomination as "boss" material.

"'Effective training,'" she continues reading aloud, "'can be commenced at any age. Even despite poor early inculcation, and the mature subject's determination to cling to ingrained bad habits.'"

Whew, what a relief. I mean, it'd be a shame, wouldn't it, to find out that her advanced years, lousy upbringing, and overall stubbornness disqualify her from the benefits of my tutelage? 🐾

———————⊷•◦•⊶———————

It's not as ludicrous as it seems. I mean, it would be nice, wouldn't it, to be able to let him out of the car in the country sometime with some reasonable expectation that he might come back? Okay, so Murphy's no Fido Beta Kappa like Amazing Grace. He's nothing like Big Red, White Fang, or Old Yeller. In fact, Murphy is a dog of an entirely different color. Neither wise nor willing, but simply a smartass. Surely for that reason alone, he could benefit from having some of those rough edges smoothed off?

Now, let's see here. "'A forged-link choke chain is your most useful teaching tool. It enables you to administer corrections and enforce your commands, by means of a swift, sharp tug on the neck.'"

>—·—⟨⟩—O—⟨⟩—·—<

A swift, sharp...? Oh, right. Jerking and jerking on my neck, as if I were an outboard motor that refuses to catch. This, apparently, is what I get for falling asleep during all the training videos she brings home. Like those awful episodes of something called *Amazing Grace* that she keeps trying to force me to sit still for—without dozing off.

God, I hate that smug goody-goody of a dog, and anyway, any fool can see that Grace is a guy. Most of the time, anyway. Actually, there's this whole gang of guys, each one more helpful and ingratiating than the last. Proving one more time—as if proof were required—that there's very little some of us won't sink to for a Liver Snap.

But seriously... can this gracious Grace critter be Dana's idea of a good, good dog? Is this the mark we're shooting for, out here in the yard, with all this sudden strongarm let's-see-who's-the-boss stuff?

>—·—⟨⟩—O—⟨⟩—·—<

Of course, a more reasonable way to go, with a hard case like Murphy, might be to hand him over to an expert. Someone like O'Ryan, who really seems to get off on the idea of playing Pygmalion to the egg-sucking Pals of this world. Except I hardly see O'Ryan these days. Not since Karen came on the scene to sweep him off his size-fourteen feet—in her own fervent, febrile, flesh-eating way.

Besides, Murphy—although not mine, thank God—is under my roof. And a Lassie Come Home I may never make him, but... well, how hard can it be to exert some kind of positive influence? I mean, I do it all the time on paper with *Amazing Grace*. Why shouldn't I be able to do it out here in my own backyard? "Murphy? Sit! Sit! Now,

Murphy...when I say 'Sit,' you sit, all right? Don't make me correct you every single time."

>—+—‹•›—O—‹•›—+—‹

"Make" her? Now, let's get this straight: I'm the one who's making her snap that chain collar up against my windpipe? How exactly is it that I'm doing that? What is it, some trick of the light out here that creates an impression I'm somehow winking at her to signal that it's okay to go ahead and hurt me?

And while we're on the subject, what's the big deal all of a sudden with "sit"? Totally on my own, many years ago, I figured out how sitting was done. Now, however, it's "sit, sit, sit" hour after hour—while she hauls helpfully on my neck. And at the same time, presses her palm on my haunches to give me a further hint.

"Murphy, sit!" In a tone of rising desperation that suggests we might have a real shot at world peace—if only I'd lower my butt to the grass. And then, when I fail to comply..."Murphy, it's for your own good," she says, even going so far as to look me in the eye. "It may not seem that way to you right now, but what I'm trying to give you is some independence."

Oh, right. Of course. That's absolutely what she's doing. Funny thing, but from where I (ahem) sit, it doesn't look so much that way. From here, it looks more like she's trying to give herself something. Some sense that there's someplace where she really *is* the boss.

>—+—‹•›—O—‹•›—+—‹

On the other hand, isn't the idea of "giving" independence a contradiction in terms? The tools. That's more what I'm trying to give him—the tools with which to forge his own independence.

"His own independence." Listen to me. Talking about handing it around, like Lady Bountiful. As if I were currently equipped even to pass out the tools to help anyone, including myself, to—

"No, Murphy. Come back. Don't go over there." And don't *you* go there either, Dana. That's a very dangerous line of thought. "Murphy, let's just go in the house, okay? That's enough for today."

Yes, that's enough for today. Enough of teaching the dog who's boss. Before one of us finds out for sure that those of us who can't, generally teach.

Chapter Six

It was a sudden impulse of Karen's to take me out for a walk. At least, that's the way she explained it to Dana, when she dropped over out of the blue to make the offer.

"You're kidding," Dana said, too startled even to invite her in. "Since when do you *walk*? Much less with a dog you don't even like?"

"I like him fine," Karen said. "And I walk all the TIME. It helps me think while I work on the act."

Still, Dana seemed doubtful. Then narrowed her eyes as she looked from Karen to me and back again. "This sudden yen to spend quality time with Murphy. It wouldn't, by any chance, have something to do with your equally sudden yen for my friend O'Ryan?"

Karen's own eyes were round and blank. "ExCUSE me?"

"Oh, come on. 'Talk about *his* interests.' That was always Ann Landers's advice to girls when we were growing up."

"I have NO clue what you're talking about," Karen chirped. "Now, is the idea to keep him on the LEASH?"

"That's the idea. Pretend it's O'Ryan."

"You're HILARIOUS, honey, really. Ever thought of doing COMEDY?"

***

Ambling through the ravine with Karen is nothing like taking a walk with Dana. For one thing, Karen carries a tape recorder, and keeps practicing the same punchlines over and over, right out loud. Then there's her outfit—also calculated to get us noticed.

204 • Erika Ritter

She's wearing a sweater with sequins, a pair of shiny stretch pants, and earrings shaped like bananas. The people we pass—assorted joggers, dog-walkers, birdwatchers, and the occasional old derelict—all cast an inquiring eye at her ensemble, and raise an eyebrow askance as she talks into her tape recorder.

But Karen doesn't seem to notice. In fact, she appears oblivious to everyone, including me—until she spots a man coming toward her along the path. An executive type, in a raincoat and polished shoes, gazing at the ground as he walks along. A good-looking guy. That much is clear to me, from the way Karen stops short and clicks off her tape recorder.

"Well, HI, honey. You're kind of a long way from the BOARDroom, aren't you?"

"Excuse me?" The stranger stops too, and raises his eyes from the ground. Then raises his eyebrows, as he takes in the earrings, the sequins, the dog, the tape recorder...

"It's about your corporate COUTURE, honey." She's smiling at him, though, as if these criticisms are for his own good. "You get lost in the woods on your way to the STOCKholders' meeting?"

Suddenly, the guy decides to grin back at her—making it clear he's the type who can appreciate when the joke's truly on him. "Looks that way, doesn't it? Actually, I lost some keys earlier. So now I'm back, trying to retrace my steps. Muddying up a new pair of Florsheims, I could add, but won't."

"You lost your KEYS? That's a SHAME." And Karen sounds as if it really is. With a golly-gee-gosh tone that matches her glittering smile and glittering outfit.

"Well, they're...my wife's keys. On this key ring shaped like a fish? She'll be pissed off as hell if she finds out I lost it."

"Oh." She nods, as if she knew all along the guy is married. "So your wife wasn't WITH you when the keys got lost?"

"Well, uh, no, actually." For some reason, he looks embarrassed about that. "I was just, uh, out for some air."

"Oh!" Karen is grinning even wider now, and seems to have more teeth than most people. "So you were out walking by YOURSELF.

Lonely as a cloud, and all that other Cliffs Notes stuff?"

"Something like that."

Now, I may not have a comprehensive grasp of what is going on here. Nevertheless, a couple of things are obvious, even to me: Karen not only likes this guy, she couldn't care less that he is married. While the guy is clearly beginning to like her back—and doesn't much care that he's married, either. Meanwhile, between the two of them—as they continue to stand here beaming—they're showing more enamel than an ad for bathroom fixtures.

"Well, when the dog and I come across your wife's keys, I'll be SURE to pick them up."

"Oh, I've combed the path pretty thoroughly."

"Yeah? Well, when it comes to spotting things, I'm pretty much the BEST."

"That a fact? And whence cometh this expertise? I mean, what are you, anyway—some surveillance hotshot with a two-way radio?" He indicates the tape recorder.

"No, honey. I'm a comic."

"No shit? Like on *Letterman*?"

"No, honey." Karen seems a little annoyed. "Like LIVE. At a CLUB. You should come some night and catch my act. I'll leave some PASSES at the door."

"Jesus! A standup comic!"

"Oh, yeah, it's big whup, all right. Seriously, it would be *so* cool if you'd come."

"Seriously, I'd like to do that. Look, let me give you my card."

Karen takes the card and inspects it. "'Richard Canmore. Patents and Permissions, Multi-Tron Systems Inc.' Even BIGGER whup! All kidding aside, Richard, I'll be in TOUCH." She sticks the card down the front of her sweater. "I'll keep it right next to my HEART."

"Great." But he looks, all of a sudden, a little nervous.

"Plus which, I can call you when I find the KEYS."

"Oh, right."

"They WILL turn up. TRUST me."

There is a moment during which she continues to stand there, gazing at him intently. Then, in the next moment, Richard Canmore extricates himself almost bodily from Karen's gaze, like someone hauling himself out of a swimming pool. He glances at his watch. "Christ, is that the time? Look, I . . ."

"Sure, honey. You have to punch back in. I UNDERSTAND."

"Look." He draws in a sharp breath. "I really would like to see your, uh, act, but I—"

"I told you, I underSTAND. Mind you, YOUR act could be worth catching, too." And Karen gives him a parting flick of her ponytail, before following me along the path, confident—even without looking back—that his gaze is firmly fixed on her shiny departing behind.

►─●─●─●─◄

I couldn't say how many times Karen drags me up and down that path before she finally zeroes in on the key ring, glinting in a patch of frost-bitten ferns. She swoops them up in a businesslike way, then hustles me out of the ravine and over to where her car is parked.

But instead of driving back to Dana's, which is what I expected, she pilots her Volkswagen at top speed to the outskirts of town, and through a succession of dull-looking suburbs. Until, at last, she slams on the brakes and turns abruptly into a parking lot, behind a low, uninteresting-looking building. Then switches off her motor and prepares to wait.

By the time Richard Canmore emerges from the building, it's night-time. Dana, in fact, must be wondering by now what's keeping Karen and me. But Karen doesn't seem to be thinking about that, as she slithers down behind her steering wheel and watches Richard cross the light-and-shadow-dappled parking lot, with a briefcase in one hand—and in the other, the entwining fingers of a perky young woman, scuttling along beside him as quickly as her high-heels can carry her.

The smile on Karen's face freezes, and her own fingers clench tightly around the fish-shaped key ring. She and I continue to watch as Richard reaches his car and unlocks the door. Then, he turns to the woman and gives her a lingering kiss before getting into his car and backing out of his parking spot.

As his headlights sweep past, Karen shrinks farther down in her seat. Then—once his car is out of sight—she sits up again, for a better look at the woman. Who lingers in the parking lot, staring at the spot where Richard's car used to be. Before turning and beginning to walk—in a happy trance—over to another car parked nearby.

"God DAMN the bastard!" Karen tromps hard on the gas—as if Richard's skull were under the pedal—and we shoot, almost airborne, out of the parking lot.

"So THIS is the deal!" She rages all the way back to Dana's. "So THIS is who you go out walking with, you scummy GUY! You need some 'AIR'? I'll GIVE you air, you retarded FUCK—more air than what's already between your moron EARS!" 🐾

⊱┈❖┈○┈❖┈⊰

No sooner am I certain it's the phlegmy putt-putt of Karen's old Bug, than I'm down at the curb, like something shot from a cannon. "Where the hell have you been? Do you have any idea how worried I was?"

From the driver's seat, Karen regards me with mild puzzlement. "Worried? Katie, WHY? We had a SWELL time. Tell her, Murphy. It was MINT."

Murphy, meanwhile, merely stares at me from the backseat, panting inscrutably through the glass. Worried? Why? Maybe Karen is right. My reaction does seem disproportionate. Given that Murphy means little to me, and I, evidently, even less to him. "Well, you could have called me, at least," I huff, still determined to prove some sort of point. "I mean, nobody walks a dog for seven hours. Or drives him around town for seven hours, if it comes to that."

"I'm sorry." With surprising meekness, Karen opens the passenger door and passes the loop-end of Murphy's leash to me. "I just lost track of time."

"Where have you been?" Now I really would like to know.

She yawns behind her long bony hand. "Here and there. Well, *hasta la vista*, honey. I'm ultra BEAT."

"Not too beat to call O'Ryan, I hope. He's been phoning me on the hour, wondering where you were. Naturally, all I could say was you had Murphy out for a walk. He was very favorably impressed."

"Yeah?" But Karen appears totally uninterested in this intelligence, or in anything else, as she waves at me wanly and drives off.

This is not a Karen I know—abstracted, noncombative, positively chastened. On the other hand, how can I come out and accuse her of hiding something from me? The dog, after all, is back safe and sound. From wherever the hell it was that she took him.

>—•—O—•—<

If I'm actually in this dream, I have no idea where. All I can say for certain is that it's nighttime, and Karen is once more out cruising in her car. From some vantage point or other, I seem to be watching as she drives—purposefully as always, and far too fast—through the ugliest outer reaches of suburbia. Then turns in at the gate of some industrial park, and comes to a halt in the parking lot, almost empty at this time of night.

Karen climbs out of her Bug and hurries over to one of the few remaining cars, a prosperous-looking sedan. From her pocket, she produces a key ring in the shape of a fish, selects what is obviously a car key, unlocks the driver's door, and gets inside.

My first assumption is that she plans to go for a spin. In fact, it crosses her mind, too. I can almost hear her thinking: How it would be the best, absolutely the BEST, for Richard to emerge hand-in-hand with his little girlfriend—to discover only a grease spot where his Camry used to be.

Richard? Who's Richard? No time for me to puzzle over that one, though, because now Karen has begun to rummage through a gym bag—"SO predictable!" she scoffs—on the backseat. Inside the bag, she finds (equally predictable) a handball glove, T-shirt, gym shorts, crosstrainers, and a towel. Karen whiffs the towel with her discerning laundry-buff's nose. *Too* fresh, in her opinion. She suspects that it's gotten nowhere near a gym in weeks—no closer than

Richard has. Ever since he began to indulge himself in athletics of another kind.

Digging deeper, she comes up with a cassette tape of New Age music, a razor, and a box of condoms. "SHAME on you, Richard," she scolds the thin air. "You overly prepared overage Boy Scout BASTARD, you!"

Suddenly, I hear the sound of high-heels echoing on the asphalt surface of the parking lot. Karen hears it too. Quickly, but quite coolly, she zips up the bag, repositions it on the seat, then slides down behind the steering wheel, to observe the progress of a couple approaching the car.

The man—who must be Richard—is good looking, in a vapid, middle-management sort of way. Youngish, unremarkable. The woman is even younger, and pretty. As he comes over to unlock the car door, Karen sits up with a dazzling smile. "Well, HI, honey! Gotcha, didn't I?"

"Jesus!" His expression, as he leaps back from the car, must be everything Karen could have hoped for.

"Oh, now, Ricky, honey, don't look so SHOCKED. I was shopping in the mall, and I thought I'd SURPRISE you by just turning up to ride home with you."

The pretty girl is gaping. Richard, meanwhile, struggles to gain some sort of handle on what the game is here. "Well, I... Shit, you surprised me, all right."

It's enough to make a cat laugh—let alone Karen, who can hardly contain her glee. Clearly, Richard has as little inkling as I do of what's going on. Meanwhile, the eyes of his woman friend are darting back and forth as she tries to work out the identity of this woman who calls Richard "honey"—and at the same time, strives to keep the other woman from knowing who *she* is.

"Well, golly GEE, kiddies!" Karen is taking full advantage of the fact that she is the only person present who can claim to be having a good time. "Don't just STAND there, Ricky. Let's go HOME. How about your little, uh, steno? Can we DROP you, honey?"

"No, thanks. My car's right here." With dignity, she extends her hand to Karen through the open window. "I'm Liz Connolly. It's nice to meet you, Mrs. Canmore."

Mrs. Canmore! Is this not the BEST? Karen beams at Richard with wifely pride as she grasps the other woman's hand. "Nice to meet YOU, Lyn."

"Liz. I'm Rich—I'm the firm's new paralegal."

Paralegal. Karen just loves that, too. "Oh, ARE you, honey? Well, aren't you COURAGEOUS, in spite of your handicap? I mean, DRIVING and everything!"

As for Richard, he can only stand by, like an actor forced to go on without a script, valiantly trying to work out the scene being played. As far as Karen's concerned, it's an attitude of discomfiture that looks good on him.

"Well, Ricky, honey..." She oozes wifeliness as she slides over to the passenger seat. "You KNOW how the kids will be waiting up for Daddy."

Richard knows. God, does he know that, if nothing else. And therefore he has no choice but to climb in the car, with a slight, apologetic shrug for Liz.

Who walks away, at last, reluctantly, toward her own car. Karen and Richard watch without comment as she drives away. Then, he turns to Karen and explodes: "Jesus Christ! What the hell is this?"

"What do you MEAN?" Karen manages to sound both puzzled and hurt. "I found the KEYS. Remember me? And I took the trouble to deliver them in PERSON."

"You took the...?" He tries to choke back his rage and strike a more conciliatory note. "Okay, so you found my wife's key ring. I...appreciate that. Really. But you could have called me, instead of coming all the way out here to—Oh, fuck, never mind. Just go now, will you?"

"Go!" The color is rising in Karen's cheeks. "Look, YOU'RE the one who wanted to catch my act. I mean, you gave me your CARD, to—"

"Oh, now, look here, lady. I never—"

"No, YOU look! Richard the...TURD!"

"Jesus!" Alarmed now, he tries to shrink away from her, against the driver-side door. "Okay, Funny Girl. You're nuts, all right? So why don't you just hand over my keys and—"

"Don't you mean your WIFE'S keys?"

"—and get the fuck out of my car, as well as my face!"

Karen holds out the fish-shaped key ring and jingles the keys at him derisively. "Here, big GUY. Don't worry, I didn't get them COPIED. But if I were you, I'd check out my gym shorts for ITCH-ING powder, and my CONDOM supply for PINholes! Oh, and by the way, LOSE the cornball New Age music-to-fuck-by tape. I bet even little Liz the Quadraparalegalplegic is too hip to climax on THAT lame shit!"

With that, she flings the key ring in his face, exits the car, and marches back to her Volkswagen. As she switches on the ignition and the headlights, she does not so much as glance over at Richard's car. She knows he's in there, gaping at her through the window, as she peels from the parking lot.

As surely as she knows that, tonight at long last, she really will kill at the Canada Goose. Kill them as softly and as surely—and as justly—as she's killed Richard the Turd. Who had the crust to try to pick her up—and then the gall to deny that he ever did.

Chapter Seven

It's raining, and—contrary to what Carl claims to fear—I am not the sort of die-hard cyclist who would ever elect to die hard on a patch of wet pavement, directly in the path of an oncoming car. Which means—since I am also too cheap to cab it—I have no choice today but to take a bus to meet Mark for lunch. His treat, at one of those chi-chi little "some-fresh-rosemary-for-remembrance?" joints in which the gay district abounds.

Given the wet weather and Mark's condition, I'm glad he selected a restaurant near his apartment. Even gladder, once I catch sight of him—stiff, rickety, like Pinocchio still held down by strings—as he makes his way, painfully, between the tables to reach mine, all the way in the back. Am I imagining it, or is he on a particularly rapid downward grade, deteriorating in a way that is sharply obvious from one encounter to the next?

"Whippet." As he leans down to kiss my cheek, his wheeze is audible. "I knew I could count on you to bury us way in back."

Before I can explain that this is where the maitre d' put me, the waiter is already hastening over to find out what we'd like to drink.

"Oh, hi, Matt," Mark greets him.

"Excuse me?" Our waiter smiles politely, wine list in hand. "I'm sorry, do we—?"

"Mark Bannerman. I used to come into Guantanamo Mary's, before it changed hands. When did you stop working there?"

"Oh, *Mark*! I didn't recog—well, you know what it's like when you see someone who...in another context."

Poor guy. Doing his best—which is not all that good—to conceal how shaken he is. While Mark isn't helping much by simply staring back at him, as if he can't begin to understand Matt's problem. "So, what do you think, Matt—a change for the better?"

"Oh, well." Matt gulps. "You *have* changed, but, uh, you look fine, Mark, just—"

"I meant," Mark cuts in, "your change in employment. There's really nothing new with *me*, except I'm wet and cold and dying— for a drink. Bring us a half-liter of the Pinot Grigio, will you?"

Something about his defiance of the facts bothers me. At the same time, what would *I* do in his place? Maybe exactly what he's doing: brazen it out as if nothing were happening.

"So, you're drinking?" I venture as casually as I can, once Matt's gone. "It doesn't interfere with your medications?"

"Doesn't seem to. Not a glass or two, anyway." And he shoots me the same look he fired at the waiter. "Anyway, I'm doing okay."

"Of course," I agree, too heartily. "You look just...fine."

"I know I do. I must have had a haircut or something since he saw me last, which would be enough to flummox Hi-I'm-Matt-I'll-Be-Your Waiter. Plus, I'm soaking wet." He coughs reflexively.

Is it worse for Mark because he used to be so handsome? The way beautiful women (I'm told) have a harder time facing the erosion of the years, simply because they have so much more invested in looks than the rest of us. "I'm sorry you had to come out in the rain."

"Why?" he snaps. "You think I'll melt, like the Wicked Witch?"

"Mark! Back off, will you? I'm like Matt the waiter. I don't know what the hell I'm supposed to say."

"Sorry." He grimaces as he pretends to scan the chalkboard of specials. "It's just lately...Well, now there are weird fungal infections, and stomach cramps, and dizzy spells—mostly from the 'miracle' drugs Ted scores for me on the sly. Shit, what with one thing and another, it's like 'Hatlo's Inferno.' You remember that, in the Sunday comic strips?"

"Where I grew up, the Sunday papers were on Saturday, and we called the weekend comics the 'coloreds.' But, sure, I remember

'Hatlo's Inferno.' Didn't every sinner get sent to the hell appropriate to his crime?"

"That's it. So here am I asking myself: What punishment would be most fitting for a vainglorious faggot afraid of growing old? And *voilà*: A disease that kills young—except, by the time you go, you're an old old man. Sans teeth, sans eyes, sans taste, sans everything."

"Oh, Mark. It's not *punishment*. I mean, we both know all kinds of gays who are as healthy as the day is long."

"Thanks. You really know how to comfort a guy."

There's no reason I should expect him to be any different than this: feverishly upbeat and snappishly sarcastic by turns—depending on whether it's his fear or his defiance on the ascendant at any given moment. Gone, perhaps forever, is the Mark of that night on the balcony—resigned to death and not minding too much because he'd got what he wanted from life. But that was then, and this is now, I think. Perhaps it's not the readiness that is all, but the degree of one's distance from the final curtain.

The wine, when it comes, seems to mellow him a little. "So, tell me how things are going with...Well, I can never keep your men straight. Was there some policeman you mentioned?"

"He's not a policeman, he's a..." I shrug. "Oh, never mind. Carl's...just fun. Nothing to cashier any of the others for, though. I still need...fuck insurance, I suppose you could call it."

Mark shudders eloquently. "Jesus. And *men* are supposed to be the insensitive sex?"

"What would you prefer? That I tell you I'm madly in love with Carl but fully expect him to break my heart?"

"No, not that. You're better than these clowns, Whippet. And you've got to get past them."

Oh, God, I think. He's not going to start up on that again? He is, I notice, not really eating—only redeploying his food around the plate with his fork.

"So what about...what's-his-name, in New York? I thought he was supposed to be the prime candidate. Again."

"Jerry." I find myself blushing, just as if I had something to feel guilty about. "Well, of course, he's still in Europe, and I've still got the dog. Which is sort of a drag, but—"

"Oh, come on. There's something going on there, isn't there? I thought I saw something the night you brought the dog to our place. It was cute, actually. As if you were introducing me and Ted and Gertie to a serious contender."

"Get out of here. Murphy is not a serious contender. He's not even a particularly serious dog. Or a particularly nice one."

"You want to know what I think? I think you ought to deep-six Carl and Jerry—along with your entire Volkswagen minibus full of married clowns—and just hang on to old Murphy there. He, at least, will never leave you. Not of his own volition, anyway."

"Mark...I hate when you do this. You know I hate it."

"What?"

"When you look out for me, try to provide for me somehow, after you're..." But I'm not so annoyed I can come right out with the words. Instead, I elect to drown the rest of my sentence in a gulp of cold water. "Anyway," I continue, a little more calmly, "it's insulting: the idea that a dog is as good as I can do for companionship. Especially a dog who doesn't even like me."

Mark laughs. "Then the hell with him, too. You deserve a lot more than that." And he abruptly sobers. "You always have."

Does he, I wonder, include himself in the catalog of what I have always deserved better than? "I'm glad you think so." I squeeze his hand—no longer the thick meaty paw it used to be—and in spite of myself, my eyes well up with tears.

"Oh, Whippet..." Mark sits there shaking his formerly handsome head at me. "It's not what I or anybody thinks. It's a question of what *you* think when—Oh, fuck, what's the point? God knows where your fucked-up image of yourself comes from, but it's too bad. Because otherwise, you have some nice qualities."

>—⊶●⊷—◅

Of course, being married to Mark all those years ago wouldn't have a thing to do with my fucked-up self-image. Playing the part of the drab brown wren to his splendiferous peacock. And then, when my fears about him began to form, trying to choose—from a series of unattractive options—which image of myself I could bear to live with: The unsuspicious little wife, pretending to herself there was nothing peculiar about the men who hung around her husband? The diligent detective, patting his coat pockets for telltale matchbooks from notorious bars? The brittle bitch, bent on adulterous revenge with every lay she could lay her hands on?

The rain is still falling, and continues to drum steadily on the roof of the bus, and to weep drearily down the windowpanes as I head back home from our lunch. In truth, I lack the heart to be hard on Mark at this late date. Since, as he points out, I'm the one who resists divorce, or any other step that will dissolve whatever bond it is that keeps me coming back for more of his pontification.

And as for the current state of my multifarious but unsatisfying emotional affairs, surely I can't reach back to Mark to pin the blame. After all, he's the one who claims I deserve better than this. While I'm the one who shrugs her shoulders, none too sure.

The bus grinds to a stop, and a press of teenagers clambers aboard. In uniforms, burdened with backpacks. My lunch with Mark must have run longer than I thought if school's already out.

One of the students catches my eye as she shows her bus pass. A wan-looking little girl with straggling hair, avoiding the gaze of the driver, or anyone, as she makes her way down the aisle in search of a seat.

A single seat. How do I know that? But I do. As surely as I know that skinny, chalk-faced girl herself, and every secret sorrow buried in her scrawny bosom.

With something bitter and unbidden rising in my throat, I turn abruptly away from the girl as she passes by, to stare resolutely out my rain-spattered window. But it's too late. She has brushed me with her coatsleeve in passing. I feel affected by the touch of misery that makes us kin. Now, despite myself, I am remembering.

When I was in high school, I would sometimes board a bus that stopped in front of Holy Redeemer Academy, which both my sister and I attended. I never think about those bus rides, if I can help it. Mostly, the memory stays buried, like a body in the basement. Like the corpses Carl and I joked about finding in my flat. And in fact, I didn't used to take the bus all that often. It was only when my mother asked me to come, after school, to where she worked that I was forced to face that long wretched ride.

By the time that bus picked me up at Holy Redeemer, it was already packed with boys from St. Ignatius—a neighboring Jesuit-run gulag of godliness. My brother went to St. Ig's. Although, mercifully, was never on the bus when I was. Nor was my sister—old enough to drive—on hand to witness my humiliation at the hands of the Ignatius boys.

Those St. Ignatius boys... For the better part of three decades, I have made a strenuous effort to avoid thinking about them. And when they do come to mind, I try to take pleasure in imagining them as they surely must be now: middle-aged, like me. But—if there's justice—unlike me, in running to fat and bald to a man. Failures at work and pariahs at home. Which small afflictions might at least begin to pay the bastards back for what they were then: loutish, loud, and bent on the disbursement of a species of cruelty as casual as it was without motive.

The torment would begin as soon as I dropped my dime in the farebox and started to make my way—swaying self-consciously with every lurch of the bus—to the nearest empty seat. Which was never anything like near enough.

"Hey!" one of the boys would yelp, as if pleasantly surprised to spot a familiar face. "Wouldja look who just got on? If it isn't the famous bathing beauty!"

"Beauty? Man, are you kidding me? First prize at the annual dog show. Woof, woof!"

"Hey, come on, show some respect for a big celebrity, eh? Don't you reckinize who that is? It's Rin Tin Tin!"

"Ah, go to grass! No way. That's Paul Jaeger's sister. His *twin* sister, eh? If you can believe it!"

"Bullshit! I'm tellin' yuz, it's Rin Tin Tin. Hey, Rinnie! Speak, Rinnie! Tell these wise-asses yer name!"

"No, for real, though. Poor Jaeger's her brother, and guess what else? Her sister is *Carla!*"

Exclamations all round of feigned surprise. "What? Carla the Cutie? You gotta be kidding! So what happened to Rinnie here—a switch at the hospital?"

"At the *animal* hospital! Hey, speak, Rinnie! Whatsa matter? Cat got yer tongue?"

Burning with shame, I would stare steadfastly out the window of the bus. Pretending interest in the spruces lining the Legislative Park, barely discernible through the grimy glass. Predictable a course as this torture ran, I always felt myself stung afresh. As soon as the familiar whine of voices began to circle me like angry wasps—one strident adolescent tenor indistinguishable from another.

"Hey, guys, let's make up with Dana here and shake a paw. Hey, shake, not-so-great Dana. Woof, woof, woof!"

There was never any help for my predicament. Not from the driver, feigning deafness, nor from any of the other passengers. Old ladies for the most part, who would, at best, shake their heads at the boys in timid disapproval. While I continued to press my burning forehead against the cold windowpane, and marvel with dull amazement that it was possible to survive this humiliation. Of course, I would reason, nobody ever did actually die of shame. Nor even became sick from it, probably—beyond a temporary fever of embarrassment, and a painful constriction of the throat.

Somehow or other, I knew I would manage to endure it, all the way downtown. To the stop on Eleventh Avenue, in front of Horton's Department Store. Where—when I got up to exit—I could count on inspiring the remaining boys to a farewell chorus of hoots and whistles, until eventually the bus doors folded shut behind me with a sigh.

Of course, my mother had no idea of the gauntlet I was forced to run whenever she wanted me to come to the Ladies Department at Horton's after school. My mother, in fact, had no idea at all in mind, other than to save me—in her own way—from the hell of my particularly unlovely adolescence, by picking out dresses for me that she thought might help.

Expensive dresses—absurdly expensive, even with her staff discount—and far too adult for me. It would not have occurred to my mother to put aside such dresses for my older, prettier sister, or even for herself. But it was an index of her relentless optimism that she continued to believe, in spite of the evidence, in the power of shoulders padded just so, the efficacy of a hemline cut on some peculiar bias, and the capacity of buttons judiciously placed to make up for what nature had failed to furnish.

Fresh from my trial by fire on the bus, I would face further humiliation at Horton's, as I emerged from the fitting room clad in yet another of those oddly cut and overly adult dresses that my mother had earmarked as "perfect" for me. Stepping out into the open, I could never bring myself to look at my reflection in the mirror. Much less glance at my mother, who was always flanked, on these occasions, by several other saleswomen. All waiting to see what transformation might have been wrought by a Beautiful Dress on an Ugly Duckling.

In fact, only my mother ever impressed me as a true believer. The other women seemed to be merely along for the ride. Like the villagers in those Virgin-Mary-makes-miraculous-appearance movies, visibly skeptical as they tagged along to the grotto at Lourdes, or the field in Fatima.

Certainly, in my case, there was never anything remotely inspiring to witness. Only the sight of me, standing in front of the fitting-room curtain—my scuffed school oxfords peering out incongruously from beneath the bias-cut hem, my head bowed abjectly, my hands folded in submission, with the price-tag of the improbably expensive dress dangling from the sleeve like a manacle. And a Father-forgive-them expression on my face, similar to the one worn by Jesus in the chromo of *The Mocking of Christ* that hung on the wall of the refectory at Holy Redeemer.

"Oh, it's *perfect* for her, isn't it?" My mother would clasp her hands to her heart in a transport of joy, while appealing to the rest of the sales staff for confirmation. "With her slim figure, she can really carry off that long, narrow line, don't you think?"

For the looks on the other clerks' faces, it was apparent to me that they didn't think I could carry off water in a galvanized bucket. Nevertheless, for the sake of my mother—so pretty, so stylish, so touchingly protective of her homely daughter—the good women of Horton's Ladies Wear were prepared to go to the mat by assuring Irene that I looked "real nice" in the Dress.

"But what about *you*, sweetheart? How do *you* like it?" My mother, with her glittering indigo eyeshadow and glimmering indigo eyes, would tip up my chin with a lacquered fingernail and search my face sincerely. "Shall I box it up, and we'll take it home to see what they think?"

I could readily imagine what they might think. Carla was easily as stunning as my mother, but nowhere near as nice. While my brother continued, throughout our adolescence, to deplore me on general principles. And then there was my father, the gruff realist inclined only to inquire "How much?" when confronted by the sight of his younger, plainer daughter in a dress clearly too pricey even for the two good-looking women in the family.

"No, don't box it," I'd urge my mother. "I don't want it. Let me take it off, and just go home."

For a moment, anger would flare in my mother's eyes. *Don't just give up*, her expression would exhort me. *Don't just lie down and die like this. Either refute the facts, or simply deny them. Those are the only two choices that work.*

Then—just as suddenly—she would recover her goodwill, and smile brilliantly upon me once more. "All right, sweetheart. I suppose if you don't *like* the dress, there's no point in taking it."

Poor Irene. I was, absurdly, her favorite. And yet, secretly, didn't she disdain me for just giving up? Her "creative" child, who at one time was able to conjure up an endless supply of horses—and now seemed incapable of sidestepping even the dullest and most terrible of truths. I would stand by awkwardly, watching her replace the Dress on the rack, and listen to her bright explanation to the other clerks that the Dress wasn't quite "smart" enough for her daughter, after all. And I would wonder, even then: How could my mother ever forgive me for what I could not even forgive myself? My failure to be someone bolder, happier, prettier, and—above all—someone else.

The ring of the bus's bell recalls me to the present moment. I glance around, and note the wan little schoolgirl standing at the back door, waiting to exit. With luck, once she is gone, the misery will depart with her. The bodies will slip back into their graves. And I will be my brighter, better self again. My mother's favorite daughter, barely touching the surface as I skim over it all.

Chapter Eight

Carl and I are on the last ferry back to the mainland. The only passengers out on the open upper deck—braving the damp breeze blowing across the oily waters of the harbor, in exchange for the luxury of this privilege, alone under the few visible stars.

Neither one of us has dressed warmly enough for our impromptu excursion to the Island. Like orphans of the storm, we drowse side by side on the varnished bench, as my head droops against Carl's lapel, and his hand encloses mine within the warmth of his jacket pocket.

We've spent the past couple of hours walking along the boardwalk that skirts the outer shore of the Island, stopping occasionally to neck, like teenagers with no place more private to go. At other points in our trek, we paused at various payphones, so that Carl—who'd forgotten his phone in his car—could make the calls he apparently needed to make, in order to replot the coordinates of his evening's schedule.

Now, on the last ferry back to the harbor, I am half-asleep, but at the same time conscious of the dull rumble of the engines below, vibrating from deck to deck—right up through the bare wooden bench on which we are huddled. Through half-closed eyes, I mentally trace, as I often like to do, the perfect contour of Carl's profile—tonight, neatly outlined against the sky. It's impossible to see where his nose got broken, in that long-ago incident as an army cadet. "They did a good job piecing your face back together, didn't they?" I murmur to him sleepily.

Carl stirs. "Sorry? What?"

"When you were at Sandhurst, or wherever it was you got drunk, and fell off the tank-turret, or whatever, and broke—"

"Who, me?" He chuckles. "Not likely. Mind you, there was a mate of mine—Tony Forrest—I must have told you about, who did disgrace himself that way in his impetuous youth. But *me?* Cor blimey! Do I look the Royal Military Academy type?"

"But it *was* you," I insist, feeling foolish but nonetheless convinced of my facts. "That was when you gave up drinking, remember? Because you got pissed, and slipped off the tank, and—"

Still chuckling, he shakes his head incredulously. "Sorry, sweetheart. You're mixing me up with one of your *other* men. You know, that vast brigade of blokes with keys to your flat, who come trooping round on the evenings when you tell me you're busy?"

It's a tired joke at the best of times, particularly tonight. "Carl, for Christ's sake. I know what you told me."

But do I? It seems ridiculous that I could be mistaken about such a simple story. Although equally absurd that Carl would choose to make up a lie so completely inconsequential. Either way, my response is an overreaction. A familiar reflex of mine that comes into play, I notice, whenever I come up against anything that smacks of subterfuge. Another echo, no doubt, of that sickening period near the end of my marriage.

"Come on," Carl coaxes, wrapping his arm more tightly around me. "It's not worth bickering about, is it? I thought we agreed it didn't matter—whose father did what in the war, and so forth."

"When did we agree on that?" Like a sullen child—like one of his daughters, perhaps, in a punitive mood—I refuse to allow him to inveigle me back into drowsy compliance. "My father wasn't in the war, and as for your father...Well, who knows about him? Since you were an orphan—unless, don't tell me, I've got that wrong too?"

Of course, part of what I'm upset about—if only I would admit it—has nothing to do with Carl's lack of either a military record or a family tree. It's the clandestine character of evenings like this one that has begun to get on my wick. His impromptu insistence that we head over to the Island, to roam along the boardwalk, shivering in the autumn wind, like participants in some illicit intrigue, rather than go to a movie or out to dinner, like card-carrying members of coupledom.

Then, there were the mysterious phone calls he seemed compelled to make all evening long, as though constantly rescripting his life as a work in progress. Time was, I enjoyed that air of intrigue and improvisation as much as he does. But now I find myself resenting the element of excitement he seems to need to add continually to the mix. As if the mere unfolding of the universe—and our relationship within it—were not fascinating enough in themselves. And tonight—to top it all off—he's not even planning to come home with me.

"Look, I did warn you at the outset," he says—reading my bitchiness, as he often does, as easily as a large-print book. "To get together tonight, I said, even for a few hours, was going to require me to do some rejigging. It's not that I want to give you short shrift, ever. It's just that tonight I must."

"Don't," I plead softly in his ear. "Don't go off to work. Come home with me instead. I'll make it worth your while."

"Can't be done," he murmurs back. "Not tonight. I did warn you."

The office towers that make up the waterfront skyline are suddenly looming, as menacing as a row of jagged teeth. The illuminated clock face on the Harbour Commission building floats against the sky, reproachfully displaying the lateness of the hour. Then, the final thump of reality, as the ferryboat jostles against the bumpers along the pier. And the next thing I know, Carl is walking me down the gangplank toward the fence where I left my bike.

"Safe home, all right?" No bad bicycle jokes tonight, I notice. Instead, solicitously, he tries to chafe the warmth back into my hands before permitting me to climb aboard and pedal back uptown. His thoughts, I can tell, are already firmly back on shore—turned toward tasks of his own that lie ahead.

"What about you?" I ask. "Where are you headed, at this hour?"

"Where else? To my car." He points to it, in the parking lot next to the ferry terminal. Then, without further adieu, hurries away—leaving me to stand watching him as he threads his way among the rows of parked cars, and does not once glance back at me.

Out of sight, out of mind, and other poems. At least, as far as Carl is concerned tonight. While I continue to wonder, all the long way home, where in the world he's going now. And what in the world he will be doing when he gets there that's so much more vital than coming home with me.

>─┤◆>─○─<◆├─◄

In my dream, the phone beside my bed is ringing. Which is quite a coincidence, since—in real life—the phone beside my bed seems to be ringing, too. And continues to ring and ring, even as I awaken.

"Hello?"

In the receiver against my ear, there is a sharp electronic *ping* in the dark. Long distance. No, even longer than that. It's...whatcha-macallit, overseas. If that, in fact, is what they still call it these days.

"Hello, Dana? Hello, it's me. Jerry. Can you hear me? Hello?"

Jerry. Jesus! Instinctively, I fumble for the lightswitch, as if ashamed to be caught asleep at this hour. What hour *is* it, anyway? Which day of the week? How high the moon? "Jerry, my God! Where are you?" Where am I, more to the point, and who's here with me? Ah, yes, of course, it comes back to me now: I left Carl down at the ferry dock. Only Murphy is in bed with me, deeply asleep.

I reach down, and my hand comes upon one of the dog's ears, soft and floppy like an old kid glove. At the sound of Jerry's name, however, the ear twitches briefly, as if in recognition. Or perhaps not. Maybe it's just that Murphy is dreaming—as I wish I still was.

"I'm here," Jerry replies helpfully. "I mean, I'm calling from the Continent."

The Continent. Right. There now, what did I say? Right from the outset, didn't I correctly divine that this call has originated from a great way off? "Why? What's happened, Jerry? Are you all right?"

All right, all right,... It's an echo of my own voice, feeding back into my ears from across the endless miles of—well, what? Black intergalactic space, I guess, where the electronic impulses generated by my voice and Jerry's are bouncing from star to star. If that, in fact, is how they do it these days. Personally, I prefer to think of the trusty old transatlantic cable, stretched quaintly across the ocean floor. I still believe in the miracle of that cable—can imagine it so clearly: big and thick and black, like an endless extension cord. Corroded with coral, nibbled by fish, and obscured by the sifting sand. Far more appealing to me as an image than some invisible impulse ricocheting off the featureless face of a satellite-dish floating in cyberspace. Or wherever.

"Of course I'm all right," Jerry assures me. But he doesn't sound it. He sounds fuzzy and foggy and faraway. "This seems to be a lousy connection, though. So, how are *you?* Is everything there okay?"

"Of course!" I'm shouting, trying to come across hale and hearty. Murphy, wide awake now, rests his chin on my knee and regards me with searching yellow eyes. Well, everything *is* okay, goddamn it. Since, at least, I don't have to contend with Carl lying here— while I lie to Jerry. "Is everything okay with you?"

"I told you, I'm fine." He's sounding slightly testy now, however, with the understandable impatience of someone for whom time— in this context—is quite literally money. "I just thought it was high time I got in touch, to make sure everything's okay with you and Murphy."

"Perfectly okay." My God, this conversation seems to be stuck in hopelessly echoing circles. "Murphy's right here. He says hi." Well, I'm not so sure "hi" precisely covers what Murphy is saying. Therefore, I'm just as glad to be the one in control of the receiver, and in charge of all the intelligence being relayed to Jerry.

"I miss you, Dana," Jerry is shouting back. "Can you hear me?"

"You miss me. Roger. I copy. I miss you, too. Repeat: Miss you, too. Do you read me?" And I *do* miss him, right at this moment.

There's not a word of a lie in that. I miss Jerry for the forthrightness of the way he says he misses me, in such steadfast contrast to... well, to everything that's happened since the day he left. "Do you, uh, have an idea yet when you're coming back?"

"Not exactly. By which I mean...not exactly. I...well, it's complicated."

"Complicated? Doesn't your conference or course or whatever have a beginning, a middle, and an end?"

"Well, it's a bit more...fluid than that."

Fluid? Did he say "fluid"? Ick. "Never mind. I'll take your word."

"Dana, is...Do you need a specific date here? I mean, are there problems at your end that you're not telling me?"

Any problems at my end that I'm not telling Jerry? Nah. Nothing other than the fact that I'm hopelessly embroiled with Carl, and don't have any idea what I'm going to do, whether Jerry comes back to me—or he doesn't. "No, no problems. How about you? Any problems at your end I don't know about?" As for instance, with Marta. Who, I'm thinking, may well be dunning Jerry by phone from New York for the specific date of his arrival home...unlike myself, the original Give-'Em-Space Girl.

"No, no problems here," Jerry is meanwhile insisting in my ear. "And everything with you is really all right?"

Sheesh. Haven't we covered this material more than once already? Besides, how can I answer him? It's as if Jerry were asking me whether I'm having a nice life. There are simply too many conflicting factors to summarize in a sentence. "Look, Jerry, I'm really glad you called. But you really don't need to worry about a thing here. Both dog and dogsitter are doing fine."

"Well, that's nice to hear..." Still, he continues to hover on the other end of the line. I can picture him, floating somewhere above the...what is it they have in Spain—the Mediterranean Ocean? Jerry, suspended by a long, long cord, bobbling up there in space like some balloon at the end of a limitless string. "It's good to talk to you, Dana. I'm sorry if I woke you up."

"No, you didn't at all. I wasn't asleep yet." Why do I always say that, even when it's a blatant lie? Even when there's no shame in confessing it? Maybe it's a kind of reflexive cover-up I employ for other, larger untruths. "It's good to talk to you, too. I won't ask you too specifically about the fluidity of the fluid time you're having."

"Come on." Even on a bad connection, Jerry is clearly embarrassed by my corny innuendos. "I'm glad I called. And I'll let you know, as soon as I can be specific, when I'm coming back. This call has helped a lot. Give Murphy a pat for me. Bye."

There is a disconnecting *ping* as he hangs up—and I find myself staring at the receiver in my hand, the way people in old movies do when they want to let the audience know they're wondering why they've been cut off. Although I know quite well why this conversation has ended. Because there was nothing more to say, that's why. Certainly not at international rates, and not with both Jerry and me—for our separate reasons—unable to speak to each other in any but the most inspecific terms. To the point where I can't even readily imagine why the call "helped" Jerry, as he claimed it did.

"That was Jerry," I explain to Murphy after I hang up. As if he didn't already know. "What do you think about *that?*"

Once more, Murphy flicks his ears on the cue of "Jerry," and continues to stare at me with an expression that is either preternaturally profound—or else just dopey-lidded with the weight of incipient slumber.

"Actually, Murph, I'm lying. It was Robert Redford on the phone." Aha. As I suspected, "Robert Redford" elicits a bigger ear-twitch than "Jerry." Which means that I'm utterly on my own here when it comes to assessing what is the emotional import of Jerry's call. After all, it's not as if I'm hoping he'll drop everything and race right back here. Nor is it—on the basis of one stilted transatlantic conversation—as if I'm in a position to work out whether he's more likely to hot-foot it home, if and when he does, to marry Marta. And stick me with Murphy forever and ever, because he's too afraid to face my fury as a woman scorned.

"What about that, Murphy? How would you feel if Jerry left you high and dry? And it was just you and me—and Carl, of course, too, sometimes."

"Carl," as it turns out, rates the most emphatic ear-flick of all, bigger than "Jerry" and "Robert Redford" put together. Which only goes to show...Although precisely what it does go to show, I couldn't say. Since I'm not at my best when abandoned with my bike at the ferry dock, then wakened hours later by surprise middle-of-the-night calls.

In fact, what with one thing and another, it's impossible for me to work out how I'm supposed to feel about anything that's happened to me in the days and weeks that have intervened between that long-ago morning when Jerry bade me and Murphy goodbye and this very night, when he awakened me from a sound sleep to remind me (however unwittingly) of how much has gone on in my life in the interim.

Chapter Nine

The good news about insomnia is that it precludes undesirable dreams. Whereas the bad news is that insomnia does absolutely nothing to prevent undesirable *thoughts*. Indeed, could even be said by some to go out of its way to encourage them.

Now it cannot, positively cannot, be that I am growing soft on the dog. If the prospect of Jerry's return concerns me, surely I have better reasons than losing Murphy to worry. Besides, how can I suddenly go soft on someone—other than a man—who has never stirred himself one whit to meet me halfway?

There are moments, I swear, when Murphy understands every word I say—as well as the thoughts I deliberately leave unspoken. And other moments when...well, the training fiasco speaks for itself. Moments when even simple commands like "Stop!" "Sit!" "Down!" and "Drop!" seem to strike him as too abstractly subtle even to pretend to grasp.

How can the Murphy who watches *Live from Lincoln Center* with such alert criticality be the selfsame Murphy who will amuse himself for a quarter of an hour at a stretch by rolling on the rug, snorting like a shoat? How is it that he has, without apparent effort, adapted himself to such highly evolved concepts as car rides, set mealtimes, and keeping quiet when I'm on the phone—yet cannot, for the life of him, seem to control the atavistic urge to root in garbage, bark at the barnyard sounds on *Sergeant Pepper's*, chew out the crotches of my underpants, and piddle reflexively on any sheet of newspaper left lying on the floor?

I mean, which one is the *real* Murphy? On the one hand, the civilized sophisticate, and on the other hand...well, there isn't one. Only a pair of clumsy, flailing paws incapable of deploying a doorknob, summoning an elevator, or teasing a tennis ball out from behind the couch.

Come to think of it, when I was little, what used to keep me awake at night was a similar conundrum: How could Pluto and Goofy *both* be dogs? On the one hand, there was Pluto—the chattel of a *mouse*, for God's sake—down on all fours, inarticulate, completely naked apart from his collar, and completely incapable of any activity more complex than trailing a bug with his nose.

On the other, there was Goofy—who *had* hands, albeit the three-fingered Disney cartoon kind. And a collar, only Goofy's had a tie attached. Plus, he boasted a whole roster of skills suitable to *Canis erectus et habilis*—including golfing, gardening, and doing his taxes.

Back when I was little, the foolish inconsistency of it drove me wild. To think that Walt Disney—the godlike Uncle Walt!—could have such a momentary mental lapse, during which he apparently failed to notice the Pluto–Goofy dichotomy.

But now that I'm all grown up, and now that there's Murphy, I see: Uncle Walt knew best all along. Because Murphy is indeed both Pluto and Goofy, by turns. And not only is the world wide enough to encompass both, it can embody both in a single species. Nay, in a single animal.

Well, I'll sleep better now, I'm sure. Assuming that Uncle Walt— no doubt impatiently pacing his cryonic cell as he awaits the Great Day of Defrost—can forgive me for questioning his omniscience all those years ago. Mice do not wear shorts with buttons, and probably never will. But Pluto and Goofy, taken together, are every dog who ever lived, to the life.

 It's not that I don't feel at home here. Certainly as much at home as I was with Jerry. But still less comfortable, in a general sense, than I'd like to be. I mean, the real question is: Where do I belong? With one foot—maybe several—in the Animals-Only camp, and the rest of me making the effort to pass, in low light at least, as humanoid.

Sometimes, on nights when I find it hard to sleep, I pace and pace. Or else curl up in the dark hollow beneath Dana's desk, pretending—don't laugh—that it's my den. As if I would stand any chance at all out there in the wild, running with the wolves!

After all, faking savagery with a slipper hardly qualifies me to get elected leader of the pack. Nor is stalking the plaster Bambi on the neighbor's lawn relevant on-the-job training to head up the hunt. Oh, and, of course, when I *really* want to walk on the wild side … I might take a drink from the toilet bowl.

Yes, it's all a far cry from the call of the wild. And yet … somewhere back there someplace, didn't we run together, the wolves and I? At some point in the misted past, before we parted at the fork of some long-lost river. The wolf heading one way, and I the other.

Until, in the end, I was no longer following the river at all—but some two-legged creature I'd glimpsed up ahead. 🐾

⊱────◦────⊰

Of course, I can't actually force Murphy to watch *Amazing Grace* if he doesn't want to. Not when he so clearly prefers the unadorned frankness of the Nature Channel. Even in the middle of the night, from way down the hall, under my office desk, I swear he can tell by the quality of the *click*, as I turn the TV on in the bedroom, if it's dull domestic *Grace* on tap … or the wolves. Seriously. There's no mistaking the avidity with which he races to watch whatever is wolf-related. Whether it's cute cubs tumbling endearingly about the den, or some staffer from a "relocation center," earnestly informing the camera about wolf-release programs in the National Parks.

Although, some of it must be tough going, even for Murphy. Those shots of hi-tech "sports" men, hunting wolves from helicopters. Or tapestries depicting medieval villagers in hot pursuit with hotter torches. And jumpy footage of idle adventurers in the Old West, lobbing bullets at Lobo from the windows of a moving train.

And, perhaps most sobering of all, scenes of wolf-hunting parties headed by dogs—closing in to kill their cousins. They *are* cousins, surely. So, what, I wonder, does Murphy make of such treachery against his own kind?

Mind you, it was the Native police force on the reserve who were seconded to dispatch Sitting Bull. His own Lakota tribesmen, in white men's clothing, with white men's haircuts, following white men's orders, as they confronted the old chief, their regulation-issue rifles at the ready. So why would dogs be any different, when—

When they fall asleep in front of the set, the way Murphy now has. Sound asleep. Would you look at that. He probably has been, all along. Leaving me alone to worry the question of what he shares with the wild and what he doesn't.

Which, at least, might make the beginnings of a story idea for *Amazing Grace*. I mean, since I'm still wide awake, and obviously on my own. A *good* story idea, perhaps. Imagine. Amazing Grace some-how getting lost in the wild, let's say, and meeting up with a pack of wolves, and eventually coming to terms with...well, what would we call it? Her inner wolf?

Sure, I could call it that, or something even more ridiculous. Since Murphy is sound asleep, and there's nobody else here to heckle.

Chapter Ten

It's unusual for me to be alone in the apartment with Carl. But from what I can gather, the whole point of today is to be unusual. For once, insisted Dana, Carl was going to stay in bed while she got up and went to the bakery. Then, she said, when she got back, they'd treat the weekend like a weekend for a change. Rolling around in bed all morning with newspapers and fresh croissants until such time, she said, as they were either very well read or totally covered in butter, or both.

All of which was fine with Carl. Who swore he wouldn't get dressed, on his honor he wouldn't. He wouldn't even so much as set foot out of the bed, if she was that determined to keep him in it. In fact, just to demonstrate the integrity of his intentions, he planned to go back to sleep straightaway, and stay that way until she came back to bury him under an avalanche of hot buttered pastries.

So far, since Dana's been gone, Carl has kept his word. Dana's telephone is right beside the bed, and he was able to reach for it and phone for his messages without actually having to set foot out of bed. Even while he was listening to his messages and suddenly realized he had nothing to write them down with, he was able—by hanging out of the bed and stretching halfway across the room, to reel in his leather bag by the strap—to rummage for a pad and pen. Without, technically, getting up.

Then, after writing down some numbers, he dials the phone again. "Stan Ludwig, please. Oh, Stan. Hart here. Working at the weekend again, are you? Yes, me too. Anyway, I got your message. No, you were absolutely right to call. I said you should ring, any time of the day or night, with even the most minor detail that might concern Doris or the kids, and so you should. What's happened, then?"

Carl, I must tell you, is good in this vein. Friendly, compassionate, but utterly efficient. What's more, it's clear to me that he knows he is.

"Yes, of course I remember her," he is continuing into the phone. "Mona Fredericks, your neighbor next door. Divorced, isn't she? Attractive? Great pals with your wife before she and the kids took off, isn't that right?" Just as though he has nothing else on his mind except every detail pertinent to the life of the man on the other end of the line. "And, in the time since Doris's disappearance, very chummy toward you, is your Mrs. Fredericks, yes?

"Now, Stan, let's look at that..." Carl's tone, while still compassionate, now conveys urgency, too. "You don't think this Mona may know something more about Doris and the kids' whereabouts than she's letting on? I mean, d'you suppose Doris has been in touch with Mona, or...? No, seriously, Stan. This is what you're paying me for, my expertise, right? And believe me, I've seen this one countless times before: the unattached female friend, or co-worker—or neighbor—begins to get ideas about the newly single chap whose wife's suddenly out of the picture. Well, it's understandable in its way, isn't it? That this unattached female might find herself less and less willing to volunteer any information she has about...well, the wife's whereabouts, let's say. You know, for fear—and I'm not even saying it's a conscious fear, mind—of a reconciliation between the couple that would leave her back out in the cold."

Through the receiver, I can hear—very faintly—a sound like the whine of an anxious mosquito.

"Now, now," Carl soothes. "Nobody's jumping to any conclusions here, and nobody will. Tell you what, Stan: Let me have Mona's number, and I'll see what I can do."

More mosquito whines of protest, but Carl is determined. "I understand," he keeps insisting, with the firm assurance of someone who truly does. "Look, I'll ring you straight back, as soon as I've spoken with Mona, all right? In the meantime, tell your secretary that if anyone rings you, you're not in—except to me. Have you got that, Stan? Because it will queer things entirely if our Ms. Fredericks reaches you before I do. I'll ring you back in ten minutes. Less than that. That's a promise."

Carl hangs up the phone, and whistles between his teeth, like a man happy in his work. Once more, he reaches for his bag, and from it produces a small tape recorder—even smaller than Karen's—and a tape, which he snaps into the machine.

As the tape plays, it offers up the sound of trilling telephones, a gabble of voices—mostly female—and, louder than the rest, another female voice droning: "Doctor Demchuck to Emergency. Paging Doctor Demchuck..."

As he suddenly notices me watching him, Carl gives me a conspiratorial smile. "What do you think of that, then? Hang on. There's more."

And as Carl continues to let the tape play, he dials the phone. "Yes," he says, in a very flat, almost nasal voice, completely unlike his own. "Mrs. Mona Fredericks, please." In spite of myself, I'm impressed with him. As is he, I can tell, when he settles back against the headboard, closes his eyes, and seems determined to convince himself of the absolute truth of what he is saying.

"Mrs. Fredericks, I don't want to alarm you, but my name is Gil Pritchard, and I'm calling you from the Records office at Eastbrook General Hospital. Are you acquainted with a Mr. Stanley James Ludwig?

"I'm sorry, Mrs. Fredericks, I'm only at liberty to tell you that Mr. Ludwig has been admitted to hospital, following an accident that—I'm sorry, I can't divulge details, not until his family has been contacted. Which is where I hope you can help. Mrs. Fredericks, we urgently need to locate Mr. Ludwig's wife. Do you know how I might do that?"

Carl is smiling to himself, and it seems to me that I know what he's thinking. How amazing it is, he's thinking, but how perfectly understandable too, that Mona Fredericks doesn't stop to wonder how the hospital got hold of her name, or why they think she would know where Stan's wife is.

"I am not a doctor," Carl informs her truthfully, meanwhile. "I can only emphasize again how imperative it is that I contact Mrs. Ludwig. Now, can you assist me on that score?" He picks up his pen, and rapidly begins to scribble. "Rimrock Motel...Thunder Bay...Do you happen to know the name she and the kids are checked in under? Hagen? With an *e*? Good. Mrs. Fredericks, you've been most helpful. Thank you. Goodbye."

Carl doesn't waste any time congratulating himself on his success. He clicks off the tape recorder, dials the phone again, and this time, when he speaks it is in his own voice once more. "Yes, Stan Ludwig, please. It's Carl Hart. Hullo, Stan? Look, I've got something. No time to go into it right now, but—Never mind that now, I said. Look, your friend Mona is frantically phoning you even as we speak; I can guarantee it. You can take her call now if you want, but I can promise you that she'll be quite hysterical. My advice is to tell her that some sleazy collection agency or other must have rung her just now, using one of their ruses to try to reach *you*. All right? I'll fill you in later. Cheerio, Stan."

Only once he's hung up does Carl take the time to sit back and smile at his own ingenuity. "God, I'm good at this." He shakes his head, as if surprised by the freshness of this discovery. Then looks over at me again, almost embarrassed. "If I say it, who shouldn't." He glances at his watch, then leaps out of bed. "'Treat the weekend like a weekend for once.' Not bloody likely, is it, old son?"

I'm not old, and I'm not his son, but I get the impression Carl is attempting to justify himself to me anyway. As he hurriedly gathers his clothes and puts them on. "Strike while the iron's hot. That's the ticket. Before it occurs to our friend Mona Fredericks to ring Thunder Bay and sound the alert. Panic, you see...Such a useful emotion, so cleansing. The way it cuts through layers or reason and red tape to get to the truth. But the effects don't last. And once she's put two and two together..."

I get the feeling he's now talking more to himself than to me, as he returns the tape recorder to his leather satchel, along with his notepad and pen. He is in the process of zipping shut the bag and slinging it over his shoulder when Dana comes into the bedroom, still in her coat, with a butter-stained bag from the bakery in her arms.

"Carl! What are you doing dressed?"

"Sorry, sweetheart." Carl is still buttoning his shirt as he pauses in the bedroom doorway just long enough to give her a kiss, before heading down the hall. "I've got to be on my way. It can't be helped."

"But...I bought croissants. I got the last two." She follows him to the door, still holding the fragrant bag. "Carl, I wasn't gone more than twenty minutes. What could have happened in twenty minutes to upstage our weekend?"

"I'll ring you when I get there. That's a promise."

"Get *where*? What is—"

"Thunder Bay." Carl kisses her again. Then reaches into the bag to pick out a croissant and hurries down the porch steps, his leather satchel swinging on his shoulder. 🐾

Chapter Eleven

I don't know why, but walking through the park today gives me a feeling of...finality. As though something other than the season were on the wane. Something which—unlike the season—is fading for good. Even the walk itself—this twice-daily ritual of unvarying predictability—has a different quality today. Something poignant, as if—for once—it's my walk as much as Murphy's. It's the same walk every day, but Murphy—like Heraclitus—never seems to step into the same river twice. Never fails to find new meanings in the same old messages on the same old tree trunks. Nor ceases to regard each new day as truly new.

And today, almost as intimately as Murphy himself, I feel that I am in touch with every blade of grass. Could experience the contours of the landscape the way he appears to know them—up close and personal, and quite literally down-to-earth.

Although, I still lack Murphy's cheerful indiscrimination. He sifts through the good, the bad, and the ugly with an impartial nose. While I find myself noting the discarded gum wrapper in the grass, the twisted bottle cap that mars the edge of the path, the sour cigarette butts, the dented Coke cans lurking among the asters. And find myself stopping to wonder whether I even *want* some of this stuff to biodegrade and become rolled in Earth's diurnal course, with rocks and stones and trees.

Today, there is a melancholy in the air, suggestive of the coming winter. Sober rituals are in progress, as the park is laid out like a corpse for the afterlife. The spading over of flowerbeds, the solemn, undertakerly pruning of the trees, by a brigade of men in sober gray coveralls. The drinking fountains are shut off till spring. The nets have been taken down from the tennis courts. The playground swing is festooned with chains, like funeral crape.

🐾 She seems sad today, on our walk through the park. Not absent-minded, as she often is, but attentive—even if what she's attending apparently makes her sad. Myself, I can't see why. Not when there's a pile of stale popcorn spilled behind the tennis courts, and a particular richness in the air that can only be the loamy aroma of freshly spaded flowerbeds.

The narrow pleasures of a narrow little life. Without noticing when it happened, I have abandoned the dream of pulling loose. I've come to terms with the fact that, in waking life, this is all there is and all there ever will be: these sedate little excursions through the park at the end of a leash. When exactly did that moment come, when I forgot about freedom? And what precisely did I agree to accept instead? 🐾

There's a small child dangling upside down from the monkey-bars, who could be the very same tot whose hat Murphy swiped on that mad rampage, his first day in the park. That man in the expensive Burberry raincoat with the Bedlington terrier is surely the self-same Burberry-clad man whose Bedlington briefly joined Murphy's rag-tag brigade in their ill-starred uprising. Murphy's fifteen minutes of infamy, that will no doubt live much longer than that in the annals of this quiet neighborhood. Long after Murphy himself has departed this place...

What's the point of being a dog, I wondered that day. What's the point in being a dog, if you never ever get the chance to run? All these weeks later, I still don't know the answer to that. Never will know probably, although...Today would be a day to find out. There may be winter in the air, but even so, the place is populated with enough of the hardcore faithful to constitute ample audience.

What would Murphy do if I let him loose? Would the hours of tedious tutelage out in the backyard bear any fruit? Would he come back to me, if the choice was his? Or simply run and run for all he's worth—far enough to make up for what he's forfeited, on the short end of the leash, all these years?

Which way would the park regulars bet—the nannies, the kiddies, the joggers and doggers? The customary cast of characters, each one looking compellingly familiar to me as I gaze at them across the park. Yes, indeed I see them all—Barsad, Cly, Defarge, and the rest of the crew, assembled at the base of the guillotine, as if converging there on some secret signal.

🐾 Of course, if I were going to make one final, futile, desperate dash for freedom, this might be the moment. Imagine me, if you can: Barreling through them all once more, for old times' sake. Scattering the small dogs like bowling pins, bodyslamming the bigger brutes, tumbling the toddlers, and cutting astonished adults off at the knees.

So much for the tedious tyranny of those sessions in the backyard. The relentless regimen of "Down," "Stay," "Heel," and "Come," hour after hour. Supplanted, in one glorious moment of mutiny, by the rallying cry "Up, up, and away!" 🐾

If you love something, let it go. Chances are, if Grace Goldberg were here right now, she'd quote mockingly from that earnest dictum that used to be tacked up in the communal john of every house in hippiedom. "Let it go. If it comes back to you, it's yours. And if it doesn't? Fuck it. It never was."

Easy for you to say, Grace. But what if Murphy *doesn't* come back? How am I going to feel if I let him loose, only to watch him speed away beyond recall? Like a kite escaping its string, slipping the surly bonds of Earth to dance smaller and smaller up in the sky.

Might my reaction be one of vast relief? The lightness that comes of having jettisoned all the baggage on board. The opportunity, that I always crave as much as I fear it, to free-fall to the bottom of the world. In hopes that when I hit, I will surprise myself by bouncing with the resiliency of a character in a cartoon.

Or else…what if Murphy did come back to my call? Would I be glad, I wonder—or sorry—to discover that some reflexive link has been forged after all? That I had succeeded in teaching him something in spite of himself? Something that he could use, and might remember me by for the rest of his life…long after he and I have parted company.

If I am conscious of any feeling at all, as I fumble with the catch on his leash, it is simply the desire to get the suspense over with. To sample as if in rehearsal the finality of how it might feel to suffer larger losses. To assure myself that, should Murphy defect, I will somehow survive his defection. As, later on, I will also survive the bigger betrayals that I somehow feel certain lurk up ahead. I unsnap the leash. "There you go."

🐾 There I...? Oh, I get it. It's some sick joke of hers. She pretends to unfasten the catch, but doesn't really. So that when I fall for it and go running off—arrgh! I am brought up short all of a sudden, with a sharp snap to the neck. Har-dee-har. It must be some sadistic joke out of that training book of hers. It has to be, because otherwise, there's no explanation for what is going on. 🐾

A long moment goes by, during which Murphy merely sits staring at me, his tongue protruding incredulously. Then, he seems to get hold of himself, and quite deliberately gets to his feet, shakes himself from head to tail—and goes trotting off in a kind of daze.

At first, he keeps stopping to look back at me, as if he still can't believe I meant what I said. Then gradually he picks up his pace, and glances back less and less often. Until, at last, he goes racing madly off—before I can change my mind.

With one accord—or so it seems to me—every head in the park snaps to attention to follow his trajectory. All eyes seem glued on him to see what he'll do next. What he does do next is what any dog in a similar circumstance might: he ranges around and around the park, reveling in the pleasure of what it is to feel freedom—so long deferred—beneath his feet.

🐾 Heads up, kiddies. Murphy's back. Rejoice, O ye downtrodden of the earth, your leader is nigh to sever your chains. Tremble, ye mighty, who are about to fall, because...because...Oh, hell, I can't. I'm having too much fun to stop and foment revolution. 🐾

My heart is in my mouth as I watch him gallop headlong toward a cluster of dogs, perhaps planning to broadside them as in the bad old days. But now—like the good new dog he suddenly seems to be—he veers off at the last possible second, and continues his care-free canter around the park.

But, oh look out now...As he approaches a group of children, being shielded by their nannies. Who scream—evidently recognizing this monster from his previous rampage. And yet, this time—my God, I can barely believe it—he skirts them all. And with a harmless, comradely wave of his tail, lopes off in quest of other adventures.

🐾 Unless, of course, this is some test she's cooked up for me, all by herself. To see if I'll come running back. In which case...well, the revolution lives. Since I *won't* come back, and have no plan in mind except to keep on running. Beyond the range of all the voices that might ever call me home. And when I do come back—if I ever do—it will be because the voice that summons me home is *mine*. 🐾

Murphy's melted from sight around the side of the tennis courts, at the farthest end of the park. Oh, God. Panic time. This is *not* what I want, after all. All that crap about the exhilarating finality of loss...it was just so much crap. Goddamn it, just forget what I said. Because the truth is, I want the bastard back. Want, above all, not to have to explain to anyone—and it's Jerry, of course, who comes to mind—how it was that Murphy simply vanished one day, like an ever-decreasing dot, eventually evaporating on the horizon.

"Murphy, come!" I am not even aware of having taken the decision to issue this order. But when I do issue it, I recognize it as formulated according to what's recommended in the training book: the dog's call-name, followed by a (preferably monosyllabic) word of command. We practiced it, God knows, often enough, Murphy and I, within the fenced perimeter of my backyard. The only part that's fresh is the fact that—this time out—compliance is totally at his discretion.

🐾 "Murphy, come!" Who said that? Gee, but I wish she hadn't. Not right this minute. Not in front of everyone, not with the eyes of the entire canine populace of the park upon me—egging me on to do what they lack the nerve to do for themselves. I know what the drill is, of course. I know what she wants. But half the fun—hell, the only fun—out in the backyard was in knowing what she wanted, and always doing the opposite. How can I throw all that away in an instant and come meekly back, just because she tells me to do so, right out loud? I am not like the others; I never have been; she doesn't own me. So, please…let's not make it so apparent, shall we, that she does? Not here, not now, not right out loud. 🐾

"Murphy, come!" Well, I've just broken the cardinal commandment of the training books, by repeating the order. Shit, by *screaming* it, in a hysterical tone definitely not recommended in any book. I know that he can hear me. Even at this distance, I can see him hear me as he rounds the tennis courts—and briefly breaks stride. Hesitates, but does not come back. There's a hush, as if the park is holding its collective breath. Or is that just how it seems to me? As if everybody and his dog—and me, of course—were waiting breathlessly to see what will happen next.

🐾 "Murphy, come"? Oh now, look, that's the second time. Doesn't she remember that the book always said it's like admitting you're not the boss? But, hey…boss, schmoss. What has either one of us got to prove here? I mean, is it *really* what she wants deep down—to be burdened with the weight of my unconditional love, assuming that it's in me someplace to give? Wouldn't she just prefer to keep on traveling light—and leave me to do the same? 🐾

"Murphy, come!" Okay, there, goddamn it. That's three. And now nobody within earshot in the entire park believes that Murphy is ever coming back. Oh, Murphy, for once in your life—while you're still in *my* life—do it for Dana. Make Mama proud. Forget every fugitive thought of mine you've ever intercepted that might have seemed to suggest I don't want you and never did. Because what I don't want—even more than I don't want *you*—is the loss of you. No matter what happens in the future, this is what I'd like both of us to have to remember: you coming back to me when I called.

🐾 "Murphy, come!" Excuse me—*three*? That's it. I can't take it anymore. So sue me, what can I do? Regardless of everything I've ever thought or said, irrespective of all those moronic mouth-breathers panting at me for guidance on how to throw off the yoke…Well, sorry, guys. Seek another messiah. Because I'm afraid she's got me over a barrel, with the oldest trick in the book. I simply can't not come. I'm a dog, goddamn it. Compliance is me. Subservience is what I do, will I or no. Who am I—any more than the rest of you—to buck the tide, or defy the course of canine history, or lift my leg defiantly on a million millennia of conditioning?

I mean, what the hey...Look at her—at the tears, honest-to-God *tears*—rolling down her face, as I come running back. Look how absurdly little it takes to make her happy. Let her try me on this trick again tomorrow and I might run away. But just this once, just for today...I'm a good, good dog. And just for today...what can I tell you? It feels very good to be good. 🐾

Ahhh! The park lets out its collective breath, and there is even a smattering of applause as Murphy comes running toward me from the far reaches of the park with his tongue fluttering in the breeze like a banner. "Oh, Murphy, good dog! You good, good dog, you!" Ridiculous tears are running down my cheeks as I open my arms to him and let him rush in. While the crowd cheers wildly, as if in the closing scene of some particularly heart-warming episode of *Amazing Grace*.

There have been, God knows, bigger triumphs in my life. Moments of greater significance, I'm sure. But I cannot, right this second, recall a single one. In a blur of tears, all I can think about is snapping Murphy's leash back on his collar and hustling him the hell out of the park—while the getting out is still good. Before he changes his mind and goes dashing off—suddenly determined, on second thought, to break my heart.

🐾 Okay, so it turns out there's no need for her to be sad today in the park. Or for me to feel melancholy, once more within the narrow confines of my narrow life, at the end of a short short leash. Because surely what we've both learned today is that I won't go. I know that now. Been there, done that, can't dance, don't ask. At long last, I have a place that I call home.

And now, the only question is: What happens when she looks into her heart, and finds me there? Staring back with an unwavering gaze that asks: "What next?" What will she call that invisible leash that binds us together—the promise of freedom, or the threat of indenture? 🐾

Chapter Twelve

On our way back from the park, I spot a familiar-looking Honda parked on my street. Almost simultaneously, Murphy sights it too. There is a buoyant lift of his ears and a tentative wag of the tail as he tries to work out, in his nearsighted way, what this blurry apparition might portend.

I glance from the car up to my front porch—already knowing what I'll find there. Sure enough: Jerry, leaning up against the railing, and pinching the bridge of his nose in that gesture I recognize as a prelude to one of his bouts of nervous sneezing.

"Why, Jerry," I carol as quippily as I can, "is that a bottle of Ventolin in your pocket, or are you just glad to see me?"

As Jerry erupts in a volley of sneezes, Murphy erupts in a volley of barks. I let go of his leash and watch him race up the porch steps, to hurl himself joyously at Jerry.

Of course the dog is overjoyed. Why shouldn't he be? There's no room for recriminations in his straightforward system. No capacity to blame Jerry, retroactively, for his unexplained departure—nor to question the suddenness of his return. I should not be surprised if, as it turns out, Murphy is only a dog, after all. What does surprise me, however, is the pang of betrayal that I feel—watching him fawn so uncritically on Jerry, whose dog, let us not forget, he actually is.

I hang back from the touching reunion, grateful at least for the chance to collect myself and begin to formulate some response to Jerry's surprise reappearance. Am I glad to see him? It would seem so. At least, glad enough to fake it with a smile and a somewhat mechanical kiss. He looks good to me, certainly—if rather jet-lagged and highway-worn. It's just that it seems so many years since he left. And refusing to think ahead to this moment has not prevented it from arriving all the same.

As I usher Jerry and his overnight bag into the apartment, I am already doing a rapid mental inventory of whatever evidence of Carl's casual occupancy may be lying out in plain view. No razor on the sink, no toothbrush parked proprietarily beside mine, no tell-tale robe on the closet door. In fact, as I stop to think about it—very hastily, as I must, under the circumstances—I am amazed to tally how very little of himself Carl has left in my apartment. As compared to the length of the skidmarks he's left on my life.

"I hope this is okay," Jerry is asking meanwhile. "Just showing up on impulse. I mean, you seem a little...dazed."

"Flabbergasted, actually. Sure, of course it's okay. Just hard to compute. God, when did you get back from Europe? Did you get a chance to sleep, even, before leaping in your car to drive up here?"

"Not much. As soon as I landed at Kennedy, I was more or less on my way up. I guess maybe I should have called ahead, but—"

"No, no need. I told you, it's great that you just came straight here." Although I doubt that Jerry's lady dentist friend would share that opinion. Since—judging from what he's telling me—he can't even have made time to see her since returning from Spain.

"I'm glad I did, too," Jerry says. "Believe me, our phone conversation the other night, or morning, or whatever it was, put a lot of things in place for me."

Phone conversation. Only dimly does it dawn on me what he must be talking about: that surreal, submerged-sounding transatlantic call that came from him in the middle of the night...What on earth could *that* conversation have put in place? What did I say, half-asleep, that might have inspired him to conclude his trip, bypass Marta, and come roaring up the Thruway to claim me as his prize?

And I'd put some of these questions to him, I really would. Were it not for the irrational annoyance I feel at Murphy for nuzzling so shamelessly at Jerry's ankles. Were it not for my rising fear that Carl could turn up at any moment to complicate the scenario further. Coupled with the sudden, sickening realization that Murphy may soon be taken away, whether Carl turns up or not. Surely, if not for these complicating emotional factors, I would be more willing than I am to quiz Jerry about what exactly I agreed to the night he phoned. Instead of finding myself feeling wary, defensive, circum-spect—like some probational mother faced with a surprise visit from Children's Aid.

"Well, I'm so glad," I hear myself telling Jerry inanely. "And I want to hear all about ... everything. So, why don't you sit down here on the couch, and let me put on some cof—some herbal tea?"

>—+—+>—·0·—<+—+—<

As Jerry and I sit on the couch sipping our tea, Murphy makes a move to scramble up beside us.

"Murphy! Off!" I bark the command reflexively, yet with no ex-pectation in the world that I will be obeyed. However, to my aston-ishment, Murphy—equally reflexive—leaps down and retreats meekly to a corner.

"Jesus!" Jerry stares wide-eyed at his dog. "He just does what you say, without making a megillah?"

"Sometimes," I admit, with reasonable honesty. "Actually, we've worked on a couple of things. Murphy? Down!"

Murphy circles twice, and then settles down, with an ostenta-tious thud of hipbones on hardwood.

"Jesus!" Jerry reiterates.

Truthfully, I am as amazed as Jerry. And even Murphy looks a lit-tle startled at his own compliance. Still, I can't help swaggering with the becoming pride of one who has no reason to expect any less from her four-legged friend. "He's learned quite a lot, in fact. Haven't you, Murph? Sit, stay, down, roll over ... He's good at that one. Murphy, roll over."

Murphy rolls over in a bored way. Then yawns elaborately and closes his eyes—as if to indicate that I can wake him up, when I'm ready to move on to something more challenging, like quantum physics.

It's all I can do not to swoop down on him, to squeal my commendation. But, of course, in front of Jerry, I can't let on how unbelievable it is to me that this Mensa graduate can be the same Murphy I've been living with—and suffering with—all these weeks. It's as if he's suddenly become a different dog.

"He's like a different dog," Jerry declares, but warily. As if he's beginning to suspect that his Murphy has been body-snatched and replaced by some perfectly behaved pod double. "I mean, he seems almost...brainwashed."

"Of course he's not brainwashed! The fact is, he likes to learn!" Why is it that I am starting to sound like Anne Bancroft in *The Miracle Worker* pleading on behalf of poor half-wild Patty Duke? "Murphy's capable of much more than humping legs and slobbering in people's faces, and it's unfair to him not to teach him some...enabling skills."

Enabling skills. Ugh. Even in my own ears, it sounds unbearably hokey. Not to mention a touch far-fetched—given that, up until so very recently, I was in despair of the dog myself.

Jerry shakes his head mournfully. "What the hell has been going on here since I left?"

It's my turn to stare goggle-eyed. "You mean, in the weeks since you took off to Spain and left me lumbered with your dog? Oh, not much. Although, it's nice of you to drop by and inquire."

Jerry has the sense to flush beet-red. "Look, Dana, don't be defensive, please. I'm just...taken aback, that's all. Everything seems so different now. You, as much as Murphy."

"What do you mean?" Oh, God, here it comes. The smile I gave him when he arrived, the kiss...Evidently, he wasn't buying.

"Well, if you'll remember, we had this...conversation before I left."

"Yes, I remember. About things we agreed to put on hold."

"Right. Although I did promise to do some thinking while I was away. And I did. That's why I came back, in fact, on such short notice."

Let's try *no* notice. Besides which, I'm boxed here in ways that Jerry can't possibly begin to appreciate. So what's the upshot going to be: Offering him a cup of herbal tea for the road before he exits my life with Murphy? Or attempting to entertain some declaration of love that he seems on the verge of making, but which I am no longer in the same position I was to field?

"Look," Jerry is continuing, "when I called you from, uh, abroad that night—or morning, or whatever—you told me that you missed me. You sounded as if you meant it, and it was the confirmation I needed, of everything I was feeling myself. Of course, if you weren't telling the truth—"

"Naturally I was telling the truth. I wouldn't have said it otherwise." Well, not necessarily, but we'll let that one pass. "It's just... well, there's a lot to talk about, and you took me by surprise. Maybe I better put on some more hot water."

"You make it sound like it's a baby we're having here. 'Get me boiling water, lots of it, and some towels.'"

"Just thought I'd make more tea. If you'll excuse me a minute."

Once I've set the kettle to boil, I steal into my bedroom, where I switch off the bell on the phone and turn down the volume on my answering machine. It would be just like Carl to choose the worst possible moment to call, and—failing to find me—to leave some suggestive message on the tape. Once Jerry has gone to sleep—which, given his current state of exhaustion is bound to be soon—I'll play my messages in secret. Hiding out in the bathroom with my machine, like some drug dealer, or housewife-turned-hooker. And hoping like hell I can head off Carl if he wants to come over.

How is it, I wonder, as I twiddle the volume-control on the machine, that I've managed—in practically no time at all—to go from being a woman too much alone to a woman with far too much male companionship? Yet continue to feel like a woman alone, all the same.

"What about Marta?" I demand to know, in the spirit of someone schooled in the rule of scrimmage that a good offense makes the best defense. "While you've been abroad, did you also figure out how you feel about *her*?"

Jerry and I are seated at the table in my dining room—where all the really serious pow-wows in my world take place. Since the living room seems consecrated to light chitchat, the bedroom dedicated to colloquy of a largely nonverbal kind, and the narrow kitchen so constricted that all that goes on in there is preparation of the refreshments that facilitate communication in all the other rooms.

"It...didn't work out with Marta," Jerry replies, his face flushed with emotion or hot tea, or both.

"But, I don't understand. How could it not work out, while you were out of the country? And if you haven't even seen her since you've been back..."

Jerry blushes an even deeper crimson. "I, well, I saw her, as it happens, over there."

"In Barcelona?"

"No." Jerry winces. "Barcelona was Mel's idea of a cover story. I've...been in Norway, with Marta. And her family. Mel's thought was that you wouldn't agree to take Murphy if you knew, and... well, what can I say? I knuckled under, and lied like a bastard. I'm sorry, Dana."

He's sorry. To say that a whole complex of dazzling emotions is spinning around in my head like a glitter-ball at a discotheque would be to short-change the impact of what Jerry has just said. The circuitry of my brain seems to be sizzled, flashing on and off to Overload and back again as I attempt to assess the situation. On the one hand, there's good news: Jerry lied to me about his entire trip. On the other hand, I've been lying to him too, about the depth of my emotions. Meanwhile—back in the good-news column—there's the advantage I gain by Jerry's not knowing I lied. Yet, at the same time, more bad news, in the form of my relationship with Carl.

Who hasn't yet come up for discussion, but who—I feel sickeningly sure—is bound to trump Marta when he does.

"I see," I say at last, when it becomes apparent to me some response is required. "I see" is what wronged women say on those network Movies of the Week I pretend I don't watch. The ones in which Judith Light or Connie Sellecca or Valerie Bertinelli is forcibly faced with the awful intelligence that her husband has other wives, or has been sleeping with the daughters of his other wives, or has contracted AIDS from sleeping with the sons of his other wives, or... Or, as in my own case, is forcibly faced with the awful intelligence that she has been stuck with the dog of her off-again-on-again neurasthenic New York boyfriend while he was osculating in Oslo with his glacially blond Nordic girlfriend. "I see. So you've been with Marta all this time."

"Yes," he says miserably. "But believe me, it's been no picnic."

I nod with that species of quiet dignity that I've learned from Judith Light and Connie Sellecca and Valerie Bertinelli—along with so much else. "So, it turns out that your relationship with Marta isn't exactly the relationship that you 'ought' to be in?"

Jerry winces again, as I suspected he might. "I remember everything I said last time I was in this apartment with you. Including that I hoped you and I could reconnect, if things didn't work out with Marta. Well, I still hope we might—when you get over being mad at me for lying."

It's my turn to wince, as I pour us both some fresh tea. "Well, I'll get over it, I suppose, in time." More than that, I cannot say, since it's still impossible for me to tell where any of this is going. Except, probably nowhere I ever craved to visit.

"I hope you do get over it. Last time I was here, you told me that you loved me. Even if you couldn't seem to spell out *why*, exactly."

"Yes, I know what I said." As I get up from the table too abruptly, my head starts spinning. And continues to spin when Jerry gets up too, and approaches me tenderly.

"Come on, Dana. I've admitted that I lied, and I said that I'm sorry. Which I am. Although, if I hadn't spent that time with Marta in Norway, I wouldn't be so certain of what I'm telling you now. So the lie was actually in a good cause. Assuming, of course, you still feel the cause is good."

"I..." I step back from his embrace. Would it be right, feeling the way that I do—which is akin to no feeling at all—if I just invited him to bed? On the other hand, would it necessarily be so wrong? "I'm sorry. This is all so sudden. You just appearing, and everything you've said...Maybe we shouldn't do any more talking right now... I'd like to be with you. Just be with you. Only, uh, give me a minute first, okay? A minute to myself to think."

Jerry looks baffled, as well he might. But only for a moment. Then, an expression of surety crosses his face as the penny seems to drop. "I think you need more than a minute. Dana, it's possible, isn't it, that you don't love me? That you never did. In spite of what you claimed the last time you saw me?"

"Jesus, Jerry! Be fair. I told you, I just need a minute. You've had weeks with Marta in Norway. While I've been here all by my—" All by my what? Unable to conclude the sentence, I leave it to trail after me as I hurry out of the room.

In the bedroom, I discover the red light of my answering machine now blinking, with silent insinuation. Carl? But I don't have any appetite to play back the message, not right this minute. In fact, right this minute, I have no real appetite for anything.

A moment later, Murphy's piebald face appears at the door. Wearing the mildly inquiring expression of a concerned third party, uncertain how best to assist the course of true love, running unsmooth just at present.

"Don't look at me like that," I instruct him in a tense whisper. "As if you couldn't imagine what-on-Earth. Of everybody in the entire world, who knows better than you do what I'm going through, and why?"

>─┼─<>─O─<>─┼─<

"Dana, this is no good." Jerry is in my bedroom, sagging on his feet with fatigue, even as he unbuttons his shirt. Poor Jerry. There are dark furrows of exhaustion under his eyes—not too surprising, all things considered. What is surprising is that he hasn't collapsed long before now.

"I know. You're dead on your feet. So just get into bed, and get some sleep, and we can pick up where we left off in the morning."

"What's to pick up? I told you, you're not in love with me and you never were, end of story."

His face is closed against me; I can see that his mind is now firmly made up. And at this moment—with all the perversity that's in me—I feel closer to wanting him that I have since...when? Since the last time he seemed about to reject me for Marta. "I *want* to be in love with you. How about that?"

He snorts, eloquently. "How about this: you *are* in love. But it's not with me. And don't try to bullshit me, because it's written all over you."

Where? I wonder. Where is it written? Or is Jerry just making a lucky guess? "I...well, it's true I've become more attached to your dog, just lately, than I ever expected I—"

"Screw the dog!" Such a crudism is completely out of character for Jerry. "It's not Murphy I'm talking about. You're in love, at long last. With some other man. And you can take a look at your face in the mirror, if you don't believe me. All that's not spelled out is his name."

All of a sudden, I feel as worn out as he must. "It doesn't make any difference what his name is. If it's any consolation to you, this is not the relationship I 'ought' to be in, either."

In spite of himself, a flicker of something like hope crosses Jerry's face. "Meaning what?"

"Meaning, I'm going to wind up getting the chewed end of the pencil on this one. At which point, men of good conscience like you can rejoice at my richly deserved undoing."

"Oh." His voice sounds thick. It's as if—in the light of what I've said—a battle is raging within him. Between wanting to protect me from hurt because he cares for me, and wanting to see me hurt because I care for someone else. "But you do love him, whoever he is. And I can tell you something else, too..." Clearly, the desire to hurt me has finally won out. "If I were to ask you what it is about this guy that you love, I bet you could answer me. No problem."

Into my mind comes an image, vivid and involuntary: Carl, lying on this very bed, his eyes closed, his dark, almost improbably long lashes against his cheek, as he reaches for me, confident his hands can find me and pull me, down, down, down... "Yes," I admit. "I could answer you. No problem."

Jerry casts one brief, intuitive glance at the bed, then begins to rebutton his shirt—methodically, unhurriedly, like someone getting ready to go to work. "I don't want to fight with you. You know that fighting fucks my respiration up." With studied precision, he concentrates on fastening the very top button, as though everything in his life depends on how well he performs this task. "Under the circumstances, I think I'd better just go."

"Go? *Now?* What, are you crazy? Drive ten hours back down to New York, you mean? On transatlantic jet-lag, with no sleep, and no intelligent discussion of something perfectly... negotiable?"

He walks out of the bedroom and, with steady resolve, carries on to the vestibule, where his valise, still packed, is sitting. "Oh, right. With you, discussion is always a prelude to something perfectly negotiable. It's what you *don't* discuss that would make for a revealing interview."

"Jerry, look... We both have our wrongs to reckon here. You lied to me; I omitted to tell you the truth. All the same, you shouldn't leave just like this."

"Just like this?" He rounds on me, amazed. "What is there left to talk about?"

"Murphy, for one thing. Jerry... would you let me keep him here a while longer?" I am, by the way, as surprised as Jerry to hear myself saying this. Even more surprised, when I recollect myself as the same person who, not so long ago, actually flirted with the notion of what relief it might afford me to watch Murphy running away through the park, never to return.

"Keep him? Dana, what are you talking about?"

"It's not such a crazy idea, is it? You said it yourself: he's a different dog."

"I said it's more like he's lobotomized. Besides, that's not the point. He's not your dog."

"I'm not asking you to give him to me outright. Couldn't we work out some kind of...I don't know, split-custody deal?"

"Split custody? Of a *dog*? That has to be the craziest thing I've ever heard." Actually, Jerry is more hurt than outraged, and I think I understand why. After all, here he is, walking out of my life forever—and all I appear to care about is whether or not Murphy will be accompanying him.

"What's so crazy about it? You don't want him. You never did. He was just...an unfortunate side effect of some forgotten relationship. Like a case of crabs."

Jerry flinches. "Attractive simile."

"You know what I'm saying. What you don't know is that there really is this...bond between him and me. It was in the park, when I let him loose. You won't believe it, but—"

"When you let him *loose*?" Jerry seizes this up as the last straw. "After I expressly told you not to? After you saw what happened that first day, when you—"

"That first day, when *you* dumped him on me and left—on some bogus radio conference that actually turned out to be a prolonged frolic in the fjords?" Clearly, my cause is lost. I might as well shed the gloves, get down in the mud, and wrestle with Jerry, *mano a mano*.

"Jesus, that does it! I am *not* giving my dog to you, of all people. I wouldn't put you in charge of a pet rock. You're irresponsible, Dana, in every way. You're vindictive, you're dishonest—"

"Jerry..." In one last-ditch effort, I suddenly drop my dukes and reach out to touch his arm pleadingly. "You know you're not upset with me for letting Murphy loose. Not really. You're upset with me for being in love with someone else." Even now, I'm thinking, there might be some way to turn this around, if only I knew which button to push. Jerry doesn't want the dog, not any more than he ever did. If I could somehow find a way to minimize my feelings for Carl, with some persuasive lie... But for the life of me, I can't seem to deny Carl. No, not even for the life of me.

"I'm sorry." Jerry removes my hand from his sleeve, then removes his glasses and rubs his eyes blearily. "I can't talk about this anymore. Believe it or not, there's a limit to how many break-ups I can handle in the space of twenty-four hours. Even when I spread my farewells out over two continents."

"At least wait until morning to drive," I urge him. "You can sleep in my office—or I will—and then tomorrow, when you're rested—"

"No, I'm leaving now. I have No-Doz in the glove compartment. Now, will you please do me a favor and get Murphy's things?"

Chapter Thirteen

It's not the act of gathering Murphy's meager effects that clutches at my heart. It's the objects themselves: his chew-toy, his balding tennis ball, his brush, his metal dinner dish—the entire inventory of one dog's modest earthly accumulations. The short and simple annals of one uncelebrated, unassuming life.

Murphy's departure is a scene which—one way and another—I've always known I would have to play. And in playing it, I pride myself on remaining dry-eyed as I bundle his belongings out to the curb, then stand watching as Jerry stows them in the hatch of the Honda with characteristically painful precision.

It's becoming dark; a ragged hunter's moon strives to shed itself of a few straggling clouds. "I really wish you'd wait till morning," I repeat to Jerry for the dozenth time at least. "It's too far to drive twice in a single day."

"Don't worry," Jerry says. "I won't get into an accident. I know how much Murphy means to you."

I am determined not to take this parting crack as a parting crack. Instead, I concentrate on trying not to cry. Jerry, I know, abhors female tears, even more—to quote his friend Mel—than he hates shorts that bind. More important, I feel I have no right to break down in front of Murphy. Who sits in the back of the car, fogging the windows with his breath, and seeming unaware that anything untoward is going on. Good old Murphy—for whom the present moment is all the time there is. And in whose evaluation—presumably—a world in which he never sees me again will simply become a world in which I never existed to start with.

As for me, however... Once again, I find myself approaching impending loss with the cautiousness of someone stepping out onto rotten ice. Once more rehearsing an experiment I've previewed so many times already: the gingerly assessment of how far I dare venture from shore before the frozen surface of the lake begins to groan and give way beneath me. "Maybe you'll call me when you get there," I suggest to Jerry.

"Maybe. Or maybe I'll let the dust settle a little."

Or maybe he won't call me at all, ever—certainly not any time soon. This is a far cry—and "cry" may soon be the operative word—from the note of hopeful civility we managed to strike the morning Jerry departed, *en route* to Europe. This time, little remains between us, except the dog. Murphy, whom Jerry never wanted and still doesn't want, but seems determined to stick with, nevertheless. Murphy, whom I was so wary of having palmed off on me—and who now threatens to break my heart as he peers shortsightedly out the back window of Jerry's Honda.

Jerry gets in, buckles his shoulder harness, and rolls down his window for his farewell speech. "Let's not hate each other, okay?"

"I don't hate you," I reply quite truthfully. "I just hate what's happened between us."

"Me too, but... Oh, shit. Look, Dana, can we say I'll call you, and just leave it at that?"

"Okay. Please drive carefully."

"I will, and... Look, nutty as this sounds, thanks for taking care of Murphy. Goodbye, Dana."

"You're welcome. Goodbye, Jerry."

Although I can't swear to it, I think there are tears behind his glasses as he rolls up the window, turns on the engine and the lights, and then pulls away from the curb. The last thing I am aware of, as the car moves down the street and out of the range of the streetlamps, is Murphy's nose, pressed against the rear windowpane, like a flat, black mushroom.

Long after the taillights of the Honda have been swallowed up in dark, I continue to stand on the sidewalk in front of my house, staring after the departed car. Then, as cautiously as someone feeling for broken bones, I head back to the house, warily assessing my condition.

So far, not bad. There is a trace of the panic I felt in the park, watching Murphy speed out of sight, but only a trace. Mixed with the more familiar and manageable sense of emptiness I generally experience when observing the departure of one of the Marrieds.

Overall, I feel blessed by a sensation of numbness. Which either means that the ice has buckled beneath me, and I'm submerging in half-frozen water, or am merely chilled from standing outside on a cold autumn night, clad in nothing more substantial than a sweatshirt and a pair of jeans.

I mount the porch steps, go back inside, then proceed to prowl from room to room, switching on the lights—just to prove to myself that the place is indeed empty. When I reach the bedroom, there is the message light on my answering machine, still blinking like a friendly beacon offering assurance of safe harbor just ahead.

But I still can muster no enthusiasm for my messages. Not even if it's Carl who's called, to record some declaration of irresistible ardor. Blithely unaware, of course, that the irresistibility of his ardor has now caused me to forfeit emotional currency of a more bankable kind.

Soberly, I drift into the kitchen. Where, under the lurid glow of the fluorescent light, I discover Murphy's water bowl—apparently overlooked in the grim flurry of Jerry's departure. The plastic rim is scarred with toothmarks, where Murphy picks it up, whenever it's empty, and brings it to...

Somehow, it's the sight of that gnawed dish, more than anything else, that hits me squarely in the chest. I sink down on the kitchen floor, pick up the dish, and hug it fiercely to my heart. Water slops over the rim, onto the floor, and down the front of my sweatshirt.

At long last, I am crying. Not joyously, as I did when Murphy came bounding back to me in the park of his own volition. But with a kind of ragged misery, as I face—belatedly—what it would have meant to me if he hadn't returned.

PART FOUR

Sex, Lies, and Audiotape

Chapter One

🐾 "Excuse me" is Mel's response to his discovery that I'm back. "Correct me if I'm wrong, Glass, but...didn't you have a real shot there at unloading the hairy bastard once and for all?"

"I'd rather not talk about it," Jerry says.

"I mean, if Dana was actually willing to keep him longer, then what the hell difference could it possibly make that it turns out she didn't want *you* back on a bet? Seriously, what do you care? So long as she winds up with the mutt and you're home free?"

"Didn't you hear me, Arlen? I'd rather not talk about it."

"Unless, of course, there's some cockamamy notion of revenge in play here. Like, for instance, you actually believe—for some demented reason—that you might have been *punishing* her by taking the dog?"

"You don't take a hint, do you?" Jerry asks.

"Or...how about this? Yeah, maybe *this* is more on point: You've been offered, in essence, a choice between—on the one hand—untrammeled freedom. And on the other, eternal bondage. Unfortunately, you turn out to be the sort of schmuck who—for some quirky, creepy genetic reason of his own—opts for the made-to-measure chains. Kvetching all the way, mind you—you always do. But holding out your wrists for those handcuffs, nevertheless. Sure, that's what's going on here, all right. Even so, I must say, I just don't get it."

"I don't get it either," Jerry says.

Which makes three of us. Since I, essentially, appear to have made the same choice as Jerry, for motives equally mysterious. There I was in the park—poised between the joy of running wild, and the servitude of coming back when called. So, what did I choose? Well, you remember, I'm sure, as well as I do.

What I don't understand—particularly now—is why I chose the way I did. Why I elected to behave like a good, good dog, if this is all the good it did me. I'm back at Jerry's—sadder, but effectively no wiser. In the same old rut, at the end of my same old rope, with Jerry holding grimly to the other end. And as for Dana . . . well, where is she, now that I actively need her to call?

"Although . . ." Even as Jerry and I are escorting him—somewhat pointedly—to the visitors' lot behind the building where his car is parked, Mel continues to concoct theories to explain the bizarreness of Jerry's actions . . . "For all I know, this may finally be that elusive 'mature' relationship you claimed to be seeking.

"Think about it, Glass: you and Murphy. Why not? Stranger things happen all the time on daytime talkshows, right? I mean, let's review what you've got going with the dog: lots of hassles, no days off, no hope of parole, no consensual sex—or so we hope.

"Christ, it's just like marriage. Certainly no worse. Of course, when you and the dog decide you'd like to make it legal, you might have a little trouble lining up someone to perform the ceremony. Although I hear some of those Unitarians can really be flexible."

"That," says Jerry, as he shuts Mel into his car, "is about the stupidest thing I've ever heard. Even from you."

"Which does not," says Mel, settling himself behind the wheel, "make it necessarily an untrue thing." Whereupon, he waves a jaunty farewell to Jerry and me, and backs out of the parking lot.

"The stupidest," Jerry repeats to himself. Then checks his watch, as he always does before taking me on my brief tour around the pie-shaped slice of grass across from the apartment. "All right, Murphy, you've got eleven minutes until the opening kickoff, and I've got twenty bucks on the Patriots. So the sooner you get down to business, the better."

And wouldn't I like to get down to business? To cross her mind some night when we're both sound asleep. In my dreams, I find myself searching for a point of entry. Snuffling the sill of every closed door I encounter, on the off-chance that one of those doors might open—and lead me to where she's hidden from me, to ask with my eyes: Why, why, why?

So far, no luck searching her out. Both asleep and awake, she seems to be hurrying on just ahead. Leaving no scent for me to follow, no lingering aroma of guilt, to suggest she even knows what she's done.

"Come!" she commanded. Well, I did. And now—even though she is no longer calling my name—I find the habit hard to break. 🐾

Chapter Two

Ordinarily, I hate family-type restaurants as much as O'Ryan loves them. Where the greasy aroma of burgers and Buffalo wings hangs heavy, and the kid whose booth backs on mine can always be counted upon to keep up a rhythmical kicking for the duration of my meal.

But today, any place beats my apartment—where Murphy's conspicuous absence would be bound to provoke O'Ryan to questions. Questions which, for some reason, I cannot yet face. Probably for fear the answers wouldn't look all that good on me.

"Jeez," O'Ryan is remarking, as he slots onion slices the size of LP records into the bun of his burger. "And to think, at first, we were goin' such great guns, her and me."

He's talking about Karen, of course. Just as he warned me he wanted to. One thing I'll say for O'Ryan: he'll generally announce his agenda up front, and then stick to it, regardless. Another thing I'll say for him is that nothing—including romantic calamity—ever appears to adversely affect his appetite.

"Well, I did try to tell you about Karen. She's just not like other people."

"I'll tell the world she's not. I mean, weird as this is gonna sound to you, Dana, I'm starting to get the definite feeling the nicer I am to her, the less she likes me."

"That's Karen," I agree. "What Winston Churchill called a mystery inside a riddle wrapped in an enigma, or however he put it."

"Yeah." O'Ryan is apparently ready to accept without question that Karen might have been as much a topic of interest to Churchill as she is to him. "She's a caution."

Isn't she just? But for all my disclaimers about Karen not being like other people, I can't help shifting uncomfortably. A woman with limited use for nice guys, eh? Yep, she's one for the books, all right.

"A real caution," O'Ryan continues, scooping up his hugely burdened burger in his two huge hands. "Most women I date complain I make myself too scarce. But Karen, she's just the opposite."

As he bites into his burger, I watch rivulets of assorted juices and condiments form a multicolored puddle on his plate. "Well, that's the trick, then. Try making yourself less available to her. Some women prefer men to be elusive." Gee, but I'm just a goldmine of interesting information, aren't I? If somewhat contradictory. Considering that I just got finished saying how little resemblance Karen bears to any other woman. Including, by implication, myself.

"Uh-huh," says O'Ryan, somewhat muffled by his bun. "Elusive." As if he may not know the precise meaning of the word, but is prepared to guess. "Well, whatever it is turns her crank, I better buy me a bottle of it and splash it on good. 'Cause, shit, Dana. Otherwise, I'm losin' her."

"I'm sorry." And I genuinely am—forgetting for the moment that if it's Karen we're talking about, O'Ryan is far better off for the loss. "But are you sure it's falling apart?"

"I got feelings about it. Like, maybe there's somebody else. Somebody's she's sweet on, only...maybe she's not gettin' any back?"

His leathery face is working as he brings out these painful conjectures. And I marvel—as if the idea were brand-new to me—at the amount of misery wrought by the refusal of those with whom we are obsessed to be obsessed with us. Especially when—as in O'Ryan's case—it's perfectly possible that the object of his obsession is as capable of being obsessed with some third party as O'Ryan is with her.

"Some other man..." I am probing his wound as delicately as I can. "What makes you think so?"

He shrugs. "There's just times...Dana, now, you gotta promise to stop me, okay? If this starts to sound too loco? It's just sometimes I get this feeling that, when she leaves my place, she's plannin' to... hook up with someone else. Or, not hook up, even. More like... follow 'em."

"Follow?" I find myself squirming even more uncomfortably. "As in...stalking them? Is that what you mean?" It's what *I* mean, anyway. Blurry, disjointed images out of my dreamlife begin to swim in front of my face, and I feel on the verge of needing to step outside for some air.

"Yeah, I guess," O'Ryan is saying. "I don't mean with, like, nightvision goggles or camouflage and shit like that, but...Jesus. Look at you. You think I'm crazy, right?"

Not that crazy. It's my own sanity that I'm calling into question right at this moment. These things I've caught myself concocting in my sleep...As bad dreams, they don't seem so farfetched. But somehow, the idea that I might actually know Karen better than I'm letting on...

"Look, O'Ryan," I tell him hurriedly, "you probably ought to trust these qualms. You're too nice a guy to—well, you're too nice a guy. Period."

"Yeah. That would seem to be the problem, all right." He grins at me bleakly, before demolishing his side of fries. "Anyways," he continues, chewing resolutely, "I appreciate the insight."

"Insight." I shrug deprecatingly.

"Come on, you're one savvy woman, and you know it. That's why I knew I could talk to you. Even if Karen's no more like you than...well, push is to shove."

"Yeah?" I'm grinning back at him now, or trying to. "So which one am I—push or shove? You can mull over your answer while we have dessert."

O'Ryan scans the menu, frowning, as if all the concentration he possesses is required to translate the written descriptions of the desserts into gastronomic sensations he can anticipate. I can so easily imagine him, alone in the night, frowning into space as he continues—despite my savvy insights—to try to puzzle out how to fix what's gone wrong. How it is that Karen cannot be broken with gentleness, or lovingly wrangled into compliance, or smoothed from the roughest of diamonds into the most willing of women...?

Why, I wonder—and not for the first time—could I myself not ever be content with a man like him? My recollections of our brief affair do not enlighten me on that score, any more than the affair itself did way back when. As some species of gentle giant, is how I recall thinking about O'Ryan then. Utterly blind in his guilelessness, like his namesake in mythology.

Long ago, for fun, I looked up the legend of Orion, with some notion of sharing it with the O'Ryan I knew. But, once I'd read the story, decided to pass on the sharing part. There was something too sadly apt about the blind giant, accidentally slain by his lover, the goddess Diana. Who was, in turn, tricked into it by Apollo, her scheming twin...

Not that I have ever hurt O'Ryan, unintentionally or otherwise. But I must have always suspected I could. And, perhaps, for all I can remember, that's why I ended the affair. If I, in fact, was the one who did.

Funny how I can't seem to recollect how it was O'Ryan and I stopped sleeping together. Even though I still recall so vividly how Orion and Diana ended up. Full of remorse, the goddess cut her slain lover into stars and placed him up in the heavens, along with his cloak and his club. And, of course, his faithful dog, who became a bright star in his own right, a dog star named—

"...*Amazing Grace*?"

"Pardon?" As I come to, O'Ryan is gazing at me expectantly, and looks as if he has been doing so for some time.

"That scrip fer *Amazing Grace*," he repeats. "I asked, how's it comin' on?"

He is inquiring, I know, only in the interest of conversational reciprocity. With no idea in the world that my own self is the last topic I wish to discuss today. "Oh, it's...coming along."

"It's the one with wolves, right?"

Wearily, I run my hand over my eyes, and try to remember what I've been working on. Or what, in the last day or so, I've been doing at all, apart from expecting to see Murphy's particolored face appear at various locations around my apartment. "Yes, the one with wolves. God knows what possessed me to try *that* on."

"I know what." O'Ryan beams with the smugness of a therapist breaking through the resistance of a particularly stubborn client. "You're hooked now."

"What, on *Amazing Grace*?" I scoff, and begin searching for my wallet to help with the bill. "Hooked on regular meals and making the rent. That's all any of it means to me, or ever did. Ask Karen, if you don't believe me."

"Problem with you, Dana, is you never let on what you care about. Like that big old dog of yours you always low-rate."

He means that big old dog I have forever forfeited the right to low-rate. Through my fault, through my fault, through my most grievous fault. I refrain from correcting O'Ryan on Murphy's ownership, as he slides a couple of loonies under his saucer for a tip and precedes me to the cash register.

Outside, I wait wordlessly while he fumbles for the key to his awful old car. A big bumbling stationwagon—of similar bulk to O'Ryan's Pontiac—is pulling away from the space just ahead. And I note it only because it seems familiar somehow.

I catch a fleeting glimpse of a gaggle of children, a blond woman, and a dark-haired man behind the wheel. Surely it's Carl. But surely not. Carl's been suddenly called out of town. At least, according to the message on my machine I finally got around to retrieving.

Now, as the car disappears down the street, I can't even be certain that the driver was a man, much less a man I know. Or, for that matter, whether the car was actually all that similar to the one that belongs to Carl's wife.

All I'm left with, as I climb in beside O'Ryan, is a lingering impression of a homely old stationwagon full of what may have been a couple of adults and some kids. Possibly fresh from a family-style outing—at the selfsame restaurant O'Ryan and I have just now departed. Which, if true, only confirms it couldn't have been Carl. Since I would have noticed him, on my way in or out.

"...in or out?"

Once again, belatedly, I realize that I am being spoken to. "Sorry, O'Ryan. What did you say?"

"I said, maybe it's time I took a stand with Karen. Once and for all ask her if she's in or out. What do you think?"

"I think," I say without hesitation, "that you should do precisely that. Confront her with your suspicions, pin her down about her feelings. Whatever it takes to put an end to these endless speculations."

My vehemence startles me as much as it does O'Ryan, perhaps even more. "What I mean," I amend, "is that the hell you know is generally preferable to the one you don't."

Oh, really? And if I'm so sure about that, why don't I follow my own advice? Because Carl has gone to Halifax, that's why. And to imagine anything else is sheer lunacy.

"Could be." O'Ryan nods soberly as he navigates his way around a stalled U-Haul. "Could be that's the way to go. I mean, since it's a little late fer me to start playin' hard-to-git, right?"

I have the feeling I should be paying closer attention than I am to O'Ryan's problem. In view of my status as the "one savvy woman" in his life. It's just that right at the moment my mind is on Carl. Who has most definitely arrived in Halifax by now, and will soon be calling me to prove it. And that's an end to it.

"You don't need to play at anything, O'Ryan. Yourself is plenty good enough. And at this point in the relationship, some honesty is surely in order."

"Right." He is still nodding along as he signals a turn onto my street.

"Oh, don't bother turning. This corner is fine."

"Come on. I'll take you to yer door—maybe stop in, say hey to ol' Murph."

"Here is just fine," I repeat, with a sick sinking feeling as I prepare to lie to my old and dear friend. "You can say hey to Murphy some other time."

270 • Erika Ritter

"Dana...is there something wrong?"

"Not a thing. Thanks for the ride."

But surely he can't help noting that I'm not meeting his eye as I swing shut the heavy car door. Then hurry off with sudden, unexplained urgency.

Chapter Three

Ring!

I'm not asleep. Not really. Not until Carl's call comes, as promised, to confirm that he's in Halifax, where—although it's an hour later—he can't possibly get to sleep, either, until—

Ring!

—until he's called to let me know that, even a time zone ahead, the moments without me are crawling slowly by as he—

Ring!

"Hello?"

"Hullo yourself. Sorry to waken you."

"No, no you didn't. I was reading." One of my customary lies. The lights are out; the book's been splayed on my chest for an hour or more. But instead of admitting that, I switch on the lamp beside the bed—for some reason intent on giving Carl the impression, even at long distance, that I'm still open for business, whatever the hour.

"You got my message, then, did you?"

"The message where you said you'd been called away suddenly on business to Halifax? Yes, I got that message. Boo. Hiss."

"Yes, 'boo, hiss' exactly. I'd far rather be with you. All warm and compliant under the covers." His voice is right up against my ear. As suggestive as ever, slightly husky, with that familiar roughness of a scratchy wool blanket.

"It sounds almost as if you are here. As if you're right around the corner. Are you sure you're all the way out in the Maritimes?"

"Am I sure?" He chuckles into my ear. "Well, now, let's review: fog for miles, constant rain...Yes, I reckon it's the Maritimes, all right."

I can, in fact, hear a foghorn through the receiver, somewhere in the background, groaning faintly in anguish like some prehistoric animal trapped in a tar pit. "I wish to hell you'd invited me to join you, Carl. Instead of leaving me with nothing but a jaunty little message on my machine. 'I say, gone to Halifax for a bit. Will ring. Not to worry. Cheerio, and all that.'"

"Come on, that's *not* how I said it—not like something out of an Ealing comedy."

"You did. 'Carry on Sleuthing,' or whatever. Anyway, the point is, if I were there, we'd be having this conversation bundled up in bed together, listening to those foghorns and feeling no pain. Too bad you never thought of asking me along."

"I did think of it. Mere moments before I thought of what you'd dream up by way of excuse for not coming along. Murphy, most likely, and the lack of anyone masochistic enough to mind the old flea-motel in your absence."

I still can't bring myself to admit out loud that the old flea-motel has exited my life. Not that Carl would be all that devastated; it's simply that I can't trust myself to relay the news without sounding devastated myself. As if Carl needs to be protected, somehow, from evidence of my emotions—including and particularly the extent to which my emotions are inextricably twined around him.

"Be that as it may," I say instead, "if I *were* there, we'd be having fun. Right?"

"Fun! Don't even speak of it, sweetheart. Not when I'm looking like being stuck here a few more days."

"More days?" My groan competes with the foghorn. "Why? What's this case you're working on out there, anyway?"

"Oh, the case is simple enough. Some...dead-beat dad. The usual story."

"What story is that?"

"Oh, you know, poor misunderstood bloke, no longer able to

front up like a man and take responsibility for the kids he's sired, or the mess he's made of—Well, never mind."

"No, wait a sec. 'Misunderstood,' you said. How's that? Sounds more like you've got him all figured out."

"Yes, indeed." Carl laughs, somewhat harshly. "I've got him dead to rights, poor bugger."

I feel a sudden sense of uneasiness. As if Carl and I both know the poor bugger he's talking about, almost too intimately. "That's good," I say quickly. "I mean, you'll be coming back, now that you've got him, right?"

"Well, I would be. Only now, see, the airport's fogged in. Which, in these parts, is no laughing matter."

"I'm not laughing, believe me."

"There's no telling when I'll get out. The word is, by mid-week the fog'll clear off. Personally, I'm clinging to that."

I, meanwhile, am clinging to the receiver, trying to coax compensatory warmth from Carl on the other end. "You do sound nearby, though." I switch off the light, the better to attend whatever blandishments I can wheedle from him. "Talk to me, Carl. Tell me what we'd be doing right now, if I were there with you in your hotel."

"Oh, Christ." His sigh is gusty in the receiver. "It doesn't bear thinking about, does it?"

Nevertheless, it's all I *am* thinking about. As I cuddle deeper down in bed, willing him to talk such a good game to me that both of us can go around the links together—even at this remove—at about five strokes under par. "Just tell me. I miss you so much. What's your hotel room like?"

"My room? Quite lovely, actually. Much more old-fashioned than the Arlington. Here, for instance, there's this quaint old claw-footed bathtub, the approximate size of a velodrome. D'you know what I've always fancied doing in a tub like this? I'll tell you: ordering down to room service for—I don't know—at least fifty banana cream pies. I mean, I reckon fifty would do it, don't you?"

"Well," I reply, "that depends." And I settle even deeper in the dark, nuzzling the receiver cheek to cheek. "On what you plan to do with fifty banana cream pies, in a big old bathtub."

"I don't know. Suppose you tell me."

"Well, maybe—and this is just a thought—maybe what you'd like to do is climb into that tub with me and all those pies, and...I don't know...lick the filling off me, inch by inch?"

"Christ, woman. Your tongue."

"Funnily, I was thinking more about yours. Like, really *thinking* about it."

"Oh, you were. And what were you thinking, specifically?"

"Come on, I thought this was *your* fantasy. Climbing into the tub with all those coconut cream pies."

"Banana cream, I said. Pay attention. You see, first I'd order down to room service. For about—I don't know—let's say fifty banana cream pies. I should think fifty would about do it, don't you?"

"Wait a minute. Isn't this where I came in?"

"I don't know, sweetheart, is it? Just so long as you came."

"Oh, God, Carl, this is ridiculous. When are you coming home?"

"I told you, as soon as I'm able. As soon as my erection permits me to walk. As soon as this bloody fog lifts."

Suddenly, I'm uneasy again, and a shiver passes through me. Almost as if I were in a hotel bathtub—all by myself, naked and cold on a foggy Maritime night, under a chilly mountain of creepy, gelatinous cream pie filling. "Look, about this dead-beat dad you brought to bay. Why *isn't* he able to front up and take responsibility for the kids he's sired and the mess he's made?"

"I really couldn't say. Sweetheart, what's all this about?"

I really couldn't say, either. Absurdly, I'm seized by the urge to tell Carl about the stationwagon I saw earlier, and the man at the wheel that I thought was him. "Carl," I say, still fighting the urge, "do you...Is it really lonely without me, in Halifax?"

An almost audible twitch of impatience on the other end of the phone. "What sort of question is that?"

The sort of question I could kick myself for asking. Yet, no topic seems safe right at the moment, so I might as well plunge on. "Listen, when you get back, I have an idea."

"So have I. You don't think I was joking about those pies?"

"An additional idea. I...Isn't it time I met your kids?"

There is an intake of breath on Carl's end. "I beg your pardon?"

I can tell, however, that he's heard me quite clearly. "Your children. They're so important to you, and yet...I wouldn't even recognize them if I saw them on the street."

"Look," he says, very carefully, "I've no idea what you're on about, but can we not wait to discuss it till I get back?"

He's right, of course. And no more than he do I have any real idea of what I'm on about. Or why, tonight of all nights. "When you get back. Whenever that is."

"I told you, when the fog lifts and—"

"And oh, God, let's not run through all that again."

"No, let's not. In fact, I think we ought to ring off. I've a hankering to take a midnight plunge in the hotel pool."

"There's a pool in your old-fashioned hotel? Open at this hour?"

"Even so. In fact, the claw-footed bathtub apart, this is a most up-to-date establishment."

"Sounds perfect. If I didn't know better, I'd say you made up this hotel in Halifax, and furnished it to your own specifications."

"Of course, if I *were* inventing a hotel, I reckon I'd plunk it down on the Riviera in season, and give the rain and foghorns a miss."

I reckon he would, at that. "And you're really going to go swimming in the middle of the night?"

"Not for long. Just a few quick lengths, all by myself."

As he says so, I can picture the cool, streamlined rush of his body, cutting through the blue-tinted water of the pool as cleanly as a porpoise. I can imagine him diving down and down beneath the surface, far below the sound of my voice. And beyond the reach of all the other voices calling and calling to him from the apron of the pool. I can see him growing smaller and smaller, moving farther and farther out of focus—like a dot disappearing on a screen, like that small fuzzy shape that was Murphy that day in the park dancing on the edge of the horizon, and then out of sight.

"Carl..." I strive to keep any tinge of panic from leaching into the telephone wires that connect me to him. "Come home as soon as you can. I'll be waiting. In the bathtub, under a mountain of banana cream pies."

"Yes? Now, that's a promise. I'm holding you to it, sweetheart. Holding you and holding you."

"I love you."

"And I you. Surest thing you know. G'night."

Just before I cradle the receiver, I hear a departing chorus of foghorns at Carl's end, offering the gloomy promise of at least another day—and more—of fogbound loneliness. I burrow far beneath the blankets. Down and down, like a deep-sea diver—to where Carl, warm and constant at the bottom of the ocean, waits to wrap me in his arms.

Chapter Four

In my dream, it's as if I've managed—without effort or explanation—to trail the stationwagon full of Carl's kids from the curb where I first spotted it, to a huge family-type restaurant way up on the highway.

It's the kind of place about which I know nothing in waking life yet in my sleep am readily able to recognize. Where at least one child in tow is required as a ticket of admission to a fantasyland of Formica tabletops, plastic chairs bolted in place, and decals of dinosaurs smiling folksily from the walls. Kids are milling everywhere, in big baggy shorts and baseball caps worn peak-to-back. There are dads in T-shirts, moms in jean jackets, and grandmothers along for the ride in pantsuits of pastel hues, like Necco wafers.

Even more amazingly, unaccompanied adult though I am, I am allowed inside and permitted to sit where I want. When I choose my table, I realize that I am right next to Carl and his family. They are seated by a big panoramic window, through which dull afternoon sunlight comes streaming, to touch the bright hair of his two daughters. Contrary to what I said to Carl on the phone, I would know his children anywhere. Including little Toby—dark like Carl, his face streaked with condiments of ghastly shades not found in nature, his eyes full of obvious appreciation for Good Old Dad.

Good Old Carl, that is, seen here in the role in which, I sense, he likes himself best: as a purveyor of low-brow treats, and an instigator of impromptu outings. He glances my way, and I stiffen. But then, as his glance carries on past me, I recollect with relief that here I am invisible. The Other Woman, who for all intents and purposes does not exist.

Carl is smiling the general smile of someone used to keeping up appearances. He is, I instinctively understand, a seasoned veteran of such jaunts as this. Trips to Wonderland, to Marineland, to Safariland, to Frontierland, and to all the other lands that lie in between. A survivor of every species of magical kingdom in which an obliging parent can expect to be nuzzled by dolphins, perched on by parrots, molested by mandrills, and drenched by his own offspring as they come screaming down the World's Wildest Waterslide.

All of which Carl relishes as a rule. Yet, today, seems unable to give himself over to as wholeheartedly as he should. As if there is some elusive corner of his mind (and I am so close to that place I believe I can map it) toward which his thoughts keep sliding, unbidden.

He has barely as yet even glanced at his wife. Prettier in a pouty way than I would have chosen to imagine her, and determinedly languid, as highly strung women so often are.

"Look here, kids." Vivien speaks up so suddenly that I jump. "Why don't you all run off to play for a bit? Gemma, be a darling and take them off to that playroom, with all those masses of Styrofoam balls to jump in. You'd like that, Toby, wouldn't you? Off you go, then."

The children exchange a quick look, then obediently disappear to the other room. Leaving his wife to smile brightly at Carl. "Well! Alone at last. A bit more of a novelty for *me*, of course, than for you—getting shed of the kids."

"Look," says Carl, "before you start in—"

"Who's starting in?"

"I'm serious, Viv. You promised: no *Sturm und Drang*, provided I came back home for a few days. Well, I've done that—more days than I'd planned on—and now it's—"

"And now it's back to the swinging bachelor life."

"Hardly that."

"Oh, right. Pull the other one, Carl. It's got bells on it."

"Oh, Christ, Vivien, there's no point in running over it end-lessly, is there?"

"None whatever. Not until you leave off pretending that you don't bring women to your little lair and screw their brains out. Which—given the sort you fancy—shouldn't be much of an under-taking."

Her voice has risen to a combative register that prompts Carl to pitch his own lower, as a cue to her to do the same. "Not much of a compliment to yourself, is it, old darling?" he observes softly. "A crack like that?"

Nor to me, either. Although, under the circumstances, I can hardly expect him to defend the caliber of woman he screws.

Vivien falls silent, and begins to pick at a scab of loose plaster with her fingernail. Carl, I can tell, feels genuinely sorry for her. At the same time, I can sense his rising anger. *Stop picking at the paint, will you?* he longs to snap at her. And for a moment, he is seized by the desire to reach over, shake her, and roughly demand that she do some ironing once in a while, organize the kids' lunches for a change, at least run the Hoover up the stairs. And then—only then—come at him with her litany of accusations.

In my dream, I can tell all this, and yet also readily deduce that he is not the sort who could ever bring himself to manhandle a woman. Instead, he is the sort who chooses to choke back his anger, to soothe and cajole. Only once that strategy has failed can he be counted on to retreat into his private life, within his private self. Like a runaway child hiding out under the stairs, where no one can find him out.

"Sod you," Vivien declares at last, in a quiet voice almost with-out rancor.

"Christ, your language. Do you go on like that in front of the kids?"

"If you stayed home once in a sodding while, you might sodding well know how I go on in front of the kids, mightn't you?"

She has, at least, given up picking at the plaster, and the anger seems to have drained from her face, if not from her words. Carl—looking at the woman he used to love and perhaps still does—considers the extent to which what has happened between himself and Vivien is his own fault. Especially since, by anybody's reckoning, he's emerged as the lucky one. With his own place, however hotly contested, his own life, however fragmented, and a job that brings with it a steady supply of fresh adventures.

On the other side of the ledger, there's Viv. Stuck—as she laments often enough—in a raw, uncouth country she's never taken to. In a neighborhood she regards as poky, and in the house all day with a pre–school-aged child—conceived, Carl has always suspected, through some desperate design to keep her marriage at least somewhat intact.

"Viv," he says, with enough real feeling to startle them both. "I'm sorry. Truly I am. For everything."

At that, she reaches out—quite suddenly—beneath the table, to cup her hand just behind his knee, in an old, familiar gesture of affection. Then marches her fingers up his leg, toward his groin. Which startles him even more.

Equally surprising is his own response. Since he is—in spite of every resolve he's ever made—powerfully aroused. Still available to her in this one arena as he is no longer available to her in any other. Sitting at the next table as I am, witnessing what I wish I were not seeing, I cannot decide who's sorrier—Carl or me—to perceive how his passion for his wife remains on active duty, no matter what.

"Oh, sorry, is it?" she whispers across the table. "How sorry, I wonder? I'd be interested in some proof of the pudding."

"What?" Carl can't help laughing. "Here and now, you mean? On a Formica tabletop, amongst the kids and the clowns and the wilted chips? You know, sweetheart, you really are barking mad."

"Never mind *me*," she replies, her fingers teasing their way farther up his pantleg. "What about you, you selfish get? Are you in, or out?"

Carl cannot seem to resist. Next thing he knows, he's leaning toward her across the cluttered tabletop, until his lips are almost against hers. "In," he whispers harshly. "What do you think?"

"Yes?" Suddenly cool, she pushes him away, smooths her skirt, and regards him dispassionately. "Well, that's something to keep in mind, isn't it? Oh, look..." Without even turning around, she has anticipated the return of the two girls and Toby, red-cheeked and breathless, to the table. "Here are the children, fresh from that room full of colored balls. And what color are *yours*, I wonder, Carl, right at the moment? An interesting tinge of blue, I should expect."

More furious with himself than with her, Carl tries to will away the erection she's coaxed from him purely for spite as he forces himself to smile at Andrea, Toby, and Gemma, all slithering back into their bolted plastic chairs. Thank God at least for them.

He is prompted to wish—and not for the first time—that the love of his three children could, somehow, be enough. Despite the fact that—even as he wishes for it—he knows it is not. Not even at this moment, sitting in a fast-food family restaurant up on the highway, basking in the straightforward devotion of his kids, with the uncertain sunlight slanting through windows slightly filmed with dust. Already Carl has begun to think of being someplace else, is already beginning to hanker to be on his way. If not on the way to bed with his wife, then on his way to bed with someone else.

Perhaps with me. Perhaps nestled in my arms, reveling in the pleasure of my ferocious devotion. Finding himself a moment of respite, a safe harbor, before his craving to be yet somewhere else overtakes him again, and forces him out of my bed and back to his kids—strewing alibis like rose petals along his path.

The moment the children have settled back down at the table, Vivien gets up—as if on cue—to head for the Ladies'. There is a hint of conspiracy in the glance she shoots at Gemma before she departs. And sure enough, no sooner has their mother disappeared from view than Carl finds all three of his offspring gazing at him with naked expectation.

"Well?" he demands jovially. "Is the world-famous Bill E. Bee up to snuff? Or is it—"

"Daddy..." Gemma, clearing her throat, assumes the role of the eldest, forever fated to play bad cop in her dealings with delinquent Dad. "How long are you planning on having your own room?"

Carl winces at the accuracy of that. A "room," I suspect, is really what it amounts to: a place that's no great distance, from which he can be recalled at a moment's notice, whenever his presence is required at the family fireside.

"I don't know," he tells his daughter truthfully.

All three of them continue to stare at him, unimpressed with this response—even Toby, who may be merely at the age where he's learned how to ape his sisters' more adult disapproval.

"But it's been so nice the past few days," Gemma points out. "Having you back home every night with Mummy and us. Quite like old times, really."

Quite like...? Oh, Christ, he thinks. That's Viv's voice talking. He doesn't blame Gemma, not in the slightest. Rather, his heart aches for her. His eldest, his favorite, with her round dark eyes that make her look to him like a Madonna in miniature. For whom the crumbled world of her parents' failures must always remain something of a sorrowful mystery.

"Look," he hears himself arguing, "I *have* invited you to my... room to spend the night, whenever you'd like."

"But we'd have to sleep in sleeping bags on the *floor*," Andrea informs him with disdain. "Mummy says we'd catch our death."

Gemma shifts in her chair, plainly impatient to steer this meeting back on track. "The point is, Daddy, we'd like you to be living at home all the time."

"I know what you'd like," he says, feeling like the derelict father in some old melodrama, whose children have no choice but to seek him out at the bar-room door. "And I've tried to accommodate by spending as much time with you as I can. But the point is..."

The point is what, precisely? How can he possibly explain to them what he fails to understand himself: how it is that he continues to crave, more than anything, to be a kid again. Like them. *Kids*, he would like to entreat them, all three. *Kids, don't put me on the other side of the barrier with the grownups. Or, if you're determined to put me there, at least, for my sake, keep yourselves on the children's side for-ever. Make it your mission to succeed somehow, where I have failed, by simply staying young forever.*

"All right, Daddy," Gemma is continuing briskly. "What about stretching out *this* visit a few more days? Because, you know, Mummy cries. She cries when you're not home."

Crikey, thinks Carl, it *is* a bloody melodrama. "Sweetheart, did... did Mummy tell you to tell me about the crying?" There really is no way out, he thinks meanwhile. And with that thought comes a cold clutch of dismay grasping at the back of his neck. The dismay of the habitual runaway, once more frog-marched out of his hiding place.

"Of *course* I didn't tell her to tell you!" Unnoticed, Vivien has re-turned from the ladies' room. "I can't help it, can I, if she's old enough to observe that the way we're living is no way to live?"

"Look," says Carl, in as controlled a tone as he can manage. "Hadn't you and I best talk about this privately?"

"When? Her smile is painfully bright—as if she, not he, were conscientiously keeping up appearances in front of the kids. "Just give me some idea when, and we'll talk."

When? All he can think about, right this minute, is how badly he needs some time to himself, talking to no one. Away from all his women—short and tall, young and less young, reproachful or fero-ciously devoted.

"Carl," Vivien prompts. "Pay the check, and when we get home, we'll set the kids up with a video and have a chat. How's that?"

Carl is, I can readily see, holding on just barely to some idea of a space—or at least the illusion of a space—in which he can continue to breathe. "All right, but I can't stay over. See, I've got work wait-ing that won't wait. Something out of town, and I've not even packed."

"Oh? This is the first I've heard of it."

"Even so." He concentrates on peeling bills from his wallet. "I'm on my way out of town. To Halifax."

"And *after* Halifax?" This from Gemma, as avidly on the case, it seems, as any detective. "When you come back, will you stay home with us?"

"Oh, sweetheart..." With infinite tenderness, Carl reaches out to stroke the cheek of this child whose dark eyes always threaten to drown him in their sorrowful depths. "Just let me go and come back. Then we'll talk about what's next."

As Vivien hustles Toby into his jacket and herds her brood out of the restaurant, I can't help but note how Carl casts the slightest glance in passing at my table, as if puzzled to note that it seems unoccupied. Before hurrying to the cash to pay, and then continuing to hurry after his departing family.

The next thing I know, Carl is through the front doors and gone. Still unaware that I've followed him in my sleep—to a place neither of us ever dreamed we'd wind up traveling together.

Chapter Five

The bedroom where Carl and I lately lay, making languorous morning love, is still heavy with the odor of intimacy. Sex hangs in the air like gunpowder; the entire room seems in a state of shock, like the site of some recently committed crime.

What an idea. I allow my mind to trace a chalk outline on the mattress—where our two bodies once sprawled—and run a police-line-do-not-cross tape around the posters of the bed, in order to secure the scene for further investigation. As if, any minute now, the boys from forensics might arrive, to dust for prints and snap a few photos.

The notion of photographs, for some reason, appeals to me. Like images to develop in the darkroom of memory—and then consign forever to some album of oblivion marked "The Past."

Which is, of course, ridiculous. Since Carl has only left for his office, not for good. Within the hour, he'll likely be calling me to tell me how wonderful it was to come back last night. Within a few more hours, I'll be hearing him bounding up the front steps. And within an hour of that, we'll be back in bed again.

Even so, this peculiar feeling of postmortem seems to linger. I find myself reluctant to get on briskly with the business of the day, unwilling to obliterate the evidence of the love we've made. Instead, I continue to stand and stare, the crumpled comforter I intended to smooth across the bed still hanging lankly in my arms.

Last night, when Carl turned up unexpectedly at the door, with a smile of triumph on his face and airline tags dangling from his luggage, it was—simultaneously—as if he'd been gone forever and no time at all.

"Taken you by surprise, have I? Yes, that was the plan. I came straight from the airport, haven't even shaved—sorry. I was that desperate to see you. Plus, of course, eager as always to catch you in the act."

He couldn't resist hamming it up by checking the closets for the other men he likes to pretend I accommodate in his absence. Although the truth is that since Carl has been somewhat steadily on the scene, I've not been much at home to the Marrieds. The Marrieds are a little disappointed by that, although not, of course, crushed. While, for me, this new and unexpected appetite for fidelity is something I don't like to think about. Not even last night, as I stood by pretending to be amused while Carl pretended to be suspicious.

"I was *hours* in bloody Halifax airport," he went on to explain, rummaging in his bag for the gifts he'd brought. "Waiting for the fog to lift, and *determined* this time not to go back to the hotel until it did. Then, when it did, all of a sudden, I'd only a moment to snatch up a couple of stupid things on my way to the gate."

He thrust at me a plastic bag from "In-Flite Boutiques Inc." "It's only some scent. Sorry. None too original. But the gift selection wasn't what it might be. Still, I even managed to find something for Murphy. Look: a plastic Pluto, filled with bubble-bath. Where is he, anyway, the old flea-motel?"

"Gone," I said. "My—his owner came and took him home."

"Oh!" I could see Carl striving to keep his expression neutral as he tried to evaluate the effect of this development on me. "Did... Was that okay, then?"

I shrugged, equally neutral. "As I told you, the arrangement was only temporary. Anyway, I'm happy *you're* here, all right?"

As Carl wrapped his arms around me, I could feel the warmth of his body through his coat. And could detect the faint, not unpleasant, tang of his sweat. Unlike the other men of my acquaintance who choose not to wear deodorant out of some odd allegiance to their masculinity, Carl has not made a choice that someone should take him aside and frankly discuss. He smells good to me always, no matter what. Never better than last night, when I stood there clinging to him as though I'd literally reclaimed him from the fog.

And now, this morning, standing in my bedroom, which is still rich with the recollection of what happened next, I smile reminiscently into space. And yet still cannot seem to rid myself of the notion that something is out of whack. Not evidence of a crime, exactly, but some detail, some niggling inconsistency that doesn't quite fit the rest of the picture.

So that when I actually notice the bag in a corner of the bedroom, it is with a sense that I have been aware of it for some time. It's a leather shoulder bag of Carl's that I vaguely recognize. In fact, I can almost recall it hanging from his shoulder when he arrived last night. He must have forgotten to take it this morning, when he put his valise in his car and headed for work.

Or else, he's left it here intentionally. Since he is, after all, planning to come back tonight. For all I know, this bag contains his shaving kit, a toothbrush, a change of underwear. The overnight accoutrements of a part-time lover—suddenly seized by the impulse to stake a firmer claim by leaving a few things behind.

That idea makes me smile even more broadly. It's not a bit like Carl, and yet it is: the notion of him leaving the bag behind—accidentally-on-purpose—as a way of informing both me and himself that he'd like to ratchet the affair up another notch.

It's an appealing notion, and it would make sense for me simply to go with it. To leave the bag in the corner where Carl left it, and see what he says about it tonight. And yet...

Even as I walk over to it, sit down on the floor beside it, and frankly begin to explore its contents, I can't explain to myself what I think I'm doing. Or why I think I should be doing it. There's no excuse for this intrusion. No one has conferred on me the right to play Pandora, or treat Carl's personal property like evidence I've collected under warrant. Nevertheless, it's what I seem to be doing.

Inside the bag, I find a handful of airline baggage tags. YUL, YYX, EWR, LGA, LAX...Along with the tags, I find several more In-Flite Boutiques Inc. bags folded flat, identical to the one in which Carl brought my cologne and Murphy's bubble-bath. Otherwise, there is only the mini tape recorder I recall from the Arlington, and a modest array of tapes, each one with a minutely printed label. "Hospital B.G" reads one. "D'town Bar," says another, and "Fog. Hbr. B.G." still another.

"Fog. Hbr. B.G" What does that mean? Nothing much to me, as I juggle the cassette thoughtfully in my hand. I feel self-conscious, painfully reminded of myself, years ago, both seeking and yet lacking the will to seek the truth about my marriage. Now, as then, suffused with embarrassment, as if I were being observed on the brink of choosing between criminality and cowardice.

Thank God that at least Murphy's not here to stare at me with steady reproach. Or else—more likely—to pant encouragement. Well? his yellow eyes would demand scornfully. *Well? What are you waiting for? Let's do it.*

"In a minute," I promise aloud. Just as if he were on hand to hear me.

In a minute? If Murphy were indeed on hand, he wouldn't put up with the old stalling routine. Instead, he'd sit here wondering, with wordless eloquence, exactly what I think I can establish about this tape simply by holding it—apart from its probable weight.

All right, then, Murphy. You win. Let's do it. Deliberately willing myself to conclude nothing negative, I snap the "Fog. Hbr. B.G." cassette into Carl's tape recorder, and hit the Play button. After a moment, a sound that I instantly recognize begins droning on the tape. The long, intermittent groaning of foghorns. The same sad cacophony I remember hearing in the background when Carl phoned me from his hotel in fogbound Halifax. Sounding as if he were right around the corner.

My mind jumps impulsively to a conclusion—and then shies abruptly away, like a horse refusing a difficult fence. How is it possible to love someone the way I love Carl Hart—and still not know the first thing about him? Or not want to know. In a panic, I begin to whisk away the evidence. I eject the cassette from the machine, bundle tape recorder, tapes, and airline tags back into the shoulder bag, and shove the whole affair back into the corner. "This is all your goddamn fault," I storm irrationally at the unseen Murphy. "Now look what you made me do."

But Murphy, invisible except for the lingering memory of those knowing eyes, only continues to stare back at me. With that characteristic expression of his that suggests he hasn't seen anything in the last few minutes that he hasn't already seen a dozen times before.

⊱┈◈┈○┈◈┈⊰

It takes a moment for me to register the sound of footsteps on the porch, and then the jingle of keys. I have no idea how long I've been sitting here, on the edge of my as-yet-unmade bed, with my hands folded foolishly in my lap.

"Hi!" Carl rushes in, a little breathless. "I was virtually downtown, would you believe it, before I realized I'd left something."

"Yes, you did." I can only marvel at how steady my voice sounds, as I reach for the shoulder bag and hand it to him. Although, there may be something amiss in my manner at that—judging from the way Carl hesitates to accept the bag. As though suddenly wondering whether it contains a bomb.

"Is something the matter?" he asks.

"I...Carl, I looked inside."

"Did you?" He is smiling—a little puzzled, perhaps, but not in the least alarmed. "Whatever for?"

"That's what I wonder myself. Whatever for?"

"Well, I've always said as much..." He comes toward me, intending to forgive my curiosity with a kiss. "There's a bit of detective in all of us."

"Carl..." I turn away from the kiss. "I played one of those tapes. The foghorns."

If this is meant, however obscurely, as an accusation, Carl is certainly not taking it as such. Too late, it occurs to me that I'm going about this all wrong, just as I always did with Mark: blurting out my perplexity in ill-formed fragments, and at the same time begging him with my eyes to elude me in a way that will enable us both to slip off the hook.

"Ah, right, the foghorns. I taped them down at Halifax harbor. Did I not tell you that I do that sometimes—the way someone else might snap a photo, or buy a souvenir postcard?" And now Carl is literally closing the case by zipping the bag firmly shut and hoisting the strap over his shoulder.

"And those baggage tags, and the plastic bags from the airport giftshop? More souvenirs of your trip?"

Carl continues to take a light-hearted approach to this mini-inquisition. "Yes, all right, if you like. Nicking anything that's not nailed down...It's another quirk of mine. A legacy, perhaps, of my years in law enforcement. The old copper-helping-himself-to-an-apple-from-a-pushcart routine." Suddenly, he seems to be explaining too much, and yet saying nothing.

"But you came all the way back here, just for this bag. Why?"

"Dana..." No longer smiling, Carl puts the bag down on the bed. "What on Earth is this about?"

"I...don't know." My voice has gone tremulous, like a child's. "It's just...Carl, I think you're cheating on me with your wife." And then—as if to shield myself from the absurdity of what I've said—I bury my face in my hands and begin to cry.

"Good God." Carl sits down beside me on the bed and takes me in his arms. For a moment, it's a liberty I permit. For a moment I allow myself to feel the familiar rough caress of his wool jacket against my cheek, to breathe in his familiar aroma, to take familiar shelter in his embrace. As if to impress on myself—firmly and finally—that this is how it felt to be loved by Carl Hart.

"You know, sweetheart, I've been accused of many things in my time. But never of being too much the family man."

"Still...it wouldn't be so hard, would it? To convince me—or your wife, if it comes to that—that you were out of town. Any time you wanted to be out of touch?"

"No, I suppose it wouldn't. Except, as it happens, I *was* out of town. Look here." Carl now seems to be over his puzzlement, and has grasped what is required of him. He continues to sit on my bed holding me in his arms, and speaks to me in a voice that is husky and tender and utterly, utterly believable. "You mustn't do this. You absolutely mustn't. I was stuck in bloody Halifax days longer than I expected to be, and missed you every sodding second. You have no cause to believe anything else."

I was—I now begin to realize—rifling his bag in search of some secret weapon. Some antidote to the panic that's come of building my love on such shifting sand, in a wholly mutable realm, where Carl might be with any one at all—and might *be* anyone at all—despite what he claims to the contrary.

Yet, along with the panic has come a craving for him expressly bred by his elusiveness. Something exhilarating in that deep deep dive that never quite takes me to the bottom. Today, what has come clear at last is how much I've actively required the uncertainty of this enterprise that has brought with it its own kind of assurance. What I have with Carl—*all* I have with Carl—is the comfort of knowing that I am free to love him as much as I want. With the surety that, however much that is, it will never be enough.

With the Marrieds, I've long been in the habit of knowing my need for limits. Even with Mark, I came to see how much I counted on elusiveness as part of his charm. But Carl? I haven't wanted to want him that way. Or haven't wanted to believe it of myself. But the truth is, much as Murphy seems to be here even when he isn't, Carl isn't ever here—not quite—even when he is. And up till this minute, that's been fine with me.

"Carl, I'd like to believe you, but…the stories keep changing. I mean, now it's your years in law enforcement. You never told me that."

"Certainly I did. My stint with the police force, up in Scotland. You must remember that?"

"No, I don't. Was it before or after you fell off that tank-turret and got cashiered?"

"No, no, it was the *cops* who cashiered me. In Leith, it was. Not a word of a lie—just like the old tongue-twister: 'The Leith police dismisseth us.' Now, surely, you remember my telling you?"

Where the panic comes in, even now, I see, is when the reflexive desire to know him completely, to possess him entirely, collides with the dizzying realization that the more he lets slip, the less I actually end up knowing—or need ever know. Whatever Carl seeks to bring me, he can't make a present of himself. He can't bundle up the truth in an In-Flite Boutiques Inc. bag and hand it to me with a convincing flourish. And for me there's as much relief as regret in knowing that. "No," I tell him. "I can't recall you ever reciting the old tongue-twister. Anyway, shouldn't it be—grammatically—'The Leith police *dismiss* us'?"

"Dana, for Christ's sake. I really have no idea what you're on about."

Why does he keep saying that, when he knows as well as I do what I'm on about? About nothing and everything—and the very thin line that separates them. "I don't want to be lied to anymore, Carl. At least, I've maybe come to the point where I *think* I don't. But just to be on the safe side...you ought to get out of here, before I decide I prefer to be lied to, after all."

The look on his face is now one of bafflement and pain. "You... want me to leave? For good?"

"It doesn't *feel* very good. But I hope it will."

"Look, I know that I seem to have upset you, and I'd like to make it up, whatever it is. Because the last thing I ever want to do is hurt you."

I nod in sober accord. "I'm not too crazy about that idea myself." Today, for the first time, Carl looks his age to me. There's a glint of gray in his dark hair that I never noticed before, and some strained-looking lines around his eyes. Although, for all I know, they may well have been there all the time.

"I have not lied to you, and I'm not lying now. But perhaps what you want is a bit of...breathing space. A few days off from me. God knows, I could afford to spend some evenings at home with my kids."

Has he spoken of it as "home" all along? Or is it simply that today I am noticing that he's never really lived any place else? Which may have suited me, too, his willing co-conspirator. Don't ask, don't tell, don't pursue, and other poems.

"I've got a better idea. Why don't you just move back home once and for all? Instead of running yourself ragged with cover-ups?" But no matter what I am saying, I am also continuing to cry, quietly and unspectacularly, like a leaking pipe.

"Don't cry, sweetheart. For Christ's sake, don't. I'm not worth this *Sturm und Drang*. And I'm not the master criminal you give me credit for being. In actual fact, I'm just...ordinary."

Yes, I would like to believe that. A conventional man, for the most part, whose bids for freedom are circumscribed, and manifest themselves in petty larcenies, in modest embellishments of the facts, in lies that are largely inconsequential. I would also like to think that he's just some short, dark, sexy, husky-voiced, priapic guy I fell for because I had nothing better to do, and that may well be true, too. But what does it change? "The feelings I have for you are far from ordinary."

"Far from it." Carl is staring out my bedroom window, where there is nothing to see but my backyard, with its trashcans, toolshed, and gnawed-looking trees. "I'll grant you that. And I don't want to lose you. Unless, that is, you truly would be better off if I left."

"No!" I retort. "I've taken a lot from you, but I won't take this. You will *not* walk out of here insisting that it's for my own good."

"All right." He is tired now, willing to concede, and his arm is no longer around my shoulder. "But I will walk out of here, if that's what you want."

"It's not what I want. It's just what's happening."

Carl allows a moment of silence to fall between us, arid and empty, before he gets to his feet. "But this is not the end. Not by a long chalk."

If I don't accept that this is happening, I think to myself, as Carl walks out of the bedroom and down the hall toward my front door, then it won't actually happen. Even now, I could call him back. Or he could turn around and come back, with some perfectly plausible explanation.

I am listening, meanwhile, to the echo of his heels on the hardwood floor. Deliberate, precise, and measured—utterly unlike the jaunty sound of the footsteps that have always heralded his arrivals and departures to and from my life.

A moment later, I hear a metallic *chink*, like the sound of a coin hitting the bottom of a collection plate, and I am puzzled, briefly. But only briefly. It's my spare key, clinking into the ceramic dish on the table in the vestibule. Carl's propitiatory offering to the gods, perhaps. His hope that a graceful exit today might increase the likelihood of a joyous reunion tomorrow. Either that...or he knows, despite denials, that it is the end.

After that, I hear, only faintly, his tread down the porch stairs— slow and sober, one step at a time. And after that, nothing at all.

This makes twice that I have spared myself the necessity of watching him actually depart. Which means that my alliance with Carl may, after all, represent progress of a sort. If I've at least learned it's best not to look.

Chapter Six

I have never regarded technology as a close friend of mine. In fact, the sole concession I have made—and ever intend to make—to the Electronic Age is my answering machine. Which, alone among technological toys, to me represents a genuine advancement in the quality of human life on Earth. After all, why shouldn't even a cyber simpleton like me consider it a boon to leave an insensate machine in charge to field the phone calls for which I have no stomach myself? Especially now that I've arrived at the point where there is absolutely no one from whom I wish to hear.

Ring!

"Hi. You've reached Dana's House of Messages. Please leave yours, after the beep." *Beep.*

"Sweetheart, look, it's me again. Are you absolutely certain you're not at home? I've thought of stopping round, but...well, if you aren't inclined to return my messages, I can't think you'd be overjoyed to see me in person. So...just pick *up* for once, why not? Or ring me back. Just to keep the lines of communication open, sort of style. After all, it isn't—"

Often, when it's Carl calling, I switch off the machine in mid-sentence and leave him talking into thin air, sort of style. Not because I have any particular desire to be nasty, but simply because there's a limit—no, really, even in my case there is—to the amount of pain I'm prepared to inflict on myself in Carl's name. However, after some time has elapsed, I usually switch my machine back on—

out of rank curiosity to eavesdrop, from a safe distance, on whoever else might be calling.

Ring!

"Hi. You've reached Dana's House of Messages. Please leave yours, after the beep." *Beep.*

"Dana, it's Mel Arlen. Glass's friend? Look, Glass would kill me if he knew I was cwalling, but...Well, let me put it like this. If I hadn't of phoned you in the first place to take the dwog...Which is, I realize, spilled milk under the bridge...But, notwithstanding that...If I hadn't of phoned you in the first place...Look, Dana, I guess what I'm trying to say is that I think it's a goddamn shame, whatever went down up there between you and Glass. Because, apparently, whatever it was, you and Glass aren't even friends anymore.

"Which really is a goddamn shame, if you ask me. Even though I'm aware you aren't asking. Me, that is. After all, why would you? What do I know about anything? Well, on second thought... maybe a little. Because even if you think that you're perfectly okay with all of this—that you are relieved, somehow, to be unloaded of Glass and his dwog at one fell swoop—well guess what? Somehow, I feel that you're not. Relieved, I mean.

"No more than I believe Glass is 'perfectly fine' with everything, as he claims to be. Personally, it's my impression that he misses you. The dwog also, for all I know. Although, frankly, with Murphy, it's anybody's guess *what* goes on in there.

"In fact, it's anybody's guess about everything, right? I mean, like the fat lady says: It ain't over till it's over. Anyhow, here's hoping that you and Glass sort it out. Meanwhile, it's been nice talking to your machine, and I'll quit now before I run out of tape, or something to say, whichever comes first. So long, Dana. I'm just...well, what can I say? Sorry as hell."

Well, hell, Mel, what can I say? Me too.

Ring!

"Hi. You've reached Dana's House of Messages. Please leave yours, after the beep." *Beep.*

"Oh, yawn, Katie. I mean, if I have to hear that LAME Dana's House of Messages message one more TIME... I mean, how often do I have to keep CALLING before you pick UP? I mean, it's not like there's some running SORE festering between us, is there? Apart from your good old buddy O'Ryan, that is, who no doubt came CRYING to YOU the minute I dusted him.

"Well, I HAD to dust him, Katie. He left me no choice. It was either MAJOR commitment time or fade to black. And since I'd rather commit to the nearest saniTARium than to a cornball like him...

"Anyway, he'll get over it. O'Ryan is a big boy. Like, a REALLY big boy where it counts, as I'm sure YOU recall from the misted past. But tell me: Was he already such a major ASShole, back in the seventies?

"Although, who CARES? These guys are just GUYS, right? While you and I, we're SOLID, since way back when. So CALL me, 'kay? Because I'm SERIOUSLY splitting, for the Coast. This time for SURE. You phone me, Katie. While I'm still a LOCAL call."

So O'Ryan, it seems, has taken my advice—with more alacrity than I did myself. Apparently he confronted Karen, and in the process lost what little he had. Still, who's to say that he—like me—is not better off for having confronted, whether sooner or later? As for Karen... well, I suppose I'd call her to say *bon voyage*. If I believed for one single minute that she's any more serious about California than she ever was about O'Ryan.

Ring!

"Hi. You've reached Dana's House of Messages. Please leave yours, after the beep." *Beep.*

"Dana! Hi! Lyle here. Lyle Trumbo—just in case it's been *that* long since I called. Actually, looks like I'm going to be in town—*your* town, that is, and hopefully *our* town when I get there—around about next Thursday. Look, I have no idea of your schedule, but do you think you could give me a quick buzz—at my office number? We can compare calendars, and whatever else comes up, ha ha. Bad joke. I mean, it's *meant* to be a bad joke, so... Well, just phone me. I'll be—"

Of course, at a certain point it occurs to me that maybe switching off the machine on a more permanent basis might not be such a bad idea at that. Leaving the phone to simply ring and ring—so that whoever is calling will eventually conclude that they've dialed a government office by mistake.

Yet, once I've done it, and am without even messages to listen to, I find time hanging heavier on my hands, as I continue to hang limply about the house, like leftover Christmas lights in mid-July. Wearing the same sweatsuit day in and day out, with my unwashed hair falling around my face in greasy clusters, with the drapes drawn in my living room, and the TV set—perennially on, but with the volume down—gibbering quietly to itself in a corner, I sit slumped in precisely the posture women in my situation are supposed to adopt. Once they've lost everything, and have decided to accessorize accordingly.

Now, if I were Grace Goldberg, I would—naturally—handle such a circumstance differently. Grace, God knows, would never be caught dead *playing* dead. Gorging on cornchips with self-destructive gusto as I am doing, wallowing in smelly sweat-togs and sour regrets. Instead, she'd be out shopping—intent on spending her way out of a Depression, just as the economists always prescribe. Or else, she might be found cackling with glee as she mounted photos of her lost love on her fridge, to fire on with a rubber-dart gun. Either way, by dinnertime, you can be sure that Grace would be feeling just fine.

But I'm not Grace—as both Grace and I know too well. My own approach to a situation such as the one I'm currently in is, first, to finish off the cornchips. Then, start nibbling at my cuticles, while wondering if it's too late to take up smoking. The one diversion from despair I permit myself is a brisk mental retrospective jaunt around the track that rings the memory of every awful relationship I've ever been in. Every faceless encounter never truly faced in the light of day. And every bad date that only went to worse.

Men who webbed their own lawn furniture, or boosted hubcaps, or brought their cell-phone along on a wilderness weekend. Men who snorted when they laughed, or laughed when they snorted. Men who called out to Anna Nicole Smith in their sleep. Men who cursed when they came, or who came when they cursed. Men who didn't come at all, not even when called.

Was it that Carl and Jerry and Mark—and even the assorted Marrieds, with all their assorted flaws—were better men than these rankest of the rank and file? Or was Murphy the best deal I'm ever going to get? At least Murphy always barked when he wanted out. Instead of just leaving me a note and cleaning out my purse. At least Murphy, for all his—

But no. I won't think about Murphy right now. Won't think about him missing me, when I don't deserve to be missed. Won't think about him back at Jerry's, drowning his sorrows in frozen yogurt, licking the bottom of his bowl so clean that the "Good Dog!" legend glazed on the bottom disappears along with the last milky drop. Don't want to think about Murphy happy without me, either. Just don't want to think about him.

I always wanted to be the sort of woman who would, *in extremis*, simply rip the telephone jack out of the wall—and feel immediately better for it. Instead, I am the sort of woman who feels compelled *not* to rip out the phone, just in case my mother calls—and then hops the next plane East in a panic because she got no answer three times in a row. It is for that reason, and that reason alone, that I eventually feel a further compulsion to turn the machine back on.

Ring!

"Hi. You've reached Dana's House of Messages. Please leave yours, after the beep." *Beep.*

"Sweetheart, it's me again. I know you're there, because you keep switching off the machine when I'm in the midst of leaving a message. Look, the only thing I'm asking is that you ring me back, drop a line, send a fax . . . Even if you spew vitriol in my ear, that would be welcome, compared to this business of cutting me off in the middle of—"

On the other hand—for your basic garden-variety-non-phone-jack-ripping type of woman such as myself—instead of keeping my callers under constant audio surveillance, the simplest expedient of all may finally be to leave the machine on, with the volume down, check through my messages hourly for ones from my mother, and erase the rest.

><del>·</del>+·◆·-O-·◆·+·<del>·</del>◄

Somehow or other, I've managed to lose track of whether it's been months, or mere minutes, since I started hiding out. The only constant is the sight of my own sweatsuited knees, nubby with grime. From that, I can deduce that I've been here a while, and extrapolate how the rest of me must look by now. "I am so *ugly*!" I declare out loud—and am amazed to discover that my vocal cords still work, more or less.

"Boy, are you ever."

I wasn't expecting a reply. But the voice has a familiar twang to it—as flat and uninflected as the bald, bald prairies of my past. Like the brittle, joyless sound of a plastic plate dropping, then rattling to a standstill on patio bricks.

Startled, I glance over to my office rocking chair to discover someone seated in it. Not Grace Goldberg this time. Today's occupant is a teenage girl, skinny and wary looking. With a sullen blemished face, and greasy bangs overhanging her eyes. She wears a shrunken T-shirt and worn-out pedal-pushers—the kind you'd never catch kids dead in anymore.

My first response is indignation. "Excuse me, I don't see what business it is of yours how I look. How'd you get in here, anyway? And why don't you leave?"

To that, the girl says nothing. Merely continues to survey me from beneath her sweaty fringe of hair—as if waiting for me to ask a question worth her while to answer.

"Besides, I don't usually let myself go like this," I go on to explain. "But the fact is, I'm having a kind of...rough time. Not that that's any business of yours, either."

The girl lifts her head, allowing me for the first time to get a good look at her face. "How come you keep saying it's none of my business? Of course it is. Since we're twins, practically."

Quickly, I get up from my office chair and pace the room. "We are no such thing. I already have a twin. His name is Paul, and he looks nothing like you. Or me, either."

"I know. I have a twin named Paul, too. And he's real good looking."

"Now, look..." I am becoming very agitated, and am beginning to suspect this girl as the symptom of some sort of breakdown I'm having. "I'm getting a little tired of this, being accosted at every turn in my life by females all claiming to be my doppelgänger."

"Your...? Hey, no fair using words I haven't learned yet."

"How am I supposed to know what words you've learned?"

"Come on, you *know*. Look at me. You know who I am."

To face her, to name her, to claim her as mine... it seems more than I can bear to do. Yet, the door is open; the lid is off the coffin; the body, so long hidden, is exposed to the light. "I, uh, suppose you're going to tell me you're me."

"No, you're *me*. Except, of course, much, much older."

"I told you," I huff defensively. "I don't usually look this bad. It's just that I'm—"

"Having a rough time. Well, to tell you the truth, I've been having kind of a rough time myself lately."

The raw, undiluted pain on her homely face clutches at my heart. "I know," I whisper. "I know you are."

"Oh, yeah?" She rounds on me, rolling her eyes sarcastically— much as I used to when I was her age. "So *now* you know everything? You're all caught up, no need to review?"

"No," I say simply. "It's just that I haven't thought about you in a long time." Or, more accurately, have made every effort not to. But how can I admit to my bygone self what I've never confessed to another living person? In fact, what is there that I can trust myself to say to this skinny kid? I could tell her she's a lot cuter than I remember. But the truth is, she isn't. And as for that smart mouth on

302 • Erika Ritter

her...well, if memory serves, she does not need *that* brought to her attention, either.

"So, you've been too busy to think about me, eh? Busy with what?" Meanwhile, she is glancing around my office with the same lack of enthusiasm that everything else about me has so far inspired. "Boy, and Mum calls *my* room a zoo!"

"Oh, come on. When the place is straightened up a little...Well, it cleans up nice. Just like me. Just like *you*, I mean. And it's mine."

"But what do you *do* in here?"

"On a good day—not today—I do quite a bit. I..." But as I look over at her, still slumped in my rocking chair, I can't quite bring myself to tell her that I write TV trash. Somehow, I vaguely recall that's not quite what she has in mind for her future. "Well, what would *you* like to do, when you grow up?"

"What would I like? I'm sort of hoping to become a stunt pilot. Or a world-famous vet. Or maybe a gun moll, with an Arabian horse farm on the side. Do you do any of those things?"

"No." I feel embarrassed. "But I've done my best." On a good day, I feel sure, I could defend my record with more conviction. However, on a good day, my teenage self would not have shown up.

"Well, are you married, at least?"

"No." This, I am certain, is not the moment to bring up Mark and the endlessly postponed divorce. "Anyway, matrimony isn't one of your goals, is it?"

"How about a boyfriend? Torrid affairs without benefit of wedlock...that *is* one of my goals. Remember?"

Yes, I do remember. Yet can't imagine the tired round of Marrieds as precisely filling this child's bill. "Well, I've had relationships, of course, but I—"

"Don't have one at the moment," the girl supplies impertinently. "I figured as much. How about a dog, then?" And she looks around again, as if expecting one to come suddenly bounding into the room.

"There *was* this dog, but...oh, forget it." All of a sudden, I find myself heartily fed up with Little Miss Ghost of Christmas Past here, who's come waltzing in, in her klutzy pedal-pushers, to crap all over my adult self. "Anyway, I thought it was horses you're crazy for. Sorry, I'm fresh out of those, too—even the imaginary kind."

My younger self stares at me, goggle-eyed. "You don't remember? You don't remember about the dogs?"

What I remember is sitting in torment on the Eleventh Avenue bus, being pelted with taunts by St. Ignatius boys. "Woof, woof! Speak, not-so-great Dana!" It's what I remember, but only on those rare occasions when—as now—I slip up in my vigilant efforts to forget. And even now, remembering, how likely is it that I'm going to breathe a word of my misery to young Dana, of all people? Who, I am sorely afraid, is bound to find out for herself soon enough, if she hasn't already. "No, I'm sorry, I don't."

"I can't believe it." She shakes her head. "They follow me. Whole packs of them, to the park."

A dim recollection, growing brighter, of myself at her age, enticing the neighborhood dogs to the Legislative Park. Luring them with... Milk-Bone biscuits, wasn't it? My God. She's right. It's unbelievable that I could have forgotten all that. Such a happy memory. Supplanted, it seems, by what came so hard on its heels.

"Carla calls me a werewolf!" my younger self is recounting, with genuine pleasure. "And Paul...well, what*ever* I do, he dies of shame. 'Mum, Mum, she's running with a pack of dogs!' God, I tell him, I could do worse for company! God, I wisht I was a dog!"

No, I think. No, you won't wish any such thing. Not when the word is ringing in your ears.

Still, her sudden quality of joyfulness is alluring. I can see it all quite clearly now: myself, in T-shirt and pedal-pushers, marching toward the park, with a dozen or more dogs following in a friendly convoy. Little dogs boiling around my ankles. Medium-sized dogs pressing their noses behind my knees. Big dogs, as big as Murphy, bumping their bony skulls against my bonier elbows. While I rattled and rattled the biscuits in the box, as my irresistible Pied Piper refrain.

"Yes, I remember," I assure her. "Now that you mention it. Only...once you get to the park with all those dogs, what do you do?"

No longer capable of being shocked by the ignorance of my questions, she merely shrugs. "What else? Study up on my breeds."

"Breeds? Of dogs, you mean?"

She reaches down beside the rocker, into a school bag, and from it she extracts a clothbound book, which she proffers by way of response. "I borrow it from the library, whenever I want. Hardly anybody else takes it out. It's the complete listings of the American Kennel Club."

Of course. This I recognize as much by smell as by anything else. The musty, oaten aroma of the pages, the gluey odor of the binding. "You mean you—I—take this book to the park? Along with the biscuits and all those dogs?"

But she isn't required to corroborate this with more than a nod. I am there now, down by the creek bank in the Legislative Park, perusing the Kennel Club book, while the dogs who've followed me there lie dozing in the sunlight, like a pride of oddly assorted lions.

Young Dana reaches over impulsively, to open the book to a random page. "I'm doing real good with my breeds. I'll show you. You tell me the number of the page, and I'll tell you what's written on it." Her face, transformed by enthusiasm, is almost attractive.

"Well, okay...It's page two-twenty-eight."

"Oh, that's an easy one. 'Retriever, Curly-Coated. Probably descended from the Irish Water Spaniel, and, more latterly, the Labrador. Head: Long, well-proportioned—'"

"Jesus!" I am truly impressed. As much by what this girl remembers as by what I evidently do not.

"Try another one." She is almost begging. "Any page you like."

"Uh, okay. Page forty-seven."

"'The Basenji,'" she says promptly. "'The barkless dog of Africa. Height: Seventeen inches at the shoulder. Weight: Ideally, betwee—'"

"Okay, okay, you've proved your point!" For the first time in what seems like months, I am laughing. But it's laughter closely akin to tears. Not because I find this child so sad, but because I find her—all of a sudden—so much more admirable than I ever expected. With her sternly imposed self-improvement projects, and her wistful standards of canine perfection. My God, where has she been, all the time I've been strip-mining dog movies for story ideas, struggling with training manuals, and scanning Murphy's impassive face for some trace of what he might be thinking? "Is it possible," I ask her in wonderment, "that you're really so much better off than I remember?"

"Sometimes," she whispers back fiercely. Then, as I glance over at her, she looks away. "And sometimes not."

It's started, then. The misery of an adolescence now beyond her abilities to imagine away. "Dana..." In a rush of compassion, I reach over to touch her bony shoulder. "Believe me, sometimes things are okay later on, too. More than okay, and more than sometimes. Even if—on this particular day—I'm not your best witness."

Her face still averted, she shrugs off my hand. "It's just...well, I just kind of hoped maybe I'd turn out...prettier."

Even across the gulf of decades, there is power in "prettier" to wound us both. Somehow, that realization makes me sadder for her than for myself. "Look...later on, there are qualities that count much more than just looks. There's, uh, intelligence, and...character, and...let me see...oh, yes, generosity of spirit. Not that I'm claiming to possess those in abundance either, but...Well, my point is, mere appearance is not such a big deal."

Young Dana doesn't look as though she cares to credit this—and why should she? At her age, appearance *is* a big deal, goddamn it. Especially when you're forced to endure well-meaning sermonettes from adults like me—who have done their very best to forget what it is to be her age and patently plain.

"Listen," I continue, "I could lie to you, and tell you that you're going to do better with your life than I've done. But you're too smart—believe me—not to see the illogic of that. You're stuck with me, just as much as I'm stuck with you. But please believe me that it's not all awfulness. Sometimes there's satisfaction. Sometimes, success. And—once in a great while—love."

"But no husband."

"No, not at the moment."

"And no boyfriends?"

"Not anymore."

"And no dog, even?"

"No," I admit, looking her right in the eye. "No one but me."

And as I say the words, I hear how empty and echoing my own voice sounds. It's true. There's no one here but me. No matter how much—at this moment—I actively wish there were a fourteen-year-old urchin in a stretched T-shirt scowling werewolfishly at me from the corner.

Chapter Seven

The car traffic is sparse today, as I pedal slowly past storefronts decked out for Christmas. Christmas! Surely even Hallowe'en hasn't happened yet? On the other hand, during my recent hibernation, who's to say how many seasonal shifts I've managed to miss?

Today, however, I no longer want to miss anything out here in the world. Today, even those tired tinsel angels and sprigs of plastic holly look lifelike to me. The smiling Santas seem like old friends, and I may have a good hour in me before the repeated refrain of "Silver Bells" sets me to screaming.

It's amazing, actually, how the will to live has suddenly returned. It's not precisely that I've forgotten why I barricaded myself in the house in the first place, eavesdropping at a distance on my answering machine, and conducting in-depth self-interviews in my office. It's more that the novelty of mourning my life has worn off. At least to the point that I woke up this morning feeling the urge to shower, to change my clothes at long last, and head out-of-doors in some kind of creditable parody of a functional woman.

Eventually, windowshopping from the seat of my bike is not good enough. I dismount and wheel the bike along the sidewalk, the better to assess the displays in the windows I pass. Out of the corner of my eye, I am aware of the reflection of a woman trudging in my direction. A bag-lady. Although, in this case, it's a bag-lady devoid of bags. One of those who's opted to wear her entire wardrobe—several sweaters, slacks, skirts, assorted scarves and hats—rather than bothering to lug it.

In spite of myself, I shudder. I'm not sure why. It's a queasy sensation I believe is common among women when we encounter what seems to be a distorted mirror image of ourselves. A path not taken, perhaps. Or, a path not taken yet.

Oh, dear. This bagless bag-lady talks to herself. But at least she's smiling and nodding as she talks. She's not old. Maybe not even unattractive, under all those layers. In fact, let's see: if we lose the bulky sweaters and skirts (to say nothing of that pile of hats!), there's really nothing all that outlandish here. Nothing to distinguish this woman from any other female of forty-plus—including, of course, myself.

Be that as it may, I don't exactly want to be caught comparing reflections with her in the store window. Before she can reach me, I'm going back to play in the traffic.

Hey, now, how about that? A whole two blocks, three maybe, before I get caught by a red light. Now, that's gotta be—Oh, my God. Look at that: no, *don't* look. It's the bag-lady—surely it's the self-same woman? And she's kept pace with me. Trudging slowly along, talking and nodding…How can it be that she's caught up to my bike? And now she seems to be looking right at me, as if she knows me.

But you know what? I may have seen her before, too. Always in this part of town. Except, this is the first time I can recall her looking at me like this…

It's a green light! Thank God. If I get back into the traffic, and put on a little speed…Ah, terrific. I'm really moving now, lights all in my favor, block after—Shit! Oh, well, at least another red light means I can catch my breath. Oh, fuck. I don't believe it. It's her! She's caught up again. And this time, she really *is* looking at me. Smiling, right at me. Like an old, old friend.

"Hiya! So, how you been, all these years?"

"Uh, fine." All these years? Christ. Which is creepier, I wonder? Her air of *bonhomie*, or her apparent ability to cover entire city blocks in a single bound? Change, light. Goddamn you, change!

"Fine? That's all you can come up with, after all this time?"

Her teeth, when she laughs, are actually decent. Surprisingly intact. "I'm sorry, do I—?"

"Now, don't pretend like you're not knocked for a loop here. This really is *me*, y'know."

She seems pretty sure about it—thumping herself on the chest as confidently as King Kong. That voice...Whose accent does...? No, not Jerry, precisely. Mel? Closer. Something very New Yawkish, certainly, and there's also something else that... "Look, I'm sure it *is* you. I just don't happen to be exactly clear who you are. But, if you think you know me, then—"

"If I 'think' I know you? I don't believe it!"

Christ, that's quite a show-stopper of a laugh she's got. Like a guffaw, and loud enough to turn heads, even on a noisy shopping street. The laugh...don't I know the laugh? Isn't it—Oh, come on now, look at me: green light, and still I'm standing here like I've taken root.

"I really don't believe this. You mean to stand here and pretend you don't reckinize me? Your old best buddy, your friggin' psychic *soul*mate, for fuck's sake!"

Oh, my God, the roll of the *r*s, the clang of that *g*... "Uh, are you originally from Long Island, by any chance?"

"Now, where the hell *else* would I be from? I *told* ya, you know me. Christ, we're twins, practically."

The shape of the face, the slant of her eyes, the curve of...Am I only imagining it, or do I really see the resemblance? Under all those layers of clothes, the heap of hats, the big loony laugh... is there some similarity? I mean, I'm not sitting in my office, all by myself, trying to imagine how she'd look now, after all these years... "Grace?" Did I say it right out loud? Did she hear what I said? Does she...? No, it can't be. Because if she looks like Grace Goldberg, then she looks like me, and if she looks like me, then—

"Grace! Bingo! Gawd, it sure the hell took you long enough. 'Course, you always were slow on the uptake."

"But you can't be Grace Goldberg. She—"

"Grace Goldberg. Well, duh. Who *else* would I be, I'd like to know?"

"But...you can't be."

"Oh, no?" As if I've offended her. "Can you give me one good reason why not?"

Because Grace would never wind up this way, that's why not. Because if something like this could happen to Grace, then it could—by extension—happen to me, and I absolutely will not let anything like this happen to me—or to Grace. "Look, obviously we've both mistaken each other for someone else, and so we—"

"So we what? Forget all about what happened between us? I'm sorry as hell, you know. Sorry that I never even wrote to say I'm sorry."

She's strong. Her hand, squeezing my wrist...But not unfriendly. Could I possibly be wrong about...? "Did you say 'write'? What would you write me to say you're sorry about?"

"You know. The guy thing. With...what's-his-name."

"Jules? The French boy?" No, no, Dana. Not like this. Not telling her. Make her tell you.

"Yeah, that's the one."

"Okay, and what happened with Jules, Grace? If you are Grace... Where did you and he go?"

"Christ! Where'd ya think? To Lon Gyland!"

Bullshit. She's saying Long Island because I said it first. Grace never took Jules back to the States. I know she wouldn't. I...I've got to get away. From this lunatic. Because she's clearly a lunatic, and that's all that she is. With her fingers squeezing my arm... "Look, Grace, it's been nice seeing you, but—"

"But what? You'd rather see me than be me? Like the purple cow?"

Oh, brother, what did I say? Wacko. "Please let go of my wrist, because I—"

"Yeah, you'd rather see one than be one, right? Well, don't be so friggin' sure, sister, that it's your choice to make."

You see? Now she thinks I'm her sister. But at least I've got my arm back. "I'm not your sister."

"I know that. What's the matter with you? I'm your psychic soul-mate, your transcendental twin. We're the last surviving members of the Doppel Gang, for fuck's sake!"

No. No. I did not hear her say that. I only imagined it. She's just one of those . . . savvy street types, is all. Accosting strangers, making lucky guesses based on what they feed her without even knowing it. "I'm sorry. I have to go."

"That's all you got to say to me after all these years? 'I hafta go'? This is the end of our Hayley Mills moment?"

I will not listen to any more of this. I have no idea how she does it, but I am not required to listen. I'm going away, as far as I can, as fast as I can. Because this is *not* Grace Goldberg, and the quicker I get out of here, the surer of that I'm going to be. "I'm not the one who fell out of touch! I'm not the one who took off with Jules!"

"Joowels? What do you mean? You're the one who took off with *my* joowels!"

There, you see? A crazy woman. She thinks I'm talking about jewelry now. Besides, even if she did mean Jules, I didn't take off with him. She did. And I went back home to marry Mark.

"You come back here! You come back here, goddamn it, and you deal with your old friend Grace!"

I can still hear her voice shrilling in my ear, no matter how fast I pedal. I can feel where her fingers pinched my arm—even hope that she left a mark. Something to prove to me later that there really was . . . Ugh. No, on second thought, I don't really want to think there was this loony woman on the street.

Just get away, that's the ticket. Standing up in the saddle, pumping like a kid. Try and catch me if you can . . .

Shit. Now, what's *he* doing? Some stupid truck driver muscling in. The light's still green, though. I can still get by him, unless—

Unless he turns. Turning? *Turning?* With no signal, no nothing, the son of a bitch. Turning right, as if I, for all intents and purposes, did not exist.

"Hey! Hey, you up there! Don't you see . . . ?"

But he doesn't. There's nobody up there on the passenger side, next to me. The windows are cranked shut, and the music is cranked up. I can barely see the driver, bopping along to the beat as he hauls hard on the wheel—and pulls right up against me.

"Hey, *hey!* Down here, on your right! On your *right*, goddamn it!"

I feel the scorching breath of the engine, right through my jeans. Throw myself clear, isn't that the idea? Throw myself right on the sidewalk...Oh, fuck. The skin scraping right off my elbows onto the pavement. Never mind that, though. I'm clear.

And then...this metallic crunch. What is it? My bike, my beloved bike! I don't want to look, but I ought to look, just to make sure there's nothing besides the bike still in harm's—

My leg. Did that even hurt? It must be hurting, just somewhere so deep I have no nerves to feel it. My shoe, peeled off neatly, like a banana skin. And that big knobbly truck tire pressing my ankle into the curb. And now, this sound. What is this sound? Like someone twisting gristle.

Like someone being run over by a truck. People use that expression all the time. "I felt as though I'd been run over by a truck." As if they knew how that felt. Well, I do. Now I know exactly what it feels like. In fact, it doesn't feel like much of anything at all.

The truck has roared off in a smelly blue haze, its driver none the wiser. I can still hear—I *think* I hear—the tinny sound of his radio, growing fainter as he rumbles out of sight. Meanwhile, above me, a circle of concerned-looking faces is looming larger and larger. Strangers. Staring down at me as if I were on TV, gazing at my leg with expressions of open horror that they really ought to downplay, since I'm *not* on TV, and haven't even managed yet to pass out.

The bagless bag-lady...Her face is nowhere to be seen, thank God, in the throng ringed around me. Of course, the fact that she's not here now doesn't prove she never was. Doesn't even prove she's not Grace. Since not being here is something Grace quite often...

God, I'm tired. If I could just get comfortable on the curb, nestle into the concrete, close my...Oh. Well, that's a nice touch. Someone lifting my head, putting it down again, on...what? A folded-up coat, maybe, for a pillow. "I'm all right. It really doesn't hurt. Not nearly as much as you might think." Just to reassure them. They're being so kind. And I'm not even lying. It really doesn't hurt that much.

Of course, now that I've got a minute here to mull it over, I realize that woman never was Grace Goldberg, not for a single second. For one thing, Grace is only twenty-two. And always will be. In her white Courrèges boots, her Carnaby Street mini, frozen in time. Frozen some place in the Pyrenees, with Jules. Two tiny figures in a snow-shaker. Poised on the slope of a miniature mountain, amid the swirling silvery flakes of...

"Hi. Can you tell me your name?"

"Who wants to know?" That's the idea. Play it cagey. Don't even so much as open your eyes.

"Ma'am? I need to know your name and where you live."

The hell he does. "I know why you're asking me that: you want to establish if I'm in shock. I'm not. Just a little...surprised."

"Ma'am." The voice sounds tired now. "I'm asking you because I'm a police officer, and I'm here to help."

Police officer? Sure enough. Now that I've opened my eyes, there's the blue uniform cap, the badge. "From the Leith police, I presume?"

"Ma'am, there's an ambulance on the way, okay?" He is forming his words with what strikes me as unnecessarily painstaking articulation. "If you'd give me your name, I could notify whoever you want that you're being taken to the General."

"Just like the old tongue-twister. 'The Leith police dismisseth us.'" That's the ticket, all right. Give nothing away. Not even your name. Especially not to a Leith policeman.

"Okay, ma'am, you just wait for the ambulance."

Good. He's going away.

"Hi. Want to give me a smile?"

Good God, who now? I've just been run *over*, for Christ's sake. And who's this—some TV reporter, with a video camera, leaning down and smiling and pointing his lens-eye right in my face!

"Hey, you look kind of familiar." He pans to my ruined bicycle, then back to me again, still smiling. "Do I know your face from show business or someplace?"

"Sure. I'm Amazing Grace."

"Hey! Jesus!" It's the cop again, chasing the reporter off. "This isn't some goddamn movie premiere!"

"Oh, I don't know," the reporter says. "She claims to be in show-biz. Grace something or other?"

"Ma'am?" Cheese it, it's the cop. Squatting down beside me again, his baby blue eyes filled with concern. He is a baby, at that, my Leith policeman. More to Karen's taste than mine—off the children's menu. "Ma'am, they're gonna put you in the ambulance now, okay? But before they do...is your name Grace?"

Oh, why not? Someone has to be, right? Someone in her right mind who can do a decent job of it. "Yes."

"Okay." And he writes it in a notebook, just like a real cop on TV. "Grace what?"

Oh, no, you don't. Not again. "Just Grace. You know us good-time girls. One name is generally all we need."

There, he's closing his notebook. That stopped him in his tracks. I knew it would. It always does.

Chapter Eight

Murphy, what are you doing here? Dogs aren't allowed in church, not even to attend the funerals of their near and dear—as you'll no doubt recall from *Greyfriars Bobby*. Not even when the service is being conducted way down here, in the Little Chapel Under the Lake. Where the rolling waves of organ music literally are rolling waves.

🐾 Come on, this isn't a church. It's an operating room. Don't you remember? You were hit by a truck. I came as quickly as I could.

Good old Murphy. You came, even though I don't deserve it. Clever dog, too—to think of disguising yourself as a scrub nurse. Only I would recognize those unmistakably yellow eyes, peering over the top of your surgical mask. But I'm afraid you got here too late. Can't you smell the sickly sweet aroma of lilies?

🐾 Your sense of smell never was worth squat. That's the odor of green onions. The chief surgeon briefed you on that—how the last thing you'd smell as you went under would be an aroma like green onions.

I can't say I remember that. Although, I do have a fairly clear recollection of the chief surgeon. Tall. Gray. Good looking. I *knew* I should have shaved my legs today before I set out on the bike. You can never tell when you're going to be hit by a truck and wind up with your stubble exposed to a tall, good-looking medical man. Ugh. The chief surgeon must have thought he was operating on an Airedale. Luckily, now that I'm in my casket, my legs don't even show.

🐾 Will you get off this funeral kick? I'm telling you, you're not dead yet.

Oh, no? So, what's my mother doing in the front pew? I'm sure she's brought along some of her famous date squares, to serve to the mourners afterward. In which case...I hope the funeral-home people brought a few extra caskets, because there may be several more interments before this day is done.

🐾 I don't see your mother here. In fact, I don't see anybody, apart from hospital staff in gowns and masks.

Come on. What about Jerry? In that pew right by the door? So he can slip out if the lilies get the better of his allergies. It was nice of him to drive all the way up here for the funeral, wasn't it? Even if only for the opportunity to file past my coffin and mutter how it served me right for riding a bicycle in downtown traffic.

🐾 It was never Jerry who gave you a hard time about the bike. It was Carl.

Carl. Right. Speaking of whom...You'll notice who hasn't even so much as bothered to send along a wreath?

🐾 Give the guy a break. Even if you were dead—which I'm telling you you're not—how is Carl supposed to know about it? Since you never returned a single one of his calls.

Yes, what a shame. Just think what a nice farewell message he might have left on my machine. "Hullo, sweetheart. Sorry I'm so late ringing you. Though...well, it seems if anybody's 'late' it's you now, isn't it? Come on, what's all this about you being dead? Surely not. Hmm! Just as well we broke up when we did, then, isn't it? Only goes to show how everything always works out for the best, sort of style."

🐾 Of course, once the anesthetic starts to wear off, you won't be so quick with the merry little quips.

Are you still there, Murphy, disguised as a scrub nurse? Because I have the funniest feeling that my eyes have just opened, and you're beginning to look more like...Carmelita Pope.

🐾 No, no, that's the recovery room nurse. I'm the one who's been curled up at the end of your bed all this time, like Flush, the spaniel.

Come on. That's not you at the end of the bed. It's my *leg*, goddamn it, propped up on a pile of pillows, like something from a display of the Crown Jewels. Speaking of whom...what ever did become of Jules, anyway? Or Grace Goldberg?

Murphy, are you still there? Murphy? It would be nice if you'd answer me. If you'd come when I call, the way I taught you. Even if I don't deserve it. Even if I'm dead when you arrive. Because even way down here under the lake where the green onions grow, and I can still smell their aroma on my hands, I'll know it's you when you get here. Even if I'm not dead, but just sound asleep, I'll know exactly who you are in my dream.

⊱┈◈┈◯┈◈┈⊰

Just beyond the window of my hospital room, a full moon that looks like a lozenge is rising fast. Actually rising, before my eyes. A moon that struggled, initially, to disengage itself from the wire grating that covers the lower part of the window. And then managed to float free—up and up, until it was too high in the sky for me to keep track of anymore.

Ever since I discovered Demerol on demand, I must say, I don't keep track of much. "Asleep" and "awake," "here" or "there," "then" versus "now"...They've become distinctions too nice to draw.

My leg, encased in its shell of hard white plaster, lies self-importantly on its pillow, like an exotically shaped egg in no particular hurry to hatch. Sooner or later, I'm sure, it will start to hurt. At which point—just as surely—the doctors will take me *off* Demerol on demand. That's the logic that operates in here: everything's permitted, until you need it. Come to think of it, the hospital is a little bit like life that way.

But not too much like life, thank God. Not for the moment, when I'm still being left to my own vices. In my happy self-administering haze, scarfing pain pills like Smarties from the little paper cup on the nightstand. Serene in the knowledge that the cup will be replenished—no questions asked—by the same smiling aide who brings in the bedpan. Always with the same worn-out joke about how she's just taken it out of the fridge.

And, by God, I laugh. Not just to be polite. But because—in my continuously copacetic state—I find the joke funny, each and every time it's cracked by the aide. Like an egg, in no particular hurry to hatch. In the shell of its white plaster cast, in the—

🐾 In the Here and Now. Or is it the Then and There?

Oh, God. Not again.

🐾 Oh, that's nice. That's gratitude.

Look, Murphy, if it actually were you, I would be grateful. But it's not. At least, it won't be, once they take away my Demerol.

🐾 It is me. I'm There. Waiting for you to come. It's a long winding road that leads almost directly to Jerry's front door. I ought to know. I've traveled that road. Crammed in the hold of Jerry's Honda, with my nose pressed against the rear window, black and wet, like a mushroom.

That's right, you're There. And I'm Here, in my hospital room. All alone.

🐾 You're confused. I don't blame you. It's a...metaphysical kind of thing. Hard to explain to the uninitiated.

Well, la-di-da. Look at you, the metaphysics major. Who took an entire three weeks to grasp the concept of "Fetch."

🐾 But who did learn to come. Which is more than can be said for you.

Now, be fair. It'll be a week at least before I'm even allowed out of bed.

🐾 The road is long and winding, but well maintained. It would be a cinch to drive.

Aren't you forgetting something? I don't drive. A person could get hurt, driving a car.

🐾 As opposed, for instance, to riding a bike?

That's completely beside the point.

🐾 Everything is, besides the point: it's a long road, but at the end, I'm waiting. Like a dropped glove, like a boot abandoned at the Lost and Found. This time, it's you who has to come when called. Limping heroically, like Lassie Come Home.

Ring!

Oops, that's my phone. I have to answer it.

🐾 "Have to"? Because it's ringing? My, what a field day Dr. Pavlov could have had with you.

Oh, shut up. "Hello?"

"Sweetheart! How are you?"

"Oh! Fine, Mum." Shit, who told my mother that—?

"I'm just calling to make sure you're all right."

"Of course I am. Never better."

🐾 Yeah? Then why are you throwing a blanket over your cast? Afraid your mother will see down the phone line, and through several time zones?

Murphy, please.

"I must say, sweetheart, you sound awfully well."

"Well, it was my leg. My vocal cords, meanwhile, came off unscathed."

🐾 Whoa! Sarcastic.

Look, there's just this way my mother has, all right? Of driving me around the bend.

🐾 Yes, but if you could do the driving...

"Oh, Dana, not your leg! Your legs were always among your best features."

You see? Just the way she used to be, when I was a kid, emerging from the fitting room in one of those godawful dresses.

"Mum, it was a very minor mishap."

🐾 Minor mishap? Hopeless cripple is the way you've been selling it to me.

"Well, you know, Dana, there may be something to learn from this. Maybe it's time to scrap the bike."

"I'm afraid the bike's already scrapped, big time."

"Pardon?"

"Nothing, Mum."

"If you decide to get a car instead, be sure to consult your father before you buy."

"I will, Mum. But in the meantime, I have to walk before I can drive."

"Walk? What do you mean? I thought it was a minor mishap."

"It was. Look, it's really late here, and I need some sleep. Call you tomorrow, okay? Bye." Phew. I've got to lay off the Demerol. If I keep lying like this, people are going to start taking me for a man.

🐾 Lying? Just now?

Like a rug. What, I'm going to admit to my sweet little mother that I expect to spend the next few years in rehab?

🐾 And what you said to her about learning to drive—

It was my *mother* who said that.

🐾 But There I am, waiting at the end of that long winding road. Like a dropped glove, like—

Murphy, please. I'm so tired. Dog tired. Let me lie. Like a sleeping dog.

🐾 Seems to me all you do is lie. One way and another.

Only now and then.

🐾 But When else is there?

I don't know. I don't keep track. Not here in the hospital. Not since I discovered Demerol on demand.

PART FIVE

Received in Graceland

Chapter One

It's only now that I'm allowed up and around that I can fully appreciate how much better off I am than most of the other convalescents I encounter. Burn victims, for the most part, with harrowing tales to tell of electrical wiring gone awry, exploded cauldrons of boiling fat, and freak mishaps with radiator pans. By virtue of the plastic surgery involved in the repairs to my leg and foot, I am a nominal ward of the Burn Ward, too. Unlike most of the gauze-wrapped, cotton-gloved, and Vaseline-smeared inmates of this floor, however, I have an injury that is trivial, as these things go.

A fact I am reminded of by all and sundry. As for instance, late at night, when a few of us more ambulatory types forgather in the common room—for a game of Hearts, among those who gamble, and a round of cigarettes, for those determined to play with fire to the bitter end.

"I wisht I had that laig of yours," one of my favorite burn victims tells me. He is a young electrician, back in hospital for a third round of grafts to an area that seems to encompass his entire upper body. As well, his face is in purdah behind a veil of dressings, and his hands are wound in bandages, like a boxer's. "Man, ridin' around in yer wheelchair like friggin' Ironside...Even after they send you home, and you barge into walls, and you can't take a shower, or even make it through the door of the john...So what? You got no worries, sister. 'Cause, shit, it' only a *laig*, eh? Located friggin' *miles* from where you live yer life."

I think about how right he is, as I go cruising carefree along the corridors in my hospital-issue wheelchair. In fact, that is precisely what I'm thinking about—the moment that I bump, almost literally, into Mark's boyfriend next to a bank of elevators.

"Dana? Dana! For God's sake!"

"I...well, hi, there, Ted! I totally forgot this is where you work." So closely does Ted resemble all the other doctors that I've been seeing so much of lately that it takes me a moment to differentiate him as someone from some other walk of my life—back in the days when my life *had* a walk. And another moment to retrieve his name and identity from my Demerol-abused memory bank.

"Dana, what happened? My God, Mark and I have been wondering where you disappeared to!"

As I fill him in, more or less by rote, another part of my mind is occupied with reflecting on how strange it is to encounter Ted—for the first time I can remember—in some other role than as my ex-husband's significant other. With the obligatory stethoscope hanging out of his pocket, and a look on his face—as I recite my prognosis—indistinguishable from all those plastic surgeon wannabes looming over my bed to discuss my injured appendage, just as though there was no one attached.

"I see," he says, once I complete my recitation. "Well, if you *had* to fall off your bicycle, you picked the right part of town to take a tumble. The General does far and away the best reconstructive work in the country."

Right. Exactly what was going through my mind when I decided that it might be fun to check out the truth of the General's claims for myself. "I'm sorry I haven't called you and Mark to let you know, but...Well, to tell you the truth, up until lately, they've been keeping me pretty blissed-out on painkillers. My whole hospital sojourn has seemed more like a...vacation from reality than anything else."

"I understand," Ted tells me. "Unfortunately, reality marches on, regardless." And his expression, suddenly, is both sober and personal. "Mark's a patient here, too. That's why we were trying to get in touch with you."

"Mark! Where is he?"

"On the seventh floor," Ted says crisply.

By now, I've been in the General long enough to know what a stay on the seventh floor betokens. "Oh, Ted. What happened?"

He shrugs. "Just the usual. Mark got a cold; he didn't have the resources to fight it off. And then it turned into—well..." He shrugs again. "Either he fights it off, or he doesn't."

What is it about doctors, I wonder dully, that makes them favor the *che sarà, sarà* approach when breaking the news? Even in cases—if Ted's an example—that involve their near and dear. "Mark will fight it off," I assure him. "The last time I saw him, he looked—"

"Dana," Ted interrupts, "the last time you saw Mark, he looked *terrible*, and that was weeks ago. Now he looks a hell of a lot worse than that. I've seen this often enough, believe me, and sometimes they go on for months, even years, seeming perfectly normal. Then they take a sudden skid. Chances are, if Mark comes out of this one, he'll go through another cycle or two of good-health, bad-health. But the fact is, there's no rule of thumb. At the moment, all I can tell you for sure is: our boy Mark is one sick puppy. So, since you're here anyway—and right next to the West Wing elevators—maybe you should take a ride up to Room 786, just to say hi to him."

>–⊷•–O–•⊷–◄

Rolling my wheelchair along the corridor on the seventh floor at the General reminds me a little of a particularly bleak section of Manhattan expressway Jerry and I drove along once. Passing patients parked here and there along the hallways—with their IV stands attached to their walkers, and a look of futile becalmment in their eyes—is not that different from driving past cars abandoned at some underpass, as they wait with resignation to be looted and stripped.

Each room along this corridor is a private room, with a huge trash basket outside the door labeled, euphemistically, Red-Bag

Waste. As unmistakably a sign of contagion as a black mark on the doorsill in the time of the Plague, as eloquent a proclamation of doom as a skull-and-crossbones on the label of some household product.

Too late, it dawns on me that I could have stopped first at the giftshop for some flowers. But as a patient myself, I hadn't thought in conventional "visitor" terms. To my relief, when I wheel into Mark's room, I see that the place is already awash with flowers. As well as cheerfully bobbling Mylar balloons, and a succession of well-wishing teddy bears ranged along the windowsill. Before Mark came out, he would have puked if anyone had ever thought to gift him with a winsome plush bear. What is it about the recognition of his homosexuality, I wonder, that has turned him into Sebastian Flyte in the eyes of his friends?

Mark is lying in the bed, as lightly as a pile of dry sticks. His hair—growing in from that awful concentration-camp cut he's favored in recent years—seems sparse and tufted, like chicken down. In fact, he has so utterly declined—even from the ailing person I saw mere weeks ago—that the substitution is almost laughably improbable.

As I brake my wheelchair beside the bed, I become aware of two young men across from me, cuddled up together in the same vinyl-upholstered armchair. Two curly-haired youths, identically dressed in maroon sweatshirts that say Beaver Canoe and black sweatpants that don't say a word.

Neither do the two young men, who are sitting more or less in each other's lap, with their arms baroquely entwined, like Siamese twins. Both are gazing at Mark unwaveringly—as if awaiting some oracular utterance. Even the fleeting mutual-friends-of-the-patient smile they offer me seems abstracted.

"Mark?" I lean toward him, speaking in a cautious whisper.

Effortfully, he raises his head from his pillows, his shoulders jutting like skeletal wings. He attempts to focus, squinting at me critically, then frowns. "So, who are *you?*" he demands querulously. "You in the wheelchair. Don't tell me...Deborah Kerr—*after* she looks up at the Empire State Building in the middle of the traffic." As he laughs hoarsely at his own joke, the two young men laugh along with him.

Christ. Can it be the drugs? Or does—

But now, with even more strenuous effort, he is waggling his finger at me, to beckon me closer. "Are you all right?" he breathes, as I incline my ear toward his face. He smells stalely of medications.

"Of course," I tell him, choked by his concern. "It's you we have to take—"

"Because," he rasps on, "if you need anything, please drop a line. The world is divided into sections, you know, like an orange. And, since the globe is rotating on its axis all the time...Well, if you send a letter special delivery, it'll get here before you mail it."

It's more than pharmaceuticals, I think dully. Mark's mind is gone, and Ted didn't tell me. I cast a referential glance at the two young men in the armchair. Both are nodding and smiling appreciatively at Mark, as if the observation he's made is particularly apt. So maybe I'm the crazy one here. Which would, in a way, be preferable.

"Oh, Mark." Eventually, I can't help it. I hide my face in my hands, and begin to blubber, quietly. "I'm so, so sorry."

Sorry? I say it as though it's something I've done. But what? It's not even a case of who left whom, all those years ago, or a matter of who fell and who was pushed. A moot point, Mark and I agreed long ago, when contemplating our break-up in the aftermath, like an undifferentiated mound of bones, lying at the bottom of an airshaft.

Technically, I suppose I was the one who walked out. But it was Mark who, out of guilt, wanted to be the one who got left. In any case, when I left, I hurled myself out of the relationship with kamikaze zeal—and straight into the arms of someone I hoped was Mark's polar opposite. Which he was, if nothing else.

If I had gone back to Mark at that point, could I have prevented what's happened since? Can that be why I'm insisting on being sorry today? Mark—what's left of him—seems to have drifted off to sleep. As I sit in my wheelchair, staring at the sunken deathmask of his face, I ponder, for the first time in a long time, whether things between us could have ended up differently.

God knows, no sooner had I moved—in defiance—out to Vancouver with my new boyfriend, than I wanted to get away. But I held on, determined to make a life without Mark in it. Equally determined was my new boyfriend, who told me that if I tried to leave, he'd have to kill me. Which, initially, seemed almost flattering. Until the day I decided to leave.

When he surprised me in the act of packing, he kicked my suitcase across the room. It was the hard-bodied Samsonite number that my parents had given me as a graduation gift, and was supposedly up to the rigors of the road. However, on this occasion, it exploded on impact with the wall.

I recall staring, fascinated, as my clothes came spewing out like guts. My soon-to-be-ex-boyfriend stood staring too. Then recollected his mission and turned to me—almost apologetically—to make good on his threat.

Actually, he didn't care enough about me to kill me, or even try to. All he wanted to do was to kick me down a short flight of stairs and then throw what was left of my luggage after me. By the time I picked myself up and dragged my battered suitcase out onto the street, I could feel a bruise forming on my face, and my head was clanging like a school-bell.

I took a taxi to an inexpensive hotel, checked in, bolted the door of my room—and immediately called Mark long-distance, to beseech him to meet my plane from Vancouver the next day. To my relief, he seemed somewhat startled, but pleased.

Encouraged by that, I mused on strategies of reconciliation all through my flight, and even on arrival, as I stood at the baggage carousel to claim my kicked-in suitcase. Then, something made me turn in mid-muse, to see a good-looking, obviously gay man hurrying into the baggage-claim area.

It was a shock when I realized that the good-looking gay guy was hurrying toward *me*, to take me in his arms. "Whippet!" said Mark. "You look *terrible*. But it's so great to see you."

Of course, we hadn't seen each other in months. And now, in the airport, I viewed him as a stranger would. The frat boy I'd dated, the young man I'd married, the faithless husband I'd left mere moments before he left me... none of them existed any longer. In their place was this warmly smiling gay man—the kind about whom women sigh, "What a waste!"

It was—I remember thinking as I stepped into his embrace—as if Mark had died. At least, the Mark I had known was dead.

And today, in his hospital room, where I sit by what could well be his deathbed, I am positive there is nothing I can do, or could ever have done. Mark is simply slated to be a man who dies twice. Once, that day in the airport. And any day, any week, any month now... once again. Now that the good-looking stranger has been supplanted, in his turn, by this bony pile of sticks. So why is it that, through all these deaths, rebirths, and transformations, I remain the same person, still clinging to my role as his college sweetheart?

>–+–◆–○–◆–+–◄

"Don't cry."

The two identical young men are escorting me and my wheelchair back to the elevator, and on the way they take turns offering symbiotically entwined phrases of consolation. "He's actually having one of his *good* days." "We've seen other friends so much sicker." "We've lost, what, maybe thirty—" "More. Make that *fifty*." "—of our closest friends in the past few years, and..." "We know how you feel." "Really. We feel the same as you."

No, I think. You don't. Not about Mark.

But I thank them, and squeeze their hands, and tell them I'll see them next time. It's only later, when Ted drops in to my room, that I find I can't help railing at someone. "It's wrong! You know that. Mark is the brightest person I know. It's wrong to see him reduced to... well, *reduced*. Mentally, even more than physically."

"Yes, it's wrong," Ted agrees wearily. "But what, in your opinion, would be the correct medical response? Some days are good, some days are less good. Obviously, this is one of the less-good days. You see, his brain is beginning to swell, even as the rest of him is shrinking. And now he's—"

"And now he's babbling. Mark would hate this, if he knew. If he *knows*. Christ, who's to say he doesn't?"

Ted has pouches of exhaustion under his eyes. "So what are you telling me exactly, Dana? That it's up to me—or to you—to determine the appropriate moment to shut him down?"

Of course, when it comes down to it, I utterly abdicate. "It's just... when I look at him the way he is now, I ... miss Mark."

An expression that is almost penetrable crosses Ted's smooth, affectless face. "Me too."

Ted is younger than Mark and I. Yet so much more willing to be grown-up that it comes as a shock to me to recollect how much younger. Today particularly, with both the medical and the personal aging him before my eyes. "Of *course* you too. I'm sorry, Ted."

It is the first—and quite probably the only—meaningful exchange of feeling between the two of us. To our mutual credit, however, we do not hug.

"I miss Mark," Ted repeats. "But you tell me: What the hell am I supposed to do with who's left in that bed on the seventh floor?"

Chapter Two

When people remark that I must be glad the hospital is behind me, I tell them I'm even gladder the bedpan no longer is. Murphy, more than anyone, could relate to that, I think. The awfulness inherent in being expected to perform your bodily functions on command.

At first, after I got sent home, I was trapped in my wheelchair. Maybe my electrician friend from the Burn Ward was right, and I had no real worries. But what I did have was a lot of time on my hands. He'd have laughed—at least I think he would have—to see me wheeling around in tighter and tighter circles in my living room, pretending, out of sheer boredom, to be Joan Crawford in *What Ever Happened to Baby Jane?* right after her sister served up the canary. Or was it a rat?

Now that I've graduated to crutches, life is both easier and harder. Easier in that I can do things for myself to a greater extent. But harder as I try to figure out how to do those things without benefit of hands.

Getting around isn't the problem. On my crutches, I can swing my way to the grocery store, say, readily enough. However, once I arrive, the simplest act of consumerism becomes remarkably complicated to execute. Hippety-hopping up and down the aisles, pausing to steady myself as I fill up the canvas sack slung around my neck. Then, once I've paid, having to transfer the entire load into my backpack, before I'm able to start crutching.

Only to discover, halfway home, that it's raining, or worse. Which means I am compelled to hop gamely up the steps of the streetcar, with my groceries bouncing on my back, and my ticket to ride clamped alluringly between my teeth—for the driver to pluck from me like a single long-stemmed rose.

Mind you, there are compensatory aspects to being a cripple. I am now able to hobble into the snootiest stores. Impervious—for the first time in my life—to intimidation.

Gone is my lifelong fear of the salesclerks at Yves St. Laurent and Pierre Cardin, or worse. Those women whose hair is twisted so tightly atop their heads that their eyes water. And whose refrigerant manner suggests that they might not go home at night—but perhaps hang upside-down in the cold-storage vault with the furs, in order to keep their blood temperature down. Yet, not even such women, I now discover, possess the hauteur to take on a handicapper.

Instead, they merely stand by, smiling edgily, as I hobble along the length of their counters, fingering silk scarves with impunity. Then peg my way into the fitting room with fifteen-hundred-dollar dresses I have no intention of buying dangling by the hanger from my teeth. Daring those haughty hordes of supercilious saleswomen to so much as raise a plucked eyebrow in reproof.

Of course, there are always those embarrassing moments on the street, when I run into someone I know—who doesn't immediately recognize me in my new role as the Little Match-Girl. Or when I think I glimpse someone I know, and decide to sidestep them, if I can. To obviate the explanations I find myself mostly too weary to give.

Once, I caught a glimpse of Carl. Or thought I did, which was almost as bad. Not in a stationwagon this time, *en famille*, but walking on a downtown street, not far from his office. Which made the sighting seem all the more plausible. I ducked my head and swung myself along on my crutches as fast as I could, horrified at the prospect of being viewed—by him, of all people—as a cripple.

Only then did it occur to me: precisely because I am a cripple, I am not viewed at all. In all likelihood Carl—if it was, in fact, he— would not have known me. A middle-aged woman on crutches is all he'd see. A generic handicapper, making her way, as unremarkable and as inconsequential as a stray dog skulking past.

The perfect disguise, in other words. Utterly invisible in my very conspicuousness. Just the thing, if I were to take up stalking as an occupation during my waking hours—which I most definitely am *not*. No, not even if that was Carl, strolling briskly along the street in the direction of his office.

Three times a week, I crutch up to the Outpatient Department at the General for physiotherapy. To spend a salutary hour or so lying on my back on a mat, raising and lowering my plaster leg, in order (they say) to prevent the muscles from atrophying. While some therapist's aide—more absorbed in her *Soap Opera Digest*, for which I can't blame her—drones "Up and down, up and down..." over and over.

Murphy, you can relate to that, can't you? Do you still remember the repetitive roster of "sit, heel, stay"? As if you could forget. Then picture me, Murphy, if you will: Lifting my plastered leg as high as I am able, then slowly bringing it down again. Up, down, up, down, over and over on command. Wondering, as I obey, why—in all the time I spent trying to teach you—it never once occurred to me that there might be anything I could learn from you. Such as how to move my ears independently of each other, the way you can. Or which itches are better nibbled than scratched. And what all is involved in relocating a buried bone.

Eventually, as my leg grows heavier and harder to lift, I can't help wondering whether learning how to twitch my ears or scratch my chin with my toenails might not be easier than this. "Up and down, up and down..." Good, Dana. Good, good dog. "Up and down, down and up..." There's something about the rhythm of it that lulls me into a trance. I lie here on my back, watching my plaster-covered leg rise and fall in front of my face, over and over again. Like Sisyphus rolling his rock endlessly up the hill, I feel not discontent. Feel, in some strange way, even grateful for my rock, oddly happy on the hill.

Above the top edge of my cast, however, a patch of unshaven

hair bristles alarmingly. While beneath the pastry crust of plaster, I can feel other, even stubblier, hairs growing in. Springing up under my cast like moss run rampant on a shaded log.

Surely elsewhere on my body, I can feel fur growing? Before I know it, a fuzzy pair of paws—menopaws!—may sprout from the cuffs of my sweatshirt. I'm panting, Murphy. Is that only because I'm working up a sweat? Or are these flashes of heat precursors to some vast Change of Life? No, nothing so trivial as menopause. What I have in mind is a far more ominous thermostatic shift: from a normal human body temperature of ninety-eight-point-six Fahrenheit to something closer to a hundred and two degrees. Doesn't that feel about right to you, Murphy?

Oh, God. I dare not look too closely at my reflection in the mirror that runs the length of the wall in the physiotherapy room. Nor attract the notice of the bored attendant putting me through my limited paces. For fear of finding out that I am turning into something even more improbable than what is retailed in the episodes outlined in her *Soap Opera Digest*.

I mean, in my time, I've been taken for a lot of things: a goldmine of unrealized creative potential; a psychic soulmate; a reasonably good sport, and a reasonably good lay. Sometimes, I've just been taken. But never, in my whole long life to date, have I been taken for a dog. Well...except maybe on that bus, way back when...

Murphy, if my humanity is, in fact, in recession, then you will have to be the one to teach me how to let it go. Into that companionable realm, where the past and present live side by side, mingling in cozy co-habitation, with no distinctions drawn between that which is gone and what's to come.

Today, Murphy, the hill. Tomorrow, that long undefended border of Time and Space that constitutes the one true divide between Here and There, between you and me...

God, if something like that actually happened to me, I like to think that I could take the longer, calmer view. I mean, in certain script-writing circles, it would be regarded as a real stroke of luck for a ho-hum amazing-animal-TV-series hack such as myself to find herself—one fine day in the physiotherapy room—miraculously transformed into a dog.

Talk about your George Plimptonesque on-the-spot research possibilities. Talk about your girls-who-just-wanna-have-the-fun-of-converting-the-grist-of-raw-experience-into-the-pure-gold-of-artistry happy ending story! Talk about—but that's just it. I couldn't. Talk, I mean. If I suddenly turned into a dog. Or type, if it came to that. Which, in my line of work, it most certainly would, sooner or later.

The truth is, lying here on my back on a mat in the physiotherapy room at the General Hospital, lifting up my leg and putting it down over and over again, I may well have forfeited my humanity for something more primal, something lower. But there's no guarantee what that something is.

At the same time, there's no denying I've forfeited much more than my claim to that lost art of walking upright, unassisted, on my own two feet. I've lost my claim to Murphy. Who does not hear me, no matter how loudly I shout his name inside my head. Murphy, who has no interest in how sorry I am, or how newly sensitized I've become to what he could have taught me, if I'd only cared to listen.

Murphy is no more, not even in my dreams. All that's left to me, sleeping and waking, is the fur-covered fantasy of Amazing Grace. Six dogs in one, the brightest star in Canis Major, or any other constellation, in any galaxy you care to name. Gleaming up in the firmament, like the most brightly polished diamond since a no-account collie name of Pal.

And if Amazing Grace is all I'm left with, then for her and her stand-ins and doubles I must toil on. Keeping my leg limber and free of atrophy. Keeping my invention alive, to the limited extent it can be. Hooked, as O'Ryan branded me. Not on the paycheck, but on the payoff. Doing my best, like a good, good dog. Not because Murphy is there to care, if he ever did. But because I'm still here, and now I do.

Chapter Three

It's O'Ryan's idea of a surprise to convey me up to the studio the day shooting starts on my script. He doesn't blindfold me, but that's certainly the spirit of the occasion, and the flourish with which he leads me onto the set has something of the old-fashioned prestidigitational flavor of *This Is Your Life.*

Nobody else associated with *Amazing Grace* has heard about my accident. Consequently, as I swing across the lot on my crutches, a general murmur arises from the battalions of script editors, script assistants, assistant producers, and assembled crew. As each one tries to work out whose last-minute rewrite might have resulted in the sudden appearance of a crippled character in the story, and who might be this unknown actress evidently engaged to play the part.

"Dana!" Glenda the script-supervisor-or-editor-or-whatever is the first to recognize me, and she sails toward me, clipboard in hand, with the air of a social convener on a particularly tautly run cruise ship. "Well, this is unexpected!" She indicates my crutches and cast with a vague, inclusive gesture that suggests I've chosen to accessorize in some new and startling way. "I wondered what you've been up to. You know, everybody's having such a terrific time with this script of yours!"

I'll just bet they are. Particularly the rewrite people. "I hope it's okay if I just showed up," I say. "It was Mick O'Ryan's idea to bring me up here to see some scenes with the wolves."

"By all means!" Glenda could not be nodding more vigorously if the idea had originated with her instead of O'Ryan. "Your timing is absolutely terrific, because the wolves are on set this very... Well, you'll see. I'm sure O'Ryan, or one of the other wranglers, will be only too happy to make introductions."

It's a cold gray day with heavy clouds and intermittent flecks of snow. In a large enclosure, similar to a dog-run, several timber wolves are pacing dispiritedly. Their appearance is a shock to me. These slinking creatures are nothing like what I had in mind. In most cases, I couldn't care less if what I wrote resembles what gets shot. But this time, I do. First of all, because it's what I wrote that compels these wolves to be here at all—literally pacing in the wings. But what makes me even sadder is the contrast between my script requirements—a big bold wolf to "save" Amazing Grace out in the wild—and these poor spiritless animals, who look incapable of saving even themselves.

"Oh, God, O'Ryan." I crutch closer to the pen, and find my face being scrutinized by several sets of yellow eyes, eerily akin to Murphy's. "These poor guys should be running loose, in some big wilderness preserve."

"Hey, no way. These lobos are troopers. They love t' work, as much as the dogs do. That's why all the excitement about yer scrip. Not only do we get to work these guys, but the episode is 'wolf positive,' as Brady says, and that's good for business."

"But... they look wretched, humiliated. Christ, I should never have written that script."

"Dana! Shit!" O'Ryan looks hurt, and uncomprehending. "What the hell are you talkin' about?"

But I am spared the necessity of further explanation by the arrival of a short, paunchy, pale-eyed man with a rust-colored set of muttonchops.

"Hey!" says O'Ryan. "It's Brady, my bossman. You can ask him if these here critters ain't the happiest of campers. Yo, Brady! Say hey to Dana Jaeger here. She wrote the scrip—wolves an' all—and I've been lettin' her meet the cast. Plus, lettin' her in on what smoke-cured hams these big boys are."

"Surest thing ya know," Brady agrees. But when he runs his pale eyes over me, with the air of a practiced appraiser of animal flesh, I sense that he's picked me out as a potential troublemaker. "I got me six dogs, eh? Well, you must of met the Majors at some point. And I got me four wolves. And when you see 'em workin' together on the set—dog and wolf—you're gonna be hard put, I guarantee it, little lady, to tell me which of 'em's havin' a bigger blast."

I smile wanly at Brady, then glance back at the wolves. Wondering how he or anyone can tell when they're having a "blast" of any dimensions.

>⸱⬩⸱◦⸱⬩⸱⟨

"I'm sorry," I say, wiping my eyes. O'Ryan, with infinite tact, has helped me to a secluded spot behind a trailer, where I can leak my rueful tears in private. "I wasn't expecting to react like this. As if it's all my fault. Which I guess it is."

O'Ryan pats my back soothingly. "Y'know, there's such a thing as caring too much about this stuff. I warned you about that, didn't I, the last time we talked?"

"You mean when you accused me of becoming hooked on writing this garbage? No, as I recall, you thought that was a good thing. Well, not today, certainly. Christ, if anything could put me right off it, it's—"

"You told *me* some things too, that day in that burger joint. Remember? About Karen?"

With a final shaky sigh, I relinquish all expectation of making clear to O'Ryan what so appalls me about the lot of those wolves, and my own complicity in it. Obviously, he'd rather talk about Karen. It may even be safe to suppose that one of his unspoken motives in arranging this day on the set for me was to make time for the very conversation we are about to have. "What about Karen? I haven't seen her since before my accident, or even heard from her since she left me a message to say she was about to leave town. Of course, that's our Karen. Always about to leave town."

O'Ryan squints off into the distance, like the stoical hero of the Old West he is at heart. "Truth to tell, she's gone."

"Oh! To L.A.? Honestly?"

He shoots me a swift look. "You make it sound like you don't think so."

"Well, L.A.'s a fairly common threat of hers. Usually she even invites me along, and it's no big deal that neither of us winds up going. Of course, since I never did get back to her, maybe she went away mad at me. If, that is, she went at all."

"She went, all right," says O'Ryan, pained. "Says she's fixin' to teach at some...comedy school for drivers?"

"You mean Traffic School?"

"Yeah, that's it. She says she did that before."

"She did. Apparently in California there's compulsory retraining for drivers when they lose their license. And, being California, they try to make it 'fun,' with some sort of gimmick like gourmet cooking—or standup comics as driving instructors. I'm sure Karen's good at it. But she *has* done it before. Which makes me wonder why she went back. Did she let on to you?"

He shakes his head heavily, like a buffalo, "Not in so many words."

He isn't actually looking me in the eye, though, and my sense is that—now that he's contrived to be in this conversation—he wishes he wasn't.

"But...you did talk to her before she left?"

"Yeah, only by the time she left, she started goin' real snaky on me."

Snaky. Perfect for Karen. "Snakier than usual, you mean?"

O'Ryan wets his lips, as if preparing to launch into some revelation—the breadth and depth of which he is still in the process of trying to work out. "Well," he allows at length, "the thing of it is, I done what you told me to: I tried to...*confront* her."

"It's not exactly that I told you, O'Ryan. I merely agreed with you that the time may have come to—"

"Anyways, I tried, and...well, the upshot was, I got dusted fer my trouble."

Yes, the "dusted" part I recall from Karen's message on my machine. "I'm sorry. Still, isn't it better to know the worst?"

"I guess." He shrugs, unconvinced, and it occurs to me that I've never before seen O'Ryan this close to misery. Beaten down, belly hugging the ground, like something subdued and caged. "Only... turns out it gets worse yet. See, Dana, the thing of it was, after I told her it was time she and me fished or cut bait, she told *me* she was splittin' fer the coast. Somehow, though, I didn't believe that was so."

"You mean you thought she was only saying that to make a clean break?"

"Somethin' like that." And he winces, as if the wound is still fresh. "Only fer me, it didn't feel clean, not feelin' about her the way I do. So...I started in followin' her."

"Following? You mean like...*stalking* her?"

"No, no, not like that. Not with nightscope goggles and black face paint or whatever."

Maybe not, but following her nonetheless. The idea both intrigues and horrifies me, and I carefully compose my face into an expression revealing of nothing. "Okay," I nod encouragingly. "So you followed her."

"Yeah." Again he wets his lips, embarrassed. "And it was like I thought: she never left town. Not fer a couple weeks, anyways. Seems she had way too much to do—trailing after guys she didn't even seem to know that well. Honest to God, Dana, it's the damndest thing. Remember what I told you that day in the restaurant, how I always had the impression when she left my place she was headed someplace else?"

"I remember. But what do you mean about guys she doesn't even know?"

As O'Ryan swallows hard, I can sense he's debating not telling me any more. And yet, now that he's come this far, he's thinking he might as well go the whole hog. "Well, it's not like she even *talks* to them. It's more like...she's got this list, and these guys are on it, and she has a regular routine of checkin' up on 'em. Late at night, in her car, driving up to the house, parking, turning out the headlights..."

I shiver. Both at the idea of Karen actually doing something so creepily characteristic of what I've imagined—and at the idea of

O'Ryan trailing her as she trails the obscure objects of her more obscure desire. "And these men are...men she's in love with at a distance, do you suppose? Or, men who've hurt her?"

"I can't say fer sure. Could be either one, or both. All I know is, she told me she was headed out of town, and she wasn't at all."

Oh, well, I think wearily. A comparatively commonplace misdemeanor, that. Especially when put alongside Karen's quirkier vices. "But I thought you told me she *has* left town."

"Yeah, in the end, she did. Only to get away from *me*, she said." Once more, his face is pinched with pain.

"Oh," I say as delicately as I can. "Then she caught you following her?"

"Yup. And she was hoppin' mad. Only, you know what, Dana? I don't believe I'm the reason she finally left. I think one of those guys of hers is headed down to the coast, and she's doggin' him all the way there, if that's what it takes."

For all I know, O'Ryan is right. If anyone understands the true nature of the truly hopeless quest, that person—at this point—is probably O'Ryan. And yet—at this point—telling him he's right would hardly constitute consolation.

"Well, going to California, for whatever reason, might not be such a bad idea," I essay cautiously. "I mean, some distance from Karen won't hurt *you*, and for all we know, she might work out her...obsession, or whatever it is. And come back a little less snaky. She will be back—once she gets fed up teaching Traffic School and waiting tables and cashiering at some liquor mart, in lieu of headlining at the Comedy Store."

Although, there is a certain irony in the idea of Karen in Los Angeles, helping those who've lost their driving privileges. When, for once, she could actually be useful here, helping me to claim that privilege for the first time in my life.

"Maybe," says O'Ryan, "but I'm not fixin' on waitin' to find out."

"I don't blame you. You've suffered enough on Karen's account. Just forget her."

340 • Erika Ritter

"No, I mean," he says, shamefaced, "as soon as this shoot's finished with, I'm headin' out myself."

"You are? Where to?" But I'm afraid I already know.

"Could be I'll take a drive down California way." He's blushing beet-red—or, at any rate, a more roseate shade of tanned leather—and I don't wonder why.

"Oh, God, O'Ryan. To find Karen?"

He shrugs and almost manages a grin. "Loco, right? That's what you think."

What I think is that even the mind's eye does not afford many sights more bizarre than the image I currently have of Karen's elusive quarry in his car—with Karen following at a discreet distance in her yellow Bug, and even farther behind, O'Ryan tailing her in his battered old Pontiac sedan, down some Pacific coastal highway, in a stately three-car procession.

"Well, I'll miss you" is what I elect to say instead. O'Ryan, of course, doesn't know the half of that. If and when I ever do decide it's time to learn to drive a car in order to head off in pursuit of my own peculiar destiny, I apparently won't be able to count on his tutelage, either.

O'Ryan looks at me long and searchingly. "But you're not telling me not to go."

"No, I'm not. Who knows? Out of some of the worst messes, good things can come."

Well, hell, what *should* I tell the poor sap: that the worst messes generally tend to generate something more horrific still? I mean, now at least I've got the guy smiling for the first time this afternoon.

"I'm sorry," he says. "I guess bringin' you up here to the set today wasn't such a hot-shit surprise after all."

"Never mind. You meant well. You always do."

You see? With such a gift for reassurance, I should be writing heartwarming family-adventure drama for television. Creating a positive parallel galaxy out there somewhere, in which things really do turn out for the best, week after week. For everybody, man and beast. Shucks, even for the wolves.

Chapter Four

I have no idea what sins of mine I think I can expiate by dropping in on Mark, with religious regularity, after each of my sessions of physiotherapy. All I know for certain is that some measure of comfort is availed to me in the mere act of sitting beside the bed where he lies like a cadaver, mostly silent, except for the regular hissing of his oxygen mask.

According to Ted, Mark has now slipped into the state common to long-term patients who can no longer remember any previous life. All that is visible of his face, above his mask, are his round gray eyes, protuberant and staring from his shrunken skull. Astonished is how they look—like eyes that seek you out from famine posters. Seldom when I visit is Mark having what Ted calls a "good" day, when he really seems to know me. But however uncomprehendingly, that horrified stare of his always finds me as I ease myself off my crutches and into the vinyl armchair next to the bed.

Today, as is typical, Ted's mother, Gertie, sits in her favorite corner of the room, knitting away. I hate the placid click of her needles, yet can't find the words to ask her to stop. Ted is more or less living at the hospital now—doing his rounds, then sleeping a few hours at a time on a cot next to Mark's bed. So that if Gertie wants to see her son at all, here is where she, too, has to be. And what else has the poor woman got to do but knit?

Even now, I have no idea how much Gertie knows about the specific nature of this tragedy. Perhaps it still doesn't make much difference to her what is going on. Perhaps she is simply prepared, as she always has been, to accept us all—herself included—as participants in some real-life drama, without concern for how our biographies interconnect. Ever ready, for her own part, to muck in, front up, be on side, no matter what. Any enemy of her son Ted's is her enemy, too. Which means that Mark's disease is her enemy—even if Mark himself may always have been, to Gertie, somewhat incidental.

A port has been inserted in Mark's emaciated forearm—a permanent site into which myriad drugs can drip without the constant jabbing of separate needles. More and more, his vision is failing, and one of the ways I occupy myself, sitting by his bed, is by reading out loud from the newspapers. Formerly something of a news junkie, Mark now falls asleep, even in the midst of my most spirited readings. Nonetheless, I continue to read, and with expression. Not so much in expectation of reaching him as in hopes of taking my own mind off the steady *click, click, click* of Gertie's knitting needles.

Today, however, Gertie furls up her knitting and her needles early, and declares herself "a bit peckish." "P'raps I'll pop down to the cafeteria, dear. Shall I fetch you back a sandwich?"

I tell her no thanks, but offer to accompany her as far as the elevator on my way to the john. "Ted must be exhausted," I remark, as I swing along the corridor on my crutches beside her. "It's particularly hard for a doctor, don't you think—trying to remain clinical about...such a close friend?"

"Oh, Ted's always been a sensible sort," Gertie says, with satisfaction.

I wait for more, but nothing more comes. "Well, what about you?" I venture next. "You're here almost every day, Gertie. How do you stand up to all of this?"

"Oh, well..." As we wait for an elevator, Gertie's head is bobbling tremulously, like the head of one of those toy animals people put in the rear window of the car. "The room is pleasant enough; the nurses pop in to chat, and I have all my fancywork. And, of course, Ted looks in, whenever he has a minute."

Of course. Ted, who makes it all worthwhile. In fact, Gertie doesn't see herself as at all hard done by, and perhaps with good reason. After all, in her world, widows with sons are often shunted off, or sidelined by territorial daughters-in-law. Whereas, up until just lately, Gertie had her weekly dinners with "the boys," regular as clockwork, weekends up at their cottage, even the occasional vacation—when Mark and Ted weren't headed some place too blatantly gay. All things considered, she's remarkably lucky, and even now does not seem to regard another dismal lunch in the hospital cafeteria as too much of a price to pay for ongoing inclusion in Ted's life—and Mark's demise.

Although, she seems determined not to mention Mark. Which determines me, just as stubbornly, to contrive that she should. "Mark's failing so rapidly now, though. Every time I come by, he's visibly lower."

"Well, p'raps. Still, it's good of you to stop by so often, given your own, uh, condition."

"Not so good of me. Since I'm in the building anyway—and my condition is only temporary. Meanwhile, Mark is—"

"Still, you do what you can, don't you? Which is all any of us can do, I expect."

Grr. The elevator car has arrived; the door is yawning wide to admit Gertie. I can see now there never will arise between us even as frank a moment as I shared with Ted. Gertie and I have already come as close as we ever will—no distance at all—to addressing the abiding mystery of our respective roles in this sad little drama. If Gertie realizes that I was once more to Mark than an old-shoe girlfriend, and if she understands, if only tangentially, that a deeper relationship than roommates is what exists between Mark and Ted, and if she's heard or read anything about AIDS in the past decade and a half...well, those are secrets she's apparently planning to take to the grave. And short of grasping her by the scruff of her sagging neck and forcing her to admit what she knows and when she knew it, I have no idea how to get the truth from her. Or—if it comes to that—why I think I should even bother.

"I may or may not still be here when you get back upstairs," I offer by way of inane farewell, as the elevator doors begin to slide shut. "If not, I'll see you next time." And the last thing I see this time, as the doors come together, is Gertie's benignly nodding head, and her face as round and calm as the Buddha's.

On my return to Mark's room, I am startled to find him sitting up, uncharacteristically alert, with his oxygen mask pushed up, almost raffishly, to the top of his head.

"Mark! Put the mask back on. You shouldn't be—"

"Come here, Dana," he says, wheezy but firm.

Obediently, I make my way over to his bed, where, bolstered by a pile of pillows, he has a transcendent aspect, like a saint shortly on his way to Paradise.

"What can I do?" I am grateful both for this moment of privacy with him, and for his sudden, apparent lucidity.

"Dana, you know how I worry about you. The way you latch on to those clowns. The way you never seem to get on with your life."

"Yes." I am more than startled by his miraculous reconnection to his old, pontificating self; I am thunderstruck. So thunderstruck that I don't even object to what he's saying. "But don't worry about me right now. Just worry about getting better. And God, this moment you *seem* so much better!"

With a grimace, he shifts in the bed. "Look—do you remember crazy Uncle Fred? Who had the cabin out in the Maritimes?"

"Of course I remember your uncle Fred. He gave us a pool table as a wedding gift—for our one-room apartment. I always liked him for that. But I don't recall anything about a cabin."

"Well, he had one. And when he died last year, he willed it to me. I haven't been there yet, but I hear it's pretty good."

"Oh." So this is it: a dying request. He wants, somehow, to see the cabin before he dies, and I'm going to have to pretend that's possible. "Well, at this time of year, of course, it would probably be pretty desolate out there—"

"Oh, no. It's fully winterized."

"Oh." I still cannot focus firmly on the fact that I am having a conversation with Mark about his uncle's cabin—or about anything at all. "I guess when you get out of here, you and Ted can go down East and check the place out."

"Whippet!" His expression, despite his bulging, staring eyes, is almost amused. "I'm not getting out of here, and you know it, so cut the crap. I want *you* to go to Uncle Fred's place."

"Me? Whatever would—"

"Don't argue with me. It wastes my breath. Just do what I'm asking you. Take the key—it's an old skeleton key—off my key ring, on the nighttable. And you keep it. Until you're ready to go. I mean it, Whippet. More than anything, you need some place you can just... go. And I don't know how else to help."

I have no idea what he's talking about; all the same, I know that he's in his right mind. Saner than I am, probably. "Mark, I appreciate this, but you really should keep the key yourself. You know, as a kind of... badge of hope."

"Dana." With an Herculean effort, he heaves himself more upright. He is now wheezing heavily. "Let's not kid each other. Just take the key. It would make me feel hopeful to know that you have it. After all, we've loved each other, you and I."

We have loved each other. Blinded by tears, I hobble over to the nightstand and remove the key from the ring. At the same time, willing myself not to look at him—the shriveled concentration-camp victim, barely managing to sit up, even with all his pillows. Just for a moment, I want to focus on the memory of the boy I first knew. Who came up behind me one day as I stood over a frying pan, and surprised me so that I clapped my hands, smelling of onions, to my mouth. "I still do love you, Mark."

"I still love you, too." His voice is dwindling to a whisper. "But now you really have to move on."

"I know." And I do know it now, as well as he does. I haul myself on my crutches back to the bed, and bend down to kiss his brow, and replace his oxygen mask. "Mark, I'm leaving now, okay? Gertie'll be back in a minute. I'll see you soon."

And I ride the elevator down to the lobby, my eyes still blurry with tears, but with the key to Uncle Fred's cabin lying like a chunk of reassurance in the pocket of my coat.

>—+—•>—•—<•—+—<

Grasping my crutches in one hand and the railing with the other, I hop effortfully up the porch steps. Then steady myself by resting my forehead against the door as I fish out my house key. Then, I tuck a crutch back under each armpit, push open the door, and swing across the sill. By the time I've shut the door behind me, I am breathing hard with the rigor of my exertions.

The phone starts to ring, and I hustle for it eagerly, feeling grateful for its cheery peal. After a visit with Mark, I welcome any evidence of a planet still spinning in an orbit unaffected by pestilence or by the skeletal hand of memory, and I crave the prospect of someone, anyone, at the end of the line offering some robust alternative to the spectral dimension I've just returned from.

"Hello?"

"Dana. Hello. It's Leonard."

"Leonard!" Leonard, of course, is one of the Marrieds. Although it's been so long since he last came through town that it takes me a moment to turn up his card in my mental Rolodex. "Where are you, anyway?"

"At home. At least, in my car, not far from my house. Look, I won't beat about the bush here." His voice sounds remote, rushed, peremptory—an effect perhaps attributable to his car phone. Or perhaps not. "I heard you've had...a medical situation to cope with. I'm very concerned."

"Oh!" It amazes me that an out-of-towner like Leonard would ever have gotten wind of my bicycling mishap. "Well, don't worry. It really wasn't as horrendous as—"

"Dana, I'm not going to pretend to you that I'm NOT worried. Shocked, is a little more like it. I mean, I had no idea you'd even been married, let alone that...Well, it's a bit of a stunner, that's all. A bit of a stunner."

"I...beg your pardon?" I have, of course, heard him perfectly well, in spite of the static. What's more, I think I'm beginning to understand what he's trying to say. But my initial impulse is to protect myself from that fact.

"You're not denying that you have an ex-husband?"

No, but at this moment—though it shames me to admit it—I would very much like to. Not to prove to Mark that I have indeed moved on. Rather, to prove to myself that an existence in which I never married him at all is as plausible as its alternative. "I'm not confirming or denying anything," I temporize. "Not until you read me my Miranda rights."

"Are you *joking* about this? I hope not."

No, I'm not going to joke, I decide. Leonard may merit that, but Mark deserves better. "Leonard, Mark and I were split up many years before I ever met you. And, frankly, it never occurred to me that I was supposed to include him in my *curriculum vitae* in perpetuity."

"Don't be smart, Dana, I implore you. This is not an easy phone call for me to make."

"No, I can imagine not. Considering that you have to hold the receiver with one hand and drive with the other."

"Look, the point is, he's dying of AIDS, isn't he?"

"How did you ever—?"

"Never mind how I know it. The fact remains, it's a hell of a thing."

"Oh, you're telling *me?*"

"And whereas I'm sorry about the emotional effects of all this on you—I'm afraid I have to ask: What is the current state of your *own* health?"

"Of my...? Leonard, let me make sure I have this straight. Are you asking me if I'm infected?"

"Oh, come on. You're a woman of the world. I can't be the only recent partner of yours who's thought to ask? After all, without any notion of when your marriage ended, and what you've ascertained about your own level of risk—"

"Leonard, stop right there, okay? And let me ask *you* something: Don't you think that if I were at risk, I'd have notified anyone I might possibly have exposed to the same danger?"

"Well, I would hope so. On the other hand..."

"On the other hand, you don't actually know me well enough to say for sure what I'd do."

"Dana, come on, now." And Leonard actually attempts a laugh, which on his car phone comes across high-pitched and nervous. "I do know you pretty well, I think. And I believe what you're telling me. But, to me, it made sense to ask. I am a married man, after all."

"Yes, I know you are." Although how that signifies, I can't really see. Since Leonard and his wife stopped sleeping together about as long ago as I stopped sleeping with Mark. The only difference being, he and his wife still live together. Suddenly, I am no longer merely stunned by the content of this conversation, I am sickened by it. "And you know what else I know about you, Leonard? You're a real slime-bucket for calling me up like this, at a time like this, without even proffering a modicum of sympathy for a man who's dying. How come I never realized before what a slime-bucket you are?" Although, of course, I've always known what Leonard is—and what I am, by association. The only difference now is that I may have begun to want to become something else.

"Look, there's no reason for you to take this tone. Considering that I have every right to—"

"Certainly you have every right, Leonard. And don't let me keep you on the line another minute. Since you probably have what Oscar Wilde would describe as many other calls of a similar character to make in the neighborhood. I mean, I can't be your *only* out-of-town fuck with a dying loved one that you'd like to harass her about."

After I hang up the phone, I sit for a long moment, thinking absolutely nothing. Until it occurs to me that I am thinking something, after all. Am, in fact, considering alternatives. Really considering them.

One, is to go on as I am right now: sitting desolate and alone, with a pair of crutches leaning against my chair, and no real plan beyond readying myself for more phone calls just like Leonard's once word of Mark and his illness reaches more of the Marrieds.

Another alternative is to do what Mark suggests, and utterly change the scene at last. Not someday, when I'm all healed up. But right now, while it all still hurts.

After all, what am I waiting for? Mark may linger on for weeks, even months. In any case, he was clear about wanting me to go. Any day now O'Ryan will follow Karen to the coast, or—failing to find her in L.A.—to the ends of the earth, if necessary. I've given up on whatever Marrieds haven't given up on me first. And renounced true love as a star too remote ever to figure in my horoscope. Even my future as a hack is in genuine peril now that I've committed the cardinal sin of caring, if only a little bit.

When I present the case to myself like this, there is every reason to go, and none to stay. And yet, go to what, precisely? Along what road?

It's a long winding road that leads to Jerry's front door. And waiting for me at the end... Well, perhaps not waiting for me, exactly. Still, even at this late date, I'll bet there's one thing Murphy and I could agree on: it's definitely my turn to come, whether or not I'm called.

It would be something, wouldn't it? To burn all my doubts, regrets, misgivings, and bridges. In that one brief, intoxicating moment—before I step on the gas and wipe that tear away.

Chapter Five

Even as I negotiate my way up the narrow staircase that leads to Luis Da Silva's Portuguese Driving Academy, I am conscious of, paradoxically, heading downward—right to the very bottom of the barrel. Certainly that's been the implication, almost in so many words, of the instructors at all the driving schools that have so far turned me down. "Why don't you try Da Silva's?" they've suggested, to a man and a woman. "Luis takes just about anybody."

Well, just *about* anybody, as it turns out.

"Sure, sure" is Luis's initially positive response, once my crutches and I finally make it up the stairs and into his makeshift-looking office, located above Da Silva's Portuguese Groceteria. "I teach you, jes' how you like. De owdamadic trangsmissen, de stick-shiff-four-onna-floor. How you like it, is how I teach."

So far, it sounds ideal to me. "Well, standard transmission, if I have the choice." I beam. "I haven't actually bought a car yet, but when I do, I think, for the sake of fuel efficiency and the environment and all—"

"Sure, sure only...Now? Sorry, no. You, I don' teach now." And with that, Luis plucks the application-to-register blank, in English and Portuguese, out of my hand.

"Oh, well, okay. If you think my particular injury might be a problem, then I'll go for automatic. I can always learn the clutch business later." Firmly, I snatch back the application form, and steady myself against Luis's desk, determinedly prepared to fill it out.

"No, no." Once more, he whips the piece of paper out from under my nose. "You, like I say, I not teach. 'Cause, look, you got the leg, you know it? All fuck up, yes?"

"Well, a little." I consider making a final, futile swipe at the registration blank—then think better of it. "Which is precisely why this would be the ideal moment for me to learn to drive. Because I can't ride a bike anymore, Luis. And I can't walk very well, and even climbing aboard public transportation is a major hassle. I mean, *everyone* is entitled to some way to get around, don't you think?"

"Sure, sure." Luis's eyes are dark with compassion; at the same time, he is shrugging his shoulders. "Only, look...You come back sometime, how is that? You come later, when is good for you to drive. Okay?"

"But that's what I'm trying to tell you: once it's good for me to drive, I can do without driving. Now is when I need to learn. And as I said, I don't need my left foot to work just a brake pedal and an accelerator, do I? So, why not take me out for a spin in an automatic, and see what I can and cannot do?"

Even as I argue with Luis, I can't escape reflection on the irony of the whole situation: I, who have stood stalwartly in opposition to every single person who's ever suggested to me that I ought to learn to drive, am now reduced to begging for the opportunity to get behind that wheel and work those controls, under the tutelage of a man who is barely accredited.

Begging in vain, too, it appears, as Luis shakes his head sorrowfully. "No. No way. 'Cause, look, is like this, okay? No matter what anybody say to you—even at Luis Da Silva Portuguese Academy of Driving, you gotta walk before you can drive. You see it?"

All I can see, as I hobble defeatedly back down the stairs, is that what I really need to do is learn how to drive, whether I ever walk again or not. Which calls, I'm afraid, for extraordinary measures, and expedients more desperate than signing my life into Luis's dubious care—even if he were willing to take me on.

Resolutely, I crutch my way back to my apartment, where— without allowing myself to think too clearly about what I'm planning to do—I go to the phone and immediately dial, before I can change my mind.

"Hart."

In spite of myself, I experience a surge of pleasure at the sound of Carl's voice, which is so brisk and so characteristically uptempo, that I feel as if no time at all has elapsed. "Hi, Hart. I'm returning your call. Or calls, I should say."

A pause. Then, "Christ. It can't be, unless...Hang on. Is it April Fool's already? My, my, how time flies when one is waiting for the phone to ring." His tone, I notice, is carefully crafted to match mine—casual, cordial, unrevealing. Except, in Carl's case, the air of insouciance may well be genuine.

"All right. I admit I'm a bit slow getting back to you."

"Just a bit, sweetheart. I...look, how are you? I *was* beginning to wonder, after all this time."

It's obvious that Carl knows nothing about my accident, or any other disaster that might have befallen, since I broke up with him. "I'm fine." And I take a deep breath, to confirm for myself that I actually am. "Carl, I'll be honest. The reason I'm calling now is, I need to ask a favor."

"Name it," he says. With such gratifying promptness that it's all I can do to keep from falling in love with him all over again.

"What I want is...I want to take you up on the offer you made to me, remember? To teach me how to drive a car."

"If I'm at your place in a half-hour," he replies, "is that soon enough?"

Chapter Six

For once, Carl is as good as his word. Exactly thirty minutes after I've hung up the phone, I hear his familiar tread on the porch steps, followed by the ringing of the bell. I make my way down the hall, and pause only long enough to paste a game smile on my face before opening the door.

"My, my!" On the other side of the door, Carl is also smiling. "It's certainly—" And then his smile abruptly fades as he takes in my crutches, and my left leg in its cast, drawn up like a stork's. "Christ, what's all this?"

"I had an accident. But I'm getting better."

"What sort of accident?" Standing here on my front porch, Carl looks unsettlingly the same. It seems impossible to me—almost indecent—that he hasn't changed in the eventful weeks since our break-up. But he hasn't. The gray flecks in his hair that I noticed the last time are still there, along with the fine lines around his eyes. And the tweed coat he's wearing today strikes me as too drab for him, like something more appropriate to a colorless operative in a British spy novel. However, in a general sense, he's the same Carl who turned up on this same porch one rainy day and inspired me to fall in love with him, in defiance of all my saner instincts.

"I guess I should have prepared you over the phone," I apologize. "It looks a lot more serious than it is."

"Yes?" He raises a skeptical eyebrow. "May I say, it looks serious enough. What on earth happened?"

"Later. You promised to teach me how to drive, remember? I hope that's still on, anyway."

"Well...we can talk about it."

Carl takes my crutches and supports me down the steps. Even in this unglamorous circumstance, the touch of his hand on my arm still has the power to speed my pulse. In one way, it's a relief that my infirmity more or less takes the issue of active sexuality off the table. In another way, I can't help feeling saddened by the knowledge that I have lost even the luxury of debating whether to make love with him.

He helps me to the curb, where his car is waiting. Then opens the passenger door, settles me into the seat, and stows my crutches in the back, before sliding behind the steering wheel. "All right. Where to?"

"I would suggest," I say, "that we just see where the backroads lead us. How does that sound to you?"

There is a slight flicker at the corner of his mouth as he concentrates on adjusting the side-mirror to his liking. "That sounds to me like an admirable basis upon which to construct a philosophy of life." Then, still studiously refraining from glancing at me, he starts the car and pulls away from the curb.

Sitting in such close proximity, we both make a scrupulous point of not touching. Somehow—in spite of the time that has passed—there seems to be nothing to say. It's not that we seem awkward, precisely. It's more that both of us appear prepared to wait—not only to find out where those backroads lead, but also to discover the terms of the journey that is taking us there.

When he turns off onto a secondary highway, then onto an unpaved road that cuts across the landscape in a no-nonsense line, I can't be certain if this is, in fact, the same route we followed the last time, or an itinerary improvised afresh for this occasion. Once the gravel road has shriveled, predictably, down to a rutted path, Carl stops the car, clears his throat, and turns to me. "This accident of yours, then. How did it happen?"

"I was on my bicycle. You have my permission to go ahead and laugh."

He doesn't, though. "Bad luck."

"Oh, come on, now. Here's your opportunity to gloat: 'I told you so.'"

"Never." His hand slides across the car seat, to take hold of mine. "I'm sorry, sweetheart. What about your injuries? How serious are they?"

"I'll be on the crutches for a while, then a cane. And then... well, I suppose it's anybody's guess. But it'll end up okay."

"Your lovely leg." His hand continues to grip mine, even harder.

"It'll be my hand in a minute," I chide lightly as I extricate it. Funny, my mother also focused on my leg as a particularly tragic casualty. "Carl, I *am* going to be okay. Really." Meanwhile, I am willing myself with all my might not to be too taken in.by his apparent concern. Striving, actively, to remember that day when he obediently walked out of my life, dropping my doorkey into the dish on the table, moments after insisting to me that he wouldn't give me up, and yet offering no indication that he was prepared to stop lying to me—and my lovely legs.

"Why didn't you let me know?" he asks now. "Why did you never reply to any of the messages I left?"

To that, I have no ready response. Except, perhaps, to ask him why he deceived me. Which I have no intention of asking him, right this minute. Instead, I shrug, and then glance out my window, trying to work out exactly where we've wound up.

Here, out in the countryside, there is more visible evidence than in the city of winter's advance. Here, wisps of snow lie like salt-licks between the stubbled rows of what used to be corn. Here—for all I can tell—is precisely where Carl and I made love in the front seat of his wife's stationwagon, such a long time ago. "Carl...I'm quite serious about taking you up on your offer."

"What, learning to drive, you mean? Fine and dandy, but... today?"

"Why not today? When I phoned you up and asked you for a favor, you said 'Name it,' and I did."

"Yes, but the state you're in makes...Well, you see, you're..."

Unable to find a polite way to describe my condition, he merely gestures in the direction of my plaster cast.

"I'm what? Crippled? Nobody says that nowadays, of course. Or even 'handicapped.' What I am is 'physically challenged.' And anyway, it's only temporary. By the time I'm ready to take a road test, I'll be able to fool any examiner into believing that the crutch in the back is someone else's, and that I'm as capable as the next forty-something female first-time driver."

"All right, even whimsically supposing that...What makes you so mad keen on driving, all of a sudden?"

"Well, in the 'state' I'm in, as you so delicately term it, don't you think it's a lot easier to contemplate driving a car than riding a bike, or walking?"

"Ah, but I *know* you, sweetheart. There's more to it than practicality. With you, there's always a lot more than meets the eye."

I smile at him demurely. "As opposed to yourself, you mean?"

For a moment, he looks prepared to answer, and I brace myself for one of his peppy retorts.

But no retort is forthcoming. Carl merely continues to study me, as if debating whether to bother pushing on with any line of questioning. Then, abruptly, he opens his door and gets out.

"All right, then," he says. "Slide over and we'll have a bash at it. Or, hopefully *not*. Meaning no offense to the physically challenged, but...I'm banking on the fact that, out in the middle of nowhere, there's a limit to the amount of damage you can do at the helm—even as one-legged as Captain Ahab."

>—+—>—•—O—•—<—+—<

Carl is right. Even one-legged, driving a car is relatively risk-free out here in the country. No white lines to abide by, no lights to obey, no parking spots to maneuver into, no other cars to shake my confidence. Undoubtedly, that was the method behind my father's strategy, all those years ago, when he conducted my sister's and brother's initial driving lessons out on the bald, bald prairie.

But, unlike the prospect of learning from my father, I regard this class with Carl as actually fun. There's something so simple about our interaction that I wish the rest of our relationship could have followed the same smooth course. Carl tells me what to do, and I attempt to do it. When I succeed, he is effusive in his praise. When I fail, he is infinitely forgiving. For my part, I am eager, excited, obedient, and unfailingly grateful—in contrast to what he must regard as my normal contrarian self. Best of all, at no point in these proceedings do I feel compelled to ask: Where are we going? What happens next? How come *you* get to make all the rules?

In fact, all male–female relationships should only be as straightforward as this. Which may be what Carl sensed, way back when, the time he tried to persuade me to let him teach me to drive. This may be what he and I should have been doing together all along—instead of attempting to negotiate the tortuous turns involving conflicting personalities, individual histories, and other hidden hazards of the road.

When he directs me, at last, to bring the car to a stop and turn off the motor, I realize that we have driven to the top of a steep embankment that looks straight over the lake. "Wow! Top of the world, Ma. Top of the world. What's that, way over there—that smudge? Not the other shore?"

The day is gray, and so is the lake. So vast and motionless that it looks like a reflection of the sky, reaching out to meet itself on the distant horizon. Carl peers critically at the blurry streak I'm indicating. "Yes, the American side."

"My God." Somehow, it startles me to have that wispy foreign skyline seem so suddenly within my grasp. "It feels as if I could just... step down on the accelerator and drive right across the water."

Carl laughs. "I shouldn't risk it, if I were you. Not on your very first day behind the wheel."

No, not on my very first day. But someday, and soon. "Still, it makes you realize, doesn't it? You could just pick up and head off anywhere, almost."

"*You* could," he says. "At least, I expect you will, in time."

I turn to him sharply. "You had your chance, remember? The last time we were out here together. We talked about taking off. You promised, in fact, that once it was my foot on the gas pedal, you'd do your part, too."

"Did I say that?" All of a sudden, he looks tired, defeated.

"Yes, you did. You had your chance, Carl. But you decided not to take it."

"I *couldn't* take it, sweetheart."

"Why not?"

"Oh, Christ, Dana." He flinches with impatience. "What's the use of this now? What's the bloody point?"

"Come on, you're the one who kept leaving messages on my machine about wanting to talk. How did you expect the conversation to go?"

"I hoped it might be about what's to come, not about what's in the past."

"Well, all right. What's to come, I hope, is that you're going to tell me at last. Did you lie to me?"

"Did I lie to you when?"

In spite of myself, I have to laugh, shortly and sharply. In fact, his answer is so revealing, all by itself, that I really ought to leave it there, with the laugh. But I don't. "Well, okay, for instance: Did you lie to me about being on trips, when you were back home with your wife?"

"Listen, sweetheart..." He is, I sense, choosing his words carefully. "That was just an idea you got hold of."

"But after I got hold of it, you didn't really deny it."

"Dana, if the real question is, did I love you or not—"

"No!" I hold up my hand. "I just want to know: Were you in Halifax?"

"What, in my life?"

"You know what I mean. Carl, you could tell me the truth now. What's left to lose?"

"Nothing." Carl leans back against the headrest and closes his eyes. "On the other hand..."

"On the other hand, there is no other hand any more, goddamn it." It annoys me that I still feel sufficiently attached to him to choke back tears. "I took you seriously, and in the end, I wound up feeling just...took."

"No. You weren't 'took.' Never." He moves toward me, to wipe an escaped tear from my cheek with his thumb. "But you see, from my point of view, you make it impossible for me to defend myself. Even now. Ever since you made up your mind that we were finished...there's been no reasoning with you."

Is he right about that? Is being finished with him something I simply made my mind up to, in that moment when I decided to unzip his luggage and examine the contents? "I don't want you to 'reason' with me, Carl. I want you to tell me the truth."

"Which assumes that I haven't, up till now."

Well, he's certainly right about that. Suddenly uncomfortable, I turn to gaze out my side of the car.

"You see?" says Carl, sensing some advantage. "You can't deny it. It was a decision you took, God knows why. What we had, you and I...it wasn't what you wanted anymore. But you couldn't come out and say so."

He might be right about that, too. On the other hand, he may simply have stumbled on something that sounds right because it makes him look good. "I want the truth, Carl." I make myself look at him, as squarely as I can. "Irrespective of whether or not it matches what I've heard before."

"Here's the truth. The only truth there's ever been." And he reaches out to pull me toward him, gently.

As I allow him to kiss me, I am amazed that his lips still taste as good to me as they ever did. At the same time, I am acutely aware that it doesn't bother him as much as it should to realize that the top of a bluff overlooking the New York shoreline is as far as he and I are ever likely to get.

"I think," I say, once I've kissed him back, "that I'm ready to drive us back to where we started. And even to get us there in one piece. Which is the whole point, right?"

"Yes." He nods gravely. "That's the whole point."

As I pilot his car carefully toward the gravel road that cuts as sharply as a knife through the stubbled fields stretching on either side, I am aware that Carl has placed his hand on the knee of my good leg—and plans to keep it there. But only for as long as it takes to reach the paved highway. At which point, I know, he'll change places with me, and resume control of the wheel. For the long, wordless drive back to where we started from. Which is where he'll drop me off, before he continues on to wherever he's going next.

Chapter Seven

"Hi. I've blown town for a while, leaving this machine in charge. In case you plan to burgle the place in my absence, there's an inventory of my valuables on the hall table. Help yourself, but be sure to cross what you took off the list, so that when I get back, I can see at a glance what's missing. Thanks. And have a nice day." *Beep.*

⊱—◈—○—◈—⊰

Hey, Murphy, look at me: I'm driving. All by myself, out on the highway, in my very own car. A pre-loved Mazda 323—in case you care—paid for in cash, right off the lot, in the single most adult act of my entire life. As well as the most expensive. Especially once you fold in the cost of the insurance, which—for a first-time driver such as myself—comes at a premium that easily exceeds the carrying charges on the national debt.

Still, who's complaining? It's been worth every penny, every agonizing step in the long slow process that has brought me to where I am right this minute: out on the open road, barreling along at my own chosen speed.

Nobody out here but us disembodied heads, peering out from behind the windows of our let's-pretend cars, like so many doll-sized faces cheerfully churned out by Fisher-Price. Our painted doll eyes making only split-second contact—if any at all—as we pass one another. Before hurtling onward, blissfully unknowing and blessedly unknowable. Our secrets secured by our shoulder-belts, our identities encased in our individual capsules of metal and glass, our souls in endless orbit around the continent. Autonomous, in every sense of the word.

With the ink barely dry on my newly minted driver's license, I have embarked upon my maiden voyage. Following my own intricately devised route of secondary roads, in accordance with my guiding principle of: "Two lanes good, four lanes bad." Tracing, in my mind's eye, the web of interconnected highways that will lead me from my own front door and across that vast undefended border—all the way to yours.

Never mind the fine points of my itinerary. Suffice it to say that I'm on my way. Give or take the many pit stops—let's call them "piss stops"—that I seem compelled to make. What is it, I wonder, about being on crutches that has thrown my urinary tract into overdrive? Or is this just a habit I picked up from you—this constant compulsion to make time to stop and spritz the flowers, while traveling along the road of life?

What surprise might be in store for me at the end of *this* particular road, I try not to dwell upon. Should Jerry be unexpectedly at home when I come crutching up to his door...What will I say? Even should I try to forestall that possibility by phoning ahead and hanging up if he answers, will he somehow know who's calling and why?

What if these well-laid plans of mine fall victim to that law of yours—the one which dictates that anything that can go wrong most surely will? These are things that don't bear thinking about—and so I won't, for now.

For now, suspended as I am in time and space, out on a seamless gray highway with no beginning, middle, or end, it's easy to pretend to myself that I can just keep driving forever. Past signs that proclaim: Roadside Picnic Table Ahead, Litter Barrel 1/2 Mile, Scenic Overlook on Right, Slippery When Wet. Past peeling billboards with amateurish depictions of Homemade Hamburgers that look like brains on a bun, featured alongside unsubstantiated promises of World's Best Ice Cream. Past advertisements for circuses long since defunct, and notification of Irish Heritage Days that have come and gone. Past word of the upcoming Snowflake Festival, Zoom Flume Closed for the Season, Fun for the Family at the Haunted Caverns, and Petrified Creatures Museum Open All Year.

Such a sense of insularity as I go speeding by—feeling light-years removed from recollections of the road, as viewed up closer and more personal from the seat of my dearly departed bike. On my bicycle, when I was wont to dart like a dragonfly. Clocking potential hazards that loomed in every direction, foreseeing a dozen different disasters in the making, glancing every which way at once, with an insect's vigilant compound eye... Except that last time, when my systems failed.

Would it surprise you to learn that I still miss my freewheeling two-wheeling days? Would you be startled to know that it's with a certain regret that I have taken my place—so belatedly—in this autonomous, adult domain? As just another guzzler of gas, hog of the road, rapist of resources, and deadly despoiler of Earth's upper atmosphere. Exercising my inalienable right to exult in the octane of automotive independence, and the mundane glory of sick transit personified. Behind the wheel of this smoke-spewing, fire-breathing, dust-raising, risk-taking machine. Whose only virtue and sole saving grace resides in every revolution of its four brand-new tires—that brings me that much closer to you.

So, hey, Murphy, look at me: I'm driving. Encased in my own private bubble. Consuming my own personal allotment of petroleum products, eating up my very own stretch of long gray highway that disappears, mile by mile, beneath my wheels. Before being shot out behind, in an endless hot plume of exhaust.

I'm your Dana Come Home, rushing onward at last. With no other thought in my head than: How fast? How soon?

Chapter Eight

🐾 Even in my dream, I am aware that this is a dream I've had a dozen times. In which Dana is pulling into the visitors' parking lot behind the building. Before hobbling on her crutches, over to the residents' lot—in order to determine if Jerry's car is there.

Which it's not. So far, so good. But—just to confirm—she buzzes from the lobby. No answer, of course. Nobody home but us chickens, and we're sound asleep. Merely dreaming that the buzzer is sounding.

In her imagination, Dana has been through the drill many times—as often, in fact, as I have dreamt it. So many times that she wonders whether—once she's going through the actual motions of the crime— she will experience it merely as make-believe. The way bank robbers must surely feel in the midst of a heist that's been rehearsed once too often. As if the real thing is just one more dream—from which to awaken a-sweat, to a truth curiously less vivid than simulation.

Even after she has hopped down to the basement of the building to locate the spare set of keys that she knows Jerry keeps under an overturned flowerpot, she may continue to experience truth and illusion as one and the same. Perhaps it's only once she's upstairs that the distinction will come clear. At the very door of Jerry's apartment, turning the key in the actual lock, opening the tangible door, and steadying herself as I launch my corporeal self at her like a cannonball. Perhaps only then will the fact finally sink in: no one is dreaming anymore.

Here she is at long last. Utterly exhausted from the endless-unaccustomed hours behind the wheel, momentarily uncertain of what to do, now that she's successfully navigated all the obstacles that have stood between her and the present moment. Gradually, it will start to occur to her that there are details to face that she hasn't worked out. Such as: how a tired, disoriented woman on crutches, who has illegally entered her ex-boyfriend's apartment, can expect to convey—unobtrusively—a large, overexcited dog downstairs, out to the visitors' parking lot, and into her car. For another long drive to God knows where.

She decides to postpone the problem by making a quick rest-stop in Jerry's bathroom. Perhaps hoping to find there unmistakable signs of fresh female occupancy—to help allay her guilt about what she is doing to Jerry. A bottle of creme rinse on the edge of the tub, a few stray hairpins in the sink, a cellophane sack of ladies' disposable razors, a pair of recently laundered pantyhose hanging from the shower rod...Any or all of the above, she thinks, would serve as reassurance that Jerry's life goes on, and will continue to do so. Even after she has deprived him of the one companion he has always claimed not to want, yet—

Ah, but. This is the moment in my dream when I always wake up. Just before she switches on the light in Jerry's bathroom. This is where the dream always ends—with me suddenly awakening to find myself still alone, stretched out on the couch in the living room, with only the darkness for comfort.

Except...This one time, could it possibly be...? Could the dream, this time, have another ending? Or—even more astounding—no ending at all?

Because this time, when I waken from my dream, it is to the sound of someone buzzing from down in the lobby. Someone who continues to buzz and buzz—even after I'm wide awake. 🐾

Chapter Nine

Of course, if I were really serious about this whole operation, I would have packed a fake mustache as a disguise for Murphy, a gun for myself, and a wad of bills in various Latin American currencies—just in case I should suddenly look up from my roadmap to discover that I turned the wrong way and am now approaching the Mexican border.

Not that any precaution of mine is going to prevent Jerry from plotzing, as soon as he arrives home to discover Murphy utterly absent. He'll recover, of course—just long enough to get on the phone to Mel. In fact, that's probably what he's doing right this minute. And I can easily imagine the conversation that is likely to ensue, once Mel arrives at Jerry's, and insists on pouring him a jigger of Scotch to calm his nerves.

"Granted," I can hear Mel conceding, "that it was *my* mistake, right out of the chute, to encourage her to take the damn dwog. But that was back when you *wanted* her to take the dwog, and it was all only temporary. Anyway, *this* time out—guess what? She can't get away with it. Because I'll bet you that dwog-napping is an indictable offense in every one of the lower forty-eight—not to speak of Hawaii, Alaska, and Kyanada. And let's not even twalk about the penalties for unauthorized entry into your apartment for the purposes of committing a felony, and blah blah blah. So buck up, Glass, drink your Scotch, and let's get on the blower to the proper authorities. If, that is, you're really convinced you want the hairy bastard back, and want to see the woman who napped him stamping out license plates for a stretch of ten-to-twenty."

Jerry's only reaction to that will be to sneeze violently into his whiskey. "You know I can't drink this stuff, Arlen. Fermented barley is poison to me, complete poison. Hand me my inhaler, will you?"

Right now, the smart thing for me to do would be to get to Jerry before Mel does. In order to forestall further calamity by assuring Jerry that Murphy is perfectly all right. Even hinting that, farther down the line, I might be open to rational discussion about which of the two of us is the rightful custodian.

But as I begin to envision pulling off the highway to make that pre-emptive phone call from a roadside booth, I can't get past the paralyzing possibility that Mel is already at Jerry's—ready to clap his hand right on the phone the second it rings.

"Canine Abduction Investigation Coordination Center."

"Mel, for God's sake. It's Dana. Is Jerry there?"

"Well, well, so the bad penny turns up at last. What's this, the first ransom demand?"

"Look, will you just put Jerry on?"

"Sorry, Dana, no can do. Glass is in the midst of a major allergy attack here, brought on by the trauma of what you've done to him."

"Are you sure it wasn't brought on by serving him Scotch?"

"Look, as Glass's official legal representative—as well as his oldest friend—I'm warning you that we plan to prosecute hard in the criminal courts, sue big at the civil trial, and beat you to the punch on the book and movie deals. In the meantime, the man could sneeze himself to death, what with the shock."

"To say nothing of all the antihistamines he's probably taken along with the Scotch. Mel, I can *hear* him in the background, self-administering.

"Do you know that I asked Jerry to let me keep Murphy? Did he tell you that he refused even to consider it? In spite of the fact that I'm the logical candidate. As you yourself pointed out, way back when—when enumerating my credentials as a writer with special insight into—"

"No, no, Dana, you don't want to go *there*. In view of the fact that you've profited professionally from your association with the dwog, a very good case might be made for abuse of creative copyright. Involving unauthorized use, for purposes of personal gain, of the dwog's likeness, utterances, opinions—"

"Oh, come off it, Mel. When I tell you that Murphy is nothing on earth like that wonder dog I've been writing for, believe me, I mean *nothing*." But am I so sure about that anymore? Wasn't I, by the end, relying on Murphy if not for inspiration then at least for insight? "Anyway, I bet there's no such thing as creative copyright."

"You can tell that to the judge."

"I will. If you catch me."

"Trust me, the cops are already on you like white on rice, and if the authorities don't come across, we got backup."

"What kind of backup?"

"Well, guess what? Seems there's this private investigator up in your neck of the woods. Specializes in the abduction of minors by pissed-off parents. When I gave him the facts here, he was of the opinion that this falls within the sphere of his expertise. And another funny thing—seeing as it's *you*, the guy volunteered to waive his fee, just for the satisfaction of seeing you brought to book, as expeditiously as—"

But no. Too much. Even for me, imagining Carl in on my capture is going way over the top. Although, at some level, I probably wish Carl *were* sufficiently attached to me to consider hounding me to the ends of the earth. As for Mel...In front of my eyes, in the long white beam cast by the headlights into the thickening darkness, there bobs Mel's reproachful face, as round and as resilient as a balloon.

"You better get your tuchus on back here," he advises me ominously, as his illuminated countenance dances just ahead of my car like a will-of-the-wisp. "Because I'm warning you, the next time we communicate, it won't be in some morbid fantasy of yours. It'll be through whatever counsel the court appoints you."

In imagination, I cut Mel loose, and his roly-poly face escapes its tether, to go floating up, up, and away—far beyond the haze of artificial light that hovers in the sky above the highway like a radioactive glow. There's no way on Earth, I pep-talk myself, that I'm going to have to deal with Mel, or Jerry, or any constabulary—including former members of the Leith police force...

It's just me now, and it's the journey itself that's got me spooked. After so many consecutive hours of keeping the pedal to the metal, it's no wonder I am now starting to feel myself slipping as far backward in time as I am actually hurtling forward in space.

I suppose it's only now occurring to me to wonder what I'll do if I somehow don't make it. To say nothing of wondering what I'll do if I *do* make it—with Murphy safely stowed in the backseat of my Mazda, and the entire rest of our lives stretching ahead.

>⊷─◦─⊶◦⊷

I park my crutches against the Plexiglas wall of the phone booth, and then, balancing on my good leg, I punch up Jerry's number and charge it to my calling card.

As the connection is made, my heart starts to flutter. Briefly, I consider hanging up before he answers. It's late, and in the garish lights of the gas-station service bay, I feel like some forlorn figure elegized in a painting by Edward Hopper. All alone at night on the highway, with the telephone receiver pressed to my ear, straining to hear some sound beyond the endless swish-swish of cars speeding along the road.

"Hello, you've reached the residence of Jerry Glass. I'm not here right now, but please leave a brief message at the tone."

The shock of hearing Jerry's voice is quickly over-ridden by a rush of relief that it's just his machine. Speaking my piece will be much easier this way—like telling my sins in the dark anonymity of the confessional.

"Jerry, it's Dana. By the time you pick up this message, you'll already know why I'm calling, and what I've done. You may think I had no right to do it, but it's done, and—believe me—Murphy is quite okay.

"He and I are...well, I don't know exactly where we are. Let's just say I'm phoning you from a...an undisclosed location. To ask you please not to worry, and not to have a major allergy attack over this. Murphy is, I repeat, okay. And I promise to call you again. In the meantime, howev—"

In the meantime, however, the peremptory beep of the machine cuts in to let me know I've exhausted the short attention span of Jerry's message tape. Momentarily, I debate calling back, to buy myself another...what was that, anyway—about thirty seconds of recording time? But in the end, I decide that—even with tape enough and time—there's not much useful I could add to what I've already said.

Tomorrow, when I'm thinking more clearly, will be soon enough to phone him again. For now, I find myself out of both energy and strategy. But feel I can limp away from this payphone knowing that I've met—if just barely—the minimum demands of human decency. After all—as men always like to say in their own defense—at least I called, didn't I?

As I swing back across the parking lot to my car, I can make out Murphy in the back, waiting in prick-eared silhouette. It's just him and me now—as I've contrived it. Except that out here in real life, I am suddenly more in charge than I ever planned to be. Responsible for making all the pertinent choices for both of us.

Chapter Ten

It may only be because it's late at night, and I'm worn out, and we've already been turned away from four other places that don't take pets. But for whatever reason, the Shady Elms Motel looks right to me, right off the bat, right from the highway. I see no evidence of a satellite dish, nor any promises on the sign of Waterbeds in Every Room, VCR, Adult Movies, Magic-Fingers Massage, or Free All-U-Can-Eat Breakfast Buffet. Nor any indication of other amenities on offer that might afford the Shady Elms the right to be choosy about the phylogenetic stature of its drive-in clientele.

I drive in, to follow the arrow marked "Office." And the closer I get, the clearer I can appreciate the perfection of the place.

Clearly, the Shady Elms is the sort of down-at-heel refuge to which some B-movie character of the fifties might repair. Wearing a battered fedora, and parking an equally battered DeSoto coupe at the door of his unit. Then, as we watch him unpack his luggage—consisting of a portable typewriter and a quart of bourbon—he explains in a world-weary voice-over how he happened to wash up on this godforsaken shoal.

The woman at the desk in the office seems similarly out of something grainy, low-budget, and black-and-white. Haggard, unexpressive, in a shrunken-up cardigan sweater over a nightdress, with a couple of old-fashioned pincurls coiled under her hairnet like baby garter snakes. There may or may not be a flicker of compassion in her eye, as she glances across the counter to note the crutches wedged under my arms. A flicker, which—if indeed it did kindle at all—promptly dies, once I confide that there's a dog sitting out in the car.

"Sorry." The woman shrugs. "It says 'No Pets,' right on the sign."

I dare not risk unceremonious ouster by pointing out to her that the sign also makes reference to shady elms, even though there's not so much as a stunted sapling of any species anywhere in sight. "He's a very well-behaved dog," I fib instead. "Quiet, nondestructive. Besides, it's only for tonight."

The woman purses her lips and casts a more comprehensive glance across the counter at my crutches and cast. A look which I choose to interpret as some potential revival of her sympathy. Besides, at this time of year, surely any patronage at all is welcome at a place like the Shady Elms—which probably stays open year-round through sheer inertia, and can stand behind "Vacancy" as its sign's only truthful claim.

"How'dja come to hurt yer laig?" the woman wants to know, before rendering her verdict on Murphy's and my candidacy.

"Bicycle accident. I'm on the mend, though. Just... awfully tired, right about now."

Her nod in response seems to suggest that she can imagine—if nothing else—how it feels to be awfully tired. From behind the closed door that must lead to her living quarters, there emanates the aroma of pot roast and the muffled whine of a radio or TV set, broadcasting what sounds like religious music. Fleetingly, I wonder whether one way to abet my cause might be through some pertinent gospel reference. Perhaps a comparison of myself and Murphy to that previous pair of weary travelers, so many eons ago, denied room at the inn, at approximately this same bleak time of year...

The motel-keeper spares me the risk of attempting to make any clumsy appeal to Christian charity. "Oh, well," she allows at last, "I s'pose I kin make an exception, this late at night. So long's you keep the dog quiet, like you said, and don't let 'im chew nothin' up."

With the sound of hymns swelling in the background, I feel tempted to respond with a heartfelt "Halleluiah." But content myself with a murmur of thanks.

"Room'll be forty-three-forty-eight, with the State tax."

I am already reaching into my purse for my Visa card when I hear Carl Hart's voice, as clearly as if he were standing here. *Hang on, sweetheart. You leave a paper trail, and somebody's bound to follow the bread crumbs, sort of style...*

Oh, come on, I argue with him silently. Let's give the cloak-and-dagger stuff a rest, shall we? I mean, I know that you don't care where I've gone. And nobody else cares, either—except Jerry. And even Jerry isn't really going to hire someone to piece together all the pertinent evidence I've left strewn behind me.

Maybe not. But maybe Carl—were he actually here—would have a point: Why take the chance? "I'll pay in cash, if you don't mind," I say aloud. "Forty-three something, wasn't it?"

"Forty-three-forty-eight, with the tax."

For some reason, my fingers are trembling as I extract two U.S. twenties and a ten from my wallet, and hand them across the desk to the woman. All my paranoid fantasies of pursuit are, of course, only paranoid fantasies. In the real world, what am I, after all—a dog burglar? That doesn't even sound like a legitimate line of illegitimate endeavor. A "dog burglar" merely gives the impression of some lesser, more inept species of cat burglar, restricted to committing robberies at ground-floor level, or lower.

"There you go." The woman counts my change back into my hand. "Now, if I kin git you to fill out this here guest-registration card..."

Fill out...? While we're still on the subject of leaving a paper trail...

I pick up the pen from the counter, and chew on it as I stare at the card the woman has handed me. Now, look: even if Jerry *were* hot enough under the collar about this to track me down, how on Earth would he go about it? Since he has no idea I am now in possession both of a car and the wherewithal to drive it. Nor has he any clue about my accident. Which means that nothing Jerry knows about me is going to prompt him or anyone to make any inquiries at any motels on any highways concerning a woman on crutches.

On the other hand—as Carl would no doubt point out—what's ever to be gained by admitting the truth if you don't have to?

"Soon's you finish with that there card," the woman is prodding me, "I kin give you the key, and git back to bed."

"Oh, of course! Sorry." I brandish the pen with businesslike flourish. Let's see here... Name, Address, Make of Car, License Plate No., Company Name... It may not be that I fear supplying any of this information. Perhaps it's only that I feel, all of a sudden, that none of these questions apply to me. In fact, the longer I stand here thinking about it, the more it strikes me that nothing that's happened this entire day—nor, for that matter, during the long weeks that led up to it—actually pertains to me as I once was.

It's as if the Mazda out in front of the motel office—with the elaborate route-map that I drew up and the freshly minted vehicle permit in the glove compartment, and even Murphy, waiting out there patiently for my return—all belong to some other person, in some alternative galaxy, whose life is running parallel to mine. But which person? What galaxy? Whose life? Whose name is it that should rightfully be inscribed on the guest-registration card, here at the Shady Elms Motel?

From behind the door that leads into the motel-keeper's living quarters, the strains of spirituals continue to waft. With no immediate awareness that I am doing so, I begin beating time on the countertop with the end of the pen. "I-yi once wuh-uz lost, But now a-am found..."

"Amazin' Grace," announces the woman, out of nowhere.

"I beg your pardon?" I look up, startled, and for a wild moment, actually wonder if she's guessed my true identity as a TV-series hack.

But she is jerking her thumb in the direction from which the music drifts. "All-time favorite of mine. 'Amazin' Grace.'"

"Oh, right, the *hymn!*" I nod vigorously, and meanwhile am thinking: Right, the hymn. "Wuh-uz blind, buh-ut now I see." But what, precisely? What do I see?

Perhaps what I see is Murphy, loping toward me across the park that day as I continued to call and call his name. Or maybe it's myself, age fourteen, staring out the grimy window of a bus filled with jeering boys. Or a long leggy girl in a too-short skirt—who looks like me, in certain lights—momentarily turning from the embrace of a beautiful French boy in a railway carriage, in order to wave me a tearful goodbye. Just as her train pulls out of the station...

I once was blind. But now I know what I see. With no further hesitation, I place the point of the pen on the line of the registration card that asks for my name. And there I print "Grace."

The motel woman squints at the card. "Grace?"

"That's right. Just like in the hymn." With a how-about-that smile, I hand her the card. "Of course I don't claim to be amazing."

"Grace what?" Choosing to sidestep my little joke, she pushes the card back across the counter toward me. "You need to put down yer full name, y'know."

Of course I know. One name is not enough, not even for us good-time girls. "Oh, right. Pardon me." I pick up the pen once more, and on the card, right after where I printed "Grace," I add "Goldberg" in the same large distinct print, and finish off with an illegible signature.

Then, as the motel woman, seemingly satisfied, takes the card from me, and as gospel music continues to pour from the unseen radio or TV set somewhere in the back, I think: Amen. Somebody say Amen to that.

Chapter Eleven

At the end of the day, the best that can be said for riding in the back-seat of a car, mile after mile and hour after hour, is that it's like one long uninterrupted dream. A dream with any number of possible endings— or no ending at all, depending on how long Dana plans to keep on driving.

In one version of my dream, we spend the night at a motel called the Shady Elms that has no elm trees, and then next morning head out impulsively westward, in accordance with some nostalgic whim of Dana's to drive a car across the bald, bald prairie of her past. Her plan is simply to keep on driving in that direction for as long as her stash of currency lasts. Then, to be brought to bay in some jerk-water town in Iowa, or Alberta, or even Utah, by the authorities. Who have finally tracked us down, and who surround us with enough firepower—as they explain through their bullhorns—to blow us up six ways from Sunday. All the way to Waco, Texas, or to Jordan, Montana, or to Armageddon— whichever comes first.

In a second—and admittedly less spectacular—version of the dream, we depart at dawn from the same Shady Elms Motel, and by noon are back up at the border. Where Canadian Customs and Immigration wave us through—despite Dana's inability to furnish them either with an up-to-date certificate of my latest rabies vaccination or a plausible explanation of how it is she has managed to spend an entire twenty-four hours in that consumers' mecca, the United States, only to return with absolutely nothing to declare. By late afternoon, we're back at her apartment. From which she immediately calls Jerry once more—in order to offer him amicable terms under which they can share me on a mutually agreed-upon timetable.

And, in yet another alternative ending to the dream, we wind up— Dana and I—way down East, on a small island she's somehow heard about. On this island, there's a cabin to which, for some reason, she has the key, and there's not much else. But it's a wonderful place, despite the desolation, and in this version of the dream—which I personally prefer to any of the others—we spend hours on the windswept beach together, Dana and I. Where she's willing to keep bending down on her crutches to pick up a stick to throw for me, for as long as I'm willing to keep fetching it—which is quite a long time.

In fact, I'm just in the midst of a fetch when I catch a glimpse of something or someone on the brow of the hill that rises up behind the cabin. The day is clear, and nearsighted as I am even in my dreams, I am able to make out a small dark speck, which begins to take on shape as it moves toward us. Meanwhile, Dana—whose eyesight is sharper than mine at any time—has also noticed the speck, and moments before I do, she discerns that it is a person approaching. Seconds after that, she identifies it as a man, simply by the gait.

But because I—not only in dreams but everywhere else—have a superior sense of smell, I will be the one first able to determine precisely what man it is who is coming down that hill toward us. It may be Carl Hart, the experienced sleuth, who has tracked Dana down. And now turns up, unexpectedly, to try to win her back. Or perhaps it's Mark, miraculously restored to the beautiful young man that she remembers marrying so many years ago. Even good old Derek is a possibility— dropping by just to let her know that his general health is much improved, and he's booked into a corner suite at an even nicer hotel than the Arlington. Or...could it be a repentant Leonard, or the shower-whistler, or amiable Mick O'Ryan, or even some blond French boy with a canvas backpack?

Or...is it Jerry? Which is by no means out of the question—since nothing is out of the question, way out here in the realm I inhabit in my sleep. All of these alternatives, along with so many others, are equally plausible—or not.

For me, there is not much distinction to be drawn between "then" and "now," between "could" and "did," between the things that happen, the things that don't happen, and the things that ought to happen and may well happen soon. In fact, there are very few distinctions at all, when I'm sound asleep, running in place on the rug. In the worlds I straddle between Sleeping and Waking, between Man and Beast, between Time and Space, all or none of the above is equally trustworthy—and equally suspect.

For all I know, it may be that I'm still sound asleep in Jerry's apartment, waiting for the downstairs buzzer to sound. As yet only dreaming in Technicolor the further adventures of a black-and-white dog of disputed ownership. A dog who once ran amok in the park—or may do so yet, unless some voice he will obey calls him back.

Whereupon, that dog that I am dreaming may hesitate in his tracks—while he debates whether to keep on running, as wild as a wolf. Or whether to turn, and come racing home. Whiskers a-tremble, eyelids a-flutter, all four legs churning in place—in my eagerness, even in my sleep, to answer the call. 🐾

Acknowledgments

My thanks to many friends and colleagues—including Susan Feldman, Christine Foster, Arnie Gelbart, Anne Gibson, Graham Harley, Gay Revell, Rick Salutin, John Sawatsky, Susan Swan, Audrey Thomas, Eleanor Wachtel, Diane Walker, Merrily Weisbord, and Cathy Wismer—who have seen me through this process and much that preceded it with their expertise, insight, sympathy, succor, support, and outright nagging.

My gratitude to my editor, Barbara Berson, and publisher, Anna Porter.

I'd also like to acknowledge the invaluable assistance of both the Canada Council and the Ontario Arts Council, whose support on projects of mine in the past helped enable me to take on the writing of this book myself. As well, I'm grateful to CBC Radio and CBC Stereo, for offering me intelligent diversion while I was writing, and stimulating employment when I was not.

And particular thanks to Marvin Frankel for taking *me* on while I took on this book.

Biography

Erika Ritter's immensely popular debut novel, *The Hidden Life of Humans*, was originally published in 1997. She is the author of the newly published nonfiction book *The Dog by the Cradle, the Serpent Beneath: Some Paradoxes of Human–Animal Relationships*, and *The Great Big Book of Guys: Alphabetical Encounters with Men*, chosen by Amazon.ca as one of the best books of 2004. Ritter is also a columnist, broadcaster and award-winning playwright.